DARK EVIL RULED
UNTIL THE COURA
WOMEN FOU
FREEDO

SETH—Disguised as a traveler he slips back into an Egypt of treachery and terror to play out a fearful destiny—a deadly duel with a sorcerer and a battle with his own tormented heart.

MARA—Egypt's proud queen, possesser of a dangerous secret about a Prince's birth and of an obsession for a forbidden lover that will jeopardize her land . . . and her life.

APEDEMEK—Evil magus of the Nubian lands, his power is so awesome that even devils obey him . . . and only a Child of the Lion knows the way to destroy him forever.

PRINCESS THARBIS—Hot-blooded daughter of a cruel king, she will discover that true love can conquer all—even in the face of death—if she has the bravery to embrace it with her whole soul.

MOSES—Thebes's last Prince, ignorant of his own past he is raised to rule the Egyptians—yet fate will lead him to another people where only the very hand of God can help him survive . . . and win.

THE DELIVERER

Volume IX

THE
DELIVERER

PETER DANIELSON

Created by the producers of
**Wagons West, White Indian,
America 2040,** and **The Kent
Family Chronicles.**

Book Creations Inc., Canaan, NY · Lyle Kenyon Engel, Founder

BANTAM BOOKS
TORONTO · NEW YORK · LONDON · SYDNEY · AUCKLAND

THE DELIVERER

*A Bantam Book / published by arrangement with
Book Creations, Inc.*

Bantam edition / September 1988

*Produced by Book Creations, Inc.
Lyle Kenyon Engel, Founder*

ISBN 0-553-27459-7

Published simultaneously in the United States and Canada

Bantam Books are published by Bantam Books, a division of Bantam Doubleday
Dell Publishing Group, Inc. Its trademark, consisting of the words "Bantam Books"
and the portrayal of a rooster, is Registered in U.S. Patent and Trademark Office
and in other countries. Marca Registrada. Bantam Books, 666 Fifth Avenue, New
York, New York 10103.

PRINTED IN THE UNITED STATES OF AMERICA

O   0 9 8 7 6 5 4 3 2 1

Cast of Characters

Nubian Expedition
Moses—Young prince of Egypt
Seth—Child of the Lion, Moses's tutor
Khafre—Military commander
Geb—Khafre's adjutant

Nubians
Nehsi—King of Nubia
Balaam—Usurper
Apedemek—Evil magus
Princess Tharbis—Balaam's daughter
Het—Nehsi's ally

Egyptians
Kamose—Drug-addicted king
Amasis—Regent, cult adept
Neb-mertef—Amasis's principal assistant
Nemaret—Overseer of Amasis's country estate

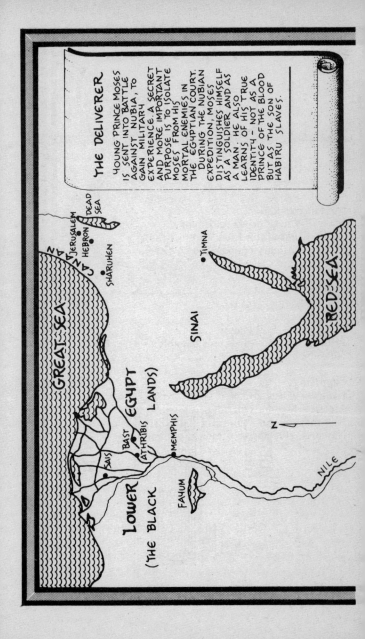

THE DELIVERER

YOUNG PRINCE MOSES
IS SENT INTO BATTLE
AGAINST NUBIA, TO
GAIN MILITARY
EXPERIENCE. A SECRET
AND MORE IMPORTANT
PURPOSE IS TO ISOLATE
MOSES FROM HIS
MORTAL ENEMIES IN
THE EGYPTIAN COURT.
DURING THE NUBIAN
EXPEDITION, MOSES
DISTINGUISHES HIMSELF
AS A SOLDIER AND AS
A MAN. HE ALSO
LEARNS OF HIS TRUE
IDENTITY— NOT AS A
PRINCE OF THE BLOOD
BUT AS THE SON OF
HABIRU SLAVES.

DEAD SEA

JERUSALEM
HEBRON
SHARUHEN

TIMNA

RED SEA

SINAI

GREAT SEA

EGYPT

BAST
ATHRIBIS
SAIS
MEMPHIS

Lower

(THE BLACK
LANDS)

FAYUM

NILE

N

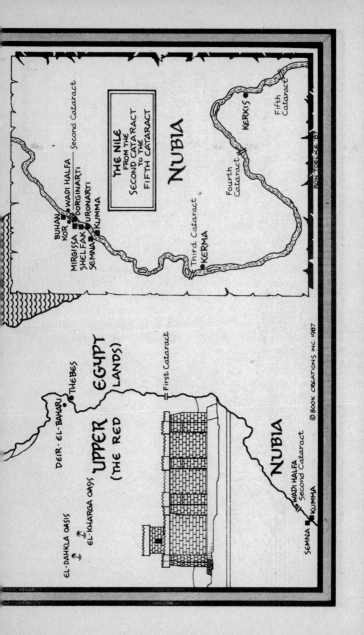

Prologue

The caravan had encamped deep in the desert and far from the sea, yet the dusky skies above the little oasis were thick with raucous gulls. These and other birds, which nested in the tall cliffs above, had gathered over the spring-fed pond as the sun's rays died, to swoop and dip, seeking insects in the quickly chilling evening air.

One moment there was still pink in the sky; then, with the startling suddenness common to events in the desert, it was pitch dark—dark above, dark all around, dark everywhere but in the circle of golden light surrounding the guttering coals.

After the last glow in the western sky was gone, the noisy birds vanished, and the only sounds were the soft sighs of the wind in the palm branches and the crackling and popping of the embers. Somewhere a crying child was silenced as its mother offered her breast. Conversation had died. All were waiting, waiting.

Into the far fringe of the circle of light stepped the Teller

1

of Tales. Grotesquely lit from below, his strong-featured face was long and bony; the nose was a hawk's beak, and the mouth was firm and severe above his long, windswept beard.

He spoke. Out of the aged face came a voice deep and rich and virile, the bold but mellifluous tones of a spell-binder. "In the name of God, the merciful, the benevolent . . . ."

Those who looked up at him were held captive by his eyes: dark, piercing, unblinking, and mesmerizing. The eyes of a sorcerer.

"Hear now," he continued, "the tales of the Children of the Lion, the men and women of no tribe, and of their ceaseless wandering among the nations. Hear the tale of Seth, wisest of all the Sons of the Lion, and of how, having lost one son, he now gained two."

There was a murmur; he cut it short with a glare. "I have told you of Seth and his great quest to become a master of the mysterious Chalybians, the iron-makers, whom the Shepherd Kings, foreign conquerors of the lands beside the Nile, feared as they feared no other."

His voice picked up speed. "You have heard how Seth lingered in Babylon, bound by love and respect to the king of the Shinarians, and forgot his pledge to return to Egypt with the iron Sword of Glory, upon which the destiny of Egypt wholly depended.

"Ah, great was Seth's sin," he said harshly, "and bitterly he paid for it, in Babylon's fall, in the death of the king who had become a father to him, of the princess he had married, and of his dearest friends.

"Seth alone survived the fall of the city, and he returned to Egypt to give the Sword of Glory to Kamose, king of the Red Lands, who killed the last of the Shepherd Kings and swept the invaders out of Egypt to die on the edge of the mighty Sinai in a fateful hamlet called Sharuhen."

The name drew nods from the half-visible crowd. They remembered this part of the story.

He bore ever on: "But the purging of the lands to the north—Canaan, the mountains of Syria, and the coastal cities of Tyre, Sidon, Arvad, and Ashkelon—took many *years. And while Kamose and his army were away from Red and Black Lands, a deadly confrontation had been a-building."*

His voice grew ominous. *"Like an evil disease, the corrupt and dark cult of the Great Goddess spread throughout the kingdom, spawning nameless horrors. The cult had possessed Kamose's soul for some time but then lost him to the arts of war. Meanwhile it had spread across the great delta and moved steadily upriver to Thebes, where it poisoned the court Kamose had left behind.*

"In the midst of this evil conspiracy, Baliniri, great and wise vizier of Egypt, had begun to groom a new king, one uncorrupted by the cult or by Shepherd blood. For when the deformed and sickly newborn of the princess Thermutis died, a foundling was secretly adopted by the royal house—the infant son of Amram, of the Habiru tribe of Levi, the hope of Egyptian and Canaanite alike. His name was Moses.

"None knew of the boy's true parentage but the child's mother and sister, and the tiny, fiercely loyal circle around Baliniri. The court believed Moses actually to be a prince of Egypt, heir to the finest bloodlines in the Nile valley. He was the undisputed choice of the nobles and the nomarchs, the priests of Amon, and the enslaved Habiru—a boy much loved by all but the cult members, who suspected irregularities in his background but could prove nothing.

"Eighteen years passed. But alas! The boy was a blank tablet yet to be written upon, and his education must begin. So, as Kamose's battered warriors prepared to return from the North to the land they had not seen since their youth, there came in Thebes the testing of Moses, born the Deliverer.

"Into the valley of the Nile came two men—one determined to destroy the boy, one committed to save him. The first had been the wisest of the wise until his soul had turned toward the darkness. The other was a flawed and chastened wanderer who had seen much sorrow and suffering and wished to save the world from further horrors.

"The two would do battle for the boy's soul and for the future of Egypt and the world."

His voice rose again. "Hear now," he said, "of the testing of Egypt, and the great war with Nubia. Hear of the first great meeting between two sages, and of the youth and maturing and flowering of Moses, prince of Egypt. . . ."

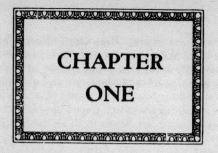

CHAPTER ONE

The Egyptian Border at Sile

I

"I think I can see the dust cloud," Psamtik said, his voice quivering. Standing at the edge of the inn's rooftop and gazing toward the east, he seemed to shudder as he spoke. "They'll be here in a little while."

"The conquering heroes return," his guest said. "An impressive and fateful day. And yet from your tone, if you'll pardon a personal remark, one would gather that you would not have it so."

Psamtik's eyes were slits as he peered anxiously across the desert waste for more definite signs of the returning army. Runners had arrived the day before to warn the city of the coming of the king and his advancing column. The warlike and triumphant lord of Two Lands, Kamose, had deserted this land eighteen years earlier on his martial errand.

"To tell you the truth, sir, I'm not quite sure what I think," he admitted. "It's not the simple thing it sounds.

5

They've been gone so long. How can we know who they are anymore? The old ones, even the ones who survived the battles, may well have died of old age or retired, taking a handful of slaves and a captured bride and grabbing a bit of surrendered land up North. The young ones who'll make up the bulk of the lower ranks won't even have been born, most likely, when Kamose left Egypt to chase the Shepherds into Sinai. They'd have joined along the way."

His visitor raised a brow. Psamtik went on. "They left an Egyptian army. As their men died—and it's my understanding that many of them died at Sharuhen—they'd have been replaced by mercenaries: Canaanites, Tyrians, Sidonians, Syrians, whoever. It wouldn't have been hard to find volunteers to pad out an army dedicated to destroying the Shepherds."

His visitor smiled, then joined Psamtik at the roof's edge. "Pardon me, sir," he said. "Who are the Shepherds?"

"Were," Psamtik corrected him, peering anxiously at the distance. "A foreign tribe from Hayastan, far to the northeast, up near Lake Van. Shepherd Kings. They invaded Egypt three generations ago and conquered the whole delta."

"Ah," his visitor replied, nodding. "We call them the Hai. I didn't know your local term for them. This is the army, then, that broke the Hai and crushed them in the North. Impressive, sir. Impressive."

Psamtik turned and looked at his visitor. Nebo, as he called himself, was himself quite impressive. He had come in with a desert caravan from across the southern route over Sinai—the hard route, the one that led up along the Great Rift from the famous copper mines at Timna—two days earlier. He claimed to be a magus from the valley of the Tigris, where the Assyrians had begun to assert themselves in recent years. Nothing else was known about him.

"Oh, yes," Psamtik said wearily. "I'm impressed that they put an end to the Shepherds, all right. Anyone would be. And I'm grateful, for all that my family prospered in the years of the foreigners' reign here. We rose from poverty to wealth, members of the landowner caste, dealing in real estate. We had our money not in farmland—that was grabbed by the government while Joseph of Canaan was vizier, so some great fortunes were lost—but in commercial property. It was the right place to be."

"Yes," Nebo agreed appreciatively. "Your servant downstairs told me. You own more land in Sile than anyone else, I believe."

Psamtik smiled, but apprehension was still evident in his eyes. "True. All the more reason for me to view the coming of the victorious Egyptian army, with Kamose at its head, with mixed feelings. Have you ever been in a city on a night when an army unit is in town, on its first leave in months?" He shuddered again and rolled his eyes heavenward. "Anything can happen. A largely foreign army, bored and thirsty after a long and punishing march through the desert, one that hasn't seen a woman, most likely, since Hebron or Jerusalem . . ."

"I see." Nebo spoke with sympathy as he watched the worry etch itself in lines around Psamtik's mouth. Nebo wore his gray beard in the style of the Valley of the Two Rivers, and his eyes, guarded and wise, seemed older than the rest of his face. "Look at it this way, though, my friend. The conquering heroes may do some damage to your property, but if I know a conquering army, they'll have fat purses. They'll spend so much money at your establishments that you'll be able to afford to pay for any repairs."

"True," Psamtik admitted grudgingly, his mind still calculating phantom losses. "But frankly, I'm sure all of us here will be glad to see them gone. When at last we sit amid the wreckage, counting the money we've made, we'll all breathe a deep sigh of relief."

"Understandably,", Nebo said. "Having been forewarned, I take it that you've been able to lay in adequate provender against their arrival?"

"Oh, yes. Food, drink, and whores. I've raided every city in the delta as far as the Damietta branch of the Nile. When I ran through all the native-born sluts and dancing girls and flute players, I started importing slaves at the auction in Athribis—whoever I could get my hands on." He shot Nebo a sidelong glance. "I even put in a stock of boys. You never know what foreigners are going to want. The Greeks who fought for King Salitis would bellow for boys, even if you waved the plumpest, most luscious dancing girl in the delta under *their* noses."

Nebo frowned. "That's a preference that never appealed to me."

Psamtik, reassured, went on. "I've scoured the area for wines of every sort, beers, and stronger stuff."

"Is that so?" Nebo said, caution in his tone. "You wouldn't be selling the juice of the poppy? The substance I understand you Egyptians call *shepenn*?"

Psamtik's eyes narrowed, and he stepped back. For the first time he began to be suspicious of this stranger. Was he what he seemed to be? Was he a spy? He thought a moment before answering. "Indeed not, sir. What do you take me for? You may not have heard, but *shepenn* is illegal, dispensed only under the most carefully controlled conditions by the caste to which you yourself belong. The official penalty for dealing in *shepenn* without official clearance from the guild of the magi is death, quick and brutal."

Nebo nodded, a mildness on his face. "We have fairly stringent laws regulating its use where I come from, but nothing so extreme, so final. Of course it's all moot for me; I'm not here to practice but to observe, to learn from you Egyptians. I hear only the best about your magi—their great successes in the cure and treatment of virulent disease. Your surgeons are particularly respected."

Psamtik, feeling no threat from his companion, now turned his face toward the horizon. "I think I can see them. I hope I haven't forgotten anything. Let's see, now. The troops and the officers mustn't be directed to the same brothels and taverns. Guides on duty will separate them one from the other. The warehouses are stocked; runners are on hand to take fresh supplies to the taverns as needed. There are fresh towels and bedding. There should be, anyhow. If anyone's neglected to stock the houses, I'll have his head."

"I can see them now myself," Nebo said. "And listen! The drums! Faint but audible."

Psamtik frowned. There was a strained look on his long face, and his eyes blinked rapidly. "I wish it were all over," he confessed. "I can't wait for it to be all done."

"Relax, my friend," soothed his guest. "What will be will

be. Think of the money you'll make." His smile was benign and untroubled. "In my country we have a saying: When your mind is troubled, close your eyes and think of gold—large piles of it, gleaming and sparkling in the sun. All of it yours, to do with as you wish. If that doesn't set a heart at rest, or ease a heavy burden, or sweeten a sour stomach, you're beyond help."

The drums beat with an insistent, throbbing rhythm, harsh and intrusive. The underofficers, marching alongside the columns of their men, bellowed out "Left!" and "Right!" to try to get the men in step. The orders were ignored.

In the third rank a tough, leathery-faced old underofficer, a career man who had been a fresh-faced boy when the army had left Egypt eighteen years before, slashed the leather tip of his braided fly whisk across the bare, scarred buttocks of a Theban soldier of the line. "Get in step there, you upriver idiot!" he bellowed. "Step lively there! Do you want leave tonight, to reacquaint yourself with what a woman looks like—or would you like to stand guard outside the general's quarters while the rest of us are playing with some fat sluts from Saïs or Bast?"

The soldier glowered at the dusty neck in front of him and muttered under his breath.

"Eh?" the underofficer said nastily. "I didn't catch that. Say it nice and loud so we can all hear it. Hey! Did you hear me? You with the bare ass! Speak up!"

The soldier almost broke step, turning his head to glare at his tormentor. "Don't you make fun of my unit uniform, you son of a whore," he warned. "We dress like this because we're desert troops. We proved our superiority to you pampered city troops in your sissy sandals and grimy loincloths at Sharuhen and Megiddo and Carchemish."

"Hah. You look like a lot of boy-loving Greeks to me."

"Another word and I'll kill you," the soldier in line threatened. "So help me." His hand went to the battered sword in his belt—other than the shield that hung halfway down his scarred back, the only item he wore. The blanket that had once hung over one shoulder had been ripped to tatters, and he had thrown it away.

"I'll tell you what," the underofficer said in a nasty voice. "Meet me tonight after roll call. Just the two of us, in the public square. We'll see who does the killing."

"Silence in the ranks back there!" an officer bellowed. The two exchanged angry glares and went back to eyes forward. The drums beat; the hard-soled feet, most of them bare now although many of the units had begun the march across Sinai booted or sandaled, pounded the earth, still out of step. The Egyptian army was coming home, heroes to all the world. But they did not look or feel like heroes. They felt like an army many times defeated, an army that had forgotten what it was they had gone so far to conquer and win. They felt like slaves, not the masters of the earth. They hated one another and had done so for months, years. The only thing that had united them and had maintained relative peace among them for lo these many leagues was the thought of coming home. But now even the joy of that was gone, lost in the endless and featureless track they had followed across the brutal and lifeless wastes of Sinai. Thoughts of family, celebrations, sex, drunken oblivion, joyous reunions, or the settling of long-standing personal grudges—all paled beside the thought of rest, well earned and long sought. Left to their own devices, they would have dropped in their tracks, most of them, and slept for two days.

"All right, damn you!" an officer called back from the front of the line. "Dress it up there! Look good! We're in sight of the walls of Sile! Heads up, now! March like heroes! Chins high! Shoulders back! Let's go through that gate looking like conquerors!"

"Conquerors," someone from the rear ranks echoed in a sarcastic voice. "You know where you can stick that sort of talk, you pompous son of a—"

"Shut up, damn you!" an underofficer yelled in a harsh bass voice. "Do you want a job digging latrines for the whole army tonight? Is that what you want? Just open that garbage mouth of yours again, and you'll get your wish!"

The drums beat harder. Somehow the backs straightened; the heads went up; the callused feet fell into step. And Kamose's victorious army, conquerors of the Hai, the terrible

Shepherd Kings, at last marched through the open gates of Sile into their home country for the first time in eighteen long and bitter years.

II

As the long files passed the inn, Psamtik, still on the rooftop, had been growing more and more restless. Finally he turned to Nebo and said, "I do hope you'll excuse me. I simply have to go. There are some things I'm not sure have been done. I have to make a last-minute check on everything. Just to be absolutely sure, you know."

"I quite understand," said his guest. "By all means tend to your business. I'm sure you'll feel more at ease once you've personally looked things over."

Psamtik turned at the stair. "If I may give you some advice," he said cautiously, "you should avoid the city streets after dark unless you're willing to hire bodyguards. It's going to be rough out there."

"Thank you for your concern," Nebo responded with friendly dignity. "But I'm an old traveler, well aware of the ways of the bad spots of the world. I'll take care." He waved good-bye and watched Psamtik disappear down the staircase.

But when the landlord had gone, Nebo went back to the roof's edge and looked down. The army was a ragged lot; there appeared to be no morale in them at all. They did not seem to care how they looked to the outside observer. It was indicative of a surliness. Things would, he decided, get rough by the middle of the night.

He turned and briskly descended the same stairs Psamtik had used and, walking not like a stranger but like a man who knew the layout of the town so well he could find his way in the dark, swiftly threaded his way through the honeycombed streets.

He reached the affluent quarters, and slowed a bit, looking for a particular house. When he found it, he walked up to the big door and knocked according to a prearranged signal: two knocks, a pause, another knock, pause, a last single knock.

The door opened. There stood before him a towering Nubian woman, a full head taller than he. She glowered down at him. He bowed, then did something quick and intricate with his hands, furtive sign language that passed so quickly, it could be recognized but not copied or analyzed.

The black woman bowed formally, then let him in and shut the door quickly behind him. "This way," she said. "My mistress is expecting you."

He was shown into a back room. Inside, a handsome, striking woman in her forties rose to greet him. "Nebo!" she said. The two embraced like brother and sister. "I trust you had a good trip."

"It was instructive," he remarked. "Not encouraging, but instructive. Do you want a report? I have to get upriver as quickly as I can."

"No," she replied. "The less I know, the less I have to hide from my husband. Did you see him? Is he coming up with the army?"

"I think so," Nebo said. "He's hard to recognize under the years. I think I knew him more by his posture than by his face. But even that has changed. If he's the man I think he is, he's lost a lot of his hairline, and his face is careworn. But the most striking difference is in the eyes. He looks drained, both physically and emotionally." He shrugged. "I could have the wrong man. But he was at the head of the rank, where the king should march on the road." He sighed. "The mighty lord of Two Lands."

"I don't feel much like a queen myself," the woman admitted. "I don't know what I'll say to him. How do I explain what's happened here since he went away?"

"He'll understand," Nebo assured her, looking the woman up and down. Queen Mara, wife to Kamose of Egypt, was still a regal-looking woman, for all that the years had worn heavily upon her and hardened her. Her eyes were the most striking feature in her face: intelligent, independent . . . and hurt. The eyes of a woman who had seen much suffering. "If there'd been time to purge the country before he left, to scour the land clean and get rid of the cult once and for all, I think he would have done it. When he finally broke free and stopped taking the drug they had been feeding him, he was at last man enough to do it. He killed his father in that duel before the walls of Avaris, so he was certainly capable of killing Amasis, purging the army and court alike, and making the country clean again."

"Yes," she said bitterly. "But instead he chose to go after the Shepherds and destroy them. Well, I'm not going to second-guess him. That was a worthy task too. And from all the reports over the years, he did a magnificent job. After breaking the Hai army at Sharuhen, he systematically took back all the northern cities the Hai had occupied over the years along the old migration route. I'm not saying that wasn't a good thing."

"No," her visitor conceded, "but in Kamose's absence, Amasis and the cult of the Great Mother have made inroads the king could never have envisioned. He'll be shocked to find how strong they are and how weak his own friends are now. If he had known that we would be reduced to an underground resistance movement, I wonder if he would have bothered to return."

Her large brown eyes held a strange mixture of sadness and bitterness. "Don't get on that particular path, please. If I ever got to thinking that way . . . look, I could simply have left Egypt and joined him in Canaan, on his way back. And we could have settled somewhere else. That would have appealed to me, if I'd let it."

Nebo bowed slightly. "But as always, duty prevailed. You know what would have happened to Egypt if you and Kamose had abandoned your responsibilities. You can imagine what would have happened to your friends the Habiru in the hands of Amasis, with all the restraints removed."

"Don't say it," she said with a shudder. "Poor souls! They have it hard enough as it is. Have you heard the latest? No, I guess you haven't; you've been away. Amasis relocated all the Habiru to Thebes. They're working in the quarries: men, women, and children. Even the elderly."

"Ach!" he said with angry indignation. "Then the pretenses are gone. They're slaves outright."

"I'm just as sorry as you are," she said. "It's not my doing or Baliniri's, either. The queen of Egypt doesn't count for much anymore, let alone the nominal vizier. Amasis runs the country. If it weren't for Baliniri's alliance with the upriver nomarchs and nobles, and with the priesthood of Amon . . ."

"Ah, yes," Nebo agreed. "The cult will never become popular with *them*, at least. Well, we must be thankful for any friends we still have. What's the news from upriver?"

"I'm afraid my news isn't up-to-date. But just before I left Thebes, I heard that Nehsi of Nubia was arming for war and had issued threats against the Second Cataract forts."

Nebo shot a significant glance at the other room, where the tall Nubian woman who had led him into Mara's back room now moved about, doing household chores.

"Oh, no," Mara assured him. "She's loyal to the Black Wind, not to Nubia. There's been something of a breach between the two entities. The Black Wind broke contact with Nubia a year ago, while you were gone. They're under the command of Naldamak, whose loyalty is always to Weret and the Desert Legion."

"I see," Nebo said. "But what would make King Nehsi want to attack Egypt now?"

"It's not clear. Our spies tell us that a dissident group, which wants different things than Nehsi, may have stampeded him into this. I can't say with any certainty whether or not this is true. Are you going upriver now?"

Nebo nodded. "I have business with Baliniri. It's time we began to bring our secret weapon cautiously and carefully into play." Seeing the concern on her face, he pressed on. "We can't hold off forever, Mara. Kamose looks exhausted. You'll see when the two of you get together. It'll break your heart."

"My heart was broken so long ago, I can't remember a time when it was whole," she said bitterly. "When Riki died . . ."

"Poor Mara." Nebo put a comforting hand on her shoulder. "You know that would not have worked out. The hand of death was on him from the day Teti died. But he gave his life for all of us, and as a result the Hai are no more."

The two pairs of eyes met, and they shared a long

moment of mutual regret. Mara had loved Riki as a friend, then as something more. But Riki, the greatest of Kamose's generals and bastard son of ex-Queen Ah-Hotep, had not long survived the death of his wife, Teti. She was the first female metalworker of the famous Children of the Lion dynasty of armsmakers. Riki had claimed to have communed with the spirit of his wife, dead of the plague, and had learned of his own impending death. From that day he had walked through the world a changed man. His mind was already in the otherworld, eagerly awaiting his reunion with beloved Teti's spirit. But before the healing death could come, he saved Kamose's life. Riki had then been murdered by the treachery of Makare, Amasis's closest and most deadly associate in the cult of the Great Mother.

"Well," Nebo said, "I have to go. You're going to meet Kamose here, then? And speak with him?"

"I must," she said. "As long as he stays free of the cult, I will remain loyal to him. It's the only way I can have any influence over him, and he's the only hope we have of winning Egypt back from the cult." There was resignation in her voice and more in her face; indeed, her very posture was that of a person forced to do a distasteful task for principle's sake. Her mouth was a straight line.

"Well, perhaps not the only hope," Nebo said, iron in his voice. "Perhaps we have a trick or two left to play on Amasis and his spies." He took her by the arms and looked into her eyes. "Keep faith with our cause and stay strong. You yourself are more of a weapon than you realize. Egypt can never repay the debt it owes you."

She stepped into his arms and hugged him close. "Give my greetings to the Habiru," she urged. "If there is anything in the world I can do for them, I will do it. Amasis would never have had the gall to move them to Thebes and strip away the last vestige of their pride if I had been there—I have a bad conscience about that. But perhaps I can still do something." She stepped back and looked at him. "If there is any strength left in Kamose—"

"You will find a good use for it," he finished for her. "I know. Keep well. Stay out of the streets tonight. This is not the same army Kamose took north to Sharuhen. From the looks of them, these are gutter scum—the sweepings of every wretched waterfront from here to Hayastan. Few have even the Egyptian cast to their features."

Mara looked out the window at the darkening sky. "It's almost sundown," she said. "Take your own advice, my friend. Don't be seen on the street. Stay here, please. There are spare rooms in the building where you'll be safe."

Nebo gave her a hard smile. "Who would attack a harmless old magus from the valley of the Tigris?" he asked. "One who quite obviously doesn't have two *outnou* to his name?" He grinned through his gray beard. "I'll be all right. I'm going upriver. A new stage of our campaign has to begin very soon, and it requires my attention. I've a boat waiting at the landing, with a stout crew of cutthroats who are more than a match for anyone who tries to stop me." He turned and went to the door, then stopped and looked back. "In the taverns today I heard a rumor. Pray it isn't true."

"What?" she asked.

"That Amasis is in the district. Here to meet his old friend Kamose and welcome the conquering hero back to a grateful country."

She frowned. "Just in case it's true I'd better get to Kamose first."

"If you do go to him, take a guard of no fewer than six people."

"I'll take Ngira," she said, indicating the tall Nubian woman. "She's worth any six men." She smiled. "Farewell. Be careful. We can't afford to lose you."

He nodded back at her, flinty-eyed, and went out the door.

Halfway down the street Nebo's path was blocked by a burly, already drunken soldier in a filthy Egyptian army uniform torn and tattered at the edges. "Hey!" the man bellowed in a rasping, alcoholic voice. "You! Old man! Come here!"

Nebo kept coming. He knew he did not look impressive. He was nearly the soldier's height but thin and trim, half his heft. The muscles of Nebo's arms were long and stringy, not bunched and knotted like the warrior's. He steered for the far side of the path, but the soldier stepped in front of him again.

"You!" the soldier repeated. "Where do you think you're going?"

Nebo stopped and looked him steadily in the eye. "You have notions of robbing me and perhaps giving me a beating," he said without emotion. "How can you do this when you can't lift your arms?"

The soldier cursed. "Can't lift my—?" he roared angrily. But it was immediately evident that he was in difficulty. "*Ahhhh!*" he screamed in agony. "My arms! What have you done to my arms?" It was as if they were sewn to his sides; he writhed back and forth, trying in vain to free them. "You sorcerer! You filthy conjurer! Wait until I get my hands on you!"

Nebo stepped forward and looked the man sternly in the eye. The angry threats slowed to a mutter and then died altogether. "One by one your bodily functions are failing you. In a moment your legs will no longer hold you up. Already they are weakening. Already they falter. Soon you will collapse to the ground, as helpless as a newborn. You will be unable to hold your bowels, and you will befoul yourself shamelessly. You will lie like a derelict in your vomit, and the pariah dogs of the street will walk around you rather than bear your smell."

"Curse you! I'll—"

Nebo considered. "I'll take away your voice while I'm at it," he said. "You can't speak. You can't call for help. In an hour when the spell wears off and you climb to your feet and head for the stews once more, you'll find that certain other bodily functions will also prove unreliable. You will be useless to any woman in Sile."

The soldier's angry, frightened eyes rolled crazily. His ugly mouth opened but could not utter a sound. And slowly, like a tree cut down, the big man pitched heavily to the ground and lay where he fell. Nebo stepped around him nimbly and continued on his way as the last rays of the sun died about him, and darkness—ominous, already foul with the clamor of faraway fighting and rowdiness—shrouded Sile.

III

The royal party—tall, hard-eyed men heavily armed and surrounded by burly guardsmen with scarred faces—swept into Psamtik's inn just as he was completing his inspection. There were already a dozen diners at their tables, and others had begun to file in through the side door. It was a higher-class inn than most; the clientele were traditionally men of affairs, traveling merchants and the like. Nevertheless, the captain of the guard called Psamtik over and imperiously commanded, "Get all these people out of here."

"I'm honored, of course," Psamtik said. "But, sir—"

"Did you hear me?" the captain demanded brutally in a darkly abrasive voice that carried across the whole room. "Get them all out of here. I will count to five. After that I will remove them myself. You won't like my methods."

Psamtik blinked. The look on the captain's face convinced him this was no time to discuss the matter. He gestured; two servants appeared close at hand. "Take all the diners to the . . . hmmm . . . the Peacock, around the corner. I'll pay for their dinners there. No charge for their food and drink here, of course. Now quickly. This is the royal party."

The servants accomplished Psamtik's bidding. He went back to the officer. "Sir, they're on their way. I'd like to say what an honor it is—"

The captain ignored him. "Clean off that table over there!" he bellowed. Three big guardsmen took charge. "Sire!" he said. "Everything will be in order in a moment."

Psamtik, wringing his hands, tried to pick out which of the three advancing faces was the king. The army had been gone so long, he could not remember any of the faces. "Sire," he ventured, choosing one, a clear-eyed, regal-looking fellow, "it is my very great privilege as owner of this establishment . . ."

The man to whom he had spoken shrugged. "Oh, don't tell me about it," he said, snorting. "I'm nobody around here, let me tell you. Passed over six times for general. Take it up with the king over here." And he jerked a thumb at a middle-aged man, balding, burly, hollow-eyed. A man with stooped shoulders, as if he carried the weight of the heavens upon his back. "Kamose! This popinjay wants to gush all over you. Are you available?"

The haunted eyes turned Psamtik's way, and there was in that first brief glance such hurt and loathing, resentment and pain that Psamtik winced. This was a man who had seen everything bad in life and no longer looked to see good. *Gods!* he thought. *Can this ruined hulk of a man be the king? The conqueror of half the known world?*

"You," the king said in a toneless voice. "Get us the strongest wine you've got." He turned to the captain of the guard, dismissing Psamtik as if he had been a servant or a slave. "Look," he said, "I didn't like what I saw in the streets on the way here. It's out of control. The lot of foreign mercenaries are loose in the stews, and that legion of cursed Greeks in particular, who came over to our side at Ashkelon and would fight for anyone who paid them one *outnou* more than their last leader, would as soon rape anything that moved as look at them. We're back in Egypt now, remember."

"Yes sir!" the captain said. "You!" he bellowed at a particularly ugly subordinate. "You heard the man! Get the word out: Any soldier who gets out of line is a dead man. You get me?"

"Yes, sir!" the guardsman said in a surly voice and turned on his heel.

The captain chuckled nastily. "He hates mercenaries anyway. And everybody hates the Greeks. Get the swine fighting each other, and maybe they'll leave the civilians alone, eh? Hey, you!" he bellowed at Psamtik. "Where's that wine?"

Psamtik gulped and turned tail. It was obvious there would be no pleasing these people. Could this bunch of smelly louts actually be the lord of Two Lands and his staff? He rolled his eyes heavenward, sighed, and called a servant. "Get them wine on the double. The best stuff, from the second cellar."

He headed for the door. But as he did, it opened and two new faces appeared there. One was heavily veiled but wore clothing of expensive cut. The other was a tall black-skinned woman from the upper Nile. "Hey!" he said in a loud whisper. "You can't come in here now! Auditions for dancing girls tomorrow at noon. Now be off with you!"

The shorter woman took down the hood of her wrap with two graceful hands. "I will forgive your insolence to your queen," she said. "You could not have been expected to recognize me."

Psamtik's heart was in his mouth. He tried to frame an apology, but the woman seemed not to be waiting for one. She peered across the room and saw the royal party. "It's all right," she said, then nodded and, with the Nubian woman in her wake, pushed her way across the room.

"Kamose!" she said, her voice deep and commanding.

The king's face went blank; then he reacted. His eyes went wide. His face puckered into a frown, which doubled the number of wrinkles on his battered, careworn face.

"Kamose," she repeated, "welcome back to Egypt."

Her husband blinked at her. "Mara," he said in a dead voice, low-pitched and rasping. "I didn't expect to see you."

Mara shot quick glances to right and left. "Leave us for now," she ordered. "All of you."

This did not bring the automatic obedience her voice might once have commanded. The generals looked at Kamose for confirmation; he nodded angrily, and they dispersed, shooting unreadable glances at her. There was an undercurrent of muttering that might have been disrespectful, even obscene, could it have been heard clearly.

"That's better," she said. She sat down across the table from her husband. The tall and silent Nubian was still within reach. Mara turned and said something in the Nubian tongue, causing Ngira to move out of earshot. "Well," she said, "hail to the conqueror."

He said nothing, but he glowered at her.

"I have heard great things of your exploits," she continued, "although I am sure they did not do you justice."

"What are you doing here?" he asked. "This is a dangerous place tonight." He sneered at the tall form behind her. "Even with your pet Nubian close at hand. How did you get her to wear clothing? Did you promise her human flesh to eat?"

Mara's eyes flashed. "I catch you in a genial mood, I see.

Well, since we haven't seen each other for eighteen years, I'll ignore your bad manners. You've earned a bit of respite from the rules of decent human conduct, I suppose. So long as you make no move to humiliate me in public."

He sneered again. "And I'll ignore that threat. Do you think that after what I've seen and done up North I can be cowed by a woman's displeasure?" He waved the thought away. "Ah, here's the wine. Would you be so kind as to pour a drink for your lord and master?" The phrase had an acid quality. "The first real drink he's had since he crossed the damned wretched Sinai with this bunch of cutthroats?"

She obliged, as skillfully and graciously as any trained servant. "There," she said. "My lord and master. Drink!" She watched him gulp noisily, spilling wine down his chin and on his garment. He backhanded his mouth with a sleeve still grimy from the road, then belched. "You're as filthy as a pig," she said. "If Sile had rooms fit for the purpose, I'd give you a wife's ritual bath. I don't mind doing such things. But there isn't a royal residence here. There hasn't been since the Shepherds came."

"Forget it," Kamose said. "I need mainly to sleep for two weeks. I don't even care how dirty I am. I plan to find a bed as soon as I've fed these scum and given the orders for their dispersal. I haven't slept well for too long."

"As you wish," she agreed. Then, "You've changed."

"Yes," he said bitterly. "I'm older. Older and tireder and uglier and sicker of the world and all the people in it. There are times when I think that if I had reliable poison that wouldn't set my innards on fire after I drank it—"

Now it was her turn to sneer. "And this is the conqueror? Give me a coward any time." But her face softened. "Pardon me. I shouldn't speak that way to you. You've had a long journey, and I should be forbearing. Forgive me, Kamose. I'll do what I can to help ease the transition for you. When we're back in Thebes—"

"Thebes!" he said contemptuously. "After these years on the road, killing and burning and smashing, I'm in no particular hurry to get back to court life. Does that make sense to you?"

She looked at him for a long moment and did not say

anything. It made perfect sense, in fact. She held no love for Thebes now; it was riddled with treason and intrigue, and every face might be a deadly enemy, particularly after an absence of nearly twenty years. "I understand," she said thoughtfully. "Perhaps I should stay here with you for a while. The court can wait." She waited, but there was no response. "That is, if it would please you to have me here with you. I'll gladly stay as long as you would like."

It was a very considerable concession, but still it drew no response, no feeling flaming up behind the dead, burned-out eyes. "Whatever you choose," he said. "It is all one."

And now out of the broad chest came the longest, most drawn-out, and alienated sigh she had ever heard. It ended in something rather like a shudder. He looked at her, and in the hollow eyes, for the first time, there was a trace of feeling. "I stopped caring," he said simply, "somewhere in Syria. Damascus? Ebla? You watch enough people turned to meat for the dogs, and after a time they all look that way to you, even the ones who are alive and walking around. I don't wish to hurt your feelings. It's nothing personal. You're a good enough woman. But I look at a man, a woman—anyone— and I see a death's-head mask. I see a corpse already starting to rot. It's just a matter of time."

She looked him in the eye and, with a horrible coldness in her veins, knew he was telling the truth. Nevertheless, she forced a smile and said, "We'll let you get a couple of days of uninterrupted sleep, and *then* perhaps we'll see how you feel."

"I can't sleep," he told her flatly. "The dreams wake me up, drenched with cold sweat and screaming." He closed his eyes wearily and then opened them again. They were red-rimmed and haunted. He tried to smile, but it did not reach his eyes at all. To her it looked like the malevolent grin of a whitened skull picked clean by crows.

It's hopeless, she thought. *I can't count on him. There's nobody left in there at all. . . .*

IV

When she had gone, Kamose sat down heavily before the big table. He poured himself a brimming bowl of palm wine, spilling half, and brought the bowl to his lips with unsteady hands. When he drank, the dark liquid stained his tunic and dripped down his scarred, naked arms.

The captain of the guard came back from the far side of the room. "Sire," he said in a voice a bit too casual given their respective ranks, "the innkeeper says entertainment is available if you're interested. Dancers? Musicians?"

"Interested?" Kamose looked up at him with eyes as empty as dry wells. Not seeing. Not hearing. Not thinking. He turned back to his wine bowl and drank.

The captain beckoned to Psamtik. "You might as well bring them on," he said. "The king probably won't even notice them, but the rest of us will. Keep the wine coming. Can you give him anything stronger than the stuff he's drinking? He has a hard time getting to sleep these days."

"I understand," Psamtik responded. He clapped his hands at the instrumentalists and drummers who had been installed in the far corner of the room for some minutes now. Instantly the music struck up, and from the two doorways on opposite sides of the fireplace came twin girls, faces veiled, breasts bared, their loins barely covered, tiny bells jingling merrily on their toes, as they performed a meticulously rehearsed dance in which each girl's every action mirrored that of the other.

Instant approval was lustily roared out from the officers. The girls smiled as their bellies shook seductively. There was already a thin film of sweat on their breasts, and under the dancing lights of the overhead torches, the effect was animal, erotic, and hypnotic.

"They're good, very good," the captain of the guard commended. "Do you have any girls skilled in massage?" Psamtik nodded and winked. "I see," the captain said. "Skilled in other matters too, eh? All the better. Bring her here. Perhaps His Majesty will take notice of her. Let's help him along a bit—the girl comes naked."

"A-all right," Psamtik said.

"And have her perfume herself beforehand. I want her reeking like the great whore of all whores. Something Damascene. *Hmmm* . . . jasmine? Yes, I think that was it. Last time we could get him interested, the girl wore jasmine and nothing else. Ah, she was something. Breasts like melons. After the king was done with her, I—but that's enough of that. And he likes them submissive. Eyes downcast, you know."

"I . . . I'm trying to remember all this," Psamtik said.

"See that you do. And where's that damned palm wine? The strongest you have, now!"

Swords and bows and war clubs had been checked in camp before the evening's festivities had begun, but soldiers were soldiers, so every man wore a dagger under his garment. It was the only prudent thing to do on a night when the frustrations of a long haul across the punishing desert were being vented in one brutal fight after another.

In the enlisted men's quarter—the Quarter of Thieves was the civilian name for it—a great battle had broken out in the Inn of the Two Walls and overflowed into the street. Already two men lay dead in the gutter, and a third sat splay-legged in the middle of the street under the torches, clutching his slit throat as if the pressure of his hand could stanch the flow of blood forever. But now two drunken combatants blundered into him and knocked his hands loose, allowing the blood to spurt wildly.

Into the pool of light staggered a burly giant, a full head taller than the other men, a bloody dagger in his huge hand. "All right!" he growled. "Who'll fight me? Step forward, you swine! Who has the guts to challenge me?"

A tall, lean soldier spat on the ground and stepped into the light. "Put the knife down," he said. "I'll fight you, hand to hand."

The big man smiled and stuck the dagger in his belt. He rubbed his hands together; but as he did, the thinner man attacked. Clapping his hands loudly to distract his opponent, he spun like a top and caught the giant in the side of the head with a terrible swinging blow from his booted foot. The big man staggered but did not fall. The thin man feinted a blow at the big man's face, then kicked him in the pit of the stomach, once, twice. The attacker recovered from each blow so quickly, he did not lose balance.

"Why you—" the big man sputtered. He rushed forward, arms outstretched, ready to give his enemy the death hug of a bear, and ran onto the outstretched sword of a guardsman. The blade sank to the hilt into his belly before the guardsman withdrew it.

The surrounding crowd surged forward angrily, then fell back. The guardsman was the first of a detachment of six. They encircled a portly figure in a dark robe, his hood pulled high to conceal his face. But as the sound of the mob's anger reached the man, he pulled back the hood to look around.

There was a collective gasp from the old soldiers in the crowd. They knew the face in the pool of light in the street, even eighteen years later—the hard unsmiling mouth, the hawk's nose, the terrible eyes . . .

"*Amasis!*" someone uttered.

"Yes," the cult leader said, his predatory eyes scanning their faces. "Look at you. As filthy as pigs rolling in their own excrement. You think you're heroes, returning conquerors, progressed beyond the disciplines of the Brotherhood, beyond the reach of the Great Mother and her servants." His tone was acid, insolent. "Little do you know! Undisciplined dogs! Jackals! The Goddess's eyes are upon you waking or sleeping! In all lands she sees your derelictions, your iniquities, your lack of faith!"

His eye transfixed a man in the front row.

"N-no, my lord," the old soldier stammered. "We've been faithful. We—"

"Silence! You can't lie to me! There's not a one of you who can look me in the eye and lie!" His voice had a sharp edge, cutting to the bone.

"Please, master," the offender said, this time with proper respect.

"Ah," Amasis said. " '*Master!*' That's better. I'll have you back in line soon." His voice rose in volume. "Tell all the army that they are back in the land ruled by the Great

Mother, and they are all answerable to me. Me! Do you understand?"

"Yes, master," several voices responded.

"I can't hear you! Do you understand!"

"*Yes, master!*" the throng roared.

"That's better," Amasis said, and with a nod to his escorts he set out through the dark streets at a pace so rapid, the guardsmen had to lengthen their stride to keep up.

The girl's hands had done their work well. Kamose now slumped over the table and was snoring lightly. He stank vilely. The girl, slim, small-breasted, and naked, looked at the captain of the guard. "He is asleep. Can I go now?" One of her hands covered her lap, and she would not look him directly in the eye. "I . . . I do not usually do this sort of thing so—so publicly."

"Oh, come on." The captain sneered. "It's a living. You'll make more money tonight than you've made in six months. Come here." He held out one large, tanned hand. "Don't be bashful. You want to be paid, don't you?"

Her eyes blazed angrily for a moment, then the flash went dead. She knew the way of the world, after all. "We can go in the back room," she suggested. "But in front of all these people . . ."

"Nobody's watching," he said. "Look around. Everybody's busy with their own affairs. Everybody who's still awake, that is. And the king is quite beyond all that. Come here."

She was about to comply, however unwillingly, but Kamose chose that moment to groan in his sleep. His hand rose, made scrubbing motions, fended off some imaginary threat. "See?" she said. "He'll wake up and want me by him. I can get him off to sleep, rubbing his neck." She shot Kamose a glance in which there was some compassion. "Poor man."

"Forget him," the captain growled. "Poor *me*. I actually have to tell a woman twice to do what I wish? I may have to beat her up a bit."

"You wouldn't," she said, but she didn't believe her own words. "Please. Couldn't you just let me go?"

"I'm getting angry," the captain said in a voice grown tight and threatening.

There was a sudden *bang* from the far side of the room, over the sound of the music and the turmoil. The captain glared in that direction. The door had been thrown open and slammed against the wall, and the doorway was full of tall, muscular guardsmen—underofficers and enlisted men. He stood, cursed, bellowed across the room. "This is officers' territory!" he said. "Turn around and—"

Behind him the king struggled to wakefulness. "Wha' . . ." he asked in a drunken voice. The captain stared wide-eyed as the guards parted to let a dark-robed man through. It was Amasis, and he stood, hands on hips, looking at them all.

"Most of you know who I am," he said ominously. "Welcome back." His voice dripped sarcasm. "Kamose! Where are you?" Then he saw the king and moved forward as the captain whirled. Kamose was sitting up, his eyes trying to get the intruder in focus, his mouth hanging open like an idiot's.

"Ah, there you are, sire," Amasis said, with neither affection nor respect. "You look exhausted." He looked over the king's head at the girl. "You. Out." She gulped and hurried out the door. Amasis turned to the captain. "Help me get him to his room."

"Wine," Kamose said. "More wine."

"Time enough for that," Amasis said. "You look like a man who hasn't slept for days."

"Weeks," the king said in a slurred voice. "Months. Don't know how long. Dreams. Bad dreams."

"Well, those days are over," Amasis assured him, lifting Kamose to his feet as the captain took his other side. "When you were with me you never had trouble sleeping, you'll remember. Well, that's the way it's going to be again. I have something for you to take that will allow you to sleep for a week. And with no dreams at all."

"No," Kamose said. "Don't want. Promised Mara no more *shepenn*."

"Just come along, now, sire," Amasis said. "Make way, there!"

The music had long since stopped, and all eyes were on the robed man and the king. The stunned crowd parted to let

them by. Amasis's eyes scanned the group, but there were
few who would look him in the eye as he moved toward the
stairs.

"There's enough moon to sail by," said the boatman.
"We can go now, if you like." With a little bow he handed
Ngira and Mara onto his vessel; then he stood with the
mooring lines in his hand. "Shall I cast off, my lady?"

Mara moved to the broad seat in the bow. "Yes. There's
nothing more for me here. I want to be beyond Athribis by
dawn."

"As my lady wishes," the boatman said. He cast off and
stepped into the boat. "Athribis it is."

"No," Mara said. "All the way to Thebes."

He calculated the cost of so great a voyage, then smiled.
His teeth were visible in the moonlight. "I have not been in
Thebes since I was a boy. Thebes it is, my lady." And he
bent to his work, unfurling the lateen sail.

Mara stared at the receding shore. "I don't know what I
was expecting," she confessed. "I should have known better
than to hope. Now there is only the one chance left for
Egypt. A child. A mere boy, unfledged and untried. If he,
too, fails us . . ."

She shuddered and closed her eyes. Suddenly she looked
her age; yes, and more perhaps. The Nubian woman moved
to her side and tried to put a comforting hand on her shoulder, but she shook it off.

Above them the sail billowed. Astern, the boatman tugged
at the tiller, and the little vessel moved upstream against the
unceasing current of the mighty Nile.

CHAPTER TWO

Thebes

I

The years had taken their toll on the once mighty frame of Baliniri, who for many years had served as the vizier of Egypt and, in his distant youth, was the world-renowned hero of the siege of Mari. The great shoulders were still broad, but bowed. The hair—what there was of it—was gray streaked with white, and his movements were slowed by age.

Nevertheless, he was still an impressive figure, addressing a hastily called meeting of his military command and the nobles and the priests of Amon who lived in the immediate vicinity of mighty Thebes. Baliniri's leonine head still was held high, and his great, jutting jaw was as firm as ever. The eyes scanning the crowd were a hawk's, missing nothing—not even the faintest hint of a change of expression—as the gathering settled down and the conversations died. Such was the authority his years of power had conferred upon him that the silence came almost instantly. He waited a beat, then spoke.

"Thank you for coming," he said in a deep voice little changed from his middle years. "I am sure you know why I have called you here. Nevertheless, there are visitors among us—observers from other nations around the Great Sea—and for their sake I will recapitulate the problem that has assembled us.

"As you know, our victorious army has returned after many years' absence, with our mighty and noble lord of Two Lands, Kamose, at its head. It is an army that has done wonders beyond the imaginings of men, having freed us from the hated yoke of the northern invaders, the Hai, whom our fathers and grandfathers called the Shepherd Kings.

"But it is also an army that suffers mental and physical exhaustion and must be allowed time to heal, to make itself whole again. However much it may pain me to say so, I must tell you that our king, Kamose, has shared its hard life as well as its undying glory, and he, too, is exhausted."

This was the first anyone in the auspicious audience had heard of some possible problem with the king, and a murmur understandably swept through the crowd.

Baliniri held up his broad, long-fingered hand, huge but misshapen with arthritis. "Meanwhile," he said, his voice rising and shaming them to silence, "trouble has appeared on our southern frontiers. A treaty of peace has been broken. Egypt has been invaded by the armies of Nubia, led by Nehsi, king of kings and ruler of all the lands above our Second Cataract fortresses."

This was not news. The rumors of the Nubian advances had been all over the city for days, but no hard facts or details had been available. After a brief eruption of angry and indignant outbursts, Baliniri again waved them to silence. "Indeed, several of our forts have been taken by surprise, and now the Nubians advance beyond the Second Cataract.

"Unchecked, they may stop at the First Cataract, where the First Nome of Egypt begins, thus limiting our loss to the buffer zone established between Egypt and Nubia by Sesostris III. Or they may advance into Egyptian territory, as they did in the days of Nehsi's father, whom the Nubians called Akillu, and whom we were able to halt at the battle of El-Kab."

Faces turned toward one another, but there was little comment.

Baliniri went on. "A breakdown of communication exists between Egypt and Nubia. Our diplomats are under arrest in Kerma, and as far as we know, this action was taken without cause or warning. The diplomats have not been permitted to send messages to us. I can only guess why this aggression has occurred: Nehsi, in recent years, has come under the influence of a strong-willed courtier named Balaam, whose reputation is one of insatiable ambition. The king may have been led astray by Balaam."

A voice spoke up from the rear of the great hall. "Your pardon, my lord. What of Nehsi's sister, Naldamak, leader of the Black Wind? Surely she must know Nehsi's mind. Have communications broken down with her as well?"

Baliniri smiled grimly. "A good question. For the benefit of our foreign guests, let me explain. Many years ago Nehsi's and Naldamak's mother, Ebana, formed an elite Nubian women's army called the Black Wind. The unit has maintained its integrity but, rather than being controlled by Nubia, it is more an independent entity. When Ebana was succeeded by Naldamak as leader of this unit, the Black Wind formed an alliance with the Desert Legion, the women's unit founded by Teti and trained by me personally to patrol the western desert and control the caravan routes to keep the Hai from sending an army secretly across the desert trails to attack Thebes."

Baliniri put his two hands together in a prayerlike attitude. "Now, to answer the question, for many years the Black Wind has been our best link with Nehsi, and through his sister we have known his mind even when diplomatic channels of communication have failed." He paused and looked around, his face somber and his eyes hard. "In the two months preceding Nehsi's move on the Second Cataract forts, Naldamak's own contact with her brother broke off, mysteriously and suddenly. It has remained broken ever since, despite her many efforts to renew it.

"Since the fall of Semna," he added in a harsh voice, "which has since become a second capital of the advancing

Nubian army, a state of war has existed between that country and Egypt."

Now the murmur rose and rose; there were even shouts from the rear. "Why don't we send the army?" a voice demanded. "They can't do this to us!"

Baliniri held up both hands. It took some moments to silence the uproar. "Please!" he said. "Please! Hear me!"

When the noise had died down, he spoke. "As I have told you, the main army lies exhausted in Sile, in desperate need of recuperation. The king, too, requires rest. A quick move by the main army force is unthinkable for us to consider, especially because of the enormous distance from Sile, on the Sinai border, to Nubia."

Another voice chimed up. "Call out the Thebes garrison! You can lead it!"

Baliniri smiled. "The Thebes garrison has been mobilized and has been augmented with troops brought up from the delta nomes, the palace guard, and the home guards of the downriver and upriver nomes. But as for myself leading them . . . thank you, my friend, for a compliment I no longer deserve. These gnarled hands"—he held them up—"will never hold a sword again. And these old legs are no longer capable of a forced march—or indeed anything more strenuous than an old man's stroll across the Temple Quarter. No, I am no longer the man to lead your army in a military move."

His eyes narrowed. "But I have given this much thought. Under the honored laws of our country, passed down by generation after generation, the army may not march against a foe unless it is commanded by a prince of the blood. And although I was married to your former queen Ah-Hotep, whose bloodlines were the finest in Egypt, my blood, alas, is no bluer than that of any man here and much less so than a good number of you."

He inclined his head to one side. "Then what to do, I've asked myself. I have consulted our astrologers and seers, military officers and learned men, and have sought the good counsel of the noble Priesthood of Amon. Only one solution has presented itself. Today I called you here to consider this possible path and, failing its acceptance by you, to ask your wise advice in steering me to an alternative that more completely meets with your approval." His tone became more serious. "Keeping always in mind that a decision must be reached immediately, as the situation grows more critical with every passing day."

"Let's hear your solution first, my lord!" someone suggested from the third row.

Baliniri smiled benignly, as if this request were a surprise and not the response he had been carefully cultivating since the first moment he had opened his mouth. "Very well," he agreed. "We have at our disposal able commanders, of respectable if not noble blood. All that remains is to put at their head a prince of the blood, who will listen wisely to their advice of experience and issue the proper orders for them to carry out.

"We *have* such a prince among us."

Now there was a buzz of real interest from the audience as face turned to neighboring face.

"But who? . . ."

"Whom could he be talking about?"

"You don't suppose? . . ."

"Friends!" he said. "Hear me! Lords, nobles, and priests of Amon, distinguished guests: Let me present to you today— Prince Moses!"

The young man who stepped forward at Baliniri's urging was tall, clear-eyed, and well-favored even among the handsome young men of the court. He had broad shoulders and a muscular frame, the result of much time spent in hunting, exercise, and sports. As he moved to a stand beside the aging vizier, his movements were easy and graceful. He smiled—a little shyly, it seemed—and looked to Baliniri for reassurance before looking out into the sea of faces.

"I was going to have the young prince make a speech," Baliniri said, "but he protests that he is soft-spoken and that those in the back will not hear him if he tries to address you. So in the way of introduction, I will tell you a thing or two about him.

"He is the son of Princess Thermutis, my wife's daughter, by the court noble Zer, who did not live to see the birth of his son. Moses is thus a prince of the blood and qualifies under the statutes of Egypt."

Baliniri's mind was working at a furious clip while his eyes sought those of the men before him, searching for signs of skepticism. His heart beat fast. . . .

Eighteen years earlier, as the great battles against the Hai, then against Amasis and the cult had begun, a plot had been hatched among Baliniri, Ah-Hotep, and Mara. Thermutis's child had been born hopelessly deformed, and it mercifully died within the day. The infant's body was secretly removed from the palace, and no one was allowed access to the princess's apartment. At almost the same moment another child had been born to the Habiru woman Jochebed, of the tribe of Levi.

Jochebed's people had lain under a terrible ultimatum issued by Amasis: All male children born among them at the time were to be killed. Because the importance of the birth of this child had been foretold by the seers and in a vision to Levi from the Habiru God, Baliniri, Ah-Hotep, Mara, and Jochebed had swiftly hatched a plot to save its life and provide Thermutis with a child of her own. And, quite by design, to give Baliniri's party a prince of the blood to raise, eventually to replace Kamose. The plot allowed for the despondent princess to find the child in a basket floating among the bulrushes where Thermutis customarily bathed. She clutched the infant to her immediately, with only a trusted few knowing that the newborn Moses was not of royal descent. Jochebed had been hired as wet nurse.

Nevertheless, there was always the chance that rumors could have circulated among the palace servants, some of whom were known to be members of the cult of the Great Goddess. Thus, as Baliniri surveyed the faces before him, his heart raced dangerously.

But none of the expressions seemed to betray any knowledge of the truth in the matter. He went on, relieved. "The prince is fit and intelligent and has had the best tutelage from the most advanced scholars and masters of the arts of war. He excels in all weapons and in chariotry and has a budding reputation, in the society in which he has been allowed to circulate, for leadership. It remains only to try him in the field, and to this end I nominate him for the post under discussion. If you approve, he will work closely with our finest officers and our wisest advisers and will give no order not made in consultation. I have little doubt that he will bring us victory, honor unstained, and the welcome news of a restored Egyptian hegemony over the lands in dispute. My lords: Shall Prince Moses lead our army south to Nubia and victory?"

The answer came, a great roar of enthusiastic acceptance. "Long live Prince Moses!" a voice cried from the rear. And one by one the ranks repeated it until the great hall resounded with their cheers.

II

After the formal meeting adjourned, a number of the assembled nobles and officials lingered on to speak with Baliniri. Standing unobtrusively to one side, Prince Moses waited patiently for the last and the least of these to go.

Baliniri took note of the prince's unwillingness to interrupt. He bade farewell to the last visitor, a rich landowner from the Fayum, watched the hall clear, and turned smiling to his young charge. "Thank you for waiting so patiently. Come. The servants have prepared a light meal for us on the rooftop. There should be a pleasant breeze. We have fresh figs and dates from the delta, right off the boat."

The young man, always affectionately deferent to his mother's stepfather, returned the smile. "Whatever you wish, Baliniri. Here, take my arm, and the stairs will not seem so steep."

As they made their way up, pausing every few steps, Baliniri grumbled under his breath. "Look at me, will you? I used to be so lively. I was too heavily built to be the fastest when races were run at the festivals, but there was a time when I could go the distance with any man and still be running when all the rest had dropped."

"There is a time for the things of youth, and a time for the things of age, Baliniri," the young man replied in his slow, thoughtful manner. It was unlike him to hurry or be impulsive about anything, and Baliniri liked that in him. "Youth is for strength and beauty, which you had in abundance when it was proper for you to have them. Age is for wisdom and authority. And now who would contest your authority or question your wisdom?" He laughed lightly and answered his own question. "Nobody, at least not while I'm around."

Baliniri snorted. "Amasis questions my wisdom and challenges my authority. He and that whole wretched cult of his." The two reached the landing and circled around to the narrower staircase, which led to the roof gardens.

"Pay no attention to them, Baliniri," Prince Moses urged. "No one with any sense listens to them."

"Oh, a few agree with him that I am senile and that my mind is gone, I know. But they do not have to believe him to be cowed enough to obey him. All the nobles you saw here today, all the army officers, even the big landowners . . . all know their households are crawling with cult informers, and few are so foolish as to oppose Amasis openly, where they can be overheard. Although the palace is overrun, I don't think Amasis has penetrated my inner circle, and to the best of my knowledge, my servants are mine alone."

At the top of the stairs the young prince helped Baliniri onto a comfortable couch beside a table laden with fruit and olives and a pair of wineskins. Then he sat down opposite the vizier and took in the view. "You're right as always, Baliniri," he said. "This is the best place in Thebes to be at this time of day. Look how lovely the light is on the river."

Baliniri took an olive from the bowl and tossed it into his mouth. "One of the few things Amasis has left alone for me is this little hideout. It was Ah-Hotep's favorite retreat. She chose all the greenery." He pointed toward the potted palms and flowering plants that flanked their seats.

"It reminds me of Grandmother, all right," the young man said. "How I miss her! And how much greater must your own loss be!"

"At my age, one has lost much. But I try to remember

how very fortunate I was to have found her in middle life and to have had her by my side another dozen years and more. Here, try these figs. They're the season's best so far."

As he watched the young prince reach for the fruit, Baliniri reflected upon the boy's use of the term *grand-mother*. The decision not to tell him of his birth and the secret that lay behind it had been made when the lad was very young; a youngster should not have to carry the heavy burden of a state secret. And, of course, there was never any question of letting the truth be known generally.

But now? Now, when Moses was eighteen and about to be tried in the field, definitively to enter a man's estate? Wasn't it time to let him know that, instead of being Thermutis's child, he was—what? The child of slaves? Of the wretched, overworked Habiru, whom Amasis had brought to Thebes to do beast-of-burden work in the quarries?

This was a lot for a young man to have to deal with, and Baliniri was not sure how the lad would react. Looking into the boy's clear eyes and noting the guileless expression on his handsome young face, Baliniri thought: *He's too honest. Not the face of a boy who would want to keep such a thing quiet.*

Reason intervened. If the word were to get out that Moses was not a prince of the blood, there could be no expedition upriver at all, not until Kamose returned. And from the report he had received only today on Kamose's condition, perhaps not even then.

No, he decided. He would wait until Moses returned from his quest on the upper Nile. There would be plenty of time for him to learn the truth . . . later.

Moses lifted a wineskin and squeezed a long line of the red liquid into his open mouth, cutting off the flow expertly when he had had his fill. Then he looked at Baliniri. "You're sure about me leading the expedition? I've never had a command. I've had very good training, but—"

"The best," Baliniri cut in. "Much of it at my own hands. And in all modesty I doubt you could find better than I have been able to give you."

Moses laughed ruefully. "I do not question the teacher. I have lingering doubts about the pupil."

"Don't," Baliniri said. "I'm surrounding you with good

men—the best adjutants and underofficers in the entire command. They're men you can count on. They'll know how to advise you. Just listen to them in all matters. In the small ones, do as they say. In the large ones, listen carefully to them, but give greater weight to the still-small voice inside your heart. You have good instincts. Learn to follow them."

"I think I understand, Baliniri."

"There's more. I'm sending another man with you. A wise and learned foreigner who's only recently come to court. I think he'll be a welcome source of advice and good counsel, and I think you two will get on. He's from my old home country, the Land of Two Rivers. Between him and the officers I'm sending with you, you'll be able to draw upon the accumulated wisdom of the two greatest cultures in the world."

"What's his name? When will I meet him?"

Baliniri took one of the dates and bit into it. "His name is Nebo," he said. "He comes highly recommended. I have spoken with him frequently since his arrival, and I find his insights acute and highly intelligent. He particularly impresses me in his knowledge of people. You will need all the help you can get in this regard. I'll be honest with you: I've done my best to eliminate from your party everyone I knew or suspected to be allied with Amasis's cult. But I can't be sure, and I think Nebo will be very helpful in this. He knows the cult's black and evil ways inside and out. If anyone can sniff out a traitor from within your circle, he'll be able to do it."

"I am in your hands and shall obey such counsel as you choose to give me." The boy smiled affectionately. "You have been father and grandfather to me since I was born. If I live a thousand years, I shall not repay the debt I owe you."

Baliniri, much touched but embarrassed, tried to shrug it off. "You've a honeyed tongue on you," he said. "May the gods protect any girl who comes near you when you reach the age of—what am I saying? You are already of age! Look at you! Are my maidservants safe? The girls of the city?"

Moses laughed. "I must admit, Baliniri, that I have begun to take notice of them." He flushed. "But while there have been small incidents here and there, nothing serious has happened. No woman has found a place in my heart. All in good time, I suppose. I have a job to do first. Perhaps after I have returned from the present expedition . . . When will I meet this friend of yours, this Nebo?"

"The day after tomorrow," Baliniri answered. "He is busy with his own affairs until then. He is a man of much learning and confers with our sages, magi, and scribes. When he has satisfied himself about certain questions, he will begin your instruction."

"Aha. Then I carry a teacher with me?" There was the mildest teasing tone in the boy's voice, but Baliniri could not get angry with him for a raillery that he would permit from no other living soul.

"The wise man considers all the world his teacher," Baliniri retorted. "There were few people who could not teach me something in this life. Even if some of them taught by bad example."

"I understand," the boy said. "When do I leave?"

"The ship sails the first of next week," Baliniri said. "The army is being outfitted now. I will keep you abreast of all the new dispatches that come from Nubia. Meanwhile, enjoy your last days of freedom. Get out in the city or go hunting, or do whatever pleases you. You'll be a slave to duty from the moment the anchor lifts and your fleet heads up the Nile. Go. Have fun. But be back here in two days, ready to begin the next phase of your education."

Prince Moses rose. "I will obey," he said with a grin.

III

At the bottom of the stairs Moses paused and stood for a moment, unable to make up his mind what to do with so beautiful a day. The balmy weather and the soft breeze atop the roof garden had cast their spell and brought upon him a languid and lyrical mood.

It was no day for the hunt, that was sure. It was no day for anything but the pursuit of idle pleasure. For a moment he considered taking a boat out on the Nile, but even the quite minor work involved in sailing was more than his present mood allowed for.

Still, it was cool on the Nile. . . .

He thought over the matter for yet another long moment and came up with a compromise. The sun played softly on the hilltops across the river. He would go—alone, without his bodyguard, if this could be managed—across the Nile and wander in the artisans' town at Deir el-Bahari. He would go dressed as an ordinary citizen so that nobody could recognize him: a loincloth of rough cloth, and papyrus sandals.

The more he thought about it, the more he liked it. He had been to Deir el-Bahari only twice in his young life, other than official visits in which he had been quite unrecognizable, one of a long line of nobles of the court in a procession, wearing the wig and ceremonial false beard of office. On the two occasions when he had visited the town informally, he had been accompanied by burly guards who had not let him do anything that had really appealed to him. This had caused him to look with envy on the carefree lives of the artists in the hillside village and wonder if, despite their poverty, they might not be more happy than he, a prince of the royal house but a boy whose every movement was circumscribed, regulated.

He had liked the look of the place. The only thing about Deir el-Bahari that he had not liked was the sight of the wretched Edomite slaves toiling in the hillside quarries outside the village. Up to that moment his life had been so sheltered that he had seldom seen how the pitiful no-hopers on the bottom of society lived.

He had learned later that various subject peoples had taken their turn in the quarries, and the turnover was tremendous, since quarry slaves did not live long. The work and the working conditions, exacerbated by the brutal treatment they received at the hands of the overseers, tended to eliminate all but the hardiest of them.

He had been shocked, and he had asked that steps be taken to improve their lot, only to be told that slaves of the state were under the particular purview of Amasis, who was not answerable even to the son of a princess. The overseers had thus not been admonished, and the suffering of the Edomites had continued.

He had pondered this for some time afterward, trying to sort out his thoughts on the injustice of having innocent people—for he knew they were not convicts—worked like beasts of burden until they dropped in their tracks and were replaced by new chattels. How could this be allowed, when someone like him lived in luxury and safety, surrounded by comforts that these poor wretches could never imagine?

It did not seem right, yet no one questioned these or any other generally accepted but cruel practices. No one had had any good answers to his questions.

That had been four years ago, and nobody took a fourteen-year-old boy's questions terribly seriously, even if he was a prince of the blood, so he had eventually dropped this line of inquiry. But now, at eighteen, he was old enough to ask again. Baliniri, he knew, would talk truthfully with him about virtually anything he wanted to know.

Meanwhile, there was this beautiful, balmy day, perfect for an adventure such as the one he had in mind. He looked around in the great hall of Baliniri's wing of the palace and saw his bodyguard waiting for him and talking with one of the female servants at the front door.

Moses thought quickly and made up his mind. He slipped through a half-open door and made his way swiftly down a narrow corridor to one of the areas that housed the palace staff. He looked around, ducked into a small room, and satisfied that no one was there, quickly doffed his outer tunic and linen loincloth. Standing naked, he reached into a clothes basket and came up with a rough loincloth. He wound this around his middle and then tossed his own clothing into a pile of dirty laundry. He kicked off his expensive buffalo-leather sandals and looked through the servant's belongings but could find no pair of papyrus sandals. The man probably had but one pair, which he was no doubt wearing. Moses shrugged and slipped out the side door barefoot.

He grinned, walked down a side alley and out into the street. He was surprised at how exotic the feeling was! Free! Unrecognized! Untrammeled!

He moved quickly, delightedly, through the city, glorying in the simple fact that for once he turned no heads at all, attracted no attention. Once, passing through a bazaar, he lingered near a vendor's stall a moment too long and was told to "get out of here, you filthy thief, or I'll call the city guards on you!" He chuckled and moved on, secure and unafraid, seeing it all with detachment and good humor.

On the quays, it occurred to him for the first time that he had forgotten to bring money with which to pay a boat-man. He frowned and thought, but no solution came to mind. He was ultimately rescued by the arrival of an old man, bent over and leaning on his stick.

"Here, son," the old man said. "If you call a boat for me, there's half an *outnou* in it for you."

He was about to tell the old man that he would do it for free but, again appreciating the humor in his situation, changed his mind. He quickly calculated the probable price of a round-trip fare and said, "Right you are, sir! Coming right up!"

Across the Nile, the artisans' village was much as he remembered it: lusty, colorful, full of life. This was market day, when all the workers put their wares on sale, and he passed, one by one, the stalls of weavers, potters, basketmakers, and the makers of clay images for use in family religious festivals. He found the vendors watching him not with the angry wariness of Theban merchants but with the amused eyes of fellow conspirators in the great game of street life.

Once he lingered near a fig-merchant's booth, and rather than being chased away, he was invited to choose the best fig and take it with him. This invitation—he could hardly believe it—was offered with a tolerant smile. Moses bit into the fig and called out a thankful salute as he strolled down the street.

At the end of the village's single street, things changed, and significantly. From here he could see on the far hillside a long line of wretched slaves, filthy in tattered rags, staggering along a rocky path. They were bent double under the bur-dens of great stones dug out of the hill quarries. As he watched, one of them stumbled and fell, landing at the feet of an Egyptian overseer. Instead of helping the man up, the overseer gave him a vicious, backhanded cuff on the side of the head that once again sent him sprawling. Moses could hear the overseer's curses, bitter and demeaning.

Moses forced himself to watch. After a moment he turned to the basket vendor manning the stall beside him and asked, "Pardon me, sir, but who are those slaves there?"

The vendor's brows rose. "You're a well-spoken lad," he said. "Manners above your station. Well, good for you; you'll rise in the world that way. The slaves, eh? Well, one day the boats pulled up at the wharf from the delta and brought us these poor wretches."

"But who are they?"

"Oh, there's a few criminals among 'em, and their kind come from just about everywhere. But for the most part they're Habiru. You know, those fellows who came down from Canaan."

Moses looked on in shock. "The Habiru?" he said.

"Yes. When they first came here during the Great Drought, they were treated with honor and were under the protection of Joseph, the vizier of the delta under King Salitis. Joseph was the son of their patriarch Jacob, and he took care of 'em while he could. But then he wound up in trouble himself, and with his protection gone, all their property was seized."

"But they were never actually slaves, were they?"

"Not until recently, no. But Amasis has it in for 'em, poor devils. He bears a grudge for the Habiru. He used to live up in their home country, and the way I hear it, they kicked him and the other cult members out. Ugh! I'd just as soon not get that black-hearted devil down on me that way. He'd be a bad enemy."

"I agree," Moses said. "I used to know two of these Habiru people when I was a child." He had been about to say, "One of them, Jochebed, was my wet nurse, and the other was her daughter, Miriam. They cared for me when I was little." But this was no thing for an ordinary man of the street to be saying. He bit off the words and stared with growing hurt and anger at the spectacle. Why, women and children were out there, carving stones out of the hillside! No distinction was made according to sex or age!

The vendor noted the look on his face. "There, now, son," he said gently. "No use getting all upset about it. There's a lot of injustice in this world. If you go around letting things like this upset you, you'll lead a most unhappy life."

"No doubt," Moses agreed. "It's just that I can't help wondering if my old friends might be among them. I think I'll go look around."

"Here, wait up," the vendor said. "You don't want to go doing that, boy. Us folks aren't allowed anywhere near a work crew. You could wind up getting in trouble. More trouble than you'd be able to talk yourself out of."

But by now Moses no longer heard him. When he had ceased to be a boy and cut the long pigtail of childhood at age eleven, Jochebed and Miriam, the closest and dearest companions of his childhood, had disappeared for good. "Gone back to their own people," the palace servants had told him. "They'll be happier there." He had missed them terribly—missed them still, if the truth be known—but he had not questioned their actions. If they were gone somewhere where they would be happier, all the better for them; he would try to be happy at their good fortune.

But what if the happy home they had gone to so trustingly had been, in fact, hopeless slavery? He was sure Jochebed could not stand up under this kind of treatment; she had been a gentle and soft-spoken woman with the soft hands of a court servant. Even Miriam, as fit and strong as she had been, had no place in this sort of life.

For an agonized moment he hesitated. Surely, he thought miserably, they couldn't have come back to this!

But he had to *know* once and for all. If by some horrible trick of chance the two dearest women he had ever known—except, of course, Mother and Grandmother—had landed in so terrible a predicament, he would have to do something about it.

Mindful of the vendor's warning, he tried to stay out of the overseers' sight, moving always on a lower level, staying whenever possible behind low scrub brush. But as he moved along the line, he searched the queue of strained, pinched, suffering faces.

How thin they all seemed! Were the overseers not feeding them? Did they not know that you got more and better work out of a servant or a slave who was treated decently?

But these poor things looked as if they had not had a proper meal in months.

Slowly but surely new feelings of anger and indignation began to grow inside him. How could one person treat another this way? Didn't these overseers realize how stupid their brutality was? Didn't their consciences bother them?

Cautiously, he moved forward down the long line of slaves, apprehensively searching each female face. Hoping, more than anything, not to find a face that he could recognize.

IV

One floor down from the roof garden, Baliniri paused at the landing, favoring an old war wound that had begun to bother him again after many years. On impulse he turned and walked slowly down the hall toward the apartment of his stepdaughter, Thermutis.

A knock brought her to the door. "Father!" she said with a smile. "Please come in. Here, let me get a comfortable chair for you."

"Don't make any fuss," he said, sitting down in the first chair he came to. "I'm here only for a moment. I wanted to tell you that I presented Moses to the nobles and officers today, and virtually every man took to him as if he'd been their own son."

Thermutis sat opposite him. "Are you sure this is the right thing?" she asked. "I know I'm just acting like a protective mother. But my son going off to battle for the first time . . ."

Baliniri leaned forward and took one of her hands. "You've known this was coming. He has to grow up some day. I told you how young I was when I went off to war."

"And it was horrible, horrible!" she said. "I should thank you for letting me have him this long." She sighed. "Listen to me, talking like someone who has had him only on loan all these years." She made a wry face. "Well, I suppose that's

the truth of it. He isn't even my own blood, and now I have
to give him up to the arts of war."

"You give him up to Egypt," Baliniri said. "That's who
he belongs to in the end, Thermutis."

"Egypt?" she asked. "Or those people he really comes
from? Baliniri, when is he going to learn who he is? Do we
have to tell him? Can't we just leave things as they are? Does
he even have to learn I'm not his mother?"

"I've been thinking of that since last night," Baliniri
admitted. "Of course I thought of you." He patted her hand.
"And I decided on a compromise. He has to know someday,
but we'll put it off until he comes back from Nubia." He
frowned. "Perhaps by then I can figure out some way to put
it that won't come as too much of a shock."

"Thank you," she said. "But what if he wants to meet his
real mother?"

"I hope I'll have a way of handling that, too, by then.
Try not to worry about him. No military expedition is perfectly safe, but I'll be surrounding him with my best men. He
won't go anywhere without protection. He won't be out there
on the front lines like a common soldier."

"I know," she said sadly. "I trust you. I'm just suffering
the same affliction that comes to every mother—even an
adoptive one. The time when her little one has to leave the
hearth. I'll bear up."

"Maybe this will make it easier," he said. "I'm assigning
him an adviser, a very wise and learned man newly come
here from the Land of Two Rivers, who will complete his
education."

He watched the growing hope in her eyes, and for a
moment wondered if he should tell her about Nebo, but
something inside him said no. The fewer people to know a
secret, the fewer chances it would leak out. It was perilous
enough to have to conceal the facts surrounding Moses's true
birth. It was in their favor that so far this wing of the palace had
not been infiltrated by the cult.

The nagging doubts resurfaced. Could he still count on
the absolute and undivided loyalty of everyone in his own
wing of the palace? Or was there the chance that one of
Amasis's people could have got through to corrupt them?

Silently he cursed the necessity for this exaggerated circumspection. It amounted to paranoia. But there had never been a time he could relax since the cult had first come to Egypt. He firmed his jaw and abandoned the idea of sharing the truth about Nebo. But he did this with a certain regret. Since Ah-Hotep's death there had been no one close to him—no one but Mara, whom he seldom saw, unfortunately— with whom he could share the confidences of the day, sitting in the cool of the evening in the roof garden.

How lonely advancing age was! This was worse than the aches and pains and the muscles and joints that would no longer do what one asked of them.

And although he was still quite competent, he was, he had to admit, beginning to forget things, mislaying things, losing the ability to keep complicated patterns clear and distinct in his mind. And his thoughts were dwelling more and more not in the troubled and uncertain present or the doubtful and worrisome future but in the manageable and unthreatening past.

He shook his head, as if to clear away the cobwebs. "I'll make sure Moses can spend some time with you before he leaves. And don't worry. You know how much he loves you. When he does learn who he is, it won't make him love you less. You've had the caring for him, the raising of him. The many hours you've spent with him will weigh more than anything else in his heart. Trust that." He struggled to his feet, cursing his creaky back and stiff joints.

She saw him to the door, and when he opened it, she was still holding his hand in hers. The new servant, Selket, was walking past in the hallway. The girl stopped to bow. "My mistress wants me?" she asked. "How may I serve her?" She awaited Thermutis's pleasure.

"No, nothing," Thermutis said, exchanging a glance with Baliniri. "You may run along." The two of them watched the girl all the way down the hall until she could no longer be seen. Thermutis drew Baliniri closer. "You don't suppose she was eavesdropping?" the princess asked, horrified.

"I don't know," Baliniri answered. "I'll keep an eye on her. What was her name?"

"Selket. She came in with the last batch from the Fayum.

She had strong recommendations, but how good the security check is these days is impossible to know."

"Exactly," he said. He gave her a fatherly embrace and moved away slowly down the hall in the opposite direction from the one the girl had taken. "Selket," he told himself. "Remember that, now. Selket."

But by the time he had reached the bottom of the stairs, he had forgotten both the name and the incident.

The girl waited an hour, although even two hours would not have been too much. Her orders had been to preserve the appearance of innocence, even at the expense of promptness. But as the noon hour passed and it came time for her midday break, she excused herself and found her way to the cellar and the cramped, cluttered office of Yalu, assistant to the staff of food-tasters of the palace. Although his responsibilities in the palace were midlevel in the overall importance of the running of things, Yalu was a very important, high-level administrator in the cult.

Selket knocked several times, in accordance with a curious pattern. Only after this, plus a brief pause, did the door open a crack at first, then all the way. "Come in," the official said. "Did anyone see you coming?"

"No," she said. "Everyone had gone outside to eat. I took great pains."

"You did well to do so," Yalu commended. He made a sign with his right hand. "Greetings in the name of the Great Mother of us all."

She returned the salutation and accepted his blessing as a priest of the cult. "I did as you said," she told him. "I was nearly caught at it. But I am sure they suspect nothing."

He shot a sharp glance at her, but then his face softened and he put a hand familiarly on her shoulder, ignoring the way she instinctively shrank away from his touch; Yalu was grotesquely fat, bald, and scarred about the face, and his reputation around the palace with the female help was notorious. "Very well," he said. "Tell me what you learned."

She contrived to move out from under his hand and stand out of reach while maintaining a properly deferent attitude. "I did not hear as much as I would have liked because other servants were making noise from down the hall. But there was something about Prince Moses. The vizier said something like, 'Don't worry. When he does learn who he is, it won't make him love you the less. All the time you've spent caring for him will outweigh other considerations.'" She pursed her lips, trying to remember more, then shrugged. "That was about all I could hear that was not just small talk. What do you think that could possibly mean?"

Yalu toyed with the loose skin of his double chins and made a face that rendered him even more unattractive. "*Hmmm,*" he mused. " 'Who he really is.' That could mean a number of things: There were rumors about his birth, but we never could verify them. There was a servant of Thermutis's who seemed about to join us, who said she had some privileged information that would be of great value to us. At the time we thought she was just trying to worm her way into the organization to act as a spy, so we backed off. Perhaps we should have taken her seriously. The next day she disappeared, and her body was later found floating in one of the canals. I think Amasis arranged that, to warn off others who might like to try the same trick."

"But if he isn't Thermutis's son . . ." Selket began. Then her face changed. "Wait. He could still be Thermutis's son. But the father may not have been Zer."

Yalu considered this. As he did, he motioned her over toward him. "There's something to that," he said. "Zer wasn't much, a weakling, while Thermutis was a girl of some spirit. Look, my dear, why don't you come over here? Sit beside me on the couch."

"I have to get back," she said. "They'll notice I'm gone. And I don't want anyone to trace me here."

He took her by the wrist, and his fat hand had a lot of strength in it. But he hesitated for a moment before drawing her to him. She had been the first spy he had ever succeeded in placing inside Baliniri's wing of the castle, and he did not wish to alienate her. Nonetheless, she was a lovely girl, and this mastery was one of the benefits of his job. His mind raced. "On the other hand," he said, "the birth was surrounded by the greatest secrecy. There could have been some sort of problem."

As he spoke he pulled her toward him. She yanked at his hand but could not break free. "Please," she said. "They'll catch me sneaking back. You don't want that, do you?"

Caution struggled with lechery; lechery won. "Time enough to think of that," he said in a voice grown husky with lust. "Quickly. Out of that dress. There's not much time. There. There, now."

She shuddered but submitted, her eyes shut tightly, her mouth set in a straight line.

V

From cover Moses watched the women lug the stones to the cart, then struggle to stack them for the drovers to carry off. The oxen seemed asleep on their feet; it was a drowsy day. The drovers lazed in the shade fanning themselves and drinking from the wineskins they had brought with them, but there was no shade for the women doing this frightful labor, and no one to offer them anything to drink.

Anxiously he scanned the faces again. More than anything he hoped *not* to see one he recognized. But the thin face of a woman in her late thirties—drawn and careworn—stirred memories. There was a vague resemblance to the face he remembered as that of his old wet nurse Jochebed, from so many years earlier. But she could not be Jochebed: This woman was much too young. This woman was more like the age Jochebed had been when he had been a boy. Perhaps this woman was a relative.

"Pardon me, sir," a voice said behind him. He started and turned to see a reed-thin girl in her twenties behind him on the lower path, bent under the burden of a heavy cut stone. "If I don't get this through, the overseer will be angry with me."

Moses's eyes flashed. "Here," he said, taking the stone from her reluctant hands. "If he gets angry, let him get angry with me instead."

But even as he took it, he was aghast at its great weight. The stone tore at his soft city man's hands, and a second wave of anger and indignation ran through him as he thought of heartless men making a girl like this carry a burden so heavy under the scorching noon sun. He walked unsteadily up the hill and put the stone in the cart, noting the frightened faces of the women, startled at the sight of a stranger interfering in their affairs.

And as he turned, brushing his hands off one against the other, he locked eyes for a moment with the woman he had been looking at a moment or two earlier. Their eyes held, and he could see that her astonishment was every bit as great as his.

She was about to speak to him, but then the drovers bellowed at him. "Hey! You! Get away from them! Get out of here if you know what's good for you!"

Moses stood staring at her, unable to move. Then he looked at the drover, and a red rage rose in him. How dare that man speak to a prince of the blood this way?

But of course the drover could not know he was speaking to any prince; he thought he was speaking to a common man in a rough loincloth and no shoes. And if a dispute arose and were put to arbitration before an armed overseer, no one would believe who he really was.

He bit off the angry retort that was already on his lips and turned back to the woman to speak with her. But she had already hurried back down the rocky path. He could barely see her disappearing around the rocky ridge. "Wait!" he called. "Come back!"

The Habiru girl he had helped touched his arm timidly. "Please, sir," she said, "you'd better go. I thank you for wanting to help. But no one can help. None but the God of our fathers, and He seems to have deserted us."

He looked into her dark eyes. "Is this your life?" he asked, feeling a great wound in his soul. "Working like beasts of burden, seven days a week?"

For a moment the hurt in her eyes mirrored his own, and then she mastered herself. "Seven days," she said, a bitter edge on her voice.

"I . . . I can't allow this," he said. But then he realized

how ridiculous that statement must seem. What could he do for her? For them all? He swallowed the bitterness in his mouth. "That woman, the one who looked at me. What is her name?"

"A slave might as well have no name," she said. Briefly a long-suppressed anger surfaced on her face. But then it softened; after all, he had tried to help her. "Forgive me. Her name is Miriam. She is the wife of Hur and is of the priestly clan of Levi."

His face was a mask of horror. "M-Miriam?" he asked. "And her mother?"

"Jochebed, wife of Amram. She's not here. They've worked the poor woman so hard for so long, she can't do this sort of work anymore."

Moses felt the color drain from his face.

"You!" the drover said, getting to his feet and reaching for his whip. "Didn't I tell you to get away from them? And you, girl! You get back to work, or I'll give you a touch of the whip."

"Please," the girl begged of Moses. "Go now. You can't help us. Even if you stop them now, they'll only make it all the worse for us when you're gone."

Moses's mouth worked soundlessly. Then he said, "Goodbye. If I can do anything at all for you, I promise I will."

But the look in her eyes as he turned to go had dismissed him as a well-meaning nobody who was soon gone and quickly forgotten. People in her world came and went, and none of them could help, or even wanted to for long. Only the work went on forever, the cruel, punishing seven-days-a-week work that had no end other than soothing death.

When Yalu was done with her, Selket, consumed with shame and revulsion, put her garment back on. She avoided his eyes. He was the kind who wanted to be told what a splendid lover he was, but for her it had been like being defiled by some loathsome animal, the sort of half-human monster one met only in bad dreams. She felt dirty. Not even the purifying waters of the great Nile could cleanse her. She reeked of his hideous sweat. It would be hours before she could wash away the foulness he had done to her.

"Here, girl," Yalu said, fastening his tunic over his bulging belly. "I have an errand for you."

Still she did not look at him. "I have to get back," she protested. "I'm new there. If I'm not where I'm supposed to be, someone will notice."

"It's all right," Yalu said. "I'll cover for you. I want you to take a message to Neb-mertef, in the Quarter of the Temple."

She finally looked at him.

"He's principal assistant to Amasis," Yalu explained. "As you progress in the service of the Goddess, you will understand what an honor I am offering you, giving you a message to take to him."

It was true that before today she would have been excited at the prospect of being asked to carry a secret communication to a man so highly placed in the cult of the Mother. But now nothing could palliate the depression she felt at having been used by so vile a man.

Yalu scowled. "This doesn't please you?" he demanded sourly. "I could find someone else to do my bidding. I could even find someone else to infiltrate Baliniri's household for me. But then I'd have to silence you, for fear that you might tell someone that I've had you spying on the grand vizier to the lord of Two Lands. There are many ways to assure your silence, aren't there? Fast ones. Or slow ones." His voice was as hard as the stones of the great pyramid. "And then to make certain you've told no one who can hurt me, I'd have to eliminate everyone close to you. Relatives, friends, your parents."

She looked at him with utter loathing, but her voice did not betray her. Only her eyes did. "Tell me the message you want taken to Neb-mertef," she said. "I will carry it for you."

"Ah," he said, "that's better. It would be even better if you smiled. And asked me very nicely to give you the message." She complied, in a voice utterly dead. "Very well," he said. "Tell him precisely what you overheard about the prince. Tell him that you and I will be watching Baliniri and Thermutis very closely. Now that I have at last infiltrated his wing of the palace, I intend to press on. He has two servants who are getting too old to be much use. I will replace them for him,

with staff of my own choosing." He looked at her and raised
an eyebrow.

"I will remember," she assured him. "Continue. Please,"
she added with a hint of sourness.

"Good. Please is always good. Tell him to reopen the
inquiry about the day of Prince Moses's birth. There's a
secret for which we must learn the answer. Tell Neb-mertef
to spare no expense but to keep the entire matter secret.
Pain of death to any who lets word slip. Make sure he
understands this."

"I will do it," she said, spitting the words out. "Thank
you for the assignment, my lord."

"In private you may call me master," he said.

"Master, then," she said flatly. "Whatever."

Night fell, and the moon rose. Two shadowy figures
slipped into the palace through different doors, thus violating
what was popularly supposed to be tight security in the great
wing where Baliniri still was thought to reign supreme, in the
absence these eighteen years of the rightful lord of Two
Lands.

There was black hatred in Moses's heart as he slipped
into the servant's room and retrieved his own clothing, tossing the coarse borrowed loincloth onto the pile of dirty clothing.

Anger was a new emotion to him. He had been raised in
an atmosphere of consistent love and concern, with people
around him whose job or pleasure it was to fill his every
need. He had seen little injustice or cruelty in the world.

But today had changed all that. He had seen women and
even children worked like oxen. He had seen an overexhausted
man beaten for falling down and dropping his burden.

He had seen . . . Miriam.

Miriam, the friend of his youth, who had played with
him as if she had been an older sister. Miriam, the daughter
of his dear old wet nurse, Jochebed, who had been like a
second mother to him.

Jochebed . . . The girl had said Jochebed was now grown
too weak to do the terrible work her daughter did all day. He

would have to inquire into this and make certain that physicians were brought to her if she were really ill.

The girl had said that they were worked like this seven days a week. This would cause them to violate the customs of their own religion, which required one day of rest.

He remembered how Jochebed had spoken of this one God, who, in one entity, made up for all the gods they did not worship. She had said He was all-powerful, all-wise, and all-seeing but would from time to time chastise the Habiru when they fell away from the faith.

Well, what their God would not do for them now, he, Moses, would try to do. To start with, he would see if their work could not be lessened. If only, at first, by a day. A wise administrator, he had been taught, always respected the religious rites of the subject peoples and allowed them their own beliefs.

This much he felt he could do immediately even though he had little direct influence over the affairs of the civilians of the city and none over Amasis and his underlings.

Beyond that, well, time would tell. He would find out more about Jochebed. Perhaps she and her immediate family could be brought back to the palace and given lighter work.

And, by an entrance even more obscure, which none of the servants knew about, the man called Nebo slipped into the palace and set out down a secret passageway Baliniri had had built when he had become vizier, before the cult had come to the lands beside the Nile.

The passageway paralleled the great hall of Baliniri's wing and came to a dead end behind a great wooden panel made of wood brought all the way from far Scythia. On the far side, Scythian wood comprised the middle panel of a triptych on which the finest painters in Deir el-Bahari had painted the events of Baliniri's life.

Nebo knocked according to a pattern long established: two knocks, a pause, another knock, pause, a last single knock. The panel slowly drew aside.

"Greetings," said the vizier of the Two Lands. "I'm glad to see you."

VI

Hearing the approach of footsteps, Selket leapt away from the door and hastily moved into the deep shadow of a tall statue of Horus at the end of the hall and far from the torch on the wall bracket. She blended into the darkness just as the newcomer rounded the corner and approached the door where she had been eavesdropping.

The knock made on the door was not the distinctive signal she had heard the foreigner make. This was the random, casual knock of a person who, visiting the grand vizier, expected to be admitted. She longed to peek out from behind the statue but dared not; once out of shadow she would be quite visible in the light of the flickering torches.

She heard the door open, then Baliniri's voice came to her: "Ah! Moses! What are you doing up this late? Come in, my boy!"

The door closed behind the young prince. Selket waited a long, long interval then poked her head out. There was no one in the hall, and conquering her fear, she moved softly down the corridor on bare soles, her sandals in her hand.

This was dangerous, she knew. If she were caught here at this time of night, there would be no way in the world to explain it. But the day's events had convinced her that she had no choice but to take the risk.

She suppressed a shudder, thinking first of Yalu—fat, gross, perverted—and then his even more dangerous cohort, Neb-mertef. It was difficult choosing which had been the greater trial. Yalu was the more disgusting, Neb-mertef the more frightening. And once soiled by Yalu, it was a small but degrading step to being further soiled by his mentor. What kind of religion was this, she wondered, that gave adepts the license to use her sexually as a matter of course? At least Neb-mertef, an incredibly wealthy man, had *promised* her something.

As she bent low with her ear to the door and tried to pick up something of the muffled conversation inside, she remembered some of what Neb-mertef had told her: "Remember, little one, an alert spy can rise quickly. An alert spy can get very rich, very quickly. Never mind what Yalu told you about your pay. You will get your bonus from me after you have received your pittance from him; the extra will be for your undivided loyalty to me. And part of that loyalty will take the form of spying on Yalu himself and of reporting to me on his activities."

That part had been exciting, at least, but of course it had been followed by the same sort of degradation she had undergone at Yalu's hands. The difference had lain in Neb-mertef's impotence and in the extra work she had had to perform in order to satisfy him. Again she shuddered.

What were they saying inside there? Something about slaves on the other side of the river. Ah, evidently the boy had gone there today, had seen things he did not like, and was asking Baliniri to aid the sorry lot of the Habiru. Well, apparently Prince Moses was a nice boy. Good for him. But he had not seen much of the harder side of life yet. She had seen the life of the quarry slaves, and foreigners or not, it was enough to break her heart to watch the way they were treated. If the boy could get them their one day a week off work, all the better. They would at least get some rest.

But hold! Where was the voice of the foreigner? Why was the boy not being introduced to the foreigner? She knew he was there, yet Baliniri and the prince were speaking as if they were alone in the room.

Why? Did the boy not see the stranger? She had heard his voice and recognized it as that of Nebo, the stranger who had come to town a couple of days earlier. She had no idea how he had found his way inside Baliniri's quarters. He certainly had not come up the stairs; otherwise, he would have passed her.

Could there be some secret access to Baliniri's apartment? She knew the stranger could not have climbed up the palace wall or come down from the roof. Palace security had ensured by design that no assassin could get to him by these means.

Well! This was interesting news! A man could come and go as he pleased, in and out of the vizier's private apartment without being seen. Perhaps until now no one had even known the trick was possible. This was something to share with Yalu.

But no! It was something to share with Neb-mertef instead. He paid better, and from the sound of things Yalu was already a man considered dispensable, replaceable. Perhaps by herself?

Selket caught her breath at the sound of Moses coming back to the door! She ran quickly down the marble hall, the tiles chill against her bare feet, and once more disappeared behind the statue. After the boy had gone, she did not linger by the door again. She had exposed herself to enough danger for one night.

After Moses had gone, Baliniri opened the panel so Nebo could step out from behind it. "I'm sorry to have been so long," Baliniri said.

Nebo smiled. "It's all right. It was a good opportunity to listen to the boy unobserved. I now have a very strong impression of him—who he is, and how it's going to be working for him. He seems like a fine young man."

"He is. Let me get you some wine," Baliniri offered. "It must have been dusty in there."

"No, thank you," Nebo said. "I haven't had wine in years. I've spent almost as much time as Kamose in crossing deserts, I think. I've come to appreciate pure water more than anything."

"Then try this," Baliniri offered, pouring from a pitcher into a bowl. "I'm afraid I don't share your ascetic ways. At my age I like a little wine now and then." He drank from a wine bowl, then wiped his mouth as a soldier might, with the back of his hand. He blew out between pursed lips. "I'm losing my grasp," he said abruptly. "In a year or two I won't be fit to lead. I hope to have the boy trained to take over by then."

"As vizier?" Nebo asked, studying the water in his bowl. "I thought you planned for him to take over the throne."

"I do. But first I need to see what shape Kamose is in when he arrives in Thebes, or I won't have any idea what my chances of success are."

"I saw him briefly in Sile. He looked like a man who'd spent twenty years in the Netherworld." Nebo snorted. "Well, he just may have. I left Mara with him, but I doubt she'll have much effect on him. I heard a rumor that Amasis was in town. If he's got hold of Kamose in that condition . . ." He shrugged. "So this Nubian thing is a trial expedition for the lad. Well, better that than something more dangerous."

"Don't be overconfident," Baliniri warned. "There's more going on than we know. This sort of thing isn't like Nehsi."

"No," Nebo agreed. "Do you think that Balaam fellow is behind it?"

"Yes, but Balaam in and of himself isn't enough to make the difference. I know the man—he was here in Thebes for a time, on some mission of state. I don't remember exactly what or when. My memory isn't what it was."

"Then train an assistant to go round with you and remember things for you. The best administrators do it." His voice softened. "You'd be less often alone, for one thing. You're lonely these days, aren't you?"

"Terribly," Baliniri confessed. "Although you're probably the only person in the world I would admit that to."

"And for good reason; I may be the only man in the world lonelier than you." The cloud flickered behind Nebo's eyes for a heartbeat, then he firmed his jaw and smiled. "I have to travel light, by the very nature of things. What's your excuse?"

Baliniri drank again. After a moment he said, "I can't trust anyone. Anyone but the boy, and I'm giving him over to your care the day after tomorrow."

"All the more reason to have someone stay close to you. I spent the day nosing around. There's a man here named Yalu—I'd keep an eye on him, if I were you."

"I already know about him."

"Good. And Neb-mertef—"

"Yes, yes. But he will always be no more than a secondary problem. When Amasis comes back, you'll have a clearer picture of how insignificant Neb-mertef is. Amasis is the dangerous one. He's older and wiser, while I'm older and less effective. There was a time when I was his equal."

"There was a time when seven of him couldn't have outwitted the one of you. My friend, you haven't lost as much as you think you have."

"I wish I could believe you," Baliniri replied. "I wonder if I'll still be alive when you return. There are so many times when I feel as though I'm in terrible danger. Well, it doesn't matter. The thing that is of importance is this mission of yours."

"You discouraged the boy from seeing his mother and sister," Nebo remarked.

"Worse." Baliniri frowned. "I made it quite impossible. Tomorrow he'll inventory supplies for the expedition, and the next day he'll spend with you. I don't want him finding out his true identity until he comes back. Use your own judgment, of course, but I don't want him thinking about anything but the campaign."

"I understand. Of course you'll see to his request?"

"I'll try to make it easier for Miriam and Jochebed, but the Habiru possess fierce pride and loyalty. Jochebed would never accept preferential treatment while the other Habiru are ground to powder by Amasis's thugs, but I'll do what I can. Now let's talk about the expedition. I also want your mind on that, not on what's going on back here."

"Agreed. All right, first I have heard that something larger, something worse, than we have suspected is going on, someone behind Balaam—someone of greater intelligence and understanding. Rumors regarding the casting of spells—"

"The cult?"

"No, there'd be no need for such secrecy if that were the case. It's something new, from another part of the world. And I intend to find out what it is." He smiled like a fox. "You didn't think I would go on a trip like this unless I had reasons of my own, did you?"

"And these are—?"

But Nebo only smiled, his face unreadable.

VII

Through the night Prince Moses tossed and turned. Unable to sleep, he got up and paced his room, trying to calm himself, trying to break the tension that kept building in him. But even as he paced, the tempo of his steps steadily increased, and his fists balled up almost of their own accord.

His heart was full of a rage and resentment new to him. He could not get out of his mind the sight of the women toiling under the sun, like convicts under the watchful eye of an overseer armed with sword and whip.

He could not get over the sight of Miriam, the childhood playmate who had been like an older sister to him all through his youngest years. Miriam, going from the soft life of the palace to the hateful, demeaning life of a slave, ordered about by brutes, the property of the state.

Miriam! And, by implication, Jochebed! How had they fallen to this terrible slavery? How had their lives fallen to such evil days?

Even as the thought once more took shape in his mind, the blood flowed to his extremities, and his fists clenched. He wanted to strike out angrily against someone, anyone. How dare they?

Ah, but who were "they"?

Who but the state itself? The state ruled by Kamose; directed—nominally, at least—by Baliniri; served, in the capacity of a prince of the realm, unofficial heir to the throne, by himself.

He once more tried to regain his calm. *Remember*, he told himself: *Baliniri agreed to try to lighten their load*. From now on, they would have a day to themselves and would not have to deal constantly with the guilt they felt over breaking their custom, which they said was dictated by their God.

Now as he thought about it, he could remember Jochebed and Miriam answering his childish questions about the customs of their people and could call to mind hearing them say how holy the seventh day was thought to be among them. It was, they had told him, the day on which their God had rested when He had created the world out of nothing.

His mind was assaulted by radical thoughts inspired by anger and frustration: Whom did the state serve? Did it exist as an entity in and of itself, all-powerful, to be served blindly as one might serve a god? Or did it exist on sufferance, a thing that men had made and men could undo? If the latter, could it not be called upon to defend its actions? Did not the individuals who made up the state have rights enforceable upon it?

He could not say no to his conscience, to the inner voice that demanded he do something quickly and decisively. In two days he would be gone, and his old friends and their people would still be in the cruel hands of Amasis and his minions.

That was a hard, hard decision to make; it meant disobeying Baliniri. But he did not see any alternative.

He abruptly stopped pacing. His rage at last mastering his indecision, he reached for the pile of clean clothing the palace servants had laid out for him at bedtime.

In the pale light of early dawn, Selket saw him leave. She had been equally sleepless all night, but her reasons were different. She had bathed repeatedly but could not wash away the feeling of having been permanently soiled by Yalu and Neb-mertef. Then she had sat up for hours, redeyed, thinking dark thoughts, all the more hateful in the almost total silence of the night, before the first pink rays had begun to show themselves on the eastern horizon past her window.

The sound of the side door opening stirred her to alertness. She rose, threw a shawl over her shoulders, and otherwise still naked from her bed, went to the window and poked her head out to investigate the source of the noise.

She recognized Prince Moses immediately. *Aha!* she thought. *So that's how he gets in and out!* This was useful intelligence, something she could trade for greater favor in the eyes of the cult's leaders.

As the thought crossed her mind it brought an instinctive shudder. The idea of returning to Yalu or Neb-mertef and having to put up with the same treatment she had gotten the day before was so disgusting that she almost shelved the notion of telling either man. But no! There was no sense in that. Since she had already degraded herself, it would be foolish not to try to reap at least some of the rewards promised for her whoring and treachery—even if it meant having to submit to the pawing of her cult superiors.

Whom should she tell? Yalu? No, she would do whatever she could to cut the legs out from under Yalu. And one of the best ways of doing this would be to pass important information directly to Neb-mertef.

But where was Moses going? Should she follow him? For a moment she hesitated. It was too dangerous. She should not do it. But a moment later, her hands were reaching for her simple servant's shift, and her feet were sliding into her sandals.

The quays at riverside were already busy when Moses arrived, and four boatmen were plying their trade at the water's edge. He hailed one of these and made his way across the Nile, his mind filled with half-coherent thoughts.

Once the boat docked, he hurried along the track toward the artisans' town, already beginning to awaken and to open its stalls. The heady aroma of breakfast cooking in the homes he passed wafted under his nose, and ordinarily this would have inspired a powerful hunger in him. But now his guts churned with unquiet thoughts.

This time he would, if possible, speak to Miriam. Perhaps he would even find his way to Jochebed and speak with her. And if anyone was mistreating her—

Passing the village and turning off onto the narrow track toward the quarries, he stepped up his pace until he was half running. The path wound around a great rock outcropping, reached a crest, then dipped into a wash on the far side.

Moses stopped at the top and looked down at a solitary worker who was being cursed by an overseer.

The prince moved silently down the path, attracting no attention. As he came closer, he could hear an angry conversation:

"Who are you to tell me to leave her alone, slave? I'll speak to whatever round-heeled Habiru slut I wish to. I'll do a damned lot more than speak to her, if it pleases me!"

"The girl is promised to me!"

"Promised?" The overseer laughed nastily. "I can break any slave's promise whenever I want to. I can have him whipped, impaled, quartered. I can have him altered so that no Habiru slut will be able to make use of him."

"You keep away from her or I'll—"

"You'll what?" the overseer snarled, reaching for the whip in his belt. "You dare to threaten me?"

The whip came out. The Habiru, unarmed but for clenched fists, moved forward, took an awkward swing at the overseer, then suffered a powerful blow on the head from the weighted handle of the Egyptian's whip. The slave fell to his knees and took a savage kick in the face, which stretched him out flat on his back.

The Egyptian's arm went back. The whip uncurled, poised for a lethal lashing.

"You!" Moses cried out in a strangled voice, tight with anger. "Stop that right now!"

The incredulous overseer paused. "Who tells me what I must and must not do? A half-grown city boy who's barely out of a pigtail?"

Moses hurried down the path and looked at the fallen body of the Habiru man, who seemed to be unconscious. "Just let him be. I'll get him back to his people."

"Out of the way!" the overseer threatened. "I'm going to take the skin off his back. And if I have to do the same to you, I'll just call it practice. Move along. This is the last time I'll tell you."

Moses heard an unfamiliar voice say in a bold, resolute tone, "Do your worst, you son of a jackal."

The voice was his own! And something new seemed to have taken over the management of his limbs. He poised on the balls of his feet, and his clenched fists rose protectively before him.

The whip lashed out, but as if it were moving in slow motion. Moses's sharp eyes picked out the uncoiling strips of braided leather, and his hand darted up and caught it. Before he could even have thought the matter over, he pulled the whip-wielder toward him, and his free fist lashed out and caught the man in the face. The overseer staggered back.

"You whore's brat!" the Egyptian growled in a voice thick with phlegm. He glanced at the whip now lying on the ground at his feet, then reached for the sword at his belt.

But he was too slow. Moses had been Baliniri's prize pupil in hand-to-hand fighting, and although he had never fought a man in earnest, his training took over and anticipated every move the overseer made. The prince's foot lashed out and kicked the sword aside. Then he drove forward, fists flailing, and smashed the overseer twice in the face with hard knuckles. The overseer pitched forward, landing prone atop the dropped sword. Moses actually had to jump back to keep from catching the falling body.

For a moment Moses stood over the overseer, the rage still hot in him. Then he heard a noise behind him and wheeled. The man in whose behalf he had intervened was sitting up, holding his head. "What happened?" he asked. "Oh, yes . . . he must have hit me. But who are you?"

"Never mind," Moses said. "You'd better get out of here before he wakes up."

The Habiru crawled on hands and knees over to where the Egyptian lay. "He won't be waking up soon, I think." He felt the side of the Egyptian's neck, then put his ear to the man's chest. He looked at Moses with wide, frightened eyes as he sat back on his heels.

"What's the matter?" Moses asked.

The Habiru said nothing for a long, long moment. "You've killed him," he whispered at last. "Now what are we going to do?"

Moses stared. "K-killed? Are you sure?"

Selket watched from her hiding place as the two men began to dig a hole in the hillside, at a place well removed from the quarry. They had dragged the body by the heels, and now it lay at their feet.

She would have to go to Neb-mertef directly. Or should she? She smiled to herself. This was too good even for Neb-mertef. This should be kept for her own private purposes. Blackmail. Extortion. Power over the prince of Egypt himself! What were the other possibilities? Rumor said that Amasis was returning to Thebes. After the fine service she had done for the Goddess, she was sure to be introduced to Amasis sooner or later. And when she was, she could contrive to talk alone with him. Then they would bargain, and her fortunes would change forever. Grinning, she took note of precisely where the body was buried.

All this before noon! Her future was made!

VIII

"What do you mean he isn't here?" demanded Khafre, general in command of the Nubian expedition. "It's mid-morning. He wouldn't be this late."

His young adjutant, Geb, threw his shoulders back into an even stiffer posture. "Beg to report, sir, there's been no sign of him all morning."

Khafre's scowl became even more ferocious, and his beetling brows covered his squinting eyes. "Well, what are you standing there for? Get someone out after him! Scour the buildings of state! Send a runner to the palace!"

"I've already done both those things, sir."

"Huh." For a moment Khafre's tense stance seemed to soften, then he barked, "Well, get him here! I don't care what you have to do. I want him here in an hour! As it is, we'll have to make up for the time we've lost!"

"Sir," Geb began, "there might be a way to avoid losing more time." One of Khafre's dark brows rose; emboldened, the adjutant went on. "If the general would approve . . . the inspection could be done by a team of surrogates, so that when the prince does arrive, all he will have to do is approve the work. As I remember, sir, there's no regulation that states that every stage of the work has to be approved personally by the prince. A wise administrator delegates some of the authority, sir, to people he can trust."

The general almost smiled but caught himself. "Very good, Geb. Very practical. Have the job done, so that Prince Moses can seal it with the royal signet when he gets here."

"Sir, begging your pardon, I've already taken the liberty of doing so. No harm done, sir. If the prince arrives now and wishes to duplicate our work, he is of course free to do so."

Now Khafre's grin showed teeth, white and unbroken despite his many engagements in battle. "I see I've picked an officer of rare understanding of the ways of the real world."

"I hope you have, sir. Of course, it could be argued, sir, that I have merely anticipated protocol set forth in our next training manual, sir, which this command will issue for general use of the garrison during the trip south to Nubia."

"Ah? And which next manual is this?"

"Sir, I've also taken the liberty to draw it up after countless consultations with other of the staff officers—and, of course, the line officers as well. Perhaps you'll be so kind as to give it a look in your leisure time."

"You cocky young scamp," Khafre said with a harsh chuckle, accepting the rolled papyrus. "I'll read your impertinent little piece of—"

"Oh, surely not impertinent, sir. I'm cocky, yes, sir; but the manual surely is not impertinent. It seems to me that the material is really most pertinent to the matter at hand. The old rules and regulations were for an army in garrison, as this unit has been ever since the battle of El-Kab. Wouldn't you agree that now is the time for a new set of rules more relevant to the affairs of an expeditionary force on the march into hostile country, sir?"

Khafre's mouth hung open. Then he took a swipe at Geb with the rolled papyrus in his hand. "Get out of my sight, you young cub!" he said gruffly. "And get me Prince Mo—" He stopped. "Here he comes," he said in a lower voice. "Out of uniform."

Geb's voice was quite low as the young prince moved awkwardly toward them, his hair disheveled, a strange expression on his face. "Neither the old rules nor, I regret, the new, sir," he intoned, "lay down unbreakable rules concerning the proper dress of a prince in nominal command of an expedition."

Now Prince Moses was upon them, returning their salutes informally. "I'm sorry," he said, puffing with the exertion. "Something, uh, regrettable came up. Something unavoidable."

"Quite all right, sir," General Khafre said, all business. "In your absence we took the liberty of certifying the manifests. They await the royal cartouche, sir, if you trust our figures."

There was a long pause while the young prince, his face distraught, glanced from one face to the other. He seemed to realize that he was undergoing some sort of test. In a more resolute voice he said, "Only an idiot signs for goods he has not personally counted and taken charge of. We'll recount."

There was a glint of approval in Khafre's eye as he said, "Yes, sir! Right you are! Ready for the inspection, Adjutant!" As Moses turned toward the field, Khafre's eyes locked with Geb's behind the prince's back. A knowing look of appreciation passed from the old soldier to the young and back again.

In the early afternoon Nebo entered a tavern by the waterfront, looked over the head of the landlord, and linked eyes with a red-bearded trader. He nodded, causing the trader to call out to the landlord, "It's all right, my friend. He's with me. Bring wine. Your best."

Nebo bowed as he approached, just a slight inclination of the head but enough to show courtesy. "Captain?" he said. "I am Nebo of Shinar. I got your message."

"Mukshash of Arvad. Please sit down. You sent for me—or, more precisely, for anyone who has been to Nubia in recent months. I have been there, sir, although I don't count it any particular mark of distinction. To be quite frank with you, I was cheated by that bunch of lying, crooked scum. I consider myself lucky to have got away with my ship in one piece and my head still atop my shoulders."

Nebo said mildly, "Then you have not done so badly. I would reflect upon that if I were you. But of course I presume. Forgive me. An old man's vagaries."

Mukshash snorted. "Cut the pig ordure. You're not old. I came because I know you by reputation. I found myself walking in your footprints in Syria. All I had to do was put my foot where you had put yours, and I made money. If I didn't think I owed you something for that, I probably wouldn't be here."

"Ah, I have grown notorious," Nebo said sourly. "Pray how did my name come up in Syria?"

"As a sharp trader. I was referred to you by one Azbuk, a learned Canaanite gentleman."

Nebo pursed his lips. "I see. And this Azbuk perhaps told you to tell me something, to demonstrate that you had his favor and could be trusted?"

"Indeed." He looked right and left out of the corners of his eyes before he spoke. "He said, 'Beware of walking too closely on the heels of the lion.' "

"Ah. And you understand what his statement means?"

"Only that it is some sort of password."

"And so it is. Now what do you have for me, that I can buy or exchange for negotiable goods, to make up for the loss you have taken in Nubia?"

"If you can make up the sum I lost," Mukshash said, "you have my compliments. But you don't look that rich. I lost a small fortune."

"If the material you have for me is good enough, a small fortune can be arranged."

"Very well," Mukshash said skeptically. He leaned forward. "The war is not of King Nehsi's choosing. He has lost ground in recent years. There have been rebellions within his ranks. Now, where once he was undisputed ruler of Nubia, he is one of what appears to be two, but which turns out upon closer inspection to be three."

"Let me get this straight: There's Nehsi, and I presume this Balaam fellow. Who's the third?"

Mukshash saw the landlord coming, so he made no answer. He took the wine jar and bowls from the man, preferring to pour for both of them himself. Then he held up a full bowl and said, "Your health, sir."

"And yours." Nebo toasted and touched the bowl to his lips but did not drink.

Mukshash drank and put the bowl down. "Whenever I would ask the identity of the third man, I would run into a dead end. Nobody would speak to me about him. Whoever he is, he seems to occupy the sort of position reserved, in Egypt, for this Amasis fellow of yours."

"He's nothing of mine. But I understand. Go on, please."

"There's not much more. Frankly, I don't know how my information can deserve all the money you promised me. Whoever the man is, he came downriver to Nubia."

"*Downriver?*" Nebo echoed. "You mean he's a black from the Sudd or the Mountains of Fire?"

"Not the way I heard it. He's been to these places, but he's white. He is spoken of as being some sort of magus. Everyone's afraid of him."

Nebo thought a moment. "And yet you have no name for this man?" he mused. "That seems strange indeed."

"All I know is that all signs point to him being the brains behind Balaam; I'd guess the two of them worked together to set Nehsi upon this destructive path. The news of the war came down just as my ship was preparing to leave for Thebes."

"Yet you managed to get away? . . ."

"In your place I would be skeptical too. I think I was allowed to escape, so I could warn someone here, strange though that may seem. Can you imagine anyone there wanting me to warn you that the Nubians are going to war with you?"

Nebo frowned. "It doesn't make much sense, does it? Why warn your enemy that you're coming?"

Mukshash shrugged, shook his head, and reached for the wine jar. But as he did so, his outer robe gaped in front and gave Nebo a glimpse of the tunic beneath, a tunic of Canaanite cut. And about his waist was an ornately tooled leather belt and a sword of curious design. Nebo leaned forward and stared at it. "Excuse me. Could I have a look at that sword, please?"

Mukshash slowly withdrew it from its scabbard and handed it over, hilt first. "It is quite unique, if I do say so myself. I am not of a mind to trade it away. It's a sword of iron."

Nebo turned the weapon this way and that, taking note of its cunning design. "It would be a rare occurrence, indeed, coming by a piece as well wrought as this. But I'm a bit of a collector, and this is unlike any design I've ever seen."

Mukshash smiled. "I'm sure it is. Would you care to guess at its origin?"

Nebo pursed his lips. "It is definitely not Hittite, and nothing at all like the designs one occasionally sees from the Greek isles or the dark lands north of the Euphrates, around Lake Van. No, this is something quite new to me. Have they mastered the smelting of iron, perhaps, in the valley of the Indus, far to the east? Because that is one direction in which my travels have yet to take me."

"Guess again. I'll tell you what: Since the little information I have given you has surely not earned me that, uh, 'small fortune' you spoke of earlier, purchase the sword from me and make up the rest with that. If you continue to study it, you may come up with some clue as to where I got it. Or you can show it to people and ask them questions about it."

Nebo looked at him sharply. "Why? What good would that do? I'm going to Nubia, not to one of the busy seaports on the Great Sea where people are likely to know such matters."

Mukshash smiled enigmatically. "Because," he answered, "it was in Nubia that I got it."

He paused to let the fact sink in.

"But this is brand new," Nebo pointed out. "Other than Teti, whose style this most emphatically is not, there has been no master of the ironmonger's craft in Nubia since Karkara of Sado. And he is dead these many years. This is like no design Karkara ever used."

Mukshash, his eyes mere slits, his face impassive, shrugged. "Be that as it may, the sword comes from upriver. An iron sword, finely made in an outlandish pattern no eye has ever seen in Egypt before you. Smelted iron, too, not meteorite iron."

"Gods!" Nebo said. "You've got a bargain, my friend. Name your price."

IX

Missing out on the morning's work meant that the job of taking inventory had to be speeded up enormously, but Moses welcomed the diversion. As long as there was detailed, high-pressure work to do, he did not have time for thought— and the last thing in the world that he wanted to do just now was think.

But as the afternoon wore to a close and he completed the tasks set before him, the time approached when he would necessarily remember the morning's traumatic incident. He had dreaded this moment and so lingered a little longer afterward to speak with Geb and Khafre.

"I won't see you until the day after tomorrow, most likely." He looked each man in the eyes and grasped each by the forearm in turn. "Thank you for your help today, and for the help I am sure you will both be giving me in the days to come."

Khafre saluted him smartly. "Our pleasure, sir. And may I say it's been very reassuring to see you pay such interest to detail, sir? I look forward to working with you."

"And I with both of you," Moses responded. "I have made inquiries about your service histories. You, General, more than live up to your reputation for alertness and efficiency, and I am sure that even the glowing reports do not do justice to your bravery and ability in the field."

Moses turned to Geb. "And I have learned from various sources that General Khafre stole you out of the staff pool of junior officers and that the other officers want you back. Today I learned why. A good officer needs a sharp-eyed man at his side to make sure he has forgotten nothing under the pressure of the moment. You are the general's good right arm, as the general will be mine. I consider us well met. Fare you well, until we meet on the docks on embarkation day." He nodded to both and strode away, his brisk and efficient steps betraying nothing of the chaos in his heart.

Khafre turned to Geb. His eyebrows went up. "It seems we have a jewel here," the general said.

"Yes, sir." Geb shook his head almost incredulously.

"This one would have made a good soldier even without connections. Of course, it's another matter how he does under combat conditions."

"He'll do all right," the general declared. "Take it from me. But something's bothering him, something big and bad that is eating at his guts."

Geb looked thoughtful. "I knew something was off." He crossed his arms over his chest and shook his head again. "I wonder what sort of desperate worries princes have. The things we ordinary people worry about all seem to do with money or powerlessness. Surely these can't be a problem with Moses."

Khafre shrugged. "None of our business, I'd say. But if he wants to talk about it on the trip south, I'll be ready to listen."

At nightfall, Nebo knocked on the hidden panel and was admitted to Baliniri's palace suite. He did not waste time. "Look at this," he said, drawing the sword at his waist and handing it over.

Baliniri took the heavy iron weapon and turned it this way and that. "Gods! Where'd you get this? What workmanship!"

Nebo waited silently for a specific, expected reaction—and got it.

"Wait," Baliniri said. "There's something about it that isn't proper. I can't tell you what it is, but it's . . . off."

"I know," Nebo responded. "There's something strange and unclean about the design, as if it were made by demons under the earth." His voice took on an edge. "Guess where it comes from."

"I don't know. Scythia?"

"A trader bought it quite recently in Nubia. And look— it's brand new."

Baliniri stared.

"Yes. I had the same reaction. Who is in Nubia that's capable of working iron? And what's the secret of this bizarre design?"

Baliniri balanced it on his palm. "The center of weight distribution is off. It should be right here, but instead it's way over here. No soldier would make a sword like this."

"Exactly. But the iron itself is splendid, far beyond the work of any smith I know. Teti couldn't have touched it on the best day of her life."

"Here." Baliniri grimaced, handing it back. "It seems there's more than one mystery in Nubia these days."

Nebo nodded. "I grow more interested in the task before me with every passing day. Something odd is going on there. There's someone behind Balaam, someone smarter than he is—"

"There'd have to be."

"But nobody will speak his name or give his description. It appears everyone's afraid of him. I suspect the trader I talked to—the one who sold me the sword—never laid eyes on him." He frowned. "Who could it be? Apparently the mystery man is a sort of magus. The equivalent of Amasis."

"Then may the gods help Nubia. What am I saying?" He smiled. "More power to anyone who brings them down."

"Not if there's a chance that the disease may spread to us," Nebo remarked. "We have enough trouble with Amasis and the cult without worrying about some outland magus powerful enough to undermine the throne of Nubia."

"Well," Baliniri said, "I'll leave the matter in your hands. You're the one on the spot." He moved to the couch beside his table, where rolled papyri and maps lay where they had fallen from his hands. "You'll be meeting with Moses tomorrow," he said, changing the subject as he sat. "I talked to Khafre this afternoon. He's very impressed with Moses, but he says something weighs on his heart. Khafre hasn't any idea what it is." He looked Nebo in the eye. "He was fine when I talked with him yesterday. See if you can find out what's troubling him."

This time Selket met Neb-mertef in the street, just outside the palace compound. "Come," he said. "The moon is bright. We can talk down by the river."

"Are you sure it's safe for us to be out on the streets after dark?"

"You will be safe with me," he assured her. "All men know my face. Anyone who harms me or anyone with me would find the full displeasure of the Great Goddess focused upon him—and his woman, and his children, and his children's children." He ignored her horrified expression and took her arm. "Come, we will walk on the quays and watch our enemies, the soldiers of the army of Egypt, make their preparations for going upriver to glory—or to death. It hardly matters which."

She tried not to shrink from his touch. "Enemies?" she said in hardly more than a whisper. "The army, enemies? I don't understand."

He chuckled; she hated that chuckle. "They are all that stands between us and the elimination of the obstacles in our path. With the army gone, those unwelcome elements will no longer have protection. You can expect to see great changes here in the immediate future."

He guided her out into the great avenue, which led to the river and the long wharves where the royal fleet was already deployed at dockside, awaiting the order to sail on the day after tomorrow.

"Look," he said, "at what remains of the might of Thebes. In two days the only military left here will be a token guard until the arrival of Kamose and the permanent cadre of the army. The mercenaries, of course, are being paid off. When Kamose arrives with my lord Amasis a week from now . . ."

She stopped listening. The casually dropped fact fell into her consciousness like a thunderbolt from above. A week! A week until Amasis arrived! "My lord," she ventured, "is there any way I can meet Amasis?"

He turned quickly to look at her. "Why?" he asked, wary. "Why? What profit would there be in that?"

"I've always admired him so," she answered offhandedly. "It would be a great inspiration to meet and speak with the all-high servant of the Great Mother."

He turned his eyes back to the street before them. "Well, I suppose that could be arranged," he responded, "but don't get any ideas about going around me to Amasis, the same way you're going around Yalu to me. If I were to catch you doing that, it would be very hard on you. That would be a very great mistake."

"Oh, no, my lord!" she promised.

"Yalu already suspected and now knows that you're reporting directly to me. He hasn't been harsh with you because I specifically told him that from now on you are responsible solely to me. You see, I'm quite aware of your plans."

He stopped, faced her, and took her by the arms, his fingers digging into her flesh like the talons of a great predatory bird. His eyes burned like glowing coals as he looked her in the eyes, and she knew a fear she had never experienced before.

"Please, my lord," she pleaded, "you're hurting me."

He ignored her. "Hear me, woman." His voice carried no farther than her ear, but his words cut like knives. "I know all your thoughts. Whatever you're thinking, I'm a step or two ahead of you. In the end you can hide nothing from me. You will never be able to hide anything from any real adept of the Great Mother."

She tried to swallow and found she could not. Her heart was beating fast.

"There is something on your mind," he said. "You know something and are debating whether or not to tell me about it or to save it and tell it only to Amasis." She tried to avoid his eyes, but this was impossible. "You will tell it to me. Now." The words pounded into her mind, one at a time: *You. Will. Tell. It. To. Me. Now.* His hands tightened on her arms until she was in pain.

"Please," she begged. "My arms!"

"Tell." Again the pressure, and it grew suddenly immeasurably greater. She cried out. *"Tell!"*

"P-Prince Moses. I saw him kill a man today. An overseer at the quarries."

Not until she had blurted it all out did he release her arms and throw her from him. She whimpered and rubbed her right arm, but the pain would not go away.

"Ah, now," Neb-mertef was saying, "this is very interesting. Shall I use it now? Or shall I save it until—"

Moses, still fully dressed, sat atop his bed and stared at the wall. The candle had gone out, and the moon was high, no longer slanting through his window and filling his room with its chill light.

He had killed a man today.

He had extinguished a human life and left that man buried in the hillside behind Deir el-Bahari. Worse, another man had seen him do it, so for the rest of his existence, his future lay in that man's hands.

And even if the man did not tell, he himself would have to live with the memory. No matter that the man he had killed had been a bad man or that the blow had been well struck. It would haunt him forever.

Angrily he shook his head. *Get a hold on yourself! You're about to leave Thebes to go to war. You'll be killing men every day. Why should one more matter, in such a context?*

But it was no use. He knew why this one would nag at him, tightening his guts and keeping him awake for many nights to come: This was the *first* one.

He had never struck a blow in anger before. And when he had finally done so, he had killed a man with his bare hands.

He held up the offending hands and stared at them in horror.

The hands of a killer. A murderer.

X

In the morning Yalu intercepted Selket in the hall. His eyes blazed; he grabbed her wrist and dragged her into an empty storeroom, closing the door behind him.

"You little bitch," he growled. "Don't you think I know what you're doing? Going behind my back like that! I brought you into the palace in the first place!"

Selket drew herself up to her full height and glared at him. "Leave me alone or so help me, I'll scream. Everyone will come running. And you know how Baliniri will take it when he hears you've been forcing your attentions on me."

He drew his arm back and would have slapped her, but

judgment stayed his hand. His whole arm shook as he mastered himself and lowered his hand to his side.

"That's better," she said boldly. "Now if you're ready to be reasonable, we can discuss this calmly."

"Calmly! When you've stabbed me in the back?"

"I'll not have you raising your voice. I'll simply not have it."

"You were planning this all along, weren't you? Planning to undermine me—"

"Calm down, now. You haven't been undermined. I'm making you look very good with Neb-mertef. He intends to mention your name, and very favorably at that, to Amasis when he arrives."

"And maybe *you'll* put in a good word for me, too, eh?" he said in a voice bitter with sarcasm. "You'll be big enough to speak to Amasis, and you'll remember your old mentor and—"

"*If* you behave yourself. And that means no more pawing me."

"Little slut!"

"And you're a fat pig. See? What good does it do for us to start calling each other names? If we work together, we can both feather our nests."

"Together! You ungrateful tramp!"

"On the other hand," she continued, "I can always have you replaced. If you only knew how many people would kill for a nice job like yours." She waited a long beat, and then added in a deceptively soft voice, "*Literally* kill for it."

For perhaps the dozenth time, Baliniri stole a sidelong glance at the young prince's bloodshot eyes and haggard features as he was taken by the arm and assisted up the stairs toward the roof. "You don't look very good," he said. "Sitting up late worrying about the expedition?"

For a moment Moses did not answer. He let Baliniri lean on him as they made it to the upper landing. "Oh, don't worry about me," he said hoarsely. "I suppose I'm a bit nervous."

Baliniri smiled. At the roof's edge a gray-bearded man with thinning hair turned to face them. "Moses, this is Nebo of Shinar. I've arranged for him to accompany the expedition. He's a man of great learning and much understanding, and you can learn from him as you'll be learning from Khafre and the other soldiers. Nebo, Prince Moses."

The stranger made an elaborate bow, ending with a practiced flourish. "My very great pleasure, my lord, which will grow a thousandfold if I am successful in serving you well."

Moses smiled, but something dark and closed remained in his expression. "I am honored," he said. "And let the first of your services be that of abandoning the formal mode of speech except on those occasions when we're expected to be stiff and unbending. From now on it is Nebo and Moses."

"Well-spoken," Nebo said, appreciation in his eye, his grin genuine, making him seem younger than he had first appeared. "I have heard much about you. I have high hopes that we will become friends."

"This too is my wish." Moses turned to Baliniri. "I completed the inventory. The supplies are ready to go. I did ask the quartermaster's advice. He suggested that I increase the rations and put in an emergency requisition."

Baliniri rolled his eyes heavenward. "The idea is a good one, but an official requisition . . . they'll be filling it about the time you return from Nubia. Tell your request to Geb instead. He'll cut through the mess and get the order filled quickly."

"Yes. I'm very impressed with him."

"And he with you. If you'll excuse me, I'm going to leave you two here. I'll carry the order to Geb myself, and you two can get acquainted." He nodded to both and made his way slowly back to the stairs, shaking off Moses's helping hand. "No, I can make it alone. When you're gone, I'll have to, so I'd better start getting used to it."

Nebo and Moses exchanged glances, and Nebo smiled and shook his head fondly.

"He's a great man. Did you know he is still famous in my homeland? 'Baliniri of the Siege of Mari.' It's a song every schoolboy learns." He grinned mischievously. "There's a tongue twister in the fourth verse, and if you sing it incorrectly, the schoolmasters rap you over the knuckles."

"I love him," Moses said simply. "He's no blood relation, you know, but my father died before I was born. Baliniri has been as close to me as a father or grandfather might have been." He smiled and looked Nebo in the eye. "He is noble and wise, a superior man."

"He has raised you well," Nebo said. "It never hurts to raise a child with much love. So few fathers, real or otherwise, understand that." He sighed. "I had a son once, and I—lost him. I think about him often, and my heart is heavy when I do. How I would have enjoyed raising him to adulthood! Teaching him about life and about the world."

His voice seemed to break, and he turned away and wiped his eyes. His shoulders fell, as a man defeated by life, but then he straightened them again and held his head high. "Pardon me," he said, turning back to Moses. "I am the prey of strong emotion these days."

"A man is less a man if he does not show what he feels." Moses laid a hand sympathetically on Nebo's shoulder. "Among friends, anyway. And I hope you can count me among that number."

Nebo looked at him long and hard. "Thank you," he said. "I find it harder to hide my feelings as I grow older. Guess my age." He did not wait for a guess. "I'm in my early forties, yet I have seen enough in one lifetime to make me a man old and bent over and senile, fit to hobble about on a crutch and mutter under my breath."

"Then you will draw upon my youthful strength as I draw upon your mature wisdom," Moses said. "We shall both benefit, one from the other."

Nebo looked at him, and his smile was suddenly that of a man who had lost no strength at all with the passing of years. "You'll do," he said approvingly. "Stand with me by the roof's edge. Look down on the fleet, lined up at the quays, waiting for the troops to muster tomorrow at dawn." Moses joined him as Nebo pointed down at the riverside scene. "It's an exciting sight, isn't it? Your first real foray from home, your first real job as a man. How do you feel about it?"

Moses seemed to be starting to speak, but then he closed his mouth.

Nebo took him by the arms and turned the young man to

face him. Then Nebo looked him in the eyes, so Moses could not look away. "Something's wrong, son. Is it something you can tell a friend? Is it a burden that two may bear more easily than one?"

Moses blinked. He tried to speak but could not.

"It'll be a long voyage, son, with plenty of time to brood. If it keeps you up at night, you'll waste away like a prisoner in a dungeon. You won't be alert, and you'll make bad decisions, which will cost lives."

"Please," Moses said miserably.

"Ah. That reaches you, doesn't it? You don't care about yourself, but you *are* concerned about harming others under your command. That's a very good sign."

Moses bit his lip.

"Well," Nebo said with a reassuring smile, "all in good time. If you need to talk about it, I'll be here." He turned back to the scene below, resting his elbows on the rooftop wall. "You've never traveled, have you?"

Moses swallowed. "No," he answered. "A trip to the delta, when I was younger, and of course summer trips to the Fayum. Mother had a villa there."

"No trips into the desert, then? I understand you like to hunt."

Moses brightened a bit. "Oh, yes. I'm good with weapons. Baliniri trained me. I'm good with the bow, and—" Again the murder intruded upon his thoughts, causing him to falter. He changed the subject as best he could. "I . . . I once went lion hunting," he said desperately. "On the edge of the Libyan desert."

"Ah! Which method did you use? Did you fire with the bow from the chariot? Did you chase him?"

"Only at first. Baliniri took me. He could still hunt then. He said that among his people—your people too, I guess—it was considered a coward's hunt to kill from the chariot. If you were a man, you would dismount and finish the animal yourself, on foot."

"And you did that?"

"Yes. First with the lance, then with the sword. He said that ideally the lion would have the same chance to kill you that you had to kill him. Otherwise you had not earned the right to participate in his death."

"Right you are," Nebo said. "Or drink his blood."

"You know about that custom?" Moses asked. "You've killed a lion, then?"

"Me?" Nebo said, then laughed. "No, I'm not a man of weapons. I left that to my friends. They were great lion hunters."

Moses glanced involuntarily at the sword in his companion's belt. "Yet you wear a sword here, at court."

"This?" Nebo said. "Take a look at it. I'm a bit of a collector, for all that fighting's not my interest." He handed it over. "See if anything like that has ever crossed your path."

"How curious," Moses mused. "This *is* unusual." He handed it back. It was obvious that he had little interest in the weapon. Or perhaps it was that whatever had been bothering him before was now back. His eyes looked beyond the hills on the far side of the river. The pinched, tight set had come back to his features.

Suddenly he turned to Nebo. "Look, if *you* had—" he began.

"Yes?"

"Nothing. I was just thinking."

Nebo looked out over the bare hills too. "I understand you've never been involved in a battle," he said. "Are you a bit apprehensive? I don't mean scared. Just unnerved about raising your hand to another human being, having to kill a man? It's a big step. I remember the first time I found myself standing opposite some big bruiser with a sword in his hand intending to kill me. Well, I was paralyzed. But then when he came at me . . ."

It was idle prattle, but it was calculated. Nebo's eyes were on him the whole time, seemingly able to look inside him, to his very soul. Moses took a deep breath and said in a wretched, tortured voice: "Nebo, I *have* killed a man." There, it was out. "With these two hands."

Nebo put a fatherly hand on the boy's shoulder. "So have I, son. And I felt terrible. Want to tell me about it?"

XI

As the day waned, the slanting lateen sail of a medium-sized cargo vessel appeared to the north. It had passed the routine inspection at the checkpoint some miles downriver, so it hardly attracted notice. It docked routinely, and its small crew proceeded to unload its cargo of dried dates from the delta islands.

No one watched as two robed figures debarked from the boat, one tall, the other short, hoods drawn up over their heads. They did not pause at dock's edge but immediately walked off into the gathering crowd that always turned up on the waterfront as the day came to a close.

Silently, purposefully they strode through the streets, past bazaar and crossroad and blind alley, wending their way through the dusk traffic with the practiced ease of old habitués of the city. Finally, in the Temple Quarter, they stopped, looked both ways, and found themselves at an undistinguished doorway, where they slipped inside before anyone could note their passage.

After a long and tortuous route through the bowels of the great building, they finally came to the panel on the far side of Baliniri's wall. They knocked according to the agreed-upon pattern and waited for some moments before the panel slowly slid aside.

"Mara!" said Baliniri with surprise. "And Ngira! Come in! When did you get to the city?"

"Only a short while ago," the queen answered, taking off her outer robe and draping it over a chair as the Nubian woman did the same. "We came right here."

"Please," Baliniri said, "sit. Tell me what's been happening."

She sat down heavily, kicked off her sandals, and drew her feet up under her. "We can forget getting any help from Kamose," she said, looking grim. "He's totally under Amasis's spell, as bad as he ever was. And he's on the drug again."

Baliniri shook his head sadly. "I was afraid of that. Nebo is here, you know."

"Well, as always he's a bit ahead of us. He as much as predicted this would happen, from nothing more than a quick glimpse at Kamose from a distance as he was entering the city."

"And there goes one of our contingency plans." He sighed and sat down slowly beside her, favoring his back. "The optimistic option."

"Yes. Baliniri, I see the fleet ready to sail, and the troops gathered within sight of the quays. They're sailing to Nubia, then?"

"Yes." He turned to Ngira. "There's some mystery man behind Balaam, and he's the one who's responsible for the invasion. Not Nehsi." The Nubian woman nodded. He turned back to Mara. "I've put Moses in charge of the expedition."

She looked at him with concern. "Will he be safe? He's all we've got now."

There was a hard glint in his eyes. "Nobody is safe anymore. In fact, he may be safer there, at war, than here. After all, Amasis will be here."

"So will the army," she said anxiously. "All but the last bunch of mercenaries. And we'll be here, and we'll have sent our only protection to Nubia with Moses." Her sigh was long and hard. "Who's the officer in charge?"

"Khafre."

"Good. He's a very sound man. But—that leaves only the army staff who are in Amasis's camp in charge here."

"Yes. I picked Khafre for Moses's side because he isn't among Amasis's adherents."

"Good for his sake. Bad for ours."

"I can't help that," Baliniri replied. "Meanwhile, we're training Moses under the very best. I'm giving him Geb as an assistant."

"Excellent. And you keep telling me you're slipping."

"Not *that* far, perhaps. Nebo and Moses apparently got off to a good start today. I saw them come in after they'd been chatting all afternoon, arm in arm like father and son."

Mara smiled. "This will be as good for Nebo as for the boy."

"I asked Nebo what they talked about, but he wouldn't tell me. It speaks of a shared confidence he promised not to reveal. Mara, the lad's in good hands. We can trust things to come out well for them, I think. The problem's here."

She frowned. "And I'm afraid we're in for quite a siege."
She let the anger come into her voice now. "Kamose! I can't
understand him! How could he be so brave—defeating the
Hai and destroying them up North the way you destroy a
snake's brood after you've killed the snake—and so weak
when he comes back to Egypt."

"You of all people should know the secret of that,"
Baliniri chided sympathetically. "The only emotion that ever
has motivated him is hatred—the driving, all-consuming en-
mity he felt for his father all those years had been transferred
to the Hai after Apophis was dead. With the Shepherds
wiped out as a fighting force, there is nothing to live for. He
feels like a man squeezed dry. He needs to have someone put
something into that empty space, to fill it up."

"There is truth in what you say. But I do not have it in
me to give Kamose what he needs from me."

"You are too much like him," the vizier remarked.

She stared. The thought had never occurred to her.
"What is that supposed to mean?"

"There was a great emptiness in you after Hakoris's
death, was there not? One that no love could fill?"

Looking at her, he could see the shock to her system as
she tried to assimilate this thought. Mara had been the daughter of a debt-ridden physician to whom the evil Hakoris had
come to have a thief's brand surgically removed from his
forehead. The operation had not worked, and Hakoris, in
blind rage, had murdered the doctor, then arranged to purchase all his assets. These had included young Mara, whom
Hakoris had taken as a slave and mistreated for years until
she had been released by Riki, then a penniless street-urchin.
For years afterward she had been obsessed by the thought of
killing Hakoris . . . and it was as Baliniri had said—she had
not known what to do with herself the moment her revenge
was complete and Hakoris was no more.

"You have looked into my heart and seen things I cannot
see there myself," she admitted bitterly. "Yes, I have failed
him, haven't I? Kamose needed a thing from me that I did
not have to give. Perhaps I could have headed all this off."

"We can give only what we have," Baliniri soothed.

"And because I could not save him, Amasis controls him.

And we are about to have a deadly reckoning with Amasis, a confrontation that we may not manage to survive." She shuddered. "Let us hope against hope that Moses can survive."

"Yes," Baliniri said with an air of resignation. "When is Amasis due to come to Thebes?"

Her words, quick and sudden, cut like knives. "Didn't I tell you? I'm at most a day ahead of him. He'll be arriving about the time the army leaves for Nubia."

Baliniri stared. "So soon?" he said in the voice of a man grown suddenly old and infirm. "I'd hoped we had longer."

Moses's face was still haggard looking when he arrived at the quays next morning, but his back was straight and his head held high. As he stood looking at the muster of the Theban guards at dockside, Nebo joined him.

"Good morning," greeted the older man. "Have you said your farewells already?"

"What?" the boy said. "Oh. Oh, yes. Yes, I said good-bye to Mother."

"And she took it well?"

"Yes, I suppose. She put a brave face on things."

"I suspected as much. She comes from valiant stock. Your grandmother's family were a gallant lot. Ah-Hotep lost a lover and a husband to war. And a son," he added with a sigh. "Riki may have been the best of them all."

"I heard the story. Grandmother's son by a soldier assigned to guard the palace, wasn't he? They tried to hush that one up, but these scandals will leak out."

"The soldier was a great man—Baba of El-Kab—and the son she bore him was even greater, for all the fact that he didn't learn who he was until he was an adult."

Moses looked at him sharply. "Excuse me," he said. "For a stranger from a foreign land, you have an amazing knowledge of the secrets in our local royalty." He smiled conspiratorially. "Is there something that you're not telling me?"

"Quite a lot. Yes, my young friend, one good confidence deserves another. But the things I have to tell you would be best passed along when we are well out of Thebes. There is more to this voyage than meets the eye. There is more to our quest than an end to hostilities with Nubia."

"What?"

"All in good time. I promise to satisfy you as the days go by. But let an old man stick to his own schedule in these things. Let me keep you in suspense a bit; it will ease the boredom of the long trip to the upriver forts." His smile was merry and mischievous. "Did you sleep better last night?"

"A little. It does make a burden lighter to share it with a friend."

Nebo clapped him on the arm. "Good. Let's hope you always remember that, so long as this particular friend is at your shoulder. Now come, let's see to the loading of the ships."

From his rooftop Baliniri watched the sailors casting off, shaking out the furled sails atop the long yard until the canvas caught the first soft gusts of wind. Mara had joined him a little after dawn and still stood beside him. He was silent for a long time.

"The old soldier wishes he were aboard, headed for war?" she guessed.

His gray-haired head shook slowly. "It's been a long, long time," he admitted, "but in the night I dreamed of being young again—young and full of vigor and strength. I haven't dreamed of being a soldier for many years. Perhaps there *is* a part of me that rides away with Moses into a new and unfamiliar world, full of fresh dangers and tests of his character . . . a part of me that longs to be back in a simpler and more innocent time, when I did not know my limitations as well as I know them now."

"You have so few limitations, old friend," she said with an affection born of years of shared perils and worries. "But I know what you mean. You long for your lost innocence, before you learned to hate and fear. Well, not I. I wouldn't be a day younger than I am just now, not if it meant relearning what I know now. All I remember of youth is how painful it was."

"What a strange thing for a woman to say," he commented. "Most women mourn for lost beauty."

"What happiness did mine ever bring me?" she asked. "At any moment I would have exchanged it for a plain face— and power."

"Curious. I had a great deal of power. I still have a little, I think. But did it bring me the happiness you think it would have brought you? I think not. I was always the restless sort, never happy with what I had. I was always searching for what I had never seen before, never experienced."

She squeezed his arm. "These are autumn thoughts, old friend," she said.

"Autumn," he repeated after her, savoring the word. "Yes. The autumn of life, of hope and expectation and faith. How appropriate. We have a winter coming, one such as you people raised on the Nile have never known. Winter will sweep across this blessed land and blight everything that lies upon it if we cannot stop Amasis and the cult." He shuddered; she could feel it through his arm, and she clung to him all the more tightly because of it.

"Baliniri, what's the matter? There's something you haven't told me."

"Yes," he confessed. "They've broken our last line of resistance. The cult has invaded our wing of the palace. I don't know who it is, but I know something's wrong. Protect yourself at all times, waking and sleeping. Don't go anywhere without Ngira, not even within the palace."

Out on the Nile the ships caught the wind and began sawing their way up the mighty river, fighting the current.

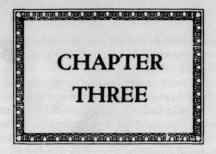

CHAPTER THREE

In the Western Desert

I

The runner was as tall and thin as a crane, without an ounce of fat to be found anywhere on her long, superbly trained body. Sweat glistened and ran down the length of her frame or flew from her in droplets as the taut muscles strained, the stringy legs pumped, and the hard-soled feet pounded the narrow path. Her overworked heart beat hard, and her lungs gulped the thin desert air in great shuddering gasps.

The woman was naked, nothing protecting her hard body from the harsh rays of the desert sun—not even the gold ornaments that were the customary adornment of the Desert Legion, the band of warriors to whom the runner belonged.

The woman was not alone. Alongside the trail, now leading, now following, broad paws unerringly finding the right place to fall, the slender form of a great spotted cheetah loped with effortless ease, in a silent companionship with the runner, which had kept the runner from collapsing these many miles. As long as the cat ran, the runner would run—unless her exhausted heart stopped and the tortured lungs accepted no more air.

The secret tribe known as the Desert Legion patrolled the desert land west of Thebes. It was a tribe of the self-chosen: women who had run away from the city, not wanting husbands chosen for them by their fathers or children forced upon them by their husbands. These "misfits" had sought refuge with the like-minded women of the desert.

The Desert Legion had been formed by Teti, daughter of Shobai, granddaughter of Kirta, descendant of Ahuni of Babylon and of the legendary Belsunu. Teti, born to the fabled armsmaking dynasty called the Children of the Lion, had learned the family trade, which had been carried down through the centuries since the remote and mythic days of Cain, the first armorer.

Like all the men of her family, Teti had been born with the famous birthmark—the paw print of a lion, a port-wine stain usually found on the back at waist height—and, on coming of age, had insisted on being taught the trade. She had quickly become adept enough to accompany the Egyptian army as armorer to the battle of El-Kab.

While accompanying the army upriver, Teti had fallen deeply in love with a young Theban soldier, Netru of Deir el-Bahari, who had died in the first wave of the battle.

In angry bitterness Teti had taken to the desert to live, with a cadre of women drawn from the slums and stews of Thebes—loners and nonconformists, outcasts like the woman she had become in her crushing loss.

She, and they, had found fulfillment living off the land in the sparest kind of existence in the desert wastes. They were armed with weapons made by Teti herself, and in time they petitioned Baliniri to supervise their training as warrior-women—a private army loyal only to him and to itself.

Little by little, they took over the great desert oasis of El-Kharga—a city in the desert, peopled by families and merchants and farmers and fed by springs that drew their waters from the far south—and the more remote oasis of El-Dakhla, where nobody but their own number was welcome.

Then, as the Desert Legion, the group worked in tandem with the Black Wind, the Nubian women's army first commanded by Nehsi's and Naldamak's mother, Queen Ebana. They consolidated total control over the desert caravan lanes, denying Shepherd access to Thebes and keeping the Hai locked up in the North.

Now, years after Teti's death, others had come to the desert lands to live and be ruled by the tall, sun-bronzed warrior-women in the gold jewelry. A small but self-sufficient civilization existed, overseen by the wise but aging warrior-woman Weret, Teti's successor and closest friend, general of the army that the legion and the Black Wind had combined to become.

Only El-Dakhla, farther to the west, remained still inviolate, a secret preserve of the women, where civilians of the El-Kharga community, male or female, were not welcome on pain of death.

Only five men had ever visited El-Dakhla and returned from it alive. Besides Baliniri, one was General Riki, who had come on army business for the vizier; he had fallen in love with Teti, married her, and taken her away to Thebes, where she had died of the plague.

Another was Teti's cousin Seth, a brilliant, restless wanderer who had not been seen for many years. He had come to the oasis to learn from Teti the secret of ironmongery, which she had learned from the legendary Nubian metalworker Karkara of Sado.

The other two men were still there. And the naked runner's mission pertained to them as much as it did to Weret.

One was Teti's illegitimate son by Netru, Neku-re, an ageless child-man, unworldly and impractical, the first of the Children of the Lion ever to forsake the craft of the clan. Neku-re's world was the world of the mind, and he was said to be able to speak with the spirits of the dead and to perform many strange feats of magic.

The other was the tiny, misshapen dwarf Tchabu, a seer of great power but no control over that power. Tchabu could sense danger before it happened. Accurate forebodings of the future could be found in his visions, but he could not predict when these fits of omniscience would come upon him and could not call for them when they would not come of themselves.

When the two men had been brought together, strange and wonderful things had happened. Although they seemed an odd pair, their minds would unpredictably, unreliably, but spectacularly mesh to provide insight into the mysteries of existence.

Weret was the heart of the combined armies of the women of the two lands, black and white; Naldamak, daughter and successor to Ebana, was the strong right arm; and Neku-re and Tchabu were the brains. To them were referred problems that arose, suspicions in need of confirmation, and any enigma that otherwise defied answering.

It was to them that the naked runner was bound. She had been on the track for hours now, having taken over for an earlier courier many leagues back. That courier had taken over from another, and so on. The relays had begun far to the south, and each runner had been expertly coached in what to say, trusting none of the message to papyrus that might be intercepted and read. None of the runners, tested and reliable women, would reveal the message to anyone but the appointed person, even under torture.

As she wound her way down an incline, signs of life began to appear in the barren desert—a green shrub here, a desert plant there. Beside the track a rivulet suddenly gushed from the rocks, creating a small creek that dripped down the hillside beside the runner's path. As other rivulets joined it, the trickle became a narrow ribbon of water, then the water became a fair-sized stream. Soon there was a merry ripple of water, punctuated by the steady footfalls of the runner and her cheetah as they made their way into the valley.

The runner could see signs of life: cultivated farmland peeping through the rocks ahead, houses, people and domesticated animals moving against the suddenly fruitful landscape. Having an end in sight gave her new wind, and she settled into a steady and unhurried lope at the canyon's bottom.

Past farm and farmhouse she ran, as the inhabitants of the southern fringes of the oasis turned to watch her. And above her head, above the cheetah's untiring bounds, flew pigeons released by scouts hidden in the hills above the entrance to the oasis—pigeons bearing messages for the commandant in charge of the main garrison, warning of the runner's coming.

The birds, of course, arrived first. Maat, the commandant, sent a messenger after Weret, and the aging general appeared with her aides.

Weret was still statuesque, proud, and athletic, her well-shaped head sitting high upon a regal neck. Her bright eyes missed nothing. As always she spoke little and listened much. She returned Maat's salute smartly and nodded at the oncoming figure.

"This would be . . . hmmm . . . Satre," Maat said. "She's one worth watching. There may be a promotion in her future soon."

The runner stumbled to a halt before them and fell to her knees, gasping. Strong arms gently lifted her and carried her to the well nearby, where her comrades splashed her naked body with water and allowed her to drink cautiously. They wanted her to rest until she got her breath back; but, impatient, she forced the issue, getting unsteadily to her feet to salute first Maat and then Weret, whom she had not recognized at first.

"Report."

"Ma'am. Satre, of the Seventh Brigade."

"I know, child. Take your time. Report. Be accurate rather than quick," Weret said, her tone stern but concerned.

"Yes, ma'am." The girl took a deep breath, then blew it out hard through pursed lips. "The compliments of my commander, Noot, of the border command. A message meant for both you and the seers Neku-re and—"

"Just summarize," Maat ordered. .

But Weret held up one hand. "No. Give it to us exactly, child. If you've memorized it properly, there may be some message in the very wording of the message."

"Right you are," Maat agreed. "Sorry."

"Yes, ma'am," Satre said. "Strong evidence exists that the Nubian court is now dominated by workers of black magic. They reportedly conjure the spirits of the dead, in order to influence the course of events. Necromancers!"

"Are you sure?" Weret asked. "This was Noot's term for it?"

"I give the message precisely as it was given to me, my lady."

"Very well, child. Go on."

"Yes, ma'am. Our spies report that strange things have been happening at the court; reliable people have seen demons, monsters, misbegotten things of the night. People have died at their hands, without a mark on them."

Maat and Weret exchanged glances.

"In the courtyard at Semna," Satre continued, "before a hundred people, a creature from the Netherworld appeared, breathing smoke and flames and standing six times the height of a man. It was enveloped in a fire that did not burn it. And as all looked on, the monster spat fire at a man in the front rank and killed him, then disappeared in a flash of smoke."

"Go on," Weret said severely.

"That's all, my lady. Except that the message was to reach Neku-re and Tchabu as quickly as possible." She stood at attention and, despite her obvious exhaustion, said, "Beg permission to take the message to El-Dakhla, my lady!"

Weret reached out and, in an uncharacteristic gesture of affection, patted the girl's cropped head. "No, child," she said. "You've done enough for one day. Get some rest. Report to us tomorrow at sunrise."

And when the girl had gone away, Weret and Maat let their eyes lock again. "Monsters?" she said in a soft voice, her right eyebrow lifting. "Demons? Creatures from the Netherworld?" She shook her graying head. "The worst part of it is, I find myself believing her. Why?"

But Maat could give no answer.

II

Weret quickly called for a fresh runner and sent along messages not only for Noot and her border guards but for Naldamak as well. This runner was bilingual, and for secrecy's sake, the message for Naldamak was given in the language of the peoples of the Land of the Mountains of Fire, ancestral homeland of Akhilleus, father of Nehsi and Naldamak. The Mountains of Fire were a thousand leagues to the south, and Nehsi had never bothered to learn that tongue; Naldamak's Black Wind, however, included several warriors from the distant land, and she had taken pains to learn every language represented in the Black Wind.

When the runner had begun her long journey to the next relay post, many leagues into the southern hills, Maat turned to Weret and said, "You told Satre to report at dawn. Are we going to take the message to El-Dakhla?"

"It won't be necessary," Weret said. "A pigeon came in from one of our posts on the western track an hour before Satre arrived, with the message that Neku-re and Tchabu would be here around sunset tonight."

"Here!" Maat said in some surprise. "They haven't come to El-Kharga in two years, at least!"

"Three," Weret corrected. "Three years and two months, to be exact. Something important must be going on, and my guess is that it has to do with the news Satre just brought us. Remember, Tchabu is growing old and doesn't like to travel— not even on the shoulders of one of our warriors."

Maat smiled at the thought. "That will be a sight. But of course he could hardly travel along the western track any other way, with his short legs. Will we speak to both men tonight?"

"I may speak with Neku-re, but it's best to let Tchabu get a night's sleep first. I have found it is best to ask questions of him in the morning, when he is still half-asleep and his mind still open to the voices in his dreams." She dismissed the aides around them and then said, "Come. We will discuss this together, the better to know what questions to ask tomorrow."

*   *   *

The desert party arrived early, quite a bit before sundown. Tchabu had had a seizure, so Dali, the warrior carrying the tiny dwarf, had increased her pace, the better to get
the little man to camp where better care could be taken of
him.

Weret hovered over Tchabu in the hammock where the
guards had placed him. Over his fitfully tossing, sweat-drenched
little body, her eyes locked with Neku-re's. "This," she said,
"is like no trance I remember him having."

"Not in many years," Neku-re agreed. "He collapsed on
the trail and toppled from Dali's shoulders. He was unconscious before he hit the ground. Dali thought he was going to
die, and to tell you the truth, I had some ill feelings myself.
I'm used to some of it—the eyes rolled back, the foaming and
drooling, the chills and cold sweats—but ordinarily he's muttering something. He's never silent when one of these things
is going on. But listen to him: not a murmur."

Weret turned to one of her aides. "Watch him. Send
someone to me if he shows any change, for better or worse."
She took Neku-re's arm and steered him up the hill to her
private arbor, where no one could listen to their conversation
without being seen.

"There's been an enigmatic message from the border,"
she said, then repeated it just as Satre had given it to her. "If
I were the sort who wagers, I would bet any sum that
Tchabu's seizure has something to do with this."

"You'd probably be right. This has been building for
days, which is why I brought him here. He's been having
terrifying dreams, and they sound suspiciously like the visions the people of Semna have been having down in Nubia."

"What of this black magic business? Where there's magic,
there has to be a necromancer to perform it."

Neku-re nodded. "Tchabu has had moments recently
when he mumbled a name—Apedemek."

"Apedemek? It's not an Egyptian name. Nor has it the
rhythm of the upriver tongues. Assyria? Elam?"

"Brace yourself," Neku-re warned. "When Tchabu was
himself again, I said the name back to him. You know that

desperate look he gets on his face when something really
terrifies him?"

"Yes. But what—"

"He recognized the name, but no more. He could not
place it with anyone, but he could tell me where it's from.
Chalybia."

Weret stared. She sank onto the stone bench under the
arbor. "But that doesn't make any sense. There isn't any
Chalybia. Seth found that out a generation ago."

Neku-re snorted. "Tchabu doesn't know that," he said
significantly, then his eyes narrowed. "Come to think of it,
you're not supposed to know that, either. Only we Children
of the Lion are supposed to know. How did you find out?"

Weret's smile was wry. "Never you mind. I have my
own secrets, after all. I can't run an army, particularly in
perilous times like these, without knowing everything I can
possibly learn about everyone."

"How much do you know about the Chalybians?"

"I know that they aren't a nation, as we once thought,
but members of a secret lodge, to which the Children of the
Lion are all supposed to belong. Your branch of the family
apparently lost contact with the order, generations back. The
family did not rejoin the order"—here Neku-re's eye lit up,
and a superior smile crossed his face, causing Weret to falter
momentarily—"until Seth finally made contact with a Chalybian
named Marduk-nasir, up in Syria, and was sworn into the
brotherhood."

This should have elicited vigorous comment, but Neku-re
only smiled enigmatically. "Wonder of wonders," he said
lightly. "Is there anything you don't know?"

"I don't know what Tchabu is going to tell us," she said
in a flat voice, then looked Neku-re hard in the eyes. "Are
you Chalybian? Were you ever initiated into the order? But
no, you're no armorer. You're a maker of golden jewelry,
with no more interest in making weapons than in making
war. Chalybians are all masters of the ironmonger's trade."

Neku-re's eyes twinkled merrily, and his smile was infu-
riating. "There *is* something you don't know, after all."

"Of course there is," she said brusquely. "And the
answer?"

"Never you mind," he said. "I have *my* secrets, too."

He was about to say something else when they looked up to see an attendant beckoning to them and pointing toward the location of Tchabu's hammock. Minutes later they were down the hillside and standing over the still-unconscious dwarf.

Tchabu stirred and began to speak. Weret and Neku-re bent down and tried to make out what he was saying, but it was all incomprehensible.

Then, suddenly, out of the gibberish came a single word: "Apedemek."

The color drained from Weret's face as she put a finger to her lips.

The tiny form tossed miserably in the open-work hammock; his short arms waved, and the stubby hands made motions as if to brush something away from the tortured face. "No!" he cried. "Tchabu not see! Tchabu not want to see!"

Neku-re knelt and took one of the fevered little hands in his own. But as he did, a strange transformation took place. His own eyes closed, and his body swayed for a moment until Weret thought he would fall. His face looked gray, and she could see, under his closed eyelids, the frantic circling of his eyeballs.

She rushed to steady him, but he suddenly righted himself and shook his head, opening his eyes. As he did, Tchabu's little body finally stopped its writhing, and the dwarf slept.

Neku-re blinked and tried to get Weret in focus.

"Are you all right?" she asked anxiously. "Come, sit down."

He accepted the seat she steered him to but did not say anything for a long moment. When he did speak, his voice was that of a man more depleted by his recent experience than Satre had been from running countless miles along the desert track.

"It's all true," he confirmed. "Believe it or not—monsters, demons, misbegotten things of the night, creatures the size of houses, which vanish in a puff of smoke."

"From the Netherworld, you say?" Weret asked, gimlet-eyed.

"I don't know where they're from. But people do see them, and they do die from the encounter. I entered Tchabu's mind, and he has been in the mind of someone at the court in Semna. Whoever it is, he's well placed in the hierarchy and gets around. He sees what the others see, and he feels their fear." His shoulders slumped, and he exhaled deeply. "The curious thing is, this unnamed person feels more fear of Apedemek than he does of the monsters—which, mind you, he believes himself to have seen with his own eyes."

"But who is Apedemek?"

"I know no more than I did, except that he's there at court. He's someone around whom even Nehsi and Balaam walk on tiptoe. Someone whom no one dares offend or even refuse." He shuddered. "Gods! I'm even a bit frightened myself." He shook his head to clear it and gave Weret a wan smile. "The rest . . . well, perhaps when Tchabu awakens, he can tell us more."

He let the matter rest. But when Tchabu awakened at last, the dwarf could remember nothing. And in the night that followed, Neku-re sat up long hours. Thinking. Brooding. Worrying.

CHAPTER FOUR

Thebes

I

Days later, Baliniri and Mara were once again atop the roof, looking down, their faces troubled and brows knit. On the quays the newly arrived boats continued to unload wave after wave of tough-looking soldiers in the uniforms of the army of Egypt. They trudged down the planks in single file from each of the four fleet-class vessels that had accompanied Amasis upriver.

"How many is that?" Baliniri asked. "I lost count."

"I'm not sure," she replied. "I stopped counting at six hundred. And there are apparently at least that many more waiting to debark."

"So few of them seem to be Egyptians," he said dejectedly. "I thought they were going to muster out the mercenaries that came back with Kamose from Syria and Canaan. But look at them, Mara. Those are not Egyptian faces. They're from everywhere around the Great Sea *but* Egypt."

100

"Strange . . ." she mused. "They don't look like the men I saw marching through the city after the return of the army from Sile. Those were tired, flat-footed men whose legs would hardly bear them. Their shoulders drooped, and their heads hung down."

"Well," he proposed, "that could just be the effect of resting up a bit. Professional soldiers have a way of rebounding from the most brutal treatment faster than ordinary men do."

"No. These look younger. And look, coming off the first boat—Hellenes! Unmistakable. Does anyone else dress like that?" She hid a smile. "I suppose I should say 'undress,' shouldn't I? Helmets and bronze greaves, and nothing else."

"Yet my spies told me of no Hellenes among the returning armies," Baliniri remarked. "That is indeed curious. And look—that's the flag of Colchis over there."

Mara turned to him. "But if they've got rid of the soldiers who defeated the Hai, and hired on new men—"

"My thought exactly," he said grimly. "They've been hired for new purposes. And unless I miss my guess, the new purposes include the final subjugation of Egypt—of Thebes and the Upper Nile nomes." He slammed his fist down on the rooftop's wall. "Where is Kamose? Not a sign of him anywhere."

"No," she said, scanning the crowd. "But look. There's Amasis!"

He looked toward where her finger pointed. The cult leader stood on the high poop deck of the command ship, his fists on hips, feet splayed, looking over the scene before him. Almost as if he knew he was being talked about, he suddenly looked up to see the two of them looking down at him. They saw the flash of his white teeth and saw his body shake with laughter inaudible from this far away. He made a mock bow at them, one too elaborate to convey respect. And then, turning his back on them—the queen of Egypt and her husband's vizier—he looked to the unloading, barked out an order, and disappeared below.

Mara walked to the top of the stairs and hit the little bronze gong hanging above the landing with her fist. "Selket!" she called. "Come up here for a moment."

The servant ran up the stairs. "Yes, my lady?"

"Please go down to the wharf and inquire whether my husband has come upriver with these people. I don't see him."

"Yes, my lady." The girl bowed and went to do Mara's bidding. Baliniri's eyes followed her until she disappeared. There was a curious, thoughtful look on his face. He was not pleased.

In Deir el-Bahari the foreman of the guard paced angrily before the assembled slaves. His eyes flashed, and one could see the violence building in him. "One of you scum knows the truth about the missing overseer. Rest assured, I'm going to learn that truth, if I have to beat it or starve it out of you."

No one spoke. The Habirus' eyes, to the last person, stared straight ahead. Nobody looked at the guard.

Their silence made him angrier. "You!" he bellowed at a slave chosen at random. It was Aaron, son of Amram. "What do you know of this?"

There was no answer.

Suddenly the foreman's fist lashed out and felled the slave in his tracks. The slave groggily got to his knees and shook his head. As he did the foreman's knee rose viciously and rammed into the slave's face. "Do you want to die? Right here and now?" the guardsman screamed. "If you do, I'm the man to oblige you! One or more of you people murdered my overseer!"

His eyes lit on a particularly tall Habiru man. "You! You look big enough to have done this! What do you know about it? Speak up, or so help me—"

"Nothing, sir," the Habiru shouted. "I wasn't even working here that day. I was on duty hauling bricks for the—"

"Shut up!" the foreman said. His booted foot lashed out and caught the tall man in the groin, doubling him over. The guard strode down the line. "Still silent?" he challenged, quivering with rage. "Very well. Half rations of bread and water for the lot of you. That includes children and old folks. And you'll still be expected to do heavy labor. This will continue for however long it takes until one of you tells me what I need to know."

He turned sharply on one heel and strode away. There was no order given to dismiss, so the long line of slaves waited until he was out of sight before breaking ranks and helping the fallen men to their feet.

Dathan, who had witnessed the killing of the overseer by the unnamed stranger, brushed off the man who had been beaten. "Aaron," he said, "are you all right?"

"I think so," said the other, touching his battered face gingerly. "My nose may be broken." He let Dathan draw him aside and watched the crowd disperse before he spoke again. "You did well not to tell him anything," he commended.

"I almost broke down when I saw the way he hit you," Dathan confessed. "Why should I stand by and let one of our own number suffer for some nameless Egyptian, even if he did help me?"

"To turn him in—even if you knew who he was—would be a wicked thing," said Aaron. "Better that a dozen of us should perish than we should betray a man who befriended us."

"Well, it's a moot point anyway," Dathan said. "I can't very well betray anyone I can't identify. He was someone I've never seen before. I'm sure he was from across the river. I know the face of every Egyptian on this side of the Nile." He frowned. "If it had been me the foreman was hitting, I honestly don't know if I would have been able to keep quiet."

"I'm sure that if it comes to that, you'll do your best," Aaron reassured, clapping him on the arm. His nose was bleeding badly. "Here, I'm going to wash this off. I'll be back in a moment."

Taking leave of Dathan, Aaron walked rapidly toward his wretched dwelling. On the hillside path, his sister, Miriam, overtook him. "Aaron! Oh, my poor dear, what have they done to you?"

"Nothing," he replied. "Don't take time out from your work to help me. One of us getting beaten per day is quite enough." He tried to smile, but that only made his nose bleed more profusely.

"Here, let me wipe it off," she offered. "This was about the killing of the overseer, wasn't it? They won't let this alone."

"So far Dathan hasn't said anything. But he's not strong. If one of them strikes him . . . well, I can't vouch for what he'll do then."

"Aaron, I didn't want to tell you, but the other day someone who fit the description of the one who killed the overseer—"

"Yes?" He took the clean rag from her, tilted his chin up, and pressed the cloth to his face, trying to stanch the flow of blood. "What of him?"

"This someone came to the quarry and asked about me. And he asked about Mother."

Aaron almost dropped the rag. He stared at her.

"What do you suppose that could mean?" he asked. "That doesn't make any sense."

She looked him in the eye and did not comment.

"Unless . . ." he began. His eyes widened.

"Yes. You're right. I saw him, Aaron. It was he. It was Moses." She paused. "It wouldn't have occurred to anyone that he wasn't Egyptian."

Aaron glanced cautiously right and left. "Easy, now," he whispered. "If anyone overheard you—"

She covered her mouth. But then she spoke softly. "*He* can't know. *He* can't have found out. They would *never* have told him. But if he doesn't know, what would he be doing over here, asking about Mother and me?"

When their unit had been dismissed, Onuris and his friend Nemti, late of the city guard of Avaris, drew aside from their fellow soldiers. "I don't feel like going out and getting drunk like the rest, do you?" Onuris asked. "Let's see if we can find something else to do."

Nemti, a year younger than Onuris at twenty-eight and half a head taller, smiled. "A good idea. I hadn't been looking forward to a stupid, drunken brawl. You know what the stews are going to be like our first night in Thebes. I'd just as soon stay away."

"Then where shall we go? There isn't going to be anywhere this side of the river where you can get away from them tonight." He sneered. "You know, I could put up with their arrogance if these weren't the dregs of the Avaris waterfront, recruited right out of the gutter, or worse."

"Yes," Nemti agreed. "Much worse. That last detachment of Syrians were fighting for the Hai when Kamose came to Canaan and captured them. Then they easily came over to the Egyptian cause. Frankly, I don't think much of a man whose loyalty can be bought as easily as theirs was." He rubbed his jaw. "Of course you and I missed the war and got pressed into service to come upriver only after Amasis paid off the bulk of his mercenaries at Sile and had to pad his army out any way he could."

The two fell in step and walked down the long quay. "I've been wondering about that," Nemti said. "Why does he need to pad them out? Why does he have to send a big unit like this upriver to his home country? Thebes isn't at war with the delta."

"Huh." Onuris snorted. "But Amasis is at war with Baliniri. Everybody knows that. And the old man just sent the city guard to Nubia. Now there'll be no one left here but us— troops loyal, in theory at least, to Amasis and not to Baliniri."

"Speak for yourself," Nemti remarked. "Baliniri's been the man for me ever since I joined the guard when I was a kid. My father served under him, and I remember how proud the old fellow was when I told him I was going to join up and follow in his footsteps. I never liked Amasis and that slimy foreign crowd that hangs around with him, always trying to drag you into that sleazy religion of theirs."

"I'm with you," Onuris agreed. "But just the same, if you favor Baliniri, I'd advise you to keep it to yourself. Nearly everybody in our unit is of the other faction, and one or two of them seem to be keeping an eye on us. I think they doubt our loyalty."

"As well they might. Forget about them. Let's go over to Deir el-Bahari. I have relatives there—distant ones, but a good lot. I met them when I was a kid. Whether they remember me or not, they'll welcome us and feed us."

Onuris looked at his friend. "Lucky you. My family are as poor as wharf rats. What do these kinfolk of yours do?"

"They're artisans. That's the prevailing occupation in Deir el-Bahari. Other than my father and me, the only sol-

dier that the family ever produced was Netru, the hero of the
Battle of El-Kab."

Onuris whistled low. "I never knew there were any
famous people in your family! If I had a Netru in my bloodlines, I'd have bragged about it by now."

"He was a cousin, not close enough for any of that heroism to rub off, I'm afraid. But we are all proud of him. Come
on, let's hail a ferryman. You'll like it over there. It's a lot
nicer place to spend an evening than Thebes." He smiled.
"The food's better, the wine's mellower, and the girls are
prettier."

"Lead on," said his friend enthusiastically. "Here! Boatman! To shore! Over here!"

II

Despite his growing difficulty with walking any distance,
Baliniri had decided to go down to the court to give formal
welcome to Amasis, the returning army, and Kamose. But
when he arrived, walking slowly and leaning on a stout hard-
wood stick, he found Amasis already there and the great hall
of the palace filled with uniformed guardsmen.

He did not know them; in fact, they did not have the
look of Egyptians at all, and as he passed groups of them
talking in the great passageway that connected the palace
proper with his own wing he overheard at least three northern languages being spoken: that of Mari, Padan-Aram, and
the Damascene valleys. This violated prohibition, going back
many centuries, against the use of foreign soldiers in the
capital.

More importantly, not recognizing him, they did not
automatically step aside or come to attention as he passed.
When one burly young captain, turning suddenly, inadver-
tently bumped Baliniri and nearly knocked him off balance,
there was no apology and no deference—just the contemptuous glare one might give a doddering old fool who had
blundered into the way.

Baliniri also took in the unusual number of new guards, a third more than had ever been necessary to deal with the entire palace and temple quarters of Thebes. What was going on?

Slowly he made his way through the crowd in the great hall toward the conspicuous figure of Amasis, who could be seen standing atop the dais where he, Baliniri, had been accustomed to holding his morning divan. The vizier raised one brow; this was dangerously close to usurpation.

Nevertheless, he had made up his mind to greet Amasis and the army's commanders with formal dignity, for appearance's sake. Any differences he and Amasis might have must be minimized for the good of the public and could best be worked out behind closed doors. He pursed his lips and steeled himself for a confrontation, which, he had decided, was not going to be allowed to become overtly abrasive.

As he approached, however, he saw that this was not going to be easy. He would be greeting Amasis from an inferior position, like one of the supplicants who gathered every morning to present petitions at his divan. He was on the lower level, and Amasis, in defiance of all palace protocol, was on the higher. Amasis would be looking down at him. This would not do. He had to make up this difference.

Thus, as he approached, he turned right and began slowly, carefully, to make his way up the long ramp that he had used for so many years to reach the raised dais. Recently, due to his difficulty in getting about, he had tended to make this trip well before the public was admitted, with a trusted palace servant or two helping him up the ramp. But he saw no familiar face at all among those in the hall, so he firmed his jaw and made the climb unaided.

Almost immediately he realized this was a mistake. His hip, stiff and painful, made every step fresh torture. Yet, clenching his teeth, he persevered, exerting every effort to keep evidence of the pain off his face.

This took some doing. It was made all the worse by the fact that, as he rose slowly up the ramp, he became increasingly aware that the prattle and chatter had quieted to a murmur and that virtually every eye was on him—on the doddering old fool staggering weakly up the ramp; a senile old graybeard among all these strong, vigorous young strangers, none of whom apparently had the smallest idea who he was.

Now, too, as he looked up the ramp, he could see Amasis's eye on him: cold, mocking, superior, and oddly triumphant. He forced a smile onto his own lips, and thought: *Wait your turn, Amasis. If you live long enough, this will happen to you, too. . . .*

Then it happened.

His foot hit a slick patch on the polished marble and slid, not accepting the weight he had put upon it.

There was a stabbing pain in his hip.

He waved his arms wildly, tottered, and fell heavily. He landed on the weak hip, then slid and rolled, landing ignominiously at the bottom of the ramp, with pains shooting all through the lower half of his body and all the breath knocked out of him.

There was a moment of silence. Then came the laughter—loud, boisterous, mocking laughter, until the great room rang with it!

His heart sank. He tried to get up, but every movement brought great, stabbing pain, the kind that made a man feel faint. He had not had anything hurt so much since his soldier days, so many decades ago. His hands clawed feebly at the slick marble but could not get any purchase.

And still the laughter rang out, and now it was accompanied by catcalls and mockery!

Suddenly, however, Amasis's voice rang out: "Silence! Silence, all of you!"

It was the unmistakable voice of command.

When the laughter had at last died, Amasis's voice barked out again: "Help him up, there!"

Rough, hasty hands reached down for him. Someone yanked at his arm. The shooting, stabbing, unbearable pain made him cry out, and he was appalled at how weak and old he sounded.

"Easy there!" Amasis ordered. "Do you think you're handling the carcass of an ox after the slaughter? Go easy with him! This is Baliniri, grand vizier of Egypt!"

The shocked silence that followed hurt, too. But the

worst thing was the condescending, patronizing tone Amasis managed to put into every word he uttered. Amasis. Talking down to him! Him, Baliniri!

The runner reached the captain of the guard, Osorkon, and his staff just as he was about to go over his plan to restrict the already meager diet of the Habiru. "Message from the lord Baliniri, sir," he said. "Very urgent. He said to deliver it in person."

The captain scowled. "What does that old fool want now?" Osorkon muttered under his breath as he took the small scroll from the runner and opened it. As he read, however, his eyes widened. "What the—?" he sputtered angrily.

His aide hovered at his shoulder, trying to catch a glimpse of the words on the papyrus. "What's the matter, sir?"

"The meddling old—" he began. But then he remembered that the runner standing there would be reporting back to Baliniri in an hour. "That'll be all," he said curtly. "No reply."

Not until the runner was out of sight did he look again at the half-rolled scroll, shaking his head incredulously. "I can't believe this. He's ordering that I give these swine the seventh day off. And to increase their rations. A flat order, just like that. The nerve of the son of a bitch! Where does he get off meddling—"

An aide pulled at his sleeve. "Sir," he whispered. "The rest of the staff . . ."

"Oh, yes. Dismissed! All of you!" Osorkon watched the overseers disperse, then turned back to the aide. "The old fool is going to go too far one of these days, mark my words."

"With our master Amasis back in the city, sir, that day is sooner than Baliniri knows. It's my understanding that Baliniri's days as vizier are numbered."

"How can that be? He can't be fired for anything less than treason—not with the powerful backing he still has from the priesthood of Amon and the upriver noble families, the landowners, and the big contributors upon whom Thebes depends at tax time."

"Trust me, sir. I've kept my ear to the ground. Big plans are in the works."

"Well, I hope you're right. Leave it up to me and I'd have the Habiru turned into pig food in no time—and Baliniri with them! I'm tired to death of everything about them. As long as they're here, I'm stuck with this idiotic job. A man of great gifts stranded in a backwater, unable to advance himself! I might as well be supervising the manure spreaders at some grubby farm in the western delta."

"And I had intended to rise with you, sir, and there was every reason to suppose that you were on your way up, and fast. While Baliniri's in power neither of us can make something of himself."

"Yes," Osorkon said bitterly. "Baliniri picked my name at random from the guard roster and stuck me with this job trying to get work out of a lot of lazy foreign scum who don't want to work on the seventh day because this grubby god of theirs claims more of their attention than the crown of Egypt does."

"Patience, sir. The palace staff, those loyal to Amasis, have told me that the return of Amasis spells disaster for Baliniri."

"How? How?"

"He's getting old. Everyone can see it. Not even the priests and the landowners want the country run by a senile dotard who can't remember where he put his walking stick. Now, whenever he does something that shows how he's slipping, our people have orders to talk it up. Soon the whole city will be making jokes about the old fool so he'll seem ridiculous. Nobody wants to back a loser."

The captain smiled slowly. "Good. Keep me informed. I swear, if I thought next year were going to go as badly as this one, I'd get out of the service."

"No you won't, sir. You're just having a rough day of it, but that won't go on forever. Things are about to undergo a big change, and experienced soldiers like you are going to be in great demand."

"We are?"

"Yes, sir. The army that landed this morning—it's all foreigners."

"Foreigners in Thebes? But I'm not sure that's legal."

"What Amasis wants, sir, that's what's legal. The king is so addicted to drugs, he barely knows his own name. Amasis has brought a foreign guard unit loyal only to himself and to Thebes. But there aren't enough native-born officers to go around. And, sir, you speak at least two of the languages of Mesopotamia, where the mercenaries mostly come from—"

"Three."

"There you are, sir. All that remains is for Amasis to find out about you. You're just what he's looking for now."

The captain scowled, thinking. Then, little by little, the scowl began to change to a grin.

III

Nemti yawned cavernously and smiled, patting his flat belly contentedly. "There, now," he said. "Wasn't that a feast to write home about? Roasted lamb fresh off the spit, the best olives in all of Egypt, and good wine." He grinned up at the portly woman hovering over their table. "Ti, you're an angel of mercy."

"Nothing's too good for a kinsman," the woman said. "Can I get you anything else? There are fresh dates."

"No, no," Nemti said. "We're stuffed as it is. Onuris and I will probably sink the boat going back to Thebes. It was all we could do to make it across going in this direction, what with this overweight partner of mine."

"Easy there, now," Onuris retorted. "You're courting a whole new set of lumps to match the ones you got in Athribis a month ago, when that jealous husband—"

"Whoa!" Nemti said. "This isn't for the ears of my virtuous relative. Save it for the campfire." He smiled at his friend, then looked up at his cousin. "Don't mind us," he said. "We act this way when we're happy, and this is certainly a good day. Sit down and talk to us, Ti. I've heard so little news of the family since I joined the military. You can catch me up."

Ti wiped her hands on her apron and took a seat opposite the two young men. "Well, it's not every day when I get
visitors from far away. I suppose I could take a few minutes
off."

"Nemti tells me you're all artists here. He's the black
sheep," Onuris said.

"Oh, no," she said, reaching out and patting Nemti's
hand. "To be sure, there are old stick-in-the-muds in the
family who still don't approve of soldiering, but we realize,
most of us, that somebody has to do the country's work."

"After all," Onuris said, "there was also your kinsman
Netru. If you're going to have an exception, it might as well
be someone of that eminence. Did you know, Ti, that they
sing songs about him down in the delta country? There's a
whole ballad about him at the Battle of El-Kab, and there's
another about Teti and him. Of course, you couldn't sing that
last one while General Riki was alive."

Nemti looked at his friend and perked up a bit. "Did you
know there's a rumor in the family that says the two of them,
Teti and Netru, had a child?"

"No!"

"Tell him, Ti."

The plump woman held up both hands. "There's not
much to tell. I personally think it's an idle story. Some
bigmouth in the family trying to season up the legend by
creating a mystery child. It was supposed to have been a
boy-child, and a Child of the Lion."

"Did you ever meet Teti?" Onuris asked his hostess.

"Once, when I was a tiny girl. She and her women came
to the town to trade the gold jewelry they made for supplies.
You know how they dressed? I thought it a bit shameless, but
it didn't seem to bother them." Ti leaned back in her chair
and crossed her arms across her ample breasts. She was lost
now in the memory of that day so long ago. "Teti was tall and
strong and bronzed, and as beautiful as the sunrise. And right
below her waist, in the back, there was that birthmark of the
Children of the Lion, dark red, looking just like a lion's paw
print."

"This is fascinating," Onuris breathed. "Nemti—I'm going
to have to come back over here again, just to listen to stories

about your family." His eyes took on a faraway look. "Imagine there being a son of Netru's. How old would he be?"

"*Hmmm,*" Ti said, counting on her fingers. "Well, if the story's true, mind you, somewhere around thirty-five or so."

Nemti stood up, yawning. "Come on, Onuris. We'd better take a long walk to work off this food." He embraced Ti warmly and kissed her on the forehead. "What was that quarrying we saw from the bottom of the road? I thought the village had some sort of dispensation that kept people from digging up the hills and making an ugly mess."

She frowned. "That was our understanding too, but Amasis doesn't seem to think he has to honor any agreements made between us and Baliniri. He's building a temple to that nasty goddess his people put so much store by. You wouldn't want to know how badly his overseers treat those poor foreign slaves he brought in from the delta."

"The Habiru?" Nemti asked. "Why can't Amasis just leave the poor devils alone? I used to know one or two of them, down home. They're decent enough people and keep to themselves. How did they get to be slaves?"

Onuris snorted. "Amasis can make a slave out of any man or woman in Egypt if he wants to, the dirty son of a—"

"Hush!" Ti warned, clapping a hand over his mouth. "There are things one may think, perhaps, but may not say—not where prying ears might overhear."

"Huh!" Onuris said contemptuously. "Amasis can rot, for all I care. He doesn't own me."

"Please don't say things like that! You don't know who might be—"

"Come on, Loudmouth," Nemti teased good-naturedly, dragging his friend by the arm. "We'll take a walk up in the hills. It'll clear that empty gourd you persist in calling your head. Good-bye, Ti. We'll see you again."

"Make it soon!" Ti said, beaming. "And bring your friend!"

"He's safely in bed?" Amasis asked.

"The physicians have him in hand," Yalu answered.

"Very well," Amasis went on. "I'll drop in and see him as soon as I've finished looking over the palace records."

"I wasn't there," Neb-mertef said. "People tell me he fell quite hard. Did he break his hip?"

"No," Amasis replied. "He's just badly bruised, from all I can tell. The worst damage was probably to his dignity. The old fool! You should have seen him!" He let out a humorless chuckle. "Flat on his back like a dung beetle some child had turned over, wiggling its little legs in the air."

"He'll resent that," Neb-mertef remarked, "and will hate everyone who saw it. I'm just as glad I missed it."

Amasis's eyes shone darkly. "Let him resent us," he growled. "Let him hate us to his heart's content. His days are done. It's all up for him, for Mara, for the whole lot of them."

There was such a terrifying threat in his voice that Yalu and Neb-mertef exchanged quick glances.

Neb-mertef finally broke the awkward silence. "Kamose is back under firm control?"

"Oh, yes. I left him at my country house with half a dozen of my most trusted attendants. The official story is that he's come down with some sort of illness of the bowels, contracted in the desert on the way home. But my lads have orders to increase his daily dosage and stabilize it at twice what I used to give him." He scowled. "I should never have reduced it, eighteen years ago. But I needed him to get rid of the Hai. Now that they're gone, he is quite expendable."

Again Yalu and Neb-mertef exchanged looks.

"You mean? . . ." Yalu began. He did not have to finish the sentence. It was painfully obvious what Amasis meant.

"Yes, the whole lot of them. Kamose. Mara. Baliniri. Thermutis and that son of hers. I haven't given up hope of confirming my suspicions about that boy's birth. There's something wrong there, something that doesn't jibe."

Neb-mertef stole a look at Yalu. *Does he know?* he wondered. *Has the little bitch told him?* His heart almost stopped. But to his immense surprise and delight, Yalu gave no sign of knowing that the prince had murdered an Egyptian overseer.

"All of them," Amasis went on. "One at a time. I wish I could simply mount a coup, but it'd be too dangerous."

"What are you going to do, then?" Yalu asked.

Amasis's eyes blazed. The smile on his face was the

deadliest thing either man had ever seen. "Baliniri's fallen. Nobody knows as yet how badly he's hurt himself. He could have internal injuries."

"We understand," Neb-mertef said, nodding.

Amasis began pacing rapidly in the great room that served him as office and reception room. "I need a new face, someone who isn't known in the palace. He has to be absolutely reliable and unquestionably loyal."

"My lord," Yalu suggested, "I have a spy in Baliniri's wing of the palace now." Neb-mertef glared at him, but he went on. "A woman named Selket. She's been listening at doors and reporting to me." At the word "me" there was an even more vicious glare. "She could perform any service you wished."

"No, no. I would prefer to use someone new, who would never be connected with either of you or with me. I want it to look as if I have installed someone selected at random."

Neb-mertef brightened. "I see. Someone who can be blamed for any mishap that might occur and eliminated the moment he has come to the end of his usefulness." Amasis's smile was confirmation. "Let me see . . . I have a long, long list of complaints from a captain of guards over in Deir el-Bahari—Osorkon's the name—who says he's been unfairly treated by Baliniri." He thought a moment, then added, "Baliniri wouldn't know Osorkon if he tripped over him, yet this fellow nurses a terrible grudge against the vizier."

"Let me have a look at him," Amasis ordered. "Don't tell him anything. Let him think that just as Baliniri chose him for a bad job, I, Amasis, have chosen him for a good one. Tell him that I have been following the reports on him and have concluded that he is a good man wasted in low-level work and deserves a more prestigious assignment."

"Right you are," Yalu said. He avoided Neb-mertef's eyes, but he could still feel them burning into him.

IV

It was Mara's regular day for visiting the Habiru camp, and on this occasion Thermutis, weary of the dull and restricted life inside the palace, had decided to come along. Mara had argued against this at first. She knew she could take care of herself but was not sure she could protect another woman if they ran into trouble going among the people. In the end, she had relented primarily out of a need to talk with another human being. Besides, they would be veiled like Bedouin women and, unrecognizable, would be safe.

Across the river and through the streets of Deir el-Bahari, the two had happily gossiped like girls half their age, pausing only to supervise the unloading of the supplies they had brought with them and hire a laborer to pull their full cart of provisions through the streets of the artisans' village, in the hills behind the main town.

Their bearer had turned an ankle very painfully, however, and could not continue. Reluctantly they paid him and watched him limp away. The two women paused at the edge of the village and looked at the heavy load that was now theirs to carry.

"Can't we just hire someone from the village here?" Thermutis suggested. "There seem to be a good number of able-bodied men along the street."

Mara pulled back her veil and fanned her face, which was beaded with sweat. "Ugh! Remind me to use a different disguise next time. How do those women stand dressing like this in hot weather?" She replaced the veil. "I don't think we could hire any villagers. They are proud and won't be hired to do anything. If they want to help you, they may volunteer, but I'm reluctant to ask. The last thing we want to do just now is to attract attention."

Thermutis stared at the cart. "We'll never be able to move all that to the Habiru camp by ourselves."

"We could take it in parts," Mara said. "It would require a few trips, but I'm sure none of the villagers would steal anything. They're scrupulously honest." She thought about the matter. "But there are other people here on the street, shoppers and off-duty soldiers. We don't know if they can be trusted."

Thermutis looked at two men heading up the street toward them, boisterously laughing and joking. "I don't know, Mara. I don't understand as much of real life as you do, having spent such a sheltered existence, but these fellows look like decent men to me."

Mara's eyes narrowed as she looked the soldiers over. "You may have a point. They're wearing delta colors, and that's in their favor. And they look clean."

She was about to signal to them, but the taller of the men caught sight of her and smiled. "Here, now, Onuris," he said. "It looks as though somebody's got a problem." He addressed Mara. "Can we help you, ma'am?" he asked.

Mara liked his open and friendly voice. She looked into his eyes and decided she liked what she saw there, too. "Yes," she answered. "We are bringing some provisions to a sick friend, but the bearer we hired hurt his ankle. I don't think we can pull this cart up the hill by ourselves."

The soldier scratched his head. "You want to go up there, ma'am? But I understood the orders were for outsiders to stay out of the slave camp. You'll get in trouble up there, I'm afraid."

Mara saw Thermutis about to speak, so she put a restraining hand on the princess's arm. "One of the slaves used to belong to my husband's household," she improvised. She exuded charm, let her voice grow husky and mysterious, and pulled the hood back a trifle, the better to let the magic of her great brown eyes work upon him. "It's a humanitarian gesture. I'm sure a nice young man like you will understand."

The young man turned to his friend. "Why not, Onuris?" he said. "We can't get in trouble here, not without doing something a lot more serious than this. The guards over here have no jurisdiction over us."

The shorter man—he looked a trifle older—snorted. "Just let them try anything. On this side of the river, I do what I please. Sure, lady. We'll give you a hand. You'll want to watch your step on the path. Nemti, escort the ladies. I'll pull the cart." He grasped the handles and pulled the heavy cart easily along the path. "You'll have to tell me where to take this."

The younger, taller man—what was the name? Oh, yes, Nemti, wasn't it?—offered his hand. Mara took it and, to her surprise, found his touch suddenly, startlingly exciting, with great strength and yet gentleness. He held her hand as if it were a delicate sculpture that could break from the slightest pressure. She stole another glance at him—and their eyes met and held. She almost stumbled.

She blushed and looked away. *Gods!* she thought. *I haven't felt that way in a man's presence for years. Not since—*

The answer came as even more of a shock. *Not since Riki,* she thought. This young man reminded her of Riki's open, free nature, generosity of spirit, and fearlessness. There was also a similar set of the head on the muscular neck, good humor in his smile, and a merry twinkle in his eye. Unconsciously her hand tightened on his. Their palms met. The contact was like a jolt. She blushed again and reluctantly forced herself to soften her grip on his broad, powerful young hand.

In the tent Jochebed stirred on her cot. "Miriam, is that you?"

"Yes, Mother," her daughter answered. "And I've brought old friends." She ushered Mara and Thermutis inside, and they immediately doffed both hoods and veils.

Jochebed, delighted, tried to sit.

"Just lie back," Mara said, sitting down on the floor beside the cot. "If you want to get well, you've got to rest."

Jochebed let herself be forced back. "What a wonderful surprise, seeing the both of you!"

Thermutis smiled and took the Habiru woman's hand in both of hers as she sat down on a chair on the opposite side of the cot. "I should have come sooner," she apologized. "I was timid. You know how little time I've actually spent outside the palace." She sighed. "I wonder how much longer I'll be allowed to live there. With Amasis back, and Kamose incapacitated . . ."

"Oh, let's not talk about unpleasant things," Miriam

urged. "Mother! You should see the food they've brought! Enough to last us a long time!"

"Please bring it inside," Jochebed said. "The soldiers—"

"It's all right," Mara assured her. "We've been befriended by two young soldiers, and they're guarding the cart for us. You should see them! If I were a few years younger . . ." She shook her head, smiling mischievously. "They have no idea who we are. If they knew, I think it'd scare them away."

Jochebed tried to sit again. Thermutis moved forward to help her and earned a tired but genuine smile for her trouble. "Mara, people tell me Moses has been here, asking about us in the camp. He doesn't know, does he?"

"He knows that the Habiru are here, yes, and that would of course include your family. But who he is and what you are to him, no," replied Thermutis. She patted Jochebed's hand. "My dear, I wouldn't mind sharing him with you; you must know that by now. He's a very loving young man, and there's more than enough love in his heart for both of us. It's just that—"

"I understand," Jochebed said, easing herself back once more. "It's much too dangerous for him to know the truth. But . . . I often worry, you know, that I might die without ever seeing him again. Without his ever knowing who I was. . . ." Jochebed bit her lip to keep from weeping.

"He's gone to Nubia," Mara said. "I hate to have to tell you this, but there's a war going on. Baliniri thought it was time to complete his education. Oh, try not to worry! He's surrounded by the best people we have. Including . . . Nebo."

Jochebed stared, then she understood. "Good," she declared. "I could hardly imagine a better person to have at his side. But my little son—*our* little son, my lady—going off to war? Fighting?"

"The Deliverer your people have been waiting for will have to know how to fight, Jochebed," Mara stated firmly. "I can't imagine your family being allowed to leave without a fight. If Moses is to become the king of Egypt, he'll have to fight his way onto the throne. Either way . . ." She shrugged.

"You're right, I know. It's not as if our people haven't had to fight. Abraham, the first of us to come either to Canaan or to Egypt, brought us across Sinai to the Promised

Land and had to defeat the four kings in the field, or we would never have been allowed to settle there." She turned to Thermutis. "That included the kings of Shinar *and* of Elam, my lady."

"I'm impressed," Thermutis said. "And, if I remember the story, he had to cast a spell on Sesostris III to get out of Egypt in the first place. I wonder what method will work this time. Egypt does not idly let valuable property get out of its hands."

"Property like us?" Jochebed inquired.

The princess reddened. "I—I'm sorry. I only meant . . ."

"My lady, you could not offend me. We share a son. I know you intended no malice. But, Mara, is Moses in great danger?"

"Actually," Mara replied evenly, "it's more like Baliniri has removed him from danger. In a very short time it's going to get to be more perilous here than at the front." Quickly she recounted recent events, from Kamose's return to the present.

"What are you two doing here?" Osorkon demanded. "Be off with you!"

Onuris looked down his nose at the captain. "Be off with yourself," he retorted. "I'll take no orders from a petty tyrant in charge of a work detail."

Osorkon's hand shot threateningly to his sheathed sword. "I'm captain of the detail. With a wave of my hand I could have six men up here."

Nemti brought his face very close to Osorkon's, did a double take, held his nose, and stepped back as if repelled by a terrible odor. "If they all smell as bad as you do, someone will die of asphyxiation," he said. "Nevertheless, I'll take the chance and call your bluff. Go ahead. Bring up a whole squad of them. I haven't had any decent exercise since a lion hunt on the edge of the Libyan desert."

"Yes," Onuris recalled for the captain's benefit. "That was the one in which my partner here rammed the short spear down the lion's throat, all the way to his fists. Once you look a lion in the eye that close, you're not about to be scared off by a bunch of sissies of the kind Amasis sets to guarding unarmed slaves he's starved half to death." Now, however, he took note of the half-drawn sword in Osorkon's hand. "Ah! The little lizard will put out its tongue at me, eh? And me without a sword?" Because his smile was the most threatening thing Osorkon had ever seen, the captain let the sword hilt go, and he stepped back. "There," Onuris said. "That's more like it. And from now on, little man, don't you ever even touch that sword around me unless you're ready to use it, and to the death."

Osorkon backed away slowly, his eyes going from one man to the other. "You're going to regret this," he promised.

V

"Excuse me," Baliniri said, trying to adjust his painful position in the bed. "I'm having trouble remembering your name. I'm sorry. I'm not myself today."

"It's Selket, sir," the girl said. "Don't fret about it. Just clap your hands for me. I'll know you're summoning me."

"Selket," he echoed. "That's right. You told me before— perhaps more than once, for all I can remember." He winced as he finally managed to get his upper body erect. "Ach! And I thought war wounds hurt!"

"You've taken a nasty spill, sir. Just stay in bed. You can send me for anything you need. I've got leave from my supervisor to wait on your needs full-time. And I'll make sure there's someone to attend you when I'm running your errands." She came around behind him and replaced the wooden headrest with a fat pillow stuffed with goose feathers. "If you don't mind my saying so, sir, it'd make things a great deal easier for me if you would give me authorization just to go out and find the best person. But the rules you've laid down for hiring in this wing—"

"No," Baliniri said. "I want to interview every one of them. I want references, and from the right people. That reminds me. Could you go over, tomorrow morning, and ask at the temple of Amon for the priest Si-Ptah? Ask him to come see me. I get my best referrals through him." He noted the look of disapproval on the girl's plain face. "Indulge me," he asked. "I'm an old man and set in my ways. I have hired personnel through Si-Ptah for a dozen years and more. You owe your present position to the fact that a relative of his advanced your name."

"Very well, sir, I'll do as you say. Now, could I bring you anything?"

He shifted himself in the bed and again felt the stabbing pain. "*Ahhhh!* I don't mind the dull aches, but that stabbing pain is terrible. As I grow older, I seem to lose the ability to bear pain gracefully. If you'd be so kind, look up the physicians and have them send me someone to deal with this pain. I can't think straight with it hurting like this."

"Yes, sir. I'll see who's on duty. Your favorite magus went with the expedition to Nubia, I'm afraid. That was Re-Harakht, I believe."

"Yes. I hated to have him leave me, but I wanted the best man for dressing a wound along on the expedition. Ah, if I'd had him with me before the walls of Mari . . . There were three key men who died that third day, who would have survived to fight again with a surgeon like Re-Harakht along."

"I'll try to find the next best man. We can't have you in this constant pain, sir."

Suddenly a silky voice spoke out from across the room. "What's this? In pain? Here, let me have a look."

Baliniri glanced up, startled, and looked directly into the dark and unreadable eyes of Amasis!

"Oh, it's all right," Baliniri hedged, wondering how Amasis had got past the guards at the foot of the stairs—guards who had the strictest orders not to admit anyone not authorized, by name, by Baliniri. "It's just a nasty bruise. There was a slick patch on the ramp. I'll be all right."

Amasis caught the undertone of annoyance in his voice and almost smiled. "Nonsense. You took a bad fall, and you may be more seriously hurt than you know. I'll have my own personal physician here in an hour. His name is Mont. You may not have met him. He hails from Ur. Medicine there is practiced on a very high level. You couldn't be in better hands. Meanwhile, you, girl—"

"Selket, sir." She fancied his eyes brightened. Neb-mertef had been talking to him, then, perhaps?

"I'll have a prescription for *shepenn* sent over. I want you to give the recommended dosage to the lord Baliniri as soon as you get it, and then again at bedtime and upon awakening. Of course, if Mont asks for a different dosage, you shall defer to his judgment. I haven't practiced medicine for many years. I only wish to spare the lord Baliniri any more pain than he absolutely has to suffer."

"I am obliged," Baliniri said, his voice not altogether free of sarcasm, "for your tender solicitude. When my unfortunate fall occurred, I had been on my way to welcoming you back to Thebes. How is Kamose?"

"I fear our good and valiant king has seen more combat than a man should see. He has been ignoring his utter exhaustion for a long time. What he needs just now is a protracted rest, with no responsibilities or problems."

Baliniri's eyes narrowed. *In other words,* he thought, *he's a prisoner. As it appears I may be, once your people have made their way into my wing.* "Well, send him my best, and my regrets as well. It doesn't seem that I'll be able to look in on him very soon." He thought of something. "Where is he, incidentally?"

"At my country house," Amasis answered. The phrase spoke volumes. Kamose, Baliniri's spies had reported, was already addicted to the concentrate of *shepenn* Amasis had given him in such heavy doses when he had first come to Egypt. Addicted, and as much imprisoned by this fact as he could be by chains or shackles. And he himself, Baliniri knew, was next on the list, if Amasis had anything to say about the matter.

"The girl isn't strong enough to lift you out of bed," Amasis said, "so I've taken the liberty of sending for one of my best men. He'll be in charge of all lifting."

Baliniri's smile did not reach his eyes. "I am in your debt. Now, if I could beg your indulgence, I think I'll try to get a bit of sleep."

Amasis saluted, bowed, and went away, very much the

man in charge. Baliniri waited until the door was closed and said, "Selket! That is right, isn't it? Selket?"

"Yes, sir," the girl said.

"I changed my mind. Go see Si-Ptah today. Right now. Tell him it's an emergency. Tell him I sent you."

So engrossed had Mara and Thermutis been, speaking to their friends inside the tent, that when they came out into the open air, they forgot to replace both veil and hood. When the two young soldiers caught sight of them, Nemti's eyes went wide, and his mouth gaped open. "My la—" he began, halfway through the elaborate flourish that began a formal bow.

"No, no," Mara said, hastily pulling the veil over the lower half of her face. "Please. Thermutis! Cover yourself!"

Mara approached Nemti and spoke softly. "Let this be our secret," she requested. "I shouldn't have put you in a position like this. I apologize."

"No need, my lady," he said. "I mean ma'am. I haven't seen a thing. Neither has Onuris here. You're just two Bedouin ladies out for a stroll, and we're being gallant and helpful."

Mara, warming to him once more, laid her fingers on the back of his great powerful hand. "You are indeed. You can't imagine how grateful we are. Could you perhaps accompany us back to the Temple Quarter of Thebes? We've stayed so long here, by the time we get back, it'll be past sundown."

"Oh, yes, ma'am," Nemti said, smiling. He covered her hand with his; then, embarrassed, he pulled both hands away. "Oh, I beg your pardon, ma'am." His smile was boyish, utterly charming. "I mean, two unescorted ladies don't want to be in the streets of Thebes after dark. Not with that foreign scum in the city."

Mara took his arm and moved closer to him. "Come along, then, Nemti. No mercenary in his right mind will challenge a couple of strong young men." She happily laughed, and it came from her chest. It was exciting. She felt like a girl again. She had not had such a feeling in years.

Coming down the main street of the artisans' village, she felt the eyes of the shopkeepers on her, and her heart beat fast. At the end of the street they found themselves approaching a man in the dress of an Egyptian officer of the lowest rank. He glared at the four of them.

Mara was about to whisper something, but Nemti broke in. "Pay him no mind. We had a bit of a brush with him a while back. Onuris backed him down. He's very unhappy with us."

"Let's have some fun with him, then," Mara said mischievously. She stopped and boldly pulled Nemti to her, pressing her whole body against him. The contact ignited her passion more than anything had done in years. "Here," she whispered, removing her veil. "Let's make him jealous. Kiss me. Kiss me hard."

Nemti complied with such youthful passion that she thought her heart would burst. Her breasts and loins were afire. Her hand stole around his waist and held him close to her, caressing the small of his back. She slipped one foot out of her sandal and sensually caressed his naked instep. He was about to pull away, but then her free hand reached up and her fingers dug into his hair and pulled his face hungrily down to hers. "*Oh*," she moaned. The feelings that raged within her tore the sound out of her, halfway between the word and a groan of passion.

"I don't understand," Selket said. "You say I'm back to working for you? What about Neb-mertef? Doesn't he have something to say about it?"

Yalu shoved his fat face closer to her; she winced at his foul breath. "Forget about him. As of today I'm on Amasis's inside track. It's me you've got to please now. And don't you forget that, you little bitch."

"I have to go," she said, edging away. "I'm on an urgent errand for Baliniri."

"It can wait. Come into the storeroom. Yes, now." He closed the door behind them, leaving them in darkness. His hands went inside her shift, clutching and clawing.

The two soldiers delivered Mara and Thermutis to an inconspicuous side entrance of the palace. Before opening the door, Mara surveyed Nemti's sweet, open young face in the moonlight. She stepped back into the street and took his hands in hers. "I hope I haven't embarrassed you," she said. "There's a spirit of fun in me that doesn't get much chance to express itself these days."

Nemti stopped her apology with a kiss. It was soft and sweet at first, then hungry and demanding. His hands, soft, gentle, yet very much in charge, left hers and went to her cheeks. Then he stepped back, his eyes on hers. "I don't care what trouble it gets me into," he said in a husky voice. "I'm not going to apologize for *that*."

When she could catch her breath, she whispered, "Neither am I. We must see each other again. I don't know how. Give me the name of your unit. I'll get a message to you. Somehow."

VI

"I'm so glad you came," Baliniri said. "I wanted to—" He suddenly noticed Selket still standing there, awaiting his orders, or—what? Listening in? "You, Selket. Go down to the galleys and bring me some fruit. I'm hungry. And some wine. My guest might like some."

"Oh, that won't be nece—" Si-Ptah began. But Baliniri's imperious frown silenced him in midthought. "On second thought, yes, that would be fine."

"Go, girl," Baliniri said. "And while you're at it, ask Yalu to set aside a dozen jars for me. The *shepenn* Amasis's friend gave me doesn't quite kill the pain. I think good wine would be a great comfort to me now."

When the girl had gone, Baliniri pulled Si-Ptah closer to his bedside, holding him by the robe. "Quickly. These days I don't trust anyone. Except you, Mara, Moses, and my wife's daughter."

The priest seated himself beside his bed. "Good heavens, Baliniri. Have things around here deteriorated to that extent? You're afraid of being eavesdropped upon even by your own maidservant?"

"I'm taking no chances. That's why I called for you. Amasis wants to saddle me with a couple of house servants of his own choosing. If I let them in here, I have no idea how long I'll last. I want to install a couple of reliable servants of my own, making his men unnecessary."

"I'll have two of my best men here tomorrow morning."

"Before then, if possible." He shifted in the bed, winced, cursed low under his breath. "I ache all over. Amasis sent one of his magi over to give me a prescription for *shepenn* that would probably put a hippopotamus to sleep. I pretended to take it."

"Baliniri! I don't mean to sound overly skeptical, but—"

"Trust me. Things are that bad. I sent away my own home guard to Nubia, so I've no defenses against them now. And have you seen the foreign bruisers he brought upriver with him? Not one in ten is Egyptian. They're loyal only to him, not to me."

"Then why did you send away your protection?"

"It's a long story. Remember what your astrologers said when I gave them the birth information on Ah-Hotep's grandchild? Prince Moses?"

"Why, yes. They said he would bring terrible grief and great liberation to Egypt. I have been puzzling over that one for many years now. Oh, I think I understand. You sent him away for safekeeping. And you sent the army with him to guard him from harm."

"Exactly. I don't fear Nubia."

The priest sat back and studied his friend's face. "You know more than you're telling me."

"You're right," Baliniri admitted. "And I'm sorry. But I have to keep some of this quiet. Suffice it to say that this lad is the key to the future of Egypt. I'm sure that his destiny is tied in very closely with ours. And if safeguarding him requires sacrificing my own safety, well, so be it. I'm getting old and have no wish to live through a doddering, senile old age."

Si-Ptah frowned. "All very easy for you to say, old boy, but in a sense you're *our* safety. If you're gone—"

"The lad will be the key, not me. I'm as sure of that as I am that you're here beside me."

"Aha. And Moses will return at the head of a victorious army, one fit and blooded and ready for whatever he asks them to do, eh? Does he know what's going on? Does he know enough to protect himself against Amasis?"

"I've taken care of that. I sent someone along with the expedition to guide him in the right direction. A personal representative of mine, a very wise man who will make sure Moses follows the proper path."

"Anyone I know?"

Baliniri cautiously abandoned plans to tell more. "I don't think so."

Si-Ptah clasped his hands together and thought about the matter a moment or two. "Very well. You've never let us down. I'll send over my own personal bodyguards the moment I arrive back at the temple. They're fourth-generation priests, and very dedicated."

"You're quite sure your temple hasn't been infiltrated by the cult?"

Si-Ptah stood. "I'd trust either of these with my own life. I'm not even sure I can find anyone to replace them, but I'll do my best. Meanwhile you'll be covered, old boy."

"Don't leave," Baliniri requested. "Not until the girl gets back. If anyone got in here while I was alone—"

Si-Ptah sat. Was this truly Baliniri, who used to be so fearless and resolute? A man afraid to be alone in his own apartments?

"You!" Amasis said. "Who are you?"

Osorkon swallowed hard and tried to speak. The first time he spoke, it came out a wordless croak. He tried again. "Osorkon, sir. You sent for me."

"Ah, yes. The fellow from the quarry. I've had an eye on you, through my various assistants. They tell me that you've been very ill used by Baliniri."

"That's my own opinion, my lord."

"Very well. I've decided to give you a job more suited to the talents you have displayed for so long despite undeserved neglect at Baliniri's hands. Just between us, the old fellow is over the hill. He was a good soldier and an able administrator once, but at the end of a long life . . ." His wave of the hand dismissed Baliniri altogether.

"I understand, sir."

There was a knock on the door. Amasis called the visitor inside and, when he saw who it was, rose and stood with him for a moment listening to whispered comment that did not reach Osorkon's ear. He frowned, then said, "Very well. Keep me informed. I'll have to change my plans."

The messenger left. Amasis stared at Osorkon, and the expression on his face was quite different from what it had been a moment ago. Osorkon felt a moment of utter panic. *He's going to dismiss me!* he thought. "My lord," he said, desperate. "I saw something today I thought I ought to mention."

"Eh? What's that?" Amasis asked ill-temperedly.

"My lord, over in the slave camp today, there were two women dressed as Bedouins. They seem to have delivered some supplies to the Habiru."

"Against my orders? And you let them?"

"They were accompanied by two soldiers of the Third Guards. Assigned to the palace."

Amasis's eyes narrowed. "Go on."

"The women weren't Bedouins, sir. One woman held up her skirt to step over a broken spot in the path, and I saw a golden anklet on her leg. Sir, I've seen that anklet before. Or one just like it."

"Can you draw the design for me?"

Osorkon did as he was asked. "And, sir, I think the other woman was of better blood than she was disguised to be. There was something in the manner of both, sir—"

"Get it out!"

"Well, sir, they were acting like a couple of sluts. Hanging all over these common soldiers. Hugging them and kissing them like street whores. Right in broad daylight!"

"You didn't see the women's faces?"

"No. They wore hoods, sir, like Bedouins. Why do you think two women of the palace caste would be over there, dressed like that, and making like whores with a couple of soldiers?"

"Who among the palace women has always taken such

interest in the damned Habiru? Indeed!" He pounded one palm with the other fist. "Listen carefully," he said, leaning toward Osorkon. "Your first responsibility has just been circumvented. But I may have other, more important work for you. Are you interested?"

"I'm your man, sir!"

"Very well. This is very important information you've brought me. I want you to speak about this to no one but me. On pain of death."

Osorkon stared. "Mum's the word, sir."

"Very well. I may know who these women are. I want you to confirm my suspicions. The conclusions you arrive at must be irrefutable."

"You can count on me, sir. You want them followed?"

"More than that. I want the soldiers identified as well. I want to know about every breath they take from now on. If you assign a subordinate to following them, he isn't to know why."

"Right you are, sir!"

"The women will be your job, personally. Do you think you'd be able to recognize them if they adopt another disguise?"

"I will if I get to shadow them everywhere. If you'll tell me who they are, sir, I'll have you a weekly report on their habits, sir."

"No. Daily."

"Daily it is, sir."

"Very well. You're dismissed from the army."

Osorkon stared, mouth hanging open.

"From now on you're in my personal service—you'll report directly to me and draw your pay from me. But nobody is to know you're working for me. You'll report here only at night."

"Yes, sir. Nobody will know a thing. Not a soul."

"They had better not. Your life will depend on it."

Osorkon took one look into these basilisk eyes and shuddered. "Yes, sir. I understand, sir."

"Don't be a fool," Onuris said impatiently. "These women are royalty, way above the heads of the likes of us. They're older, *and* the queen is married."

Nemti closed his eyes and savored the memory of having Mara in his arms. *If you only knew . . .* he thought. "Just let me dream a bit. I've never had anything like this happen to me."

"Huh! You could say that about being impaled on a sharpened stake, too. And that's what will happen if you're caught romancing the wife of the king! If these crazy women want to put on disguises and play around with commoners, that's their business. I just don't want you getting mixed up in something dangerous like this."

"She wants to see me again. She said she'll get a message to me."

"Please, Nemti! Forget her! Nothing good can come of this! You don't know if this is a game for her, if you're just one in a line of playthings. You've never had any trouble finding women. Why should this one make so much difference to you?"

Nemti wanted to tell him. The queen of Egypt! And she wanted him. Him, Nemti! How could you explain a thing like that? Even to your best friend?

CHAPTER FIVE

On the Upper Nile

I

Eighty miles up the Nile, the Theban fleet came to the end of the First Upper Egyptian Nome, where the border between Egypt and Nubia had stood for hundreds of years until Sesostris III had pushed the frontier back to the river forts near Semna.

In this land that was so completely dominated by the great Nile, the natural boundary, was the First Cataract—more accurately a succession of rapids extending ten miles south of Aswan. Here the Nile, diverted from its original course by some unknown seismic catastrophe before recorded history, had spread itself over a rocky basin, between slopes of sand on the one side and cliffs of granite on the other.

Dotted with uncountable islets and diverted into numerous channels, the river fought its way through a labyrinth of paths. It foamed over sunken rocks and eddied among boulders, always changing its speed as the bottom rose or fell away.

There was no possibility of sailing through this hazardous maze, even in high water, which was many months gone. The ships, therefore, had to be hauled up the treacherous rapids by brute strength, with the entire expeditionary force pressed into service. Standing on the banks and straining mightily on long hemp ropes purchased from foreign traders, the soldiers dragged the boats upstream inch by inch.

As the soldiers cursed and sweated, Moses and Nebo, accompanied by bodyguards, threaded their way along the banks, through great piles of multicolored granite, piled block upon block and column upon column, rising out of the water, squared and buttressed in the likeness of forts.

A few of the largest were crowned with clumps of palms, and one was completely covered with gum trees and acacias, date palms and tamarisks, all festooned together under a hanging canopy of yellow-blossomed creepers.

Moses was delighted with everything. "Nebo!" he said. "I've never seen anything so lovely! Why didn't anyone tell me we were going to pass through areas as beautiful as these?"

Nebo squinted down at the roiling waters. "Enjoy it while you can," he advised. "Upriver of the rapids it gets to be empty for a long, long spell."

"Perhaps," Moses said, "but I'm not used to this sort of thing at all. Where I've been, the Nile is so placid. Who would imagine it could be so violent?" He pointed upriver to where the current, divided into four headlong torrents by a cluster of small islets, came rushing down the slope like a living hill of rolling and tumbling water.

"You've a poet's eye for such things," Nebo commended. "That's good. A man shouldn't be all action and reaction. He should be able to notice the beauty of the natural world as he passes through it. You've no idea how few men do." He grunted. "Take me, for instance. For a long, long time in my youth I looked at things emotionlessly. Where another man might have admired a beautiful young girl, fresh in the bloom of youth, I would have seen an organism, mammalian, bipedal, and symmetrical, with fatty deposits here and there. After a certain amount of reflection, I might have taken note of her gender and made a mental evaluation as to her health and apparent efficiency as a self-contained unit." He laughed. "What a fool I was."

"I can't imagine that," Moses said with a smile. "This has to be back in the very dawn of time."

"That old I am not," Nebo retorted. "And yes, I was a fool, albeit a 'learned' one. It wasn't that long ago. I made my worst mistakes around the time you were born, and you're not exactly a graybeard. Ah! If only I'd developed some wisdom earlier in life. What pain I could have saved so many people—including, least importantly, myself."

"After my, uh, experience back in Thebes," Moses said ruefully, "I begin to understand a little of what you're getting at. How I wish all that had never happened! But you have to do what you have to do. I don't know how I could have done anything differently."

"Except," Nebo said, "by changing into someone other than who you are. And I wouldn't have wanted you to do that! If you ever lose that sense of right and wrong or forget how to tell justice from injustice, I'll have failed you as a teacher." He turned to smile at the young man as they traversed a great, flat boulder half again the size of an average Egyptian house. "And this is one assignment I do not wish to fail in."

"Nebo," Moses said, "everyone treats me as though I were . . . special. Different. Why? I'm just another court brat. I'm not even in the line of succession. My father was an undistinguished nobleman who died quite young, and while my mother's bloodlines are good, under the normal rules of succession, I would not be considered a future king."

"Mara has proved barren."

"But Kamose can take other wives any time he wants. Surely someone will provide him with an heir."

"Huh," Nebo said. "It can't have escaped your attention that something's deadly wrong with Kamose."

"All I have is hearsay. Kamose left Egypt when I was a newborn. I haven't even seen him yet, although I understand he's back in the country."

Nebo looked at the guards far behind, then squinted upstream at the advance men on the point. "They're all too far away to hear anything. Perhaps it's time to let you in on it all." Swiftly he sketched in the whole story of the cult's successful invasion of Egypt, then all about the strange, malignant spell Amasis exerted over Kamose. "If my informants are right, Kamose is back on the drug. Amasis most likely has him held captive somewhere, getting him more and more addicted to the stuff." He grimaced. "There are times I wish he'd been killed up in Syria. It would be easier on all of us—and kinder to him than this living death."

Moses looked at him, an odd expression on his face. "A lot of things happened at the same time, didn't they? My birth, the arrival of the cult, Kamose's victory over his father, the beginning of the long purging of Egypt and the northern lands of the influence of the Shepherd Kings—"

"And a lot more than that, too, that you don't know about." Nebo shot a sidelong glance at him. "I'll have to tell you all about it one of these days. After all, you confided in me. I must learn to confide in you, one item at a time."

He was about to say more, but there was a cry from below, so Nebo and Moses went to the edge of the rock to look down. A rope had broken, and one of the ships careened about, taking the whole rush of the current on her beam. The breaking of the rope had swept half a dozen men off the edge and into the white waters of the Nile, and their companions were frantically throwing ropes to them, to pull them out of the water.

"Well, that does it," Nebo said. "We've lost the rest of the day. It'll be that long before a new rigging can be put together. We might as well make camp."

"Here?"

"Yes, I know. It sounds idiotic. But by the time we can drag the ships up to calmer water, the day will be gone, and it's far too dangerous to try to do any more at night. If we can anchor in a pool between the individual cascades, we'll be able to start again in the morning."

"Good," Moses said. "Tonight will be an excellent time for you to fill me in on a few of those things I'm just about old enough to know. We can talk after dinner."

Nebo laughed. "Maybe some of it," he agreed. "As for the rest, well, I'm playing everything by ear."

Moses grinned. "Would that perhaps include something about this destiny everyone thinks I have, but nobody wants to explain?"

Nebo scowled, thinking for a moment. Then he said, "Don't be in so much of a hurry. You may not like that destiny when at last you hear about it."

They moored the ships two at a time in pools above and below the first cascade, stationed guards with the boats, and made camp on one of the islands. From the shade of a ruined temple built there by one of the early pharaohs, Khafre and Geb supervised the deployment of the troops and the setting up of the camp; Moses, mindful of all he had yet to learn about soldiering, followed Geb around and observed the procedures.

"Are the boats safe there?" Moses asked. "What would happen if a flood should come down from the mountains all of a sudden? For all we know it could have rained a day ago in the Mountains of Fire."

"A good question, sir," Geb said. "Under better circumstances we would not moor there. To our advantage is the fact that it usually doesn't rain south of us at this time of the year. But you're right, sir—it is a risk we're taking. But a worse chance would be to try to clear the rapids before nightfall."

"You're the experienced man here," Moses said affably. "I'll trust your instincts. I just feel so ill at ease."

Geb, standing atop a promontory and looking down at the two first boats, said, "Everything having to do with the Nile is unsafe, sir. You're supposed to feel ill at ease. I suspect that you've a bit of soldier blood in you." He rolled his eyes and smote himself contemptuously on the forehead. "Fool!" he said. "I have totally forgotten that your grandfather was Sekenenre!"

Moses smiled. "I feel very close to him sometimes," he said. "He was a citizen soldier, of sorts."

"Of the most valiant sort, sir," Geb responded. "A brave man whom all the army honors. He sacrificed his own life in single combat with Apophis, delaying the fall of Thebes long enough for reinforcements to arrive and save the day for the

army. Your grandfather was a noble man and a great king."
He pursed his lips in thought. "Still, sir, from the accounts I
have heard of him, he was retiring and scholarly. You, sir, are
a hunter and athlete, much better cut out for the life of a
soldier."

"I have followed the life Baliniri chose for me," Moses
explained simply. "Frankly, I do not know what my natural
bent would be if I had had the management of my life."

This said, he fell silent, thinking. Geb looked at him but
then prudently looked away and left the prince to his thoughts.

What am I? he wondered. *And who? What is this strange
and secret destiny chosen for me? Why has everyone been so
reticent about it? Why won't someone tell me what I am being
trained to do?*

He felt the frustration build within him. This had gone
on long enough. Tonight he would take Nebo aside and
demand to be told. It was time.

But even as he thought this, something inside his mind
shrank away. *Better not to know! They must have had their
reasons.*

He firmed his jaw, straightened his back, and crossed his
arms defiantly. No! He had to know! And now!

II

As nightfall approached, to Moses's surprise, unfamiliar
faces began to appear on the perimeter of the camp: black or
deep-brown visages bearing little resemblance to the Egyptians, either in the hue of their skins or in the general
architecture of their strong-featured faces. He approached
Geb. "Who are these people?" he asked.

"Nubians, sir," Geb answered, unperturbed.

"Nubians? But we have come to fight Nubians."

Geb remained calm. "These people may live beyond the
natural borders of the First Nome, sir, but they feel allied to
Egypt. The border tribes have always been free spirits, some-

times leaning toward Nubia, sometimes toward us. Since the death of Akhilleus, they have leaned in our direction. They never accepted Nehsi."

"Then they pay tribute to us?"

"When they remember. We don't force the issue. That may be one of the reasons they leaned our way in the first place." Geb smiled, watching the thinly clad blacks approach the soldiers, chattering in a half-Egyptian border tongue developed centuries before by the traders. "Nehsi may have been a harder taskmaster than our more recent monarchs up this way have been."

Moses crossed his arms over his chest, then rubbed his still-beardless chin. "What are they doing here?"

Geb shrugged. "Satisfying their curiosity, I suppose. Actually I'm glad they came. I'd have sent someone to look for them. They'll help us to haul these boats up the rapids. They're past masters of the art. They can do in one hour's time what it would take us five to do without their help. I suppose Khafre will strike a bargain with them in the morning—or he'll get me to do it; I'm rather good at that sort of thing—and we'll have the boats through the cataract in one day with the help of these boys."

"Wonderful," Moses said. "May I look on when you bargain? I think there is much to be learned from you in this matter."

Khafre, eyes narrowed, watched intently as Nebo chattered animatedly in the Nubian tongue with the chieftain of the locals. He had wandered near them a few moments earlier, hoping to join the conversation, only to learn that they were speaking not the pidgin of the border but the language of the upriver peoples.

Nebo continued to puzzle Khafre. Day by day the older man's Mesopotamian accent continued to fade, and his words tended to conform more and more to the normal speech rhythms of an educated Egyptian of the land-owning class. Was Nebo learning the normal speech patterns of the Egyptian language quickly, he asked himself, or, having feigned that accent, had he begun to drop it and end an imposture that was no longer useful or necessary?

Who, after all, was this Nebo? He knew more than a normal man could learn in a long lifetime. Khafre had tried him on all six of the languages *he* had learned in his soldiering career, and not only did Nebo know them all, but he often spoke them with a daunting facility. He knew soldiering and seamanship and weapons. He even knew a move or two of fencing. Yet Khafre would bet the next six months' pay that Nebo had never been a soldier.

He had come to Thebes a complete stranger only a short time earlier but had been accepted almost at once by Baliniri and that part of the court still loyal to the vizier. Then he had disappeared for a bit and had turned up in Thebes just in time to be put in the highest civilian position of the entire expedition, second only to Prince Moses.

Moreover, he seemed to have some undefined advisory role, connected with the completion of Prince Moses's education. Education for what? To what end?

It was no secret that Kamose and Mara had no children and no prospects for having any. It could be that Baliniri was grooming an heir. But how would the transfer of power be made? Baliniri was unlikely to live long enough to see the lad put on the throne by force, if that was his intention. And where might Amasis stand in all this? Did he not have some plans for the succession himself, regardless of his unpopularity with the priests of Amon and the property owners?

Khafre rubbed his nose and puzzled over the matter. There was another possibility: If Amasis had returned from the delta in command of the army, if Kamose were incapacitated, then Amasis could easily merge his army with the military units of the Theban command. This would effectively destroy his, Khafre's, command as an independent fighting unit, one capable of challenging Amasis's burgeoning power.

Yes! That had to be it! Baliniri had sent almost the entire Theban command away, ostensibly to take on the Nubian invasion force but in fact with the notion of keeping them intact but separate, uncorrupted by Amasis's thugs and their officers. Once Amasis had taken over Thebes this would give Baliniri a striking force of his own, capable of mounting an outside attack on the Theban army and perhaps even retaking the city from the cult's leaders. Augmented by allies drawn from the Bedouin legions, the Black Wind, and the Desert Legion, Baliniri could assemble enough troops to oppose successfully anything Amasis could put up against him.

Ah! So *that* was what the old fox was up to! He had not lost his touch after all! It made perfect sense: The army of Thebes would return to the city not only fit and able, fresh from battle and ready to fight again, but forewarned.

But that was the problem. He, the ostensible commander of the unit, had *not* been forewarned. In whom, then, had Baliniri chosen to confide?

He looked hard at Nebo.

Ah, he thought. *We're going to have to have a nice little conversation one of these nights. And well before we reach the Second Cataract, and the front.*

The sun had set, after the magical manner of the heavens above the Nile, then the lingering afterglow had been replaced, with startling suddenness, by a blackness softened by the myriad stars and a low-lying moon.

A cool breeze had struck up, and Moses, chilled, sat by the fire. One moment he was alone; the next moment he was not. "Nebo!" he said, looking up with a start. "I didn't hear you coming!"

The older man smiled. "It took me many years to learn to move silently," he said. "Now it's second nature, and I forget how disconcerting it can be."

"I was hoping you would come. I wanted to talk. There are so many questions I need to ask."

Nebo settled down next to him before the glowing campfire. "And there are things I need to tell you. But let's not try to take in too much all at once, my young friend. You'll have a lot of adjusting to do once you've heard everything. But rest assured that I will satisfy your expectations—yes, and perhaps then some."

Moses began to speak, but the expression on his companion's face made him hold his tongue. He picked up a dry stick and poked the fire.

"I want to show you something," Nebo said, suddenly standing. To Moses's surprise, he slipped his tunic over his head. Clad only in loincloth and sandals, he turned, so his back was to Moses. The warm light of the burning coals danced on his skin. "Have you ever seen anything like this before?"

Near the middle of his back there was a red stain, a birthmark. The outline was not clear, but anyone who wanted to find in its indistinct form the shape of a large animal's paw print could have done so. Nebo turned, his eyes were bright.

"My name is not Nebo," he confessed. "And I was not born in the Valley of Two Rivers. I was born in Thebes."

"But—"

"The mark on my back is that of the Children of the Lion. We are an ancient family of armsmakers, whose lineage goes back to Cain, son of the first man in the world, the man who killed his brother and had the mark of God put upon him, so that no man dare lay hands upon him without being cursed. Every man who ever killed a Child of the Lion has died for it, died violently and in great pain."

"But who are you?" Moses breathed.

"My forebears came from distant Ur, where Belsunu, the great artist of the bronze sword, learned the family trade. A slave raid left Belsunu's wife and daughter slaughtered, his son dragged off. Belsunu blamed himself for being away when the raiders came, and he spent the rest of his life looking for his son but died without ever finding him."

"I have heard a bit of this. . . ." Moses began, but it was obvious that the older man wanted to continue.

"His son, by chance, was purchased at a slave auction by an armorer named Zakir. The boy, Ahuni, became his apprentice. He adopted the lad, and they traveled to Canaan, drawn there by stories that a great leader named Abraham of Ur needed an armorer."

"Abraham! Wasn't he the patriarch of the Habiru? I think my old wet nurse once told me about him."

"You remember well. The Children of the Lion continued to intertwine their fortunes with those of the Habiru. Ahuni's son Kirta settled in Haran and fathered two sons, Shobai the giant and Hadad the cripple."

"All men know these names. The songs about them are many. Shobai, the blind armorer, and little Hadad, the cripple who saved his city and gave his life for his brother."

"Right you are. As the Shepherd hordes approached Haran, Hadad saved his wife and child by sending them south with a great leader named Jacob, founder of the Habiru nation and father of Joseph, vizier of Egypt under Salitis."

"This part I have never heard."

"You will hear much of it in time to come," Nebo said. "Joseph was kidnapped and sold as a slave into Egypt. His closest friend, Ben-Hadad, son of the hero of Haran, left his home to come find his comrade in this foreign land. He settled here.

"He had a son, a child he mistakenly thought was sired by his wife's lover. The child grew up repudiated by his father. Lonely, withdrawn, he barely spoke until he was ten years old. His mother thought him an idiot."

Moses leaned forward as he listened, drawn by the burning intensity in the older man's voice.

"Then an old tutor was hired, who learned that the boy possessed great brilliance. He grew up to be a savant known far and wide, but a man in whom any knowledge of the human heart was missing. He lacked an understanding of himself. Wisdom. Charity. Love of his fellow man. Compassion. He was a man on a collision course with a terrible and savage destiny.

"His portion in life was to rise to great power but to destroy, by his mindless folly, the greatest and most benign empire that ever existed in the history of the world."

He closed his eyes, and a great sigh came out of him.

"His name is Seth, and he stands before you," he said, in a voice in which sadness and bitterness were mingled. "I am Seth, son of Ben-Hadad. Bearer of the blood and the tradition. And of the curse of Cain, whose mark I bear."

III

In the darkness beyond the firelight, Khafre turned to Geb. "I can't believe it," he said in a low whisper. "I saw Seth as a young man, before he disappeared. This man doesn't look like him at all."

But even as he said it he looked at the graybeard, his furrowed cheeks, the hollow eyes, and thought: *Wait now. This man has surely seen and suffered much for many years.* Hard living and pain could very well change a man beyond recognition and make him gray-haired before his time. And the Seth he had seen two decades before had been a childman; he would not have kept that look forever.

Khafre shook his head as he wondered what sort of experiences could mark a man so. He had heard that Seth had returned just long enough from his quest in the northern countries to bring the fabled Sword of Glory to Kamose. With that superior weapon, Kamose had driven the Hai into the desert, where the might of the Shepherd army had crumbled.

But then Seth had disappeared. Some said he had gone to Thebes but had left almost immediately, impelled by some secret quest. Some said he had gone upriver to Nubia; others said he had gone off into the desert to live with the warrior-women's army. But nobody could speak of Seth's whereabouts from direct and sure knowledge.

"He is a Child of the Lion, though," Geb said in a whisper that carried farther than he wished it to. "Look at his back."

"Shhhhh," Khafre warned. "Listen, and learn."

"I have heard of Seth, son of Ben-Hadad," Moses said quietly in a thoughtful voice. "All men here have heard of him—I mean, heard of *you*. You are the wisest man in Egypt, and one of the few ever to visit the women's army sanctuary at El-Dakhla. But why didn't anybody recognize you at Thebes?"

"Mara did. So did Baliniri. I have withheld little from them since I witnessed the final return of Kamose and his army, whom I decided to precede into Egypt for reasons of my own."

Moses studied him and saw clearly for the first time now the deep furrows in his companion's cheeks under the gray beard. "Then you made yourself known only to them?"

The older man frowned ruminatively into the darkness. "Yes. To them and one or two others. I have taken particular pains to avoid Amasis. Although he met me only once—and it was eighteen years ago—I have the unpleasant feeling that he would know that something about me was out of the ordinary and dangerous to him."

"I can imagine something like that. Come," Moses said. "Relax and tell me everything."

"I'd rather stand," Seth said. "I shall continue. It may be good to get more off my chest."

"Whatever you wish," Moses agreed, leaning back on his elbows.

"When I left Egypt twenty-two years ago, I told everyone I was looking for the secret of iron. In truth, I had already learned how to make iron of a sort. But Kamose put great store in a prophecy that said that he would prove victorious against the Hai only if he wielded a Sword of Glory made of iron from Chalybia." His tone was weary. "After years of tracking down false leads and going on wild-goose chases, I learned that there was no such place as Chalybia and that the Chalybians were simply a secret brotherhood of armsmakers, which had jealously guarded the secret of the perfect iron alloy since the first day of its discovery."

"So you *did* find them!"

Seth nodded. "The next thing I learned astounded me: The Chalybians and the Children of the Lion were one and the same. I was one of their lot, whether I knew it or not!"

Moses leaned forward, wide-eyed. "Somehow, down the centuries, my branch of the family had been cut off from the others. And there seems to have been some reason why the Chalybian masters of the craft decided against stepping forward to share the secrets with us—not only of the iron formula, but of our heritage."

He paced before the guttering fire as the low flames lit his bare legs and flanks. "Kirta was a man obsessed with ambition. He wanted iron so badly, he abandoned his wife and children to find it. Hadad, the next generation, did not want to make weapons; he became a jeweler. Shobai made weapons, but his life was, at the beginning, vain and shallow."

"So Shobai never learned of the Chalybians?"

"I doubt it. After he came to his senses, he refused to teach my father the making of iron, saying that Ben-Hadad was not mature enough to be entrusted with such a secret."

"From your description of the Chalybians," Moses said, "it sounds as though they decided whether or not a man was ready for initiation."

"Possibly. I'll have to ask—" He was about to say a name but caught himself. "I'll have to ask a friend who has insights into such matters. When the time came to pass along what he did know, Shobai passed it along to my cousin Teti. The thing that makes me think that Shobai had not become an initiate was that he did not teach Teti the last, most difficult step of the process, which can only be learned directly from a master of the craft. And she did not teach it to me—although she much later became the first female mistress of the craft, having been initiated into the order by Karkara of Sado, the only Chalybian ever to settle in Nubia."

"Why didn't Teti teach it to you?"

"Because I was a self-absorbed, shallow idiot. Before I had learned enough of life to be accepted by the brotherhood, I was lucky enough to meet a master of the craft. He took a chance on me prematurely. I still had much of the rash, reckless fool in me when he taught me."

Moses could see, by the fire's diminishing light, the pain on Seth's face.

"Then I went to Babylon. Babylon! Ah, my young friend, if you could have seen it, the great Ishtar Gate . . ." He closed his eyes but quickly reopened them, the picture in his mind evidently too painful to contemplate. "I met there a king who made me his heir. He opened the coffers of the richest city in the world to me and told me to rebuild the city in any image that pleased me." He shuddered. "And all this while the great Hittite army, which had declared war, was inching its way across Mesopotamia toward us. Like a fool, I paid no attention. I did not arm the Babylonians with the iron weapons that could have saved the city."

"I heard," Moses said sympathetically. "Didn't the Hittites, under Mursilis—"

"They attacked. I had just married the king's daughter. When I close my eyes, I can see her. Shala! How I loved her!" He balled his hands into fists, and his words came more quickly now. "We were totally undefended. They murdered the king, the citizenry, and my only friends. All gone, gone!

And Shala . . . I never saw her again. When I escaped the city, it was dying quickly, and with it the finest civilization that ever existed anywhere. All my fault, all mine!"

"Don't," Moses pleaded. "Please. You couldn't have known."

Seth stared at him with red-rimmed eyes, a stricken look on his face. "Why did I survive the death of the city? I have been looking for the answer for many years. Perhaps I will learn before I die." His words caught in a dry throat. "If you knew the agonies I've suffered since then . . . No wonder no one can recognize me. No wonder . . ."

IV

After a time Moses went off to his tent. The man who had turned out to be Seth of Thebes, Child of the Lion and Chalybian magus, lingered for a while, staring into the fading coals. In the dark Khafre nodded to Geb, the watchers exchanging glances, and the adjutant went away, as Moses had done. Khafre himself was about to slip through the darkness toward his tent when Seth raised his head and looked right at him.

There was no doubt about it. His eyes came to focus on the figure in the darkness and showed recognition but no surprise. "General," he called, "come and join me before you go off to sleep. I won't keep you awake long."

Khafre, feeling every bit the fool, walked into the small circle of light. "How long have you known?"

"Don't worry about it," Seth said.

Khafre sat on a flat rock across the fire so the two could look into each other's eyes. "I must say, I'd never have known you. I saw you once when you were a raw recruit—"

Seth laughed at the memory. "I'd been pressed into service and couldn't do anything right. I remember you. You took up for me once when someone was cursing me out for not being able to keep in step."

"I'd known you from the bazaars. I watched you a month earlier, advising strangers how to plant their fields. I was impressed."

"So you could see through the comic figure I cut as a soldier. Remarkable."

"Now that I'm in on your secret, must I keep it from the men?"

"No need. Nobody here is going to go back to Thebes and tell. You may already have guessed that we are not going back to Thebes for some time. We are now an independent unit, not answerable to anyone—not even to Baliniri. He arranged for that, knowing how slim his chances were of keeping Amasis at bay back in Thebes. He doesn't want anyone stealing his signet ring and sending false orders in his name. He wants us to ignore any orders we get."

"Then who's in command? Me? Moses?"

"Moses, nominally. You will actually do most of the work. I am here in an advisory capacity. You and I will guide the boy's steps until he can walk independently of us."

Khafre was trying to adjust to the new situation quickly. "And what is our mission? I gather the control of the Nubians is a cover. There is something else more important than that. What is it?"

Seth stirred the dying coals with his stick. "We are now the army of Egypt—we and the women. You will meet them when the time is right. Baliniri has cut them free too, making them an independent unit. They answer to no one but Weret and Naldamak until Prince Moses has learned the lesson he came here to learn."

"Which is?"

"How to be a king."

Khafre started. His eyes opened very wide, then he forced a wooden expression over his face. "A king," he echoed. "Of Egypt? Of the empire?"

"That is not clear. There is another possible alternative. There is a seer who lives with the women—"

"Yes. Tchabu."

"You never cease to surprise me. Yes. Well, Tchabu has had wildly contradictory visions about the lad. The only thing they have in common is his overwhelming importance in the scheme of things, perhaps to Egypt alone, perhaps to the rest of the world as well. One of Tchabu's prophecies was that the boy's name will be known thousands of years from now, more widely than has any man who has ever lived in our world."

"Good heavens. And you believe this?"

"Tchabu's dreams are not idle fare," Seth replied seriously. "Moreover, they have been corroborated by—" He stopped abruptly.

Khafre leaned forward. "By whom?"

"A man like you deserves to know more, but I am sworn to silence for now. All I can say is that the evidence is very strong that Tchabu's dream is true. This lad is more important than anyone alive in the world today. Yet he knows nothing of this. He doesn't even know who he is."

Khafre's eyes narrowed until they were slits. "Gods! You're not making this easy, are you?"

"All in good time, my friend. Relax. At the front you will learn everything you need to know. We shall become partners in the noble enterprise of training a mighty leader and perhaps a king. I will depend upon your expertise, your undoubted bravery, and your legendary ability, which you will be teaching the lad—and I will be teaching him from my talents. Trust me."

Khafre frowned. "Amid such reticence and silence, that is difficult."

Seth smiled. "I know. I've thought of that. Wait here." He returned from his tent moments later, holding a parcel by his side. "I brought you a bribe, the better to enlist your sympathy for our common cause and to encourage you to give me your trust—or at least the benefit of the doubt—until I have proven myself."

"I don't take bribes."

Seth fumbled with the parcel, unwrapping it. "Actually it's two bribes instead of one." He handed the first over, leaving the other half still in its cloth covering.

"What's this?" Khafre asked. "A sword? I have a sword."

But now he hefted it, and his eyebrows rose. He shot a sharp glance at Seth as he held the weapon up by the handle. "I wish I could see this more clearly! Where did you get this? This is really quite extraordinary. The feel of it, the balance!"

He made a pass or two with it. "Gods! What a sword! You've found my price. Name your corruption, and I'll swear to it. I'd kill you to keep you from taking this back. Where did you get this? Tell me about it, eh? What is it? It isn't one of yours, is it?"

Seth smiled. The second package was in his lap, his hands resting lightly upon it. "No, I'm not capable of the likes of this. Neither is any man now alive. This is a sword of Belsunu's."

Khafre stared. The sword almost fell from his hand.

"This is a very famous sword," Seth went on. "It was made at about the same time Abraham of Ur was entering Canaan for the second time."

"The same man you mentioned to the lad?"

"Yes. At Timna, where Abraham had come looking for men to arm his sons and his slaves and to teach them the ways of war so they could fight their way into Canaan, Belsunu met an Egyptian mercenary named Sneferu. The two men became friends immediately, and Belsunu, who had found Sneferu broke and unemployed, gave him, as a gesture of friendship, this sword."

"Just as you're giving it to me."

"You catch on very quickly. Abraham called for both of them, and they said they would not hire on separately, that they were a team." He smiled. "As you and I are now. Belsunu armed Abraham's party with swords perhaps not as fine as this, but nonetheless they were weapons made by a great master of the craft. They won the war. Belsunu died, then Sneferu died. The sword was lost. Many years later it was found by Belsunu's son, Ahuni, who repaired it. When he died, the sword was thought lost forever. But it has continued to turn up here and there. I bought it from a man in Arvad who had no idea how valuable it was. It is, perhaps, the best bronze sword ever made."

"Why give it away to a man like me, whom you hardly know? You who must certainly find it hard to part with such a treasure."

"Call it a promissory note against friendship, collaboration, and conspiracy. My friend, you and I and Moses may be Egypt's last hope. When we left the city, we removed Baliniri's last defenses. He is very likely a prisoner by now. He sent us away to preserve us."

"Yes, yes. I figured that out."

"Good. We are alone in the world and will remain so until we have linked up with the women. You and I must get along, must speak with one voice, must preserve this army, and train its young leader. You and I will seal a bargain to remain true to Egypt and save her army for her with this gift. Take it with my blessing."

Now Seth began to unwrap the other parcel in his lap, taking his time. "Of course you will not wish to fight with it. Sneferu could bring it into battle because he had Belsunu there to repair it for him. You have only me: a Child of the Lion, to be sure, but a man whose artistry lies elsewhere than in the making of beautiful bronze weapons."

He unrolled the last rolls of soft cloth from the other object in his lap. "Do you want to know what it is that I *am* good at?" he asked. He did not wait for an answer. "My skills are utilitarian and ordinary, but they have their uses. And this is yet another of the reasons why I was sent along with the army." He handed the second sword over.

"Iron!" Khafre gasped.

"Yes," Seth confirmed quietly. "My work has no historical or artistic value, but this thing will cut through any bronze sword ever made, including Belsunu's. And if we conquer Nubia, we conquer a nation richer in iron ore than any I have ever found on my travels. With this ore I will make swords for this army, and Weret's Desert Legion, and Naldamak's Black Wind. And when we go back to Thebes at last . . ."

He let the sentence hang. Khafre looked him hard in the eye and nodded.

V

The morning dawned bright and beautiful, and before Moses had arisen, made his ablutions, and broken his fast, he could already hear the sounds of the Nubians at work on the river below, hauling the ships up the next stretch of rough water. By midmorning that white water had been passed, and the Nubians, having completely taken over the long ropes from the soldiers, were moving the fleet across one of the deep-water lakes formed between one cascade and the next.

Moses stood watching from a high bluff. Geb joined him, hands on hips, looking on as the unappointed Nubian overseers shouted orders to their compatriots who manned the oars and rowed the boats to the next spot where the channel came roaring down into the backed-up waters of the natural lake.

"They're an interesting lot," Moses remarked. "I'd like to know more about them."

"That's a very good idea," Geb said. "You and I could go aboard one of the boats and watch them work. They probably haven't changed much in their methods since the days when the great pyramids were being built."

"I understand they're very independent," Moses said.

"They can afford to be. Both Egypt and Nubia buy almost all of their henna from them. It's their main export. Before our civil war, people used to come all the way from the Greek isles and Crete to buy the stuff from these men of the marches."

"I can't imagine much grows here in the way of food."

"Some lentils and durra. Of course they eat a lot of fish and crocodile meat. There's some game hunting—antelope, usually. You've never seen anyone throw the javelin the way these fellows can, sir. And the boomerang! They'll heave the thing off—*away* from the target, mind you—and then the damned thing will curve way around, like this, and come whirling back at great speed, spinning madly, and slice right through the neck of the animal they want to kill." He nodded his head sagely. "Do the same thing with a man, sir. How they go about aiming something like that and doing so much damage with it, I can't say."

Moses nodded. "Let's go down later and mingle with them. You know a bit of their language?"

"Enough to make my wishes known, not enough to bargain. I'm leaving that to Seth—" He stopped very suddenly.

"You were listening last night," Moses said.

"I'm afraid so, sir. My apologies."

"Accepted," Moses said. "I suppose it's all part of a soldier's job. We'll all get to know one another pretty well this time out, I think."

"I think you're right. As you may have gathered, this is more than just a military mission. From past the First Cataract we live off the land, making do with what we can find."

"Good," Moses said. "That means providing our own food. Why should we be using up the stores we brought with us from Thebes when there's the Nile to be lived off? Tell the men to organize a fishing detail while we're here. We'll catch tonight's supper before we move on."

"Very good idea, sir! I should have thought of it myself. You're learning very fast, sir. By journey's end you'll be giving lessons to all us old soldiers. I'll pass on the word, sir, as soon as we've found our way down to the waterside. Meanwhile, would you like to go down and talk with the Nubians?"

"Yes, Geb. Lead the way."

Seth, from an adjacent height, watched as the two followed the narrow path down the steep hillside. It was good to see the lad making friends with Geb, who knew everything and had vast experience for the young prince to draw from. They seemed to be hitting it off well, and that was a good sign. No officer—and no prince of the realm, either—was going to get by without having won the friendship and respect of his generals; but even more important was the friendship and respect of seasoned soldiers like Geb, who knew his place in the hierarchy and could make or break any man assigned to lead him.

Slowly Seth walked along the high path, looking down at the scene below. He had been here before and had liked the area and the people. The scenery was among the most beautiful he had ever seen, and he had deeply envied those members of Naldamak's Black Wind who had followed the Nile to its source below the Mountains of Fire, deep down into the continent. They had told of snowy mountains with perpetual ice caps, which, when you climbed them, turned out to hide boiling, bubbling pots of pure unleashed fire in their cores—

huge holes where the earth stank and shook and rumbled. He hoped someday to see those mountains for himself.

Meanwhile, revisiting this place was quite a pleasure. He wished he were a painter, able to preserve in some form more permanent than fragile memory the magnificent sights. Sloping sands of burnished gold led down to the water's edge; placid green pools lay hidden in the middle of lupine fields and tracts of barley; mud dwellings, made according to patterns as ancient as human life itself, perched on the heights; water-washed boulders of crimson and black and purple granite were dotted with wildfowl at midday and the spread nets of the fishermen in the evening; the bronzed, nude men and the gorgeous, blue-robed, stately women moved slowly along the Nile's edge with graceful elegance, toward their tiny towns green with sycamores and tufted palms.

When he had been here before, caravans still plied the old trade routes, coming down to the water at the First Cataract to board ships bound for downriver ports. At the time he had watched, fascinated, as the stolid Nubians loaded wild animals onto a cargo vessel bound for the great cities of the world—camels, cheetahs, antelope, even a huge, towering beast the men had called an elephant. If he had not actually seen it himself, he would have doubted the word of any man who tried to describe it to him.

He had been on a quest then, too, but one in which he had never found the thing he was looking for. It was one of his bitterest disappointments, all the worse because he could not blame it on anyone else on earth but himself. It had all been his fault! His!

The Nubian whom Geb had singled out was tall, hard-eyed, and seemingly fearless. Moses stood watching the two of them talk and noted with pleasure Geb's unintimidated approach.

I must learn that, he thought. *They look like two villagers chatting on a street corner, yet they're sizing each other up, probing for weaknesses; they're in deadly earnest every moment.*

From time to time the Nubian chieftain—he had to be that, at the very least—looked the prince's way. Finally Geb called him over. "Sir," he said, "if you'd like to question him . . ."

"I would," Moses said. Approaching, he imitated the curious double handshake Geb and the chieftain had used when they had first met. He noted Geb's smile of approval when he did. "Does he know who I am?"

"Yes, sir," Geb answered. "I told him you were a young prince of an ancient and noble house and that you had come upriver to learn from the wise men of the upper reaches of the Nile."

"I see. And does he believe you?"

"No, sir. I can see it in his eyes." Geb suppressed a grin.

"Tell him we have come up the Nile to take the measure of Nehsi, the son of Akillu, and to find out if he wants to fight or merely to bluff. Tell him if Nehsi wants to fight, we will have ourselves a fine battle; otherwise, we will go back to being friends and will work it all out over a great feast."

Geb raised a brow but barked out a quick translation in the Nubian tongue. Then he waited for a reaction. "You've got his attention now, sir. Look how he's appraising you."

"How do you think I did?"

"Pretty well, sir. These folk understand plain talk."

Now the Nubian began to speak and went on at some length. When at last he paused, Moses nodded gravely and turned to Geb for the translation.

"He says, sir, that Nehsi is not the problem, that Nehsi is the friend of all men. He says that Nehsi is under an enchantment."

"What kind of enchantment? How does he know?"

Geb spoke once more to the chieftain, this time getting an emphatic answer. At its conclusion the Nubian spat on the ground. Geb looked at Moses. "The chieftain says the evil spirits have soured the wells, poisoned the crops, and made the domestic animals die. He is very angry about this and wishes you could cleanse Nubia of the demons that have infested it and bring back the normal bounty of the Nile." He elaborated. "Life here, sir, is just bare survival, as you can see. Arable land in some places beside the river is limited to an area so narrow, a man can shoot an arrow across it. Any change for the worse can make the difference between surviving for another year and dying of starvation. The only reason his people will make it through this year, sir, is that we are here, and the money they make helping us like this will be taken to our trading posts and spent for provender."

"Tell him I am glad we have been of service to him and that upon our return we shall give him and his people a bonus for their help. Tell him we shall return loaded down with spoils and that we will be generous in sharing them with such good and loyal friends."

"Well said, sir. I'll tell him just that."

Moses watched them converse, thinking. *Demons? Enchantments? What are we getting ourselves into?*

By midafternoon they were free of the cataract and were sailing upriver, sails billowing. Above the white-water area the Nile flowed deep and stately; the rocky heights that hemmed it in closely on either side were golden on the one side and black on the other as their path cut between the narrow banks.

Then the river widened, and Moses could see how the population density was completely regulated by the advance of the desert. Only as the river receded at the end of flood season did the humans at water's edge begin little by little to reclaim portions of the land for their own. A tiny patch green with lentils would grow in size as the river shrank, and the farmers would plant every newly retaken foot of land, scratching new furrows and sowing new seeds. The Nubians could not afford to let any of the meager land sit idle at any time.

Farther upstream the desert began to assume a malevolent aspect as the river cut between the dark granite cliffs on one side and the torrents of windblown sand on the near bank. The sands constantly drifted, like golden streams pouring down from the higher levels of the Libyan desert, finding new channels in every ravine and gap, here trickling in tiny rivulets, there flowing in broad torrents.

They were beautiful, these sand streams, these rivers of death that menaced all by the edge of the Nile: smooth, satiny, shiny, as fine as diamond dust, undulating and luminous, looking like a snowdrift turned to gold. As the day's shadows began to grow, they lay darkly upon the drifted sand, creating a beautiful texture, sinuous, twisting, ever shifting, rich in grays and ambers.

Moses watched from the lee rail. Seth joined him at sundown, while the sailors furled the sails and cast down the anchor in deep water. "It's awe-inspiring," Moses said quietly. "I grew up on the edge of the desert, but I know so little of it. This far from civilization, I find it frightening."

Seth put a fatherly hand on his shoulder. "I understand. This will change, however, as you come to know it. And before we return to Thebes, you will know it well. You will come to love it."

"But it's so *dead*. And so deadly."

"So it seems now, but where the untutored eye sees nothing but desolation, the habitué of the sands will find food, water—life abundant. The trick is to remember that everything is smaller here than elsewhere, but it is there." He pointed. High above the water a vulture circled. "See? Infallible signs of life. The eagle and hawk are gone from these waters. The fragile life at the water's edge is not robust enough provender for these. But this sentinel here knows that there *is* life: small, helpless, fit provisions for his weak claws and soft beak. You will learn to follow where he goes. You will find food where the hawk and the cheetah and the leopard cannot. You will know the kingdom of sand the way you knew your nursery as a child. And you will be as safe as if you never left home."

Moses listened, hardly believing but wondering: *Why? Why me? What destiny will I find in the desert? Why must my path lie within the shifting sea of sand? I, who was born in the marsh country and raised listening to the seabirds and within plain sight of the Nile?*

CHAPTER SIX

Thebes

I

Neb-mertef bent over the spread scroll on the table, trying to look as though he understood the symbols on it. "This is very interesting," he said. "Are you quite sure?"

Set-Nakht, the magus, stood watching him, arms folded across his ample chest. "In such matters mere mortals cannot ever be quite sure, for our knowledge of such things is limited. We see all things as through the thick fogs of the delta, and our eyes remain clouded in the best of times. All I can tell you is that divination is my profession and my trade, that I live by it and by it alone, and if I were often wrong, I would have starved to death long ago." He paused a moment; then, not satisfied with the impression he was making, he went on. "You'll recall I was trained in Ur, which was the very cradle of astrology."

"But . . . to act on no more than this would be very dangerous."

The magus leaned back against the wall and impassively regarded Neb-Mertef. "Indeed. And what would you call it, honored sir, if my information later turned out to be precise, detailed, and accurate—and you had *not* acted upon it? Would you not call that dangerous, too? Life itself is a danger. We are all in the hands of the gods and can only try to inform ourselves as best we can and act upon that as judiciously as possible. Beyond that, our destinies are fixed and unalterable."

"But I've never heard another of our magi prophesy anything comparable to this. They have all foretold the existence of a great leader who will depose Kamose if he is not stopped in time. And all men are familiar with the story the slaves in Deir el-Bahari believe about a Deliverer who will lead them out of their bondage. But not even Amasis has spoken of anything like this."

"That, esteemed sir," the magus responded in a voice with a slight edge to it, "is because the mighty Amasis turned me away from his door. My presence here in your apartments gives you the opportunity to know something that Amasis does not—information he needs desperately." He shrugged and changed his tone, becoming almost flippant. "Of course, if I have misjudged you and you have not the vision to see when a golden chance like this is offered—"

"Now wait. Let's not be hasty—"

"—or if, perhaps, you are so much in awe of the noble Amasis that you follow him blindly, unquestioningly . . ."

"Explain it to me again, will you?" Neb-mertef requested in the voice of a harried man.

"Certainly." The magus uncrossed his arms, leaned over the papyrus, and flattened the curled corners with broad hands. "This top chart represents the skies of one week ago. See the juxtaposition of the planets here, here, and here. This happens very seldom . . . but once before. And when did this happen? In the very month when the Hittites invaded Babylon and laid the city waste, the King Samsi-ditana and all of his line died in the one afternoon."

"Where is that again? I didn't understand."

The magus's tone was withering. "Here, esteemed sir. And here and here. Trines here, squares there. The fifth planet on the cusp, so." His fingers drummed impatiently on the tabletop. "Do you see?"

Neb-mertef was almost afraid to betray his ignorance. "Yes, I see," he lied.

"Well, then. A mighty mind had invaded Babylon, causing much disruption and changing its ways beyond recognition. This portended ill. The normal affairs of men are not to be trifled with lightly. The rhythm of the spheres is a delicate one, not to be tampered with, even by one so brilliant as Seth of Thebes."

"Yes, yes. But what does Seth of Thebes have to do with—"

"In time. Patience, kind sir. Patience. Seth was a stray, a wanderer, a meddler, a factor unaccounted for in the scheme of things. When he went to Babylon he upset the general balance, offending the gods. Samsi-ditana welcomed the man, paid him honors, even adopted him into his family. Well, he paid for such folly, and in the dearest coin of all. He and all those he loved."

"Go on."

"As you wish. If you like, next time I come here, I can show you the charts for the very day Babylon fell. I drew them up earlier this month, the better to study the present situation. They do not match exactly, but there are correspondences I would not hesitate to call ominous."

"Tell me more."

"Very well. The correspondences approximate those of the fateful date in Babylon. But see here, here, and particularly here."

"Yes, yes," Neb-mertef said. His palms were sweating.

"Very well. Now look at this." He swept the scroll off the table onto the floor, uncovering another beneath it. "This is a map of the skies, drawn up for six months from now. Chaos! Sheer chaos!"

"I don't see—"

"Here!" the magus shouted. "And *here*! Any fool could see it! But your local stargazers, ill trained, poorly prepared . . . ah, but I forget myself." He moderated his tone. "Mind you, sir, the stars impel; the man who pays attention to planetary trends, and who acts accordingly, has powerful advantage over the man not comparably armed against misfortune."

"Explain it to me simply."

The magus shrugged, then spoke as one speaks to a child. "Very recently—within a month or so, I'd say—a very great danger newly entered this domain. The person to whom the danger refers is Amasis. His luck will be extremely bad if he does not take decisive steps to nullify the effects that have been unleashed here."

"Yes, yes."

"At first I thought the problem had to do with the danger to Kamose, which we have already spoken of. But upon analyzing the matter, I found that the person whose stars are ill aspected is Amasis himself. Since I am blocked from getting the information to him directly, I find myself explaining the matter to you, sir. Of course if I am addressing a man who is but a mindless puppet of Amasis's and whose ambitions extend no further than this—"

"I'll thank you not to prod me. You forget yourself, my friend."

"A thousand pardons. I am convinced that if Amasis does not come to understand the terrible danger he is in, he will soon fall from his present pinnacle. He will be deposed as leader of the state—"

"He is not the leader of the state!"

"He will be. The charts are absolutely clear about that." The magus leaned forward over the table, looked Neb-mertef in the eye, and lowered his voice to a conspiratorial whisper. "Within a single day he will become all-powerful in Thebes. This I can tell you, although by so doing I take my life in my hands. If you denounce me as a subversive, I'm a dead man. *But* if you wish to check on whether my predictions are accurate, just wait for the night and day to pass. Within a complete circuit of the sun from this hour today to this hour tomorrow, sir, Amasis will become the wielder of absolute power in Thebes, such as none has held here since the days of the Twelfth Dynasty."

Neb-mertef eyed him skeptically. "You're willing to stand or fall on that?"

"I am, sir. And if I prove to be accurate, does this mean

we have a contract to work together, in which I will provide you and you alone with information in the months to come? In exchange for the stipend agreed upon, and the privileges and perquisites discussed earlier?"

"If you deliver on this, all that and more. If you don't—" He glared. "The crows will peck out your eyes before noon of the second day from now."

"Gladly, sir. And once I have proven myself, there is much more that I shall reveal. There is something new on the scene." He pushed the second scroll onto the floor and uncovered yet a third. "Now this, sir, is the most amazing of all. *This* juxtaposition of the planets, which depicts the night skies six months from now, indicates that the new element has borne fruit. Great and dazzling changes—ominous ones—are at work, transforming every aspect of our lives. And mark you, the danger to Amasis from this point grows daily."

"I am already half-persuaded. Please me in this, and you will have made a real believer of me. And I will be generous with my rewards, as future insights prove to be true. But mind you, I buy your absolute silence on these and any other matters. I buy your exclusive services."

"Exclusive? You mean I become a member of your household, with title and lands and a fixed sinecure, sir?"

"That and more, my friend, if you deliver. I will provide for your declining years. You will see the Fayum farmlands that will be yours, and the rents in such cities as Athribis and Avaris. I am a rich man and could give away the total income of a town like Saïs every year for ten years and not impoverish myself."

"Yet you remain ambitious."

"Precisely. What does a man want who has all things?"

"Power, sir."

"Precisely, my friend. Power. Now leave me. And come back this time tomorrow, to the hour. With the best of news."

II

Their unit had been given the rest of the day off halfway through the morning, and Onuris and Nemti were about to leave when the courier came from the palace.

"Orders," the messenger said brusquely. "You're being transferred."

"Transferred?" Nemti echoed. "What sort of nonsense is this? We only just got here. Surely nobody has any need of us down in the delta; they just sent us up here to get rid of us. And the last boat's already left for Nubia."

"You're not being sent away, never fear. Cushy duty, my friend. The sort of duty that means promotions."

"Where?"

"The palace. Baliniri's wing. The order comes direct from the old boy himself. It took me the morning to find you. He got the number of your unit wrong. I think the old fellow's losing it, little by little."

"Well, let's keep it a secret among the three of us," Nemti said sharply. "Meanwhile it would behoove us to continue to show the 'old boy,' as you call him, some of the respect he's earned over half a lifetime of service to Egypt." There was an unmistakable threat in his words, and the courier immediately snapped to attention. "That's better. Now, let's hear the details."

"Yes, sir. You're being assigned to guard the entire wing. There may be other duties. You're to report to Baliniri directly, at sundown."

"Are you sure? Nobody ever gets into that wing at sundown—certainly not a couple of low-grade officers like us."

"They made me repeat the order to make sure I got it right, sir."

Nemti and Onuris exchanged glances, then Nemti turned back to the courier. "It'll have to be cleared with the commanders of our unit."

"That's already been taken care of. You're to bring your gear. You'll be living in. Baliniri wants full-time help there.

You'll be allowed to hire men for the other shifts, but he wants to talk to you before you do."

"Very well. You may go."

The two men watched the courier turn on one heel and retreat, chastened. "Huh," Onuris said. "Do you think it's authentic?"

"It has to be," Nemti replied. "Do you think a smart aleck like that would be as easily cowed by a sharp word from me if it weren't? With my old rank, he would have sassed me all he liked. But as a member of Baliniri's personal guard? Never!"

"Well! This is good news!" Onuris stopped dead, his face blank. "Wait a minute. This is too sudden. This would happen only if somebody pulled strings. Two nobodies like us, being picked out of the muck by someone who can't even get the number of our unit right? I'll bet I know where this comes from."

Nemti pursed his lips in thought. "I'd just come to the same conclusion. And if we're right . . . well, I'm not sure this is the way I'd have chosen to rise in the service." He paused for a long moment, and his expression became serious and thoughtful. "On the other hand . . ."

When he looked back at Onuris, his friend was grinning mischievously. "You sly dog, you," Onuris teased. "You haven't been telling me everything, have you?"

"What do you mean?" Nemti asked. "I've yet to spend an hour alone with her. Not that I think I would have the good sense to refuse if she were to ask me to."

"You realize how dangerous this is."

"It could be. But, we are members of a profession in which danger is taken for granted."

"But the danger's not supposed to come from our own side. Look, do you remember that slave-driving son of a bitch we met over in Deir el-Bahari? The one I made back down a while back, the day we met the women?"

"Yes. I asked around about him later. His name is Osorkon."

"Yes. Well, I learned two facts about him: First, he's no longer attached to the slave detail; second, the bastard's been following us."

"Following us!"

"Yeah. I caught him at it the other day. Oh, I didn't confront him. I didn't let on that I knew."

"Let's go down to the quays and have a glass of wine where voices can't carry over the sound of the river and all the hollering by the stevedores. The whole damned world can hear us here." He inclined his head to one side, and the two set out in that direction through the back streets. "Let me know if you see anybody behind us. Just unobtrusively glance around every so often. I'll lead us on a roundabout course, so you'll have plenty of opportunities."

"There he is, as a matter of fact. Don't look now. I caught a glimpse of him out of the corner of one eye. But he's back there." Onuris snorted. "Turn left up here. When you do, sneak a peek back. He's in civilian dress, but that's him. Why, for half an *outnou* I'd lay in wait for him and kick him in the balls."

"You're assuming he has any to kick," his friend joked. "Come on. I have an idea. Let's pick up the pace. I want to get well ahead of him. We're going to lead him down through the brothel quarter and cut through one of the houses."

Onuris hooted. "Not *that* one."

"Right you are. Down at the end of the block."

"But that one specializes in—"

"Right again. Now don't be shocked. The proprietor's male, whether he dresses like it or not. He used to be a soldier, until he decided to declare himself. So when he starts twittering like a little bird in that deep bass voice of his, try not to giggle. I still have his marker after a long and profitable game of chance. I'm going to let him pay me back in favors. No, you ass, not *that* kind of favor. I'm going to let him work it out in trade—with Osorkon."

Before Onuris could respond they reached the door; Nemti opened it and showed his friend inside. "Now mind your manners," he whispered, "and *don't laugh*."

A large, burly person in a woman's wig and dress came toward them, painted gaudily and walking with a wiggle. "Nemti!" he fluted in a voice that broke. "What are *you* doing here, dear boy?"

"We're giving a friend a surprise for his birthday," Nemti

said ever so seriously. "He's right behind us. You know that debt you—"

"Oh, yes, I meant to—"

"Never mind. Accommodate our friend, and the debt is retired."

"Oh, how jolly. Do go on."

"The problem is this: My friend out there likes to pretend he's not . . . well, *you* know. His fantasy is that he has to be taken by force, bound and gagged and humiliated."

"Yes. Yes, indeed. Sounds delightful—"

"That's not all. Don't let him speak. Grab him from behind and rip his clothes off. Gag him and bind him. But humiliation is the main thing. He loves being whipped, particularly in front of a lot of people calling him names. You must take particular care to ridicule his sexual equipment and refer to him constantly in the feminine gender."

"Oh, he sounds like fun."

"That he is. Feel free to improvise, just as long as it involves humiliation, and plenty of it. Oh, and when he's done, you must carry him right out into the middle of the most crowded marketplace in the city and dump him there, stark naked—"

"How delightful!"

"—and with his privates dyed bright purple. Use the good dye you buy from Tyre; it takes at least six months to fade."

"This is getting expensive."

"You owe me a lot of money. Or would you rather I turned the bad debt over to—"

"Oh, no! No! I'll do it. In fact it'll be a lot of fun. Can I dye his nose and ears blue, too? I did that to a Greek once who didn't pay his bill, after he beat three of my prettiest boys until there were bruises all over their cute little—"

"I'm sure he'd really appreciate that. But don't let him talk you out of any of it, no matter how hard he screams. He won't mean any of his threats. He'll really be loving every moment of it."

"Right. That must be him at the door. You two go along, now."

Ignoring the muffled sounds behind them, Nemti and

Onuris slipped through the far door. They threaded their way through the complex interior, trying not to look at the various tableaux that presented themselves on every side.

At last they found themselves in the street. Onuris halted, turned, and stared at his friend. "Remind me never to get you mad at me."

"I'm simply assisting the dear fellow in discovering his true nature."

"You are one evil man." His grin was wide and full of malice. "Deep down inside where it really counts. Pure evil."

"You don't think the Tyrian dye was too much?"

"A trifle extravagant, actually. He must have owed you enough money to choke a camel."

"He did. But I'd never collect anyhow."

"Evil. Downright evil," Onuris repeated, still grinning.

"Say, what if he *likes* it?"

"He may, especially the part about all the purple dye on his—"

"I liked the addition of the nose and ears. That's Libyan. The Libyans do that to people caught committing the act with livestock. It does add a distinctive touch. They'll lock up the onagers and water buffaloes in every town he enters for at least six months. You know how many Libyans one runs into in the street these days, now that the western caravan routes have been closed off. And you know how Libyans talk. They're like monkeys chattering in the trees."

"You're terrible!"

"A real friend would say 'creative.' "

"All right, you're creative."

"That's better."

"But terrible."

"Then why are you grinning like an idiot?"

"Me? Grinning? Was I, really? Imagine that!"

In Thermutis's rooms, Mara and the princess stared at each other, all their expression in the eyes. "I can't believe I'm listening to this," Thermutis groaned. "Do you have any idea how dangerous this is?"

"You don't have to go along with it," Mara said. "You don't have to do anything. Just don't get in my way."

"If someone found out—"

"Who's going to find out? My husband? He's off in some dream world of his own. Even if he knew, he wouldn't be interested. He hasn't been for years. He wasn't interested even when he *wasn't* on this drug of theirs. I'm lonely. Lonely and—"

"So am I. But—"

"And you don't even have a husband to worry about. What's stopping you?"

"I don't know. I've heard the stories about my mother and her affair with Baba of El-Kab. But, Mara, we're not young girls like my mother was. We're older than she and Baba were."

"And what woman would turn down the chance of having an affair with a young soldier, handsome and strong and full of life?"

"But—"

"Just you watch. They'll be right here. All the time."

"But, Mara—"

"Look. We have Baliniri's blessing. He told me so. Obey your instincts. You know you want to."

Thermutis sighed long and hard. "I don't know," she quavered. But when Mara looked in her eyes it was obvious that some sort of decision had already been made.

III

Baliniri shifted painfully on the couch, trying to find a comfortable position. It was no use; the pain continued. He gritted his teeth and reached for the little bell by his bedside, ringing it imperiously. "Selket!" he called. "Selket, where are you?"

It was a long, long moment before the girl appeared in the doorway that led to the outer room. "Yes, my lord?"

"The pain's back. Go for my physician. Bring him here."

"Why, my lord? I can give you a portion of *shepenn*. My lord Amasis showed me how to do it."

Baliniri scowled. *That's just what I'm afraid of,* he thought. "No. I want a physician. Go to the Temple of Amon and have Si-Ptah recommend one. Now. Why are you standing there, arguing with me? Do as I say."

She turned her coolly noncommittal eyes on him and said, "As you wish, my lord. But that will leave no one here with you."

"Stop at the rooms of the queen on the way. Tell her I want to see her. If she's not available, send my stepdaughter. But do it now."

"Very well, my lord. But I'd feel better if I could give you something beforehand to stop the pain. It makes me feel bad, seeing you hurting like that and not being able to do anything about it."

"Damn you!" he said. "Who cares how *you* feel? You're not here to feel. You're here to do my bidding, and if you can't do that, I'll find someone who can."

She turned unhurriedly and moved away, each step slow and deliberate and maddening. Baliniri closed his eyes. *Listen to you,* he told himself. *You sound like a weak, cranky old man.* Well, that was what he was. He was failing daily. The memory was going, and the alertness, and with them the ability even to get servants to do his bidding.

Look how he had botched the handling of the two priests his friend Si-Ptah had sent over. They had been less than perfectly attentive, to be sure, but they had actually been better-than-average companions. And although it had been obvious they would have refused such an assignment if it had been given by anyone of lesser stature in the temple hierarchy than Si-Ptah, they had been courteous enough, and efficient.

No, the fault had been his: storming at them in his weak old man's voice, sounding like someone's ill-tempered, bedridden old uncle. No wonder they'd gone back to Si-Ptah and asked for reassignment.

Well, he hoped these two guardsmen Mara and Thermutis had foisted off on him would have more patience. They would need it, no doubt. He would have to be on good behavior when they showed up for duty this evening. No use in alienating them, particularly not if it meant getting Mara and his stepdaughter angry with him in the process.

He shifted again on the couch and, with no one to hear him, allowed himself to cry out at the pain. *Damn!* he thought. *You old fool! Taking a spill like that in front of your enemies, giving them a chance to laugh at you as if you were some sort of clown!*

He hoped he hadn't angered Si-Ptah too much. Mara had gone to the priest herself the next day to ask for his forgiveness and had come back saying the whole thing had been forgotten. So she had said. Who knew what had really transpired between them? Quite possibly Mara had told the priest that he, Baliniri, was not responsible for his actions anymore and must be humored—coddled—like the dotard he had become. Under such circumstances he could imagine Si-Ptah nodding indulgently and pardoning the "old fool," rolling his eyes heavenward as he did.

Ach! He had lived too long! How much better it would have been if he could have died before old age had set in. To have his heart give out, say, as he strode through the halls of the palace and slip painlessly off to the Netherworld—or wherever a man's spirit went when he was gone. He was not sure what he believed in. Yes, a nice quick painless death, one you did not have to take notice of . . .

But no. In the end it was better that he had made provision for things first. And that could not have been done any earlier—his honor had demanded that he strictly tend the stewardship he had embraced so many years before, when he had inherited this job from Baka: that he keep the kingdom in trust until Kamose's return, in the hope that the king would have solved his personal problems and come back to Egypt a whole man, able to run his own affairs.

So much he had done, and faithfully too. There was the matter of saving the army and saving Prince Moses with it. With officers like Khafre, a seasoned subordinate like Geb, and a brilliant counselor like Seth to guide him and to introduce him to that other independent striking force he had created so many years earlier—the women's armies of the oases—Egypt might have a future. And in that, he knew he could take legitimate pride.

The reflective mood conjured up a name, a face, a person long dead. *Tuya* . . .

No matter that it had been two other women, Ayla and Ah-Hotep, that he had married. A man's first love was the one that he felt the most, even after many years elapsed. He had never really loved until he had met Tuya, back in the golden days when he was young, strong, handsome, and relatively inexperienced in the ways of women and of how they could cut so deeply into a man's heart.

After Ben-Hadad's death, there had come an opportunity for them to rekindle their affair, but he had passed it up. Something in him had held back from making a commitment to her. He had known that it would not work between them, that he had been flattered by her intense need of him rather than by an intrinsic quality of her own.

Ayla hadn't had that need of him. Neither had Ah-Hotep. He had been happy with them. He had not felt as though he was bearing a burden in either marriage, so his attention could be given exclusively to business: first of saving the delta from the mad Salitis, then the business of saving Egypt. There had been no room in his life for a woman who needed him the way Tuya had. He had instinctively known that and had backed away from her.

He looked at the table beside him, at the vial of *shepenn* that Amasis's doctors had left for him, which he had not touched. Standing beside it was a jar of wine, also untouched, beside his cup.

All of a sudden the pains came back, strong and insistent. His hand reached for the *shepenn*. Anything, anything to ease the pain.

He stayed his hand, closed his eyes, and sighed. Then his eyes fluttered open, and with yet another sigh, he poured himself a shallow bowlful of the red wine.

Regretfully, he looked at the *shepenn* and drank deeply of the wine in his bowl, still looking at the little vial. Immediately he knew he had made a mistake.

His head reeled. The bowl fell from his hand. He clutched at his throat and tried to call out.

He sat, ignoring the stabbing pains in his back. He tried to stand but found he was not sure just which direction was up. He fell heavily to his knees, still holding his throat. For a long moment the pains were worse than any he had ever felt.

And then there was no sensation at all.

IV

"This is odd," Onuris said. "Where are the guards in the hall? This place ought to be crawling with guardsmen. We should have been stopped at least three times. You're not supposed to be able just to walk right in like this. What if we were spies or assassins?"

"I don't understand it either," Nemti concurred. "I'm not even sure we're in the right part of the palace. I've been trying to make up my mind whether or not that right turn a while back was the proper one."

"You mean we could be in the wrong wing?" Onuris asked. He came to a halt and turned to look at his friend. "Then we could be in deep trouble. I've heard what Amasis has done to people who break his rules—even people who don't know what rules they are breaking."

Nemti blew out, shaking his head. "Maybe we should retrace our steps and try to find someone to direct us?"

"We could try knocking on a door."

"No! Not until we're back in neutral territory. What would happen if we're in Amasis's wing? You remember what happened to that officer in the Fourth Troop?"

"Ugh! No thanks! You're right. Let's go."

But as they turned and headed back where they had come from, they heard footsteps approaching. "Quick!" said Nemti. "Behind here!" And the two of them slipped behind a wall hanging just as the intruder rounded the corner and entered the hall in which they stood.

To their chagrin the walker stopped at the door directly opposite their hiding place. Both men shrank back against the wall; Nemti looked down and saw that the distance between the bottom of the wall hanging and the marble floor was the width of a man's hand. Silently he cursed the fact. If someone standing in the door opposite were to look at the floor and see their feet . . .

He held his breath as the door opened.

"Ah!" said a familiar, chilling voice. Amasis himself! Nemti let his hand steal to his sword hilt. "Come in! How did it go?"

A female voice answered, "He sent me for his physician. He won't take the *shepenn* left out for him."

"Come in," Amasis invited. Nemti waited for the sound of the door closing, but it did not come. Instead the voices faded slightly, as if the woman had entered and now stood in the middle of the room but had not closed the door behind her. "That's good," Amasis said now. "If he suspects the *shepenn*, he assuredly will not suspect the wine. And he must be in enough pain to need something."

Emboldened, Nemti took a deep breath and peeked out from behind the arras. The door stood ajar by a handspan. Apparently Amasis felt so secure in this wing that he did not care who heard him. Perhaps this was the reason for the lax security. He motioned Onuris, and the two crept softly from behind the curtain.

Silently he removed his sandals and tucked them into his sword belt as Onuris did likewise; the quieter they were at this stage, the better. But as he prepared to move away down the hall, the voices became audible again. Amasis and the woman had moved closer to the door. Nemti froze, stared at Onuris, and made a silent shushing motion. The two men did not move for fear of making the smallest noise.

". . . leave some time for the stuff to work," Amasis was saying. "Then go right ahead and do what you told Baliniri you were going to do. This will give you an alibi for being absent from his rooms. Then . . ."

Nemti's eyes went wide open. He and Onuris exchanged startled glances. Was this what it sounded like? His lips formed the word: *Baliniri?* And Onuris nodded, frowning, hand on the hilt of his sword.

". . . go to the women first, as he told you to do."

"Does it matter, my lord? No one heard him say anything to me. I'm sure of that."

"You forget there's that secret passage in the wall—we

don't know where it is or how it works. There's been no opportunity to search for it. Since he got hurt he's never been away from his room long enough for us to find out. But someone just possibly could be hiding behind it at any time listening."

"You're right, my lord. I will send Mara and Thermutis to his rooms."

"Then go for his physician. Meanwhile I'll pay a surprise visit, having allowed the women to get there first. I'll bring a couple of my men as witnesses. With luck we can pin this on the women and have Baliniri's doctor show up while we're doing it, to confirm it for us."

Nemti's hands were shaking, as rage contended with indignation. He felt like a caged lion ready to burst loose, to rip and tear and kill.

"But, my lord," the woman said, "who would believe the queen would poison her counselor? Or the princess?"

"We have the evidence of their illicit liaison with the two soldiers," Amasis replied.

Nemti's eyes locked with Onuris's.

"To be sure, it's not the strongest of evidence," he continued. "The fool I sent to follow the soldiers and the women managed to get himself into the most incredible sort of condition. It will weigh against his credibility, and badly."

Nemti allowed himself a wry smile, but the tension in his body was the kind a man ordinarily felt only before a battle.

"Nonetheless, he was accompanied when he observed one of the queen's meetings with her young man, so that will help. The man with him was more reliable."

"Then . . . this murder is supposed to have been done to silence Baliniri?"

"Yes. Under our law any woman who offends against her sovereign lord in this fashion is punishable by death—even the queen, even a princess of the blood like Thermutis."

Nemti once more exchanged glances with Onuris. His friend's eyes were hard, and his face was as rigid as that of a stone statue. Nemti nodded; as if by prearranged signal the two moved softly down the hall and slipped around the

corner. Only when they were at the far end of the long hall
did they stop.

"Well?" Onuris asked.

"We're doomed anyhow. If they have evidence against
us, we have only two choices: wait until they come to get us
and be slaughtered like lambs, or give them a bit of a fight."

"Or a bit of a chase."

"Right. And we've got to warn the women."

Onuris did not demur. His back straightened, and his
jaw firmed. "We've got to get them to safety."

"Good man. Let's go. Since this is Amasis's wing, I know
where we are now. That right turn was a mistake. The first
door will be Baliniri's; the fourth will be Mara's. She told me
two nights ago."

"Well, thank your lucky stars she did. Let's go."

Nemti grinned at him. This was the old Onuris, fearless
and resolute. He felt a sudden rush of pride and affection for
his old comrade. "Lead the way," he said.

The pounding on Mara's door was loud and urgent. She
moved swiftly to open it. "Thermutis!" she said. "What's the
matter? You look—"

"Come quickly!" the younger woman gasped. "There's
something wrong with Baliniri. He was on the floor. I can't
rouse him! His pulse is barely going!"

Mara followed her out into the hall, and they hurried
toward his open door. "I don't understand. There was supposed to be someone with him at all times. Where was the
girl?"

"I don't know."

They came to Baliniri's door and went inside. Mara
rushed to the fallen man's side and bent over him. The
overturned wine bowl was near him, and spilled wine stained
his garment. His arms lay spread carelessly, and whatever
expression his face had borne in his last moments, the muscles had now relaxed into a neutral position. His mouth hung
open, and his eyes stared, wide open.

"No signs of life," she said tensely. "They got to him
somehow." She frowned. "Unless the girl herself—"

There was a sound at the door. She whirled and looked up at Nemti and Onuris. "Nemti! Something's happened—"

"No time to talk," he said. "Baliniri's been poisoned. You're to be blamed for it. Is there any way out of here other than the front entrance? By now Amasis will have sent out for his guards."

Far down the hall they heard the pounding of feet.

"Quickly!" Mara ordered. "Bar the door! Onuris!"

The shorter man moved even as she spoke, slamming the stout crossbeam into place with a single powerful stroke. Then he began dragging furniture in front of the door and piling it high, chair upon couch, table atop chair.

"The secret passage," Mara said. "Here, help me."

The two dragged at a loose block in the wall behind Baliniri's bed. As they did, pulling the block free, a wooden panel in the adjacent wall slid to the left, opening an escape route. The doorway led to a long, dark stairway.

There was a powerful pounding at the door. "Open up!" a familiar voice commanded.

"Come on," Nemti said, taking an oil lamp from beside Baliniri's bed. He ushered first Onuris, then Thermutis into the passageway and watched them go down the staircase. The violent pounding outside increased. Amasis was screaming now. Something hard and large slammed into the door, jarring it, but the hinges held. A chair atop the pile fell to the floor, but the stout crossbeam withstood the assault.

Mara suddenly reached up and kissed him. Then she slipped through the doorway.

Nemti joined her in the passageway and shoved the great panel to. From the other side, he saw the key stone slip back into place. He grinned. "This will slow them down. Where are we going?"

"There's only one door in Thebes that Amasis dare not break down," she explained. "If we can get that far, perhaps we can find time to make other plans."

Nemti, close on her heels, said, "The temple."

"Right," she confirmed. "Si-Ptah's priests can delay them; an open assault against the temple would bring about an open revolution."

"Lead the way," he said, and felt her hand steal back and

give his a quick caress as they reached the bottom of the long staircase.

"Damn them!" Amasis shrieked. "Where have they gone? You! Search that wall! Look for a lever or loose block. And you two! What are you doing standing there? Look out the window! They may have scaled their way down the side!"

"No sign out there, my lord. No ropes, no nothing. A sheer drop. Somebody would break a leg at the very least."

"The wall, damn it! Keep searching! There has to be something! If we've lost them—"

Ten minutes' pushing and pulling finally located the loose block, and at last the door came open, revealing the dark staircase. But the prey was long gone.

V

"You!" Neb-mertef said. "Where are you going? Stop! Come back here!"

"I'm sorry," Selket said, flustered, unable to look him in the eye. "I've got to go somewhere. If I'm not there in a minute or two, I'll get in real trouble."

Neb-mertef stared hard at her. Then he grabbed her by the wrist in a strong grip.

"Let me go!" she demanded. "I work for my lord Amasis. If you keep me from doing what he told me—"

"What errand did he give you? Tell me, you little slut!"

"Let me go! If he finds you've kept me from reaching a magus—"

"Magus? What for?" He stared. Then his eyes opened even wider. "Baliniri! He's having some sort of attack!"

Not answering, she tried to struggle free. He reached down, grabbed her chin, pried her face up, made her look him in the eye. "Wait. Something is fishy here. If you're going for Baliniri's personal doctor, what does Amasis have to do with it? If Baliniri's having some sort of attack, would

Amasis send you out? Where is he? At Baliniri's rooms? Answer me!"

"You're hurting me!"

"Where is Amasis? Is he with Baliniri? I'll go there to find out!"

"No! He doesn't want anyone—"

She made herself stop. He shook her violently. "Tell me, damn you!"

But then it dawned on him. He smiled malevolently. "You've killed him, haven't you? Amasis has let you kill him! And you're on your way for help. But along the way you'll do something to waste time. What's happened? Has his heart given out? Eh? Speak up, or I'll break your arm!"

"Don't!"

"Ah! You know I would, too, don't you? And in such a way that it'd never heal right."

"Don't! It's too late for you to do anything."

"Did you poison him? That's it, isn't it? I can see it in your eyes."

"Please . . ."

"Let's see. Was it in the painkiller, perhaps?" He jerked at her arm, and she cried out in pain. "No? In the wine? Ah! That was it. The wine!" He suddenly slapped her in the face, hard, snapping her head back. "So, he's dead? He'll have had plenty of time to die by now, won't he? And you—you'll be impaled for it. But you haven't figured that out yet, have you? Now that he's got you to do it, you'll be blamed for it. And there you'll be, with no defenses, the only one who could have done it. You think he'll protect you. He won't. He'll throw you to the dogs."

"No!"

"They'll have you red-handed."

"No! He's got it set up so the queen—" She bit her lip, clamped down on the rest of her ill-considered retort, and tried to twist her arm free, wincing and whimpering against the pain.

Surprisingly, he let her go; then, placing one hand on her chest, he shoved hard—so hard that she stumbled back against the wall, hit her head, and fell to the ground. She

shook her head, tried to get her legs under her, and fell
again.

"The thing about the women won't work in the end," he
said. "You have to know that. When the queen slips off the
hook, they'll still need someone to blame. This is the death of
a vizier of Egypt, after all, not some bricklayer. And what will
you have got out of it? Nothing. Some paltry sum. One that
won't buy you protection from either Yalu or me. Nor protection from Amasis either. You don't suppose he'll leave you
alive, knowing what you know?"

"My head hurts."

He threw his head back and laughed long and hard with
a fierce triumph. "So *this* is what Sek-Nahkt meant!" he
howled. " 'Within a single day,' he said. A single day! And
the prophecy is exact! All-powerful in Thebes! Ah, I'd take
his word now for a king's ransom! And I have his exclusive
services! He's mine! From now on I'll know everything, and
before Amasis does! More powerful, he said, than anyone
since the Twelfth Dynasty! How right he was! But he's walking the edge of a precipice and doesn't even know it! But I
do! I do!"

"Wait," Nemti whispered. He held the women back
with one protective arm and approached the corner, taking a
deep breath before sticking his head out at last. "I don't see
anyone yet. Where does this passage go?" he asked Mara,
beside him in the semidarkness. "I can't see much past the
next transverse hallway."

"That's all there is," she answered. "We won't want to
take the path on the left. It leads to the guardroom, where
the soldiers relax when they're off duty."

"How about the hallway to the right?" he asked.

"It's all we've got. It leads to the kitchens. We can cut
through there."

"Good." He was about to step out into the hall when she
pulled him back.

"When you enter the kitchens, bear right once more.
That'll lead you through the storerooms. Past two doors you'll
come to the vault where they store the wine. It's about a

dozen steps down. It'll be very dark. Take about half a dozen steps along the wall to your right, and you'll come to a ramp."

"I'm not sure I'll remember all this."

"You will. The ramp is the one they use to roll the wine casks down. At the top of it the door has a big bronze ring. You pull it and—"

"All right. Come on. Onuris!" His whisper was sharp. "Keep an eye on that hall to the left."

"Right."

Nemti stepped out into the hall and made his way to the transverse passage. He stole a quick look to his left; a door at the far end lay open, leaking a sliver of light into the otherwise dark hallway. He could hear rough masculine voices there. He grabbed Mara's hand and pulled her into the passage to their right.

Here, once again, the door was not entirely shut. There was another tall line of light. He approached the door cautiously, then drew back hastily. Voices inside! He put his head near the door and drew his sword.

". . . said they may have come this way. They're armed and dangerous. Keep an eye out. If they get past you, don't come to work tomorrow."

"If they come this way, I'll stop them. Never fear. I spent twenty years as a guardsman and won prizes with the sword."

"Fat chance. But mind what I told you, old man. They could be anywhere."

"Look to yourself. Don't worry about me."

Nemti turned to Mara. The light spilling through the partly open door made her face quite visible. "Who?" he mouthed silently.

"Yalu. Nobody special. A court spy."

Nemti put his eye close to the door and looked into the well-lit room. Tall ovens lined the far wall; there were two tables in the middle of the room and atop one of them a rack with an assortment of razor-sharp butcher knives.

"Come on," he said, and stepped out into the bright light.

As he did, however, sword in hand, there was a swift movement just beyond his peripheral vision, and a powerful blow fell on his sword arm, causing him to drop his weapon. A second blow fell on the back of his neck, driving him forward to stumble into the table and almost fall.

"Well," a voice said, "what have we here?"

Nemti blinked and looked at the man. He was fat and shapeless. His hand held a bludgeon used to tenderize meat. As Nemti watched he stooped and retrieved the sword Nemti had dropped.

Mara came in after him, and Thermutis, and Onuris. "No! Get back!" Nemti cried, but it was too late.

Onuris rushed forward, his sword at the ready; but the fat man had grabbed Thermutis by the hair and pulled her to him. He held Nemti's sword to her neck. "Make a move, any of you," he threatened, "and I cut her throat."

Onuris's hand shook on the sword hilt. "You do that, and you can't begin to imagine how badly you'll die. I'll send the others ahead and take my time killing you. They'll have to carry you out in two buckets."

Nemti got slowly to his feet. His hand was numb. He kept his eyes on his own sword in the fat stranger's hand. "You've got your hands on a princess of the blood. Do you know what the penalty is for laying so much as a finger on a member of the royal house?"

The fat man smiled nastily. "None of that means much around here anymore," he said. "It died with Baliniri. Oh, hadn't you heard? Mont just confirmed it. Poisoned by Queen Mara. There's a very strong suspicion that this one"—he shook Thermutis by the hair, roughly—"had a hand in it too. You're all sunk. Now throw down that sword."

Nemti suddenly feinted a swift kick at the fat man. The sword at Thermutis's throat started to cut across—and Mara, as fast as light, reached for one of the butcher knives on the table and whirled. When she came around full circle the knife was pointed directly at him. She drove it deeply into his side, just as Nemti, reacting quickly, reached him. Nemti pulled Thermutis away, and Onuris lunged forward, driving his sword into the fat man's neck. He stepped back just in time to avoid a hideous gush of red.

Yalu fell, holding his neck, trying awkwardly to hold

back the flow. Nemti retrieved his sword, then, seeing that the princess was all right, said, "Come on. Down this hall?"

"Yes. Two doors down."

They heard the pounding of running feet.

"Quickly!" Nemti ordered. "In here!"

They opened the door and dived into darkness just as the kitchen door opened behind them. They could hear the voices as guards happened upon the carnage.

"Gods!"

"Looks like some animal turned the tables on our fat meat-cutter here. . . ."

The door closed behind Onuris, and they heard no more. "Now," Nemti said, "the ramp has to be . . . yes, here it is. Watch your step. Hold onto my hand, Mara."

"The ring on the door—do you feel it? It'll be about waist high."

"Yes. Here it is. Stand back."

He pulled hard. At first the door resisted, then, slowly, it gave. Moonlight flooded the cellar.

Down the street to both sides there was the sound of furious activity. Nemti, risking a look, could see men running helter-skelter.

"What do I do now?" he asked.

"The temple," Mara said beside him. "We've got to get to the temple."

"How?" Nemti asked. "The streets are full of guardsmen."

"Over the wall," Onuris suggested. "Right over there, in the shadow between the two buildings. If you three can get there, I'll hand you up and over. On the far side is the Temple Quarter. You have to pass through a residential area first, but it'll be sparsely guarded. They'll have called in all the guards they can get to catch us over here."

"Good," Nemti said. "Now!"

He took Mara's hand again and set out across the wide avenue at a ferocious clip. When he got to the shaded space, he made a cradle of his hands. "Here," he offered. "Up you go."

Behind them he could hear the footsteps of Onuris and Thermutis. Down the street someone bellowed: "Look over there! It's them! It's them!"

"Up and over!" Onuris said. "I'll hold them off!"

"No, you won't!" said Nemti. "I'm not leaving without you."

"Well, if you're going to be that way . . ." He boosted Thermutis up and over the wall, then stepped back and made a running leap, grasping the top and pulling himself over just as a spent arrow, fired from some distance, fell short and clattered on the stones. Once on the far side they could hear the yelling behind them.

"Quick," Nemti said. "I don't know this part of town. Mara, you'll have to lead the way."

"Stay with me, now," she said.

Kicking off her sandals, she set out through the dirt streets. Nemti blinked at her agility, increased the pace, and found to his surprise that he could just barely keep up with her.

The four of them came to the end of the street and turned a corner into a new sector of the quarter just as the soldiers behind them came across the wall.

VI

On the far side of the stout oak door, the captive, pathetic king of Egypt cried out again. "No! Stop him! Cut him down! Don't let him get away! Guards! To me! To me!"

This much had, at least, a sort of coherence to it, insane though it might be. But from there the cries degenerated into wild bellowing, moaning, and in the end the pitiable and somehow contemptible mewings of a person unmanned by fear and loathing.

Nemaret, chief overseer and master of Amasis's sprawling country home, stared at the barred door and frowned. "How long has he been this way today?" he asked the maid.

"Three hours, sir. He had a bad dream and woke up in a cold sweat. He said he'd dreamed that he was back at Megiddo, supervising the slaughter of the whole Hai community. He was calling out for the killing of the women and children. 'Don't let any of them go,' he said. 'It's no good killing the snakes. You have to get their young as well.' Horrible, sir. How can men do that?"

"Just the facts, please. What did you do?"

"Why, I gave him the regular dosage, sir, just as you told me to. It was hard getting him to take it, though. He was afraid it would bring back the dreams."

"*Hmmm,*" Nemaret mused. "I'll have to consult with Amasis when he returns. Perhaps the dosage should be increased again. This isn't working as well as it ought to. He should be out like a candle flame right now, but just listen to him."

"I'd rather not, sir. If there were any way I could be reassigned to some other duty—"

"There, now, my child. I did have an idea for a better assignment. I was going to make you my own personal servant." He put one unwelcome hand on the girl's lower back. "It would pay much, much better than the present work does. But anyone assigned to my own rooms would have to be someone I could really depend upon, so it would be contingent upon your satisfactory performance of a less pleasant job, like the present one."

She sighed. It was a letdown. "I understand, sir. It's just that he's so strong, and when he grabs my arm in one of his spasms . . . well, look at my arm, sir. It's been six days, and the bruise hasn't gone away."

He caressed the arm familiarly. "A pity," he said in an oily voice. "You can't begin to imagine how deeply I regret there isn't anybody free to give this job to."

"Can't a man do it, sir?"

"I've tried that. I put the cook's apprentice on the job. He's quite strong and should have been able to handle things. But the king suddenly decided that the apprentice was Apophis, or the commander at the siege of Sharuhen. He gets really violent with a man there."

"I heard, sir. He broke the boy's arm for him. I'm just being unreasonable, sir, and I'm trying not to be. But I'm afraid of him."

"Just remember he's your king, your lord and master,

and that he's been very ill and we're trying to cure him. Be gentle with him. That usually works."

The shouting began again on the other side of the thick, barred door. "It's an ambush!" Kamose cried out. "We're surrounded! Bring up the chariots! Where is the cavalry? Archers! Archers! Where's my Third Troop?"

"I'll go in with you this time," Nemaret offered. "Perhaps together we can give him another dose of *shepenn*. Then when he's slipped off to sleep—"

"Is that safe, sir? This soon after the first one? My lord Amasis said every five or six hours. It's been three at best, sir."

"Don't worry your pretty little head over that, my child." His smile was chill and distant, and his hand caressed her waist. "I don't expect this to go on forever. My lord Amasis has . . . certain plans."

"Sir! You don't mean—"

"Never mind what I mean. If you keep your head about you and do as I say, you may be surprised at how little more of this you will have to put up with. If you can last this out and earn my confidence, you have quite a nice future ahead of you around this household."

She shuddered, and hated herself for it.

The magus Set-Nakht turned up at Neb-mertef's door precisely at the hour appointed. "Good to see you!" said his employer. "Has the news reached you yet?"

"No news, honored sir." He allowed himself to be shown into Neb-mertef's lavish palace apartment. "But I assume from the expression on your face that the news is not bad."

"Not bad!" Neb-mertef chuckled triumphantly. "It came to pass just as you predicted. It couldn't have been better." He paused for a heartbeat. "Well, yes, it could. The queen and Thermutis seem to have got away. They, and those two young men they've been playing around with."

"I don't understand, sir."

"Baliniri! He's dead!" Neb-mertef paced back and forth, his eyes focused on something far away. "Amasis had him poisoned. The maid left him alone with nothing to drink but a jar of poisoned wine. Like a fool he drank it."

"Ah! I suspected that might be the way. And was the rest as I told you, esteemed sir?"

"Precisely! It all came true, as you said, within the space of a single day! Amasis is all-powerful! Well, except for Kamose. But I wouldn't give *that*"—he made an obscene gesture, quick and contemptuous—"for Kamose's chances of living to another birthday."

The magus bowed his head in a gesture of affected modesty. "The stars do not lie, sir. Not to the man who knows the language they speak. Then I may take it, sir, that I am hired?"

Neb-mertef stopped; his eyes focused on the magus now. "Oh, yes. Continue to please me as you have done today, my friend, and your fortune is made."

Set-Nakht smiled. He looked around him very casually. "If you'll pardon a personal remark, sir, I admire your taste. These furnishings are superb. I see you have had little to do with the royal decorator."

"This?" Neb-mertef said. "Just a little place in the palace to put foot to earth, as they say. A mere hideaway, one I use when there isn't time to go home. I have a town house not a quarter of a league from here. You'll like things better there. I've given orders that if you please me, you're to be moved in there. You'll have a suite there, with servants of your own."

"Ah. So your requirements have been met, sir?"

"Yes. Yes, indeed. Why?"

"I . . . well, I had fancied something in the palace itself."

"I can arrange it quite easily. But you may not like it here as much as you think."

"Oh, I didn't mean to live here, sir. The suite you're having prepared for me at your home will do splendidly for that. There's the matter of status."

Neb-mertef's expression hardened. The magus suddenly realized he had gone too far. "Our understanding of one another may not be quite so complete as I had expected," he said harshly. "A public position for you does not figure in my plans. My use of your services is to be quite private, and your name is not to come to the attention of Amasis. I don't mind your having a place here, for it'll make you more accessible when I have need of you. But the others are not to know who

you are or what your function is. You're to be spoken of as an
assistant of mine. You will derive status from your association
with me. Do you understand?"

"I am at your disposal." The magus swallowed hard. "In
whatever guise and disposition you prefer."

"Good." There was frost on the voice. "See that you do
not forget."

When the door was at last barred, Si-Ptah turned back to
them. "You realize, Your Majesty," he said to Mara, "that
you can't stay here. The door will keep them out just so
long."

"I understand," Mara said. Her hand stole into Nemti's
and squeezed it; there seemed no reason for hiding things
anymore. Their lives were forfeit anyway. "All we need is
breathing space. I know your own position is precarious
now."

"I wish I could offer more. But we have no communication with the other temples. One of our couriers went out
two weeks ago to the delta temples, and he should have been
back already. I fear the worst. You realize that when Amasis
decided he was in a position to kill Baliniri and blame it on
you, it was a clear signal to us that our own position was
untenable."

"How long have we got?" Nemti asked.

"At most, three days."

"That settles it," Nemti said. "We've got to get away
immediately."

"Where?" Thermutis asked.

Onuris frowned. "I know what you're thinking," he said.
"It's too dangerous. Your kinswoman's home is the first place
they'd look."

"You're right," Mara said. "We have to find our way
across the river to Deir el-Bahari. But they'll be watching the
artisans' village. I know who will hide us long enough to let
us slip out into the desert along the path to the oases."

"Who?" Nemti asked.

Mara smiled. "Who are the most wretched people in
Deir el-Bahari? Whose hovels would be the last place in the
world anyone would expect to find the queen of Egypt?"

Nemti stared. "The Habiru?" But his question did not need an answer. "It might just work," he said.

"It has to," she said. "It's all we've got."

VII

In the past Neb-mertef had avoided going out into the city streets unescorted; a man of his great wealth was a natural target for robbery, kidnapping, or even assassination. But now, with the death of Baliniri and the assumption of complete power by Amasis—the one followed hard on the other, with brutal finality—all that had changed. While he retained the favor of Amasis, he was everywhere as safe as if he had bought and purchased the city and converted it all to his own uses.

The first thing he noticed now, during the afternoon of the day after Baliniri's death and the disappearances of the two women of the royal house, was the quiet order in the streets. This was widespread within the city, enforced by the massive number of soldiers now evident in the streets. Amasis, leaving only a token contingent in the main encampment of the Theban guard outside the city, had simply moved the entire unit within the city walls and given their commanders orders to enforce strictly the new rules he had issued for the conduct of citizen and visitor alike.

These were all aimed at control: control of traffic in the city streets, control of the distribution of goods, control of commerce between buyer and seller, and control of ideas and their communication. No gathering of more than three people in the city remained legal, and conversations held in the open air were monitored by every guardsman who wandered near. All of a sudden, the guardsmen, tough and hostile mercenaries fiercely loyal to Amasis alone, were everywhere.

Amasis had given the order: Any guardsmen whose suspicion had been aroused could enter any dwelling, search the premises, and carry off anything or anyone they thought merited special attention.

Since dawn these orders had been made public in many locations by the city criers, augmented by the ubiquitous guards in their heavily accented voices, and were scheduled to be announced all day. At the end of that time all who lived or worked within the city would be expected to have heard the rules, to have memorized them, and to be responsible for the keeping of them.

It was obvious to Neb-mertef, among others, that the orders had not sprung full-blown from anyone's mind in one day. The whole plan had been in place, waiting to be executed, for quite some time. It had only remained for Baliniri, the last bastion of real power standing in Amasis's way, to fall into the hands of his enemies.

All this Neb-mertef contemplated with a wry, appreciative smile as he strolled leisurely through the temple quarter, chuckling softly to himself as one patrol after another of brutal-looking, alien soldiers marched through the streets.

It was all going to work out so perfectly.

He did not fear the show of force; he welcomed it. The better developed the package of power constructed by Amasis in the weeks and months to come, the better organized would be the government Neb-mertef would simply take over, transferring Amasis's unlimited power into his own hands when the time came for Amasis's days of trial.

He was no longer in any doubt about the magus's predictive powers—not after yesterday. Now, secure in the possession of Set-Nakht's exclusive loyalty, he had only to wait, observe, and bide his time until the promised nemesis, whatever it might turn out to be, confounded Amasis's plans for the permanent consolidation of his power.

He was sure that Amasis was on a collision course with a dark destiny. From the moment he had seen Set-Nahkt's first prognostications confirmed, he had begun to feel the aura, the air, of doom that lay on the foreign usurper. Why had he never noticed it before? Amasis had always seemed so invulnerable. Now, knowing what he knew, he could not doubt the witness of his senses. Amasis had trouble coming.

But of what kind? he asked himself now. What—or

who—would be the agency that would nullify the steady rise to the pinnacle of Egyptian society? He had no idea. The magus remained vague on this. He had only an approximate date. This was in the stars, he said, and he would refine this as the days went by, supplementing the message of the stars with the results of other auguries drawn from many cultures. And only he, Neb-mertef, would know that as the months advanced in their orderly procession toward the fateful date, Amasis would be moving toward a destiny for which he was unprepared. The thought gave him great satisfaction, causing him to enjoy more fully the sight of the frightened people who had come to buy produce and other provender at a half-empty market.

He climbed the low stairway on the far side of the marketplace and stood alone for a moment on the upper-level esplanade, looking down on the two adjacent quarters of the city on either side.

His! Soon it was to be all his!

And if a man had Thebes, he had Egypt now that the Shepherds were gone. There was no doubt about this. Not even the cult would stand in his way. He was, after all, a high enough ranking official in the craft of the Great Mother to be able to assume control of it . . . even though he did not truly believe in the cult's mumbo jumbo. It had simply been expedient to join it early, and rising through the various levels of the hierarchy had paid off.

Wait, he thought now. *How many men are between me and Amasis? How many outrank me in the service of the Great Mother in Egypt? Two? No, three.*

He smiled. It was time for things to start happening to these adepts, removing them from his path but in the most delicate way.

He knew that Yalu had already been eliminated, by the soldiers who had escaped with the queen. Selket had died from the head wound he had inflicted upon her when he pushed her against the wall yesterday. She had barely lasted the night. And a good thing too: Both she and Yalu had had something on him. Now there was no one left who knew anything about him that could conceivably place him in danger. Except the magus Set-Nakht himself.

Now there was a disturbing thought! He would have to find some infallible way of binding the magus to him—by greed or fear, most likely. And he would have to create diversions to keep Amasis from noticing Set-Nakht. The promise of that palace apartment would have to be broken. It was too risky. He would convert that promise to another, perhaps one involving great riches.

Now that he thought about it, even the idea of keeping the magus with him in the city was too risky. The country home would be far better. Keep him there under guard, the way Amasis was keeping Kamose, with no communication with the outside world.

But the trick was how to keep this from seeming like imprisonment . . . how to keep the man happy where he was, inside the compound of the great country estate, having no commerce with the world of the city?

Hmmm . . . There was that rumor about the magus having a taste for sexual delights involving his own sex. Yes, there was potential in that, but how? Who? *Let's see . . . there's that fellow who used to be a soldier now running a brothel in the city. The one into whose hands that idiot Osorkon had had the misfortune to fall, with such disastrous results.*

This was not a bad idea. The man, for a fee, would surely procure him a virtually unlimited list of willing partners for the magus.

Of course there was no question of those partners ever being allowed back out of the compound once the magus had tired of them! They would have too much damning information. No, they had to be expendable. He would have to create a mechanism for their disposal. And there had to be an understanding about this with the brothel owner who did the procuring. And, of course, some means for keeping the brothel owner's mouth shut, as well. That was the trouble with these complicated schemes. There was always the possibility of a leak. But silence was, after all, negotiable. There were blackmail, threats, assassination, and bribery. These were the rungs of the ladder up which he would rise in the months to come.

And the gods protect anyone who got in his way!

*   *   *

At the fruit vendor's stand, Onuris and Nemti took note of the expensively dressed man standing at the top of the stairs. Nemti pulled his Bedouin headdress close around his face and turned to his companion. "Who do you suppose he is?" he asked. Then, answering his own question, he said, "Someone close to Amasis, that's a sure thing. Look at the fearlessness on his face, the contempt with which he views the people in the bazaar."

"All this in less than a day," Onuris said, scowling. "It's remarkable how complete the takeover has been—as if it had been meticulously planned over a long time."

Nemti snorted. "You can bet it has been."

"The greengrocer said there were half a dozen arrests this morning, and other people were beaten up by the guards. The word gets around fast."

Nemti looked around him; another detachment of guardsmen were poking about in the corner of the square. "Let's move on. I don't think I want to have to answer any questions just now."

Trying to look as nonchalant as possible, the two moved slowly through the market and exited through the other side. Once in the street beyond, Nemti looked around and cursed softly under his breath. "Damn! I should have taken the other way. Now we've got to thread our way through the most thickly populated part of town."

"That might be just the thing we want," Onuris remarked. "We can get lost in a crowd." Nevertheless, he muttered angrily as they passed down a side alley, "You know, we're going to have a terrible time getting the women out of the temple complex and across the river. Even at night it's going to be a real problem."

A dead donkey lay across their path. The flies were beginning to gather. Nemti stepped across its corpse and wrinkled his nose in disgust. Then he stopped abruptly. "Maybe not," he said, smiling. "I think I have an idea."

VIII

Two days after assuming power, Amasis, surrounded by burly guardsmen and petty officials, presented himself at the great gate of the Temple of Amon. By custom dating back from the earliest days, he was barred from entering, and the servant in charge of the entrance, bowing and observing all necessary secular protocol, bolted the door in Amasis's face before going inside to consult Si-Ptah.

"My lord," the servant said, "the lord Amasis requests permission to enter."

The priest smiled sardonically. "What a pleasure it would be to tell him to await our pleasure on the bottom of the Nile with the crocodiles. But we will settle for making him wait." He glanced at the sundial in the middle of the atriumlike inner patio, then laid his finger on its surface. "We will give him an answer when the sun's shadow is here."

"Sir, is that wise? That's a long time to make a man like Amasis wait—even for the pleasure of the high priest of Amon."

"I know. And I'm sure he'll find his way in here sooner anyhow. I just want to make it a bit unpleasant for him. He'll lose face this way, and in front of that horde of hangers-on he always brings around with him these days! Well, let him cool his heels for a while."

The servant gulped, then said, "Very well, sir. Oh, the procession is ready to go. It awaits your blessing."

"They're lined up in the courtyard, then? Is it large enough, do you think? The train, the mourners? . . ."

"I think so, sir. Shall I tell them you're coming?"

Si-Ptah shrugged. "Let them wait too. I have a thought. Now listen to this. . . ."

Amasis, standing in the warm sun, fretted and cursed. Nearly an hour had passed, and still the servant had not returned with permission to enter the temple.

"There now, my lord," Neb-mertef soothed, using the formal mode of address he had previously shunned. Now that he knew he would eventually supplant Amasis, he could afford to be courteous. "You know what a fuss there would be if we forced a confrontation with the priests."

"Indeed." Amasis's voice quivered. His eyes glittered with rage as he glared at the great gate before him. "I'll give it another minute or two, but that's all."

There was a noise inside. Slowly and amid much creaking the bolt withdrew on the far side of the great door. And even more slowly, the great door swung wide.

Si-Ptah stood framed in the gateway, bowing deferentially. Behind him a full two dozen priests—two more men than in Amasis's party—armed with stout bows whose shafts were already nocked, stood eyeing the visitors.

"Good morning," Si-Ptah offered politely. "And how may we serve the good right arm of the king?"

"Open your doors," Amasis snarled. "I have reason to believe you harbor dangerous fugitives."

Si-Ptah's eyebrows shot up, and his face reflected total innocence. "Fugitives? Surely you are misinformed, my esteemed friend. The Temple of Amon gives sanctuary to no evildoer. Only the pure in heart may—"

"Enough!" Amasis commanded. "You know perfectly well whom I seek. The women!" Saying the names of the fugitives would have been premature. The palace coup had yet to be acknowledged formally as the usurpation it was.

"Women? No women are allowed in the Temple of Amon!"

"I mean inside the compound. I know women aren't allowed in the temple proper, confound it. But the outer quarters of the compound aren't consecrated in the same way. Curse you, get out of the way. Let me in, or so help me, I'll—"

"My lord honors us with a great knowledge of the customs of our national religion, which he abstains from observing." Si-Ptah's tone was so polite that Neb-mertef suppressed a chuckle only with the greatest difficulty. And yet the high priest managed to convey with infinite delicacy his all-encompassing contempt. The word *heathen* had hung in the air unspoken, a deadly insult that both parties understood totally.

"Well," Amasis said, "let me in. Get out of my way."

Behind Si-Ptah the priestly archers aimed their weapons.

"It would appear," Si-Ptah went on, "that my lord's prodigious memory has yet to inform him that in five hundred years no secular person has ever entered even the courtyard of the temple *uninvited*. I am sure the memory of this fact will come to my lord. I'll wait."

"Look, you, the old rules are over. I'm coming in—"

Behind Si-Ptah the archers drew their bowstrings all the way back until only the bronze-tipped heads showed on this side of the belly of the bow.

"Surely my lord's memory has returned by now," Si-Ptah suggested.

He was about to continue when there came such a terrible din behind him, in the open court, that Amasis and his men were clearly startled. Drums, blaring horns, shawms whining the wailing notes of a dirge, and the uplifted voices of many people howling with grief!

"What the—" Amasis began.

But even as he said this, he stepped back. The archers relaxed the tension on their bows and moved back several paces while Si-Ptah turned and made ritualized signs with his hands, blessing the funeral procession that began to move slowly through the great gate.

"What's this?" Amasis bellowed over the howling and wailing of the family, servants, and professional mourners. "Get them out of here!"

"I can't do that, my lord. Even I am enjoined from disturbing the orderly procession of a departed soul to the Netherworld." He lowered his voice. "Besides, the deceased was of a noble family that wields great power in the provinces and contributes great sums annually to the court as well as to the temple."

He watched as slaves bearing gifts and funeral offerings moved past them, out the gateway and down the long avenue, carrying cakes, flowers, jars of wine and water, and vials of perfume. One pulled a calf with a rope around its neck for sacrifice. Yet another held up three large birds in a cage on a light saddle; these, too, would be sacrificed.

"As you can see, sir," Si-Ptah continued calmly, "this is the funeral parade of no ordinary citizen." He waved a hand to make his point. A second group carried furniture, flagons for libations, the canopic jars, masks, weapons, scepters, batons of command, collars, faience scarabs on cushions, and wooden statues of hawks. After a noisy group of mourners whose dissonant caterwauling split the air in a hideous cacophony, more slaves flitted by, these observing the fixed rituals: flicking droplets of milk on the ground for sacrifice and sprinkling the crowd with scented water from a silver spoon. And now the catafalque itself appeared, quite large, and mounted upon a sledge drawn by oxen and more slaves. To right and left the family members, weeping and moaning, flanked the ornate coffin, gesturing extravagantly and saying, "To the West! To the West! Our lord has gone to the West!"

Si-Ptah looked Amasis directly in the eyes. He shrugged indulgently. "Calculate, sir," he said, "the cost of such a procession and the wealth of the family paying for it. There has not been such a procession to the Necropolis since the death of King Sekenenre. Shall I tell them that, upon your instructions, I must impede the progress of their dear departed to the glorious Netherworld? Surely, sir—"

"Damn your insolence," Amasis muttered. "I'll be back here tomorrow, and you'd better be prepared to admit me. Me and half the guard of Thebes."

"Indeed, sir. And will they draw their swords on the Temple of Amon and its priests? I know your lordship has imported soldiers not of our faith, but there still remains a sizable cadre who maintain some observance of our religious customs. Will these fight their priests? Will they allow their fellows to fight them?"

Amasis was about to answer when Neb-mertef pulled discreetly at his sleeve.' "Discretion," he advised.

Amasis glared at him but finally yielded. "Be warned," he said in a lowered voice. "If I do find out that you're protecting the women . . ."

He let the unfinished threat hang in the air and turned to his retinue. "Come along," he said. "I have business at court."

Si-Ptah, a small and unforgiving smile on his face, watched them go. Then he turned to his servant. "Behold the value of planning ahead. Because everything was so meticulously organized in advance, we were able to slip precisely what my lord Amasis was looking for under his nose."

"I was holding my breath the whole time," confessed the servant, indulging in a low chuckle. "Imagine if he'd decided to stop the procession and look into the sarcophagus."

"Not a chance, my friend," Si-Ptah replied with a smile. "I had him concentrating on the lavish appointments of the procession. Wave money in front of a greedy person, and his attention will be fixed on it. Amasis never gave the sarcophagus a passing thought." He frowned. "The one I'm worried about is that ambitious bastard behind him—Neb-mertef. He's got so much money, he isn't awed by it anymore. I caught him eyeing me and not the procession, hoping to find a secret in my face. He wasn't convinced, I don't think."

"At least our guests are off and away, sir. That's quite an achievement, given the concentration of soldiers in the city."

"True," Si-Ptah agreed. "They're out of our hands and off our consciences, to be sure. But they're not safe yet. There's the river to span, then sneaking away from the procession. Worse is the desert to cross. Any number of things could go wrong. Let us pray for them, my friend. And for ourselves and Egypt while we're at it. These are perilous times. Perilous times indeed."

As Amasis's party wended its way through the city streets, Neb-mertef worked constantly to keep the smile off his face. He walked at some distance behind Amasis, the better to conceal his unseemly mirth.

How could the fool not have noticed? How could he have failed to see? It was quite ridiculous how they had managed to dupe Amasis.

Neb-mertef considered: Someone who wanted to escape Thebes and Amasis's wrath could not leave by boat. Patrols up and down the Nile would apprehend anyone. Going east would be suicidal. No, the only way out would be across the desert, to the oases where Mara had powerful friends who were not afraid of Amasis or the Egyptian army. If the fugitives could get as far as the domain of the Desert Legion, they were home free.

That meant crossing the river. But how could four people get past Amasis's board-and-search patrols? There was only one way: to go with a funeral party to the great Necropolis at Deir el-Bahari.

Neb-mertef smiled openly now. He had even recognized one of the two soldiers in the contingent of hired mourners. No doubt the two women were among the "family" or were inside the large catafalque. (The gods alone knew where the real mummy of the dead was, if that was the case!)

But had any of this penetrated Amasis's anger-beclouded mind? And was he, Neb-mertef, going to tell him?

He almost laughed aloud. Any enemy who escaped Amasis's grasp, the better to regroup and fight again, was a potential ally, however unwitting, of Neb-mertef's own campaign to replace Amasis. Let the queen and princess slip through his nets! Let the soldiers come back to destroy him! The more the merrier, and the faster he, Neb-mertef, would move into position for the great coup that lay ahead!

CHAPTER SEVEN

The Second Cataract

I

There came a time when the desert flanking the Nile vanished behind tall cliffs of rocks, and the river narrowed. Sail gave way once and for all to the oar. When Moses arose this day, the big sail that had brought them so far had already been taken down by the sailors, rolled in a huge ball, and placed atop the deckhouse. The main yard was situated like a ridgepole above his head, and the oars were lashed twelve on a side. On the lower deck, every alternate plank formed seats for the oarsmen.

These were the soldiers of his command. Cursing and grumbling, they raised oars at the hortator's command and awaited the first beat of his deep-voiced drum.

Seth came on deck just as Geb bellowed out the order to the hortator to begin. He smiled at Moses and joined him at the starboard rail as the first of the slow, regular beats of the drum boomed out.

"Unless I've guessed wrong," Moses said, "we must be getting close. I'd say less than a day away."

"You're right," Seth responded. "Today we'll arrive within sight of the first of the Second Cataract forts. And we have been within the domain of the army of Nubia since late yesterday."

"Yesterday?" Moses said, looking to right and left. "Then how have we not come under attack yet?"

Seth smiled. "Why should the Nubian army alert us to danger? They'll let us continue blithely past the first forts, so we'll think them unoccupied. They'll want us to feel overconfident and sail right past Buhen and Dorginarti. The *real* trouble comes after we negotiate the first stretch of dangerous water just past the Rock of Abusir. We'll have to drag the boats up the path beside Mirgissa. It will take every man we've got just to haul a boat up the ramp one handspan at a time, and we'll be unprotected while we do this—our men will have laid down their arms for the heavy labor. Then, when we're at the roughest and most arduous point in our portage—" He finished by drawing one hand across his throat in an eloquent and ominous gesture.

"But what shall we do?" Moses asked. "If they're drawing us into a trap, how do we avoid being ambushed and slaughtered?"

Seth's smile was wickedly conspiratorial as he drew out the rolled papyrus he had held at his side until now. He spread it on the gunwale and held one end of the map with one hand and pointed with the other. "Help me hold this open, will you? Here we are. All this"—he indicated the area above Wadi Halfa with a finger—"is the Second Cataract. It's more of the same thing we experienced at the First, only worse—hundreds of channels, hundreds of islands, hundreds of snags, hundreds of places where a boat can get herself broken up on the rocks or ambushed by some of those jolly fellows who have been watching us from the rocks since yesterday."

"Where?" Moses asked quickly. "I haven't seen anyone."

"That's because you haven't known what to look for. Don't worry. You'll learn fast; you'll have to. See that speck atop the tall pillar? That's a Nubian. There's another across the channel on the other side."

"Gods!"

"My guess is that we're going to be first attacked at Mirgissa. Oh, don't worry. If we're ready for them, they won't do us much harm. They don't have any plans to wipe us out, they just want to break our resolve and unnerve us. They're counting on us to be perhaps a little less organized than we actually are. They don't know who your commanders are. Khafre and Geb are two most resourceful and experienced men."

"I have great confidence in them," Moses agreed. "They have also the advantage of knowing this country."

"And," Seth added, grinning, "the Nubians don't know *I'm* here, and I am very familiar with this part of the river. I came up this way for . . . well, for reasons of my own some time back. I studied everything—the forts, the rapids . . . Now, they'll hit us here, the most dangerous place on the river, another thirty miles upstream. Between Mirgissa and the straits they'll figure we'll be nervous and jumpy, worrying about what lies behind every rock. But let me tell you, my young friend: When Sesostris III picked a site for the Semna forts, he knew what he was up to. He was a splendid strategist."

"Semna? That's down here, right? Look how the Nile narrows at the point! Is that scale accurate?"

"It is actually worse than that. The Egyptians built up the sides of the strait to dam up the Nile, then totally restricted shipping. Last, they constructed the largest, highest-walled, most impenetrable fortress ever built."

"Impenetrable? But Akhilleus and Ebana and the Black Wind took it a generation ago."

"True," Seth agreed, obviously pleased that Moses knew his history. "But only by subterfuge. It could not have been taken any other way."

"But if it's impenetrable, how can we—?"

Now Seth's smile was that of a fat and contented cat. "I specialize in the impenetrable, my boy. Trust me."

For a long time the hills to either side had been yellow sandstone, made of the fine, powdered sand from the desert beyond. The expedition had suffered through the windblown sand, which caked in their hair, got in their eyes, and added a thin film of dust over their minimal soldiers' meals. With this plague had come another: flies—hateful and ubiquitous, too thick to be driven away.

But now the scenery abruptly changed. On the western bank there appeared a fringe of volcanic mountains, as much alike as if they had been man-made. They were divided one from the other by a series of perfectly uniform sand drifts, and each rounded top was crowned with a layer of purplish-black stones, tinged here and there with patches of dull red. Some were as small as currants, others as large as loaves of flat bread. Seth took time off to climb the hills and retrieve a pocketful during a brief halt as the men cleared a passage of an underwater snag.

"See?" Seth said, holding one out to Moses as the boats once again began to move through the now-cleared channel. "At one time these mountains belched forth these rocks. Don't ask me how; it'll take all day to explain. Suffice it to say that it's a common enough occurrence a thousand leagues into the heart of the country from which the Nile sprang."

"You've gone there?" Moses gasped. "To Akhilleus's homeland?"

"Everywhere but there," Seth revealed. "There was a quest that engaged my attention." His face darkened with sudden sadness, as if a cloud had drifted overhead; but now he forced himself to continue. "I may go back. There is someone—some*thing* I have to find. On the way I learned of portents, clues. . . ." He sighed, and his shoulders slumped. Then he once more drove the mood from his mind. "Never mind. I will get to the Mountains of Fire someday. Look up ahead. See the big island dividing the river into two channels? Now look beyond that, on the banks, where the hills change their shape. Since they're no longer regular, like the ones we've been cutting our way through, we can assume that something awesome has happened here. The valley of the Nile has not always been as it is now. Strange and wondrous events have been seen here. But by the eyes of what men? My feeling is that all this happened so far in the past that we cannot imagine it. Before the pyramids. Before the first kings."

As their boat moved past the odd mountains, they did indeed change in shape if not in color. They all tapered toward the top, but one was four-sided like a pyramid; a second was scooped out in tiers of arches, while a third was crowned with a rude cairn of piled stones. Moses pointed. "Did men put those atop the cone?"

Seth shook his head. "'I doubt it, however strange that may seem. The stones look small from here, but they are too large for any ten men to lift, much less to bear to the top of a steep hill. But look. What else do you see?"

"There's a man atop it! You're right. Look at the scale! That rock he's hiding behind—"

"Right. Keep an eye open for these things. I took quite a chance climbing the hill back there. There was a Nubian not fifty paces from me at one point."

Shocked, Moses turned and looked at Seth.

"I knew he wouldn't kill me. That would only serve to alert the command and make it impossible for them to ambush us in the straits around Mirgissa."

Now the men shipped the oars as the trading post at Wadi Halfa loomed on the right bank. Here they stopped to buy provisions under palms and among the skeletons of foundered boats rotting at the water's edge. Seth went ashore for a short time and came back with news.

"I talked with one of the local chieftains," he reported to Moses as the sailors cast off and pulled anchor. "They aren't any happier with the Nubian invasion than we are. He warned me of the Mirgissa portage. I may as well talk with Khafre about it now." He went away inside the tall deckhouse.

Alone, Moses leaned on the starboard rail and watched the passing cliffs. The oars were out again, and bit by bit the expedition entered the Second Cataract proper.

After a time Geb joined him. "Look, sir. Buhen coming up on the western bank and not a soul to be found. Strange, isn't it? I mean, not only that the fort should be empty and undefended, but that there should be nobody guarding the little town at the foot of the fortress walls."

Moses realized he was being tested. "Does the village outside the walls have special significance?"

Geb smiled. "Oh, yes, sir. It's a great copper-smelting center—rich deposits of copper can be found near here. But nobody to guard it. Odd, don't you think? You'd expect the place to be crawling with soldiers, making sure we don't set up our own forges here."

Moses understood. "So the fact that the place is untended is significant. They want us to think they're nowhere near this far downriver. That way they can maneuver us into position for the coup they intend at Mirgissa."

Geb beamed. "Right you are, sir! I'm convinced Seth's assessment is correct."

"So am I," Moses agreed. "So what are we going to do?"

"Watch, sir. We've got too many boats with us for the work at hand. We're going to stop at Dorginarti, just past Buhen—I'd stake my life on its being unoccupied, too—and reorganize. We're going to leave one of the boats there, to simplify the portage. But when we do, we're going to let one of the detachments . . . well, *detach* itself, as inconspicuously as possible. When we reboard we'll be that many men light."

Moses grinned. "And that detachment will go by land and join us at Mirgissa." He stopped. "But what's to stop the Nubians from signaling ahead and warning their men?"

"Why, the very configuration of the river in the first stages of the cataract, sir. The cliffs tower right over the river, so the Nubians can signal at such distances only by smoke. And they can't do that without our seeing the smoke columns." He chuckled and wiggled his eyebrows. "Which won't stop there being columns of smoke anyhow, sir!"

"We'll send our own!" Moses said, laughing. "With false information! It's perfect!"

"Beg to differ, sir," Geb said seriously. "In war nothing's perfect. But it's hard to improve upon, given the circumstances." He shook his head slowly back and forth in silent admiration. "Seth is a marvel. I used to wonder how our forefathers conquered the world back in the days of the Sesostrises and Amenemhets. Maybe there were more people like Seth back then!"

II

As the boats dropped anchor off Dorginarti, Seth rejoined Moses and Geb. "Khafre can use you just now," he told Geb. "He'll explain what we've decided to do." He looked Geb in the eyes and smiled. "Why do I get the idea that you've already figured it out?"

"Because I have, sir," Geb answered. "I'm beginning to know a part of your mind—the part I can understand, I mean. And it's my business to know my commander's." He saluted, a small smile lingering on his lips, and went away.

"Well?" Seth inquired. "Was he right?"

Moses reported Geb's prediction.

"Not bad," Seth said, nodding. "Actually we're going to spend the night at Dorginarti and combine vessels. The detachment will slip away in the darkness. Unless the Nubians take a body count from the heights—and I'm betting on nobody doing that—it's unlikely that they'll notice we're a squad or two shy the next morning when we get back under way, since there'll be only one fewer boat, and the few spare men will be on the shore getting the boats ready for the portage."

Moses looked worried. "Is the portage absolutely necessary?"

"Oh, yes. Yes, indeed. Roughest section of the whole river coming up."

"But it seems impossible that we'd be able to get ships of this size upstream, over land. I can't imagine it."

Seth grinned, and his face looked twenty years younger. "The Nile has a thousand surprises," he said mysteriously, wiggling his fingers before Moses's eyes. "I doubt that I will ever learn everything there is to know about this great river. But I *do* know how to get the boats past Mirgissa, if I can get the Nubians to let us alone while I do it. You'll see."

"And do you think this ruse of yours will get them to let us alone?"

"Perhaps. Unless I've underestimated the force they intend to throw at us. I don't think the main force will be here."

"What might a main force consist of up here?"

Seth looked thoughtful for a moment. "Here's a chance to continue your education. Come with me. Dorginarti appears to be deserted. Let's explore it. You need to know what a river fort looks like from the enemy's side."

Moses stared. "You mean we're going *inside*? Isn't that dangerous? Do you think Khafre will let us without a detachment of soldiers?"

"Oh, come along, my boy. What Khafre doesn't know won't hurt him. You don't want a lot of soldiers tagging along. You're armed. So am I."

"But he's charged with our safety, Seth. Is it fair to him for us to take off like this without informing him?"

Seth's smile was replaced by a serious look. He put one fatherly hand on Moses's shoulder and said, "You've a good heart, which one seldom finds in a man destined to be a leader. It does you great credit to think of Khafre's reputation and career. But if something happens to us, with whom is Khafre going to get in trouble? Who will discipline him? He is supreme military commander here. We are all there is. There is no 'Egypt' anymore, where we're concerned. By now Baliniri will probably be dead, and quite possibly the king and queen and half the court. I would wager that the coup has already taken place, and Amasis is all-powerful. And is he 'Egypt'? Is he someone to whom we are subordinate?" He shook his head. "No. You're the nominal head of the entire expedition and answerable to no one left in the world. Khafre answers to you, not you to Amasis. Which," he added soberly, "is not to say that I want to see you stop consulting him and deferring to his military judgment. For quite some time you will need to rely heavily upon his expertise, and even when you have stopped needing to do so, it would be wise always to honor his wisdom and valor by treating him as a valued counselor."

Moses paled at the mention that Baliniri might be dead. If that was true, how would his mother the princess be faring? "I will do as you say," he said. "But you're a civilian. To whom are you answerable?"

Seth clapped him on the shoulder in a rough gesture of

affection. "The only men to whom I ever thought myself
answerable died far, far to the north many years ago: My
king, Samsi-ditana of Babylon, and my master, Marduk-nasir
of the order of the Chalybians, both bound me to them by
love and respect. And although I am a civilian on a military
expedition, consider me a friend, an adviser, a boon companion if you will, as the wise Criton was to me." There was a
note of inconsolable sadness in his voice as he added, "I will
try to be to you as Criton always was to . . ." But here he
swallowed hard and could not finish the sentence.

Not only was the towering fortress apparently empty,
high on its steep bluff above the river, but its great gate was
open and undefended. Rearing high above Seth's and Moses's
heads, it was an impressive sight. The gate itself was dwarfed
only by the long-fallen Ishtar Gate of Babylon, and it framed
a narrow opening along which they had to walk, totally vulnerable to any bowmen who might have been manning the
crenellated walls above. They entered across an open drawbridge after stopping to peek through the narrow windows in
the gate at the Nile-fed moat below the roadbed.

Moses walked with one hand on his sword, looking cautiously right and left. But Seth seemed unperturbed by any
possibility of danger and ambled along as if through a bazaar
in the safest city in Egypt.

Well, Moses thought as he kept a wary eye on the
interior, *apparently one of us will have to watch for two.*

It was a sort of town they were walking through, one
with paved arterial roads that divided the village into three
equal parts. Down the center of each street ran a stone drain.
Seth pointed at this. "As you can see, they have more rain
here in season than we're used to. These are for runoff.
Imagine an Egyptian town needing drains."

To one side and the other all the appurtenances of city
life presented themselves: a temple, homes, barracks, work-
shops, forges—here Seth stopped to inspect the smelting
furnaces and pronounced them fit only for copper—and storerooms. "Guess," Seth challenged, "how many fighting men
this place would support?"

Moses considered. He started to say something, then stopped himself. "Why did you stop?" Seth asked.

"I was about to say a larger number, but then I settled for a smaller one. Two thousand? Under arms?"

Seth beamed. "That's very good! You continue to delight me. Come: We'll go up on the wall and look over the defenses."

They climbed the wall by an interior staircase, narrow and steep. "How thick are the walls?" Seth continued. "And how high?"

"Oh . . . thirty feet perhaps."

Seth nodded. "And how thick?"

"I can't say until we're on top."

"Would you believe fifteen feet at the thickest point?"

"No!"

"Yes! I was just doing some mental calculations as we came up the stairs. There'd be something like ten million bricks in this. Here we are—the top at last. What do you see?"

"Gods! How could anyone ever take this fort? *Nobody* could come up this wall. Look how the loopholes work: One archer could command a field of fire of great breadth without exposing himself to hostile fire. And even if he ran out of arrows and any survivors crossed the moat safely, they'd have to scale the scarp first, then make it up the brick wall."

"Yes. There'd be men tending fires here, pouring boiling liquids on anyone who dared to try to scale the wall. As an attacker how would you handle all this?"

Moses's eyes were large and round. "I—I have no idea. Some sort of canopy or shield to protect my men from attack from above?"

"Very, very good! That is one option, but not the one taken by Ebana when her Black Wind took the fortress, losing not a single warrior in the process. The women, all black, all naked, waited for a dark night and climbed the walls. The defenders could not see them until the moment they came across the wall. By then it was too late."

"We can't do that. We don't have the advantage of dark skins. Unless we starved them out, I can't imagine how we would ever be able to take this place."

"A siege is virtually the only infallible method," Seth agreed. "But mind you, these places were planned for self-sufficiency. There are wells beneath the city streets, so one need never run out of water, and I'll wager there's enough food in those storerooms and warehouses for the normal complement of this place to last the better part of a year."

Moses's face bore a woebegone expression.

"There is another way," Seth consoled. "The best one of all. But I'm not going to tell you what it is. Tell me when *you* have thought of it."

Moses lost himself in thought, walking through a doorway that led through the upper projection of the great gate. His hand was not even near his sword when a black warrior suddenly lunged at him from out of the darkness in the long, shaded corridor. The warrior's long spear was aimed at Moses's heart.

Moses instinctively grabbed the shaft and deflected it just before it would have skewered him like a ripe fruit. He backed into the light, pulling hard on the spear as he emerged from the dark hallway, dragging the soldier with him, but then he lost his footing and fell backwards heavily as his opponent deliberately let go of the spear. The Nubian unsheathed the sword at his belt and aimed a long, swooping stroke at Moses with its razor-sharp blade. Moses rolled swiftly to one side, trying to get his legs underneath him, trying at the same time to liberate his own sword from its suddenly jammed scabbard.

The Nubian attacked and stumbled. Standing before him was Seth, blocking his path. "Seth!" Moses yelled. "No! Get out of the way! I'll handle him!"

Seth stood, hands empty, arms crossed over his chest, looking at the Nubian. He said something that must have been insulting in the Nubian tongue. The Nubian attacked and stabbed at a place a full arm's length to Seth's right!

"I'm over here!" Seth pointed out calmly. And this time the Nubian aimed a blow at a place equally far from Seth's left side!

Seth smiled coldly. He still had not moved to defend himself.

Moses scrambled clumsily to his feet and drew his sword, but the Nubian let out a horrible scream, dropped his sword, and began clawing at his body. With one last horrible cry of agony, he jumped to the top of the wall and, still pawing his body desperately, leapt to his death.

After a moment's shocked silence, Moses climbed to the top of the battlement and looked down. The Nubian had not leapt out far enough to reach the moat, and his broken body lay sprawled unnaturally, like a child's abandoned doll, on the rocks below. Moses turned and looked at Seth, knowing that it would be a long time before he would forget the red blood that coated the rocks and the horrible wound a projecting rock had made in the dead man's back.

III

When Moses finally stepped down from the wall, Seth was busily inspecting the entrance to the passage from which the Nubian had emerged. He had drawn his sword. Moses stared, openmouthed, slowly shaking his head back and forth. The Nubian's behavior just prior to his suicide—and the suicide itself—had been the strangest, most inexplicable episode he had ever witnessed.

"Uh, Seth," he ventured. "Seth, how did you do that?" Seth did not answer. He poked inside the opening with his weapon.

"You don't want to take too many chances in a place like this. You never know when one of these fellows is going to be hiding somewhere, just waiting for you to stick your nose in." He disappeared inside the passage, and his voice echoed. "But it looks as though he was the only one." He came back out into the light, returning his sword to its scabbard. "Time to get back, I'd say. It's going to be almost dark before we've made it back to the boats."

Moses, fists on hips, stood staring at him without budging. "You're not going to tell me, are you?" he said, exasperated.

"Come on. We'll talk as we go." He stepped down onto the steep staircase and motioned to Moses to join him.

Moses rolled his eyes and moved forward. "You looked at him—just *looked* at him—and drove him over the wall. How could you do something like that?"

"Weak minds are easily influenced," Seth answered matter-of-factly. "If he'd had any sense he would have avoided my eyes."

"How could you do something like that with just your eyes? Are you a wizard or something, who can get inside a man's mind? I've heard of that, although frankly, I never believed it. Baliniri told me once of a wonderful dwarf he'd known named Tchabu, who could read men's minds and see into the future. But I'd always thought he was kidding me."

"Tchabu was real. He probably is still alive. I haven't heard from Tchabu in quite some time, but if he had died, I think Baliniri would have mentioned it. Yes, he could do marvelous things." They reached the bottom of the staircase, their hands on their swords as they retraced their steps through the city streets.

"And you?" Moses asked.

Seth smiled. "I hate to disappoint you, but alas, I cannot, although such talents do run in my family. I happen to be one member of the family who inherited none of this ability at all. But Teti and her twin brother, Ketan, could feel each other's pain and fear. She even felt his death. This brought on a series of visions, in which she claimed to have seen her own future, to the moment of her own death." He paused a moment. "And beyond."

"Beyond? How can that be?"

"I have no idea." They crossed the moat, still warily watching the alcoves beside them and the battlements high above. Finally the men emerged into the fading sunlight. "Having foreknowledge of her death, she viewed the rest of her brief life with equanimity. Reportedly, she died at peace with herself and the world. This, mind you, despite the fact that she died in childbirth, of the plague."

"This is all beyond me," Moses admitted. "But why do I

get the feeling that you're telling me this to distract me from asking questions about that stunt you performed atop the fortress wall?"

Seth laughed low in his throat. "You're sharp, but not sharp enough. I've already posed you one question you haven't been able to answer. That was the one about what is the best way to breach an unbreachable wall and capture an impregnable fort. Have you an answer for that one yet?"

"No, but I'm working on it."

"As to my 'stunt,' as you so kindly phrased it," Seth continued, leading him off onto a path that ran alongside the river, "see if you can dredge up a more complete memory of the event. You have all but one of the pieces to put the puzzle together."

"I don't understand."

"Of course you don't. You won't understand until you remember. Concentrate, one step at a time, now."

Moses frowned, looking down. Now he understood why they were going to have to portage. There was no passage at all at low water for the ships. The channel was broken up by hundreds of small rock islets, too close together to accommodate a vessel the size of theirs. Between and among these, the river dashed against the rocks and sent up tall columns of spray as it roared deafeningly down the incline. He turned to Seth. "How do we get the boats up that grade? The land passage is uphill, and the ships are so heavy, the drag on their hulls will be ruinous."

Seth grinned that infectious grin that made him look so many years younger than his evident age. "You'll see," he promised. "First, take a look at the terrain. When we're out there in the plain, lugging our boats past the roughest part of the rapids on the silt floor of the deserted town, you can confidently expect to have to fight. But where?"

Moses thought for a long, long moment. "Let's see. The plain's quite empty. If they come at us before we've reached the Mirgissa fortress, we'll see them coming, and they'll lose the advantage of surprise. That channel cuts the big island in the middle of the river in half. It'd be a splendid place to park a couple of fast galleys full of bowmen, to hit us with a heavy barrage from the flank so that we can't retreat. Yes, if I were their commander, I'd have one full detachment hiding behind the southern wall of the fortress and another scattered among the temples between the fort and the river. And I'd have another group coming around the other wall of the fort to cut the expedition off from the rear. We'd be surrounded. And if they had more bowmen atop the battlements, raining arrows down on us from above . . ."

"Aha! Good! But I made it too easy. I should have asked you to look the situation over, then do all this from your memory of what you'd seen!"

Moses frowned. "You really do want me to be able to remember everything, don't you?"

"Why not?" Seth asked. They came down from atop the bluff and headed along the path to the plain below, where the soldiers and sailors were dragging one of the boats aground and readying another for the same treatment. "You have to remember that a lot depends on you. Perhaps more than you know. I'm an able enough man—"

"Able? Seth, you're a genius!"

"—and the officers we brought with us are uncommonly adept. But none of us has even one prophecy about our destinies, let alone two—"

"Two?"

Seth ignored the question. "None of us is going to be the promised Deliverer of his people. I have this not only from Tchabu the seer, whom we mentioned, but from various of our magi in Thebes *and* from the other member of my family who shares the kind of gifts Tchabu and Teti were blessed—or cursed—with. Never mind: You'll meet him soon. All of them agree that you're an important young man, one on whom the future not only of Egypt but perhaps of the rest of the whole world may depend."

Moses, incredulous, stopped dead, turned, and looked at him. "Are you sure you've got the right person? These are high expectations for a fellow who's never really done anything." A shadow came over his face as he added, "Except kill a man he'd never even met before."

"That's a heavy burden to carry, isn't it?" Seth said sympathetically. "How I wish I could wipe it from your mind! But even if I could, just to spare you pain, it would be unwise. You are going to have to learn to see and remember everything—absolutely everything. Mind you, I speak as a man who caused great damage by letting himself get distracted. I am here to train your eye, your memory, and your mind. Others will train you in warfare and leadership, and in the ways of the river, the desert, and the wild places of the world."

They walked in silence for a while, Seth lost in memory, Moses digesting the heady clues his friend had divulged about the future.

"How I wish *I* could forget," Seth said, deeply remorseful. "But I cannot. I, too, must remember everything that has ever happened to me, so it may never happen again and be charged to my account. I speak not as a wise man, but as a fool who has caused great suffering."

Now it was Moses's turn to put a comforting hand on the older man's shoulder. He marveled at the unsuspected hard muscle under the cloth. "As you have shown me yourself, burdens are sometimes made lighter by allowing another to share the weight of them."

Seth closed his eyes and did not answer. He seemed to be searching for the right words.

"Tell me about it," Moses gently urged.

Seth hesitated, then his mouth worked, but nothing came out. He closed his eyes and opened them again, and when he did there was a different, more composed expression on his careworn face.

"Come on," he said. "It's been a long day, and we have a lot of work ahead of us tomorrow."

IV

By the time Moses had struggled out of his tent in the morning, work was already under way in the camp and all the boats hauled onto land. The additional boat had been broken up the night before, and its curved timbers had been used to provide a sort of cradle that would allow each ship to be dragged onto the shore and moved up onto the beach, where now the vessels to be moved lay aligned, awaiting the near miracle that, Moses thought, would be needed to move the boats up the slowly rising slope past the terrible rapids that lay above them on the river.

With some trepidation he approached Khafre, who stood supervising the first stages of the move. Moses almost turned back. Then he forced himself to continue and came up alongside the commander and made himself speak the first word. "Khafre, I'd like to apologize for yesterday. I shouldn't have done what I did. I realize I'm in your safekeeping and that I'm your responsibility. I won't make you worry about my safety again."

The commander turned to look at him, unsmiling, not angry. "Your concern does you great credit, my lord," he said. "In truth I would appreciate knowing where you are, particularly as we approach the battle zone." Now he smiled a tight soldier's smile. "As you can imagine, Seth and I already spoke about that last night. Not that I feared overmuch for the safety of either of you—my men had already inspected the fortress before you entered it. Seth tells me they missed one man. I can ignore the danger one man might pose for the two of you, particularly when one of you is Seth."

Moses was surprised. "Did he tell you, then? He didn't even lay a hand on his own sword! He just looked at the man, and it was enough to—"

"Yes, my lord?"

"Wait a minute. I'm beginning to piece something together here." His eyebrows drew together. "Would you excuse me?" Without waiting for an answer, he took off down the hill to where Seth was assisting Geb with the boat detail. As he approached he noted every man was armed to the teeth as they wrestled the first boat up onto a curious set of parallel rails and pointed it along the track that had been constructed.

"Ah, there you are," Seth said. "See how this works? I've got a whole bucket detail bringing up Nile water."

"Later," Moses said. "I've figured out—"

"'Come on, there!" Geb bellowed sharply. "Bring up that water! Do you think we can wait all day?"

"You see?" Seth said. "They're going to pour water into this little cradle formed by the space between these two long sets of rails."

Moses, exasperated, looked where he pointed. "You don't mean to say you're going to try to float the ships uphill? That's the most ridiculous thing I ever—"

"Not at all," Seth said, chuckling. He took a bucket from one of the soldiers and threw its contents onto the ground in front of Moses. "Walk over here to stand beside me."

He had not taken three steps before the ground underfoot became as slick as wet marble. He slipped, waved his arms wildly, and sat down hard.

Seth bellowed with laughter. "Here! Let me help you up!"

Moses batted his hands away. But as he tried to get up, he slipped once more and sat down again. Scowling and humiliated, he reached down to test the ground beneath him with one finger. "Why, it's as slippery as animal grease!"

"Certainly," Seth said. This time Moses let himself be helped up, and Seth brushed off his clothes for him. "Nile silt is a fine powder of clays. This is the wonderful stuff the river deposits in the delta, and it will grow any produce you choose to plant in it. It's one thing dry, another thing wet. If you venture forth again on that stuff, you'll have trouble stopping once you've started."

"So I gather," Moses said ruefully. "Is this how the stones were moved for the Memphis pyramid field?"

"Yes. This far upriver it's even finer and becomes even slicker when wet. Now, as you can see, these tracks run on for quite some distance. It's approximately three leagues to the end of the portage. You'll be surprised how quickly we arrive there."

"What about the Nubians?"

Seth watched Geb move to the far side of the track and bellow one terse order after another. Slowly the big vessel, propelled from behind by many hands, began to move easily up the slope. "Oh, we'll deal with them when it is necessary," he said lightly. "Meanwhile, stay close to my side.

Khafre has ordered me not to undertake any more exploratory expeditions until after we've passed through the Semna straits."

"That reminds me," Moses said, watching the second vessel being loaded onto the track just behind the first. "I was thinking about those two problems you gave me."

"You've figured out how you go about taking an impregnable fortress?"

"No, the other one."

Seth turned to him and smiled half-mockingly. "You've figured out how I propelled a man to his death just by looking him in the eye."

"It wasn't just that. You *did* talk to him . . . in his own language. I forgot because I didn't know what you were saying. I assumed you were insulting him."

"Go on."

"Well, Baliniri told me once about a magus who could implant suggestions in another man's mind by getting his attention and then talking to him."

"Just how did he do this?"

"I don't know," Moses admitted. "Neither did Baliniri. But he said that once he'd seen a magus convince a man to take off all his clothing and wind it into a turban atop his head and walk all the way through a crowded party. He said it was the funniest thing the court had ever seen, and the man never lived it down."

"Indeed? And how did he convince the man to do this and remain unaware that he was doing something so embarrassing?" Seth leaned over and whispered in Moses's ear.

Moses nodded, then began to do Seth's bidding as he answered, "He talked to him, then told him he wouldn't remember having heard the command. The man would only notice, all of a sudden, that he'd already done it. And of course when he did, everybody was laughing—"

Moses stopped dead. He wheeled. Behind him everyone was laughing! As he turned the laughter stopped. But the faces before him—faces of soldier and sailor alike—bore hastily suppressed grins of irrepressible mirth. "Why are they laughing?" he asked.

"Look down," Seth said quietly.

Moses did so. He was naked. He reached atop his head. He seemed to be wearing some sort of hat. . . .

He hastily grabbed for the pile of clothing atop his head. The laughter started up again and would have continued to build had Geb not intervened, threatening every man who laughed with extra duty digging—and cleaning—latrines.

When he was dressed, Moses confronted Seth. "You tricked me!" he said half-angrily. "Why would you want to make a fool of me?"

"Forgive me," Seth said sincerely. "When I was young I never smiled. I never joked. On my long trip to Babylon, I learned friendship for the first time. My companions taught me how to be a human being, not just a disembodied mind, and what a healthy thing it is to laugh and to value the perspective that a sense of humor gives a man. It's too easy to take yourself seriously."

"Am I so limited? Am I so wrapped up in myself?"

"No," Seth answered quickly. "Not at all; not the way I was. But it doesn't hurt any of us to be the butt of a good joke now and then. It tends to remind not only us but our friends that we're human, just like anyone else. It takes the edge off resentment." He changed his tone suddenly. "Does this answer your question as to how the Nubian came to jump off the wall?"

"I know why. But I don't know how."

"Neither do I. But somehow I learned to do it, a bit. If only I could have worked with Marduk-nasir longer! The things he'd have taught me!"

"Was he so learned, then?"

"I'll never know to what extent. He took me as far as he thought I needed to be taken, then he left. If I hadn't got myself distracted by my own vanity—" He shook his head violently, as if to fling away a horrid truth. "But my journey was spoiled already. Spoiled from the first." He turned and motioned Moses to join him as he walked slowly along the track beside the slowly moving boats. "Did you know I had a son?"

"You mentioned him once, briefly," Moses answered.

"I never knew him. Before I left on my quest, I had a

brief affair with a wonderful girl named Aset, a heroic young woman who had been a member of the resistance movement inside the delta. They worked against the Hai. She, with Queen Mara, helped to liberate the little slaves of the Children's Refuge in Avaris. When I left, I thought we'd had our fun and that was all there was to it. Young men can be irresponsible about these things. I had thought I was above human folly. But I was as much a fool—a vain, self-centered fool—as anyone else."

"Ah. And when you left, Aset was with child?"

"Yes, but I didn't know it. When she bore her child—my child—the friend she'd been staying with threw her out. Too late the friend went looking for her, to take her home again, but by that time she'd disappeared."

"And you knew nothing of this."

"Not until I was back in Egypt from Babylon. That's why it did not get in the way of my marrying a princess of Shinar." He sighed. "I was in love. I thought that was all that mattered. But after my wife died—and all else with her—I learned about Aset and the child I'd abandoned. I had a long, long time to think about my actions."

"I'm sorry."

"I've got to find them. For nearly twenty years now I've scoured the world. I traced her as far as the oases, where she had escaped for a time. But she has disappeared from there, and nobody knows where she went. With my son! My *son!*"

Moses reached one hand out to comfort him. But as he did, a shrill cry rang out from the heights above.

"Attack! We're under attack!"

V

Even before looking up at the heights, Moses caught a quick glimpse of Seth's face. The change in the older man's demeanor was instantaneous and complete. He was again the man of action, his eyes alight, his face set in a fierce smile.

"The damned fools!" he cried exultantly. "They've botched the attack! We've got them!"

Moses looked up, his hand on his sword hilt, to see black soldiers pouring down the hillside, their gleaming copper swords and long spears outheld. The bowmen already visible atop the heights loosed a rain of long, slender shafts, which arched high—too high—and fell short, just paces before the advance of their own men.

Geb bellowed orders to his men, who had already fallen back to the far side of the boats. A second detachment brought up a wagon carrying war clubs, spears, and bucklers. And now the Egyptian bowmen appeared atop the decks of the boats, nocking and firing arrow after arrow into the advancing horde.

Moses fell into position beside the troop closest to him. "Steady, now!" he said. His weapon was drawn, and he assumed command smoothly. "Hold your positions! You up there—let them have another volley!" Accordingly, the men atop the boat fired their arrows, and this time fully a dozen struck home, and that many Nubians staggered forward and fell.

"Let them get a little closer!" Moses called out. "Let them get on the wet silt!"

One of his underofficers laughed aloud appreciatively. Moses was about to join the unit and move forward when he felt a restraining hand on his arm. "Let them go on without you," Seth said. "Just give the orders. You'll have plenty of chance to fight. I want you to watch this. You'll learn something of human folly in this, I believe. They've picked the wrong place, the wrong ground, and the wrong time."

Moses, deferring to his mentor, gave instructions to his men. "All right," he said, "give them three strides more . . . all right . . . now!" And, bellowing mightily, his unit rushed forward.

Seth shook his head at the Nubians' incompetence. "If they'd followed the strategy you sketched out when we were on the fortress walls looking down on this ground, they might even have saved their necks. But look at them! That was one of the stupidest maneuvers I've ever seen. Look, up on the heights! Our unit that left camp last night have come up behind the bowmen!"

Moses, looking where Seth's hand pointed, winced at the slaughter. It was a vicious thing to watch. One of Khafre's men drew back his broad-bladed battle-ax and beheaded a Nubian bowman with a single stroke. Another bowman was caught by an Egyptian spear and eviscerated.

On a patch of silt that Khafre's men had watered down a few moments before, the Nubians staggered, slid, and fell. They were cut down in waves, first by the Egyptian archers, then by the mopping-up force.

Halfway down the hill a second wave of Nubians moved into place behind the first. These split up and skirted the watered patch. But the Egyptians were waiting for them.

"Wait," Seth said, frowning. "There's something wrong here. This shouldn't be so easy. Something's badly wrong. Khafre! Khafre! Over here!"

The general moved to his side. "You see the same thing I do, eh? This isn't the normal way Nubians fight."

"No. Ordinarily they're as good as any soldiers I've ever seen in action. Get the word out: I want one Nubian officer and one underofficer spared."

"Right," Khafre said, and went off to shout out a series of orders to the Egyptians preparing to move in on the now-surrounded Nubian attackers.

"What's the matter?" Moses asked.

Seth's frown grew dark. "This is sheer insanity."

"You don't like the fact that we're winning easily?" Moses asked. "That doesn't make any sense."

Seth stared as the besiegers' circle narrowed, and as three more Nubians in the middle of the circle staggered and fell under an Egyptian onslaught. "I hope he can save a few; I want to talk to them. I have to know something." He scowled. "No! Stop him! Stop him!"

Moses looked at the scene before them. This particular group was down to three Nubian survivors, surrounded and beleaguered on all sides; then two; then one. And now as the ring around him halted its advance under audible orders from Khafre, the last remaining Nubian reversed his sword and committed suicide before anyone could prevent it.

The oddest thing was that the Egyptians had suffered almost no casualties. Three men had been hit by arrows, one fatally; two men had sword wounds, both superficial; and one man had taken a severe cut in the upper arm from a dagger thrust.

Khafre, Moses, Seth, and Geb conferred by the riverside, standing high above the falls as the unit re-formed and the boats began once more to move slowly uphill. The roar of the falls muffled their voices and kept their words from carrying to the rest of the command.

"Well?" Khafre began. "What do you think? It was like killing lambs at the spring slaughter. Does anyone have any answers?"

"Not unless one of them can be brought back to life and induced to tell us what was going on," Geb growled. "You don't suppose they were ill, do you? Some sort of disease they'd all come down with, perhaps?"

"I talked with the magus," Seth said, "and so far he has found no sign of illness in any of the men he examined. Of course, that's not conclusive."

"Then what was the matter with them?"

Seth looked Khafre in the eye. "It could be drugs. Sometimes a lax unit gets a supply of *shepenn*. I realize it's unlikely that any commander would put a lax unit in a point position. It'd be much more like the Nubians to throw a strong unit against us, to frighten us if they could."

"I agree," Khafre said. "But that leaves us where we started."

"Pardon me. I know you men must have thought of this already," Moses ventured, "but what if they first hit us with their worst to take us off our guard, then hit us again with the main unit in the shadow of the Mirgissa fortress—right where I suggested they would have done well to attack us."

Geb and Khafre exchanged appreciative glances. Khafre said, "We had thought of that, my lord, but I can't say how delighted we are to hear this kind of thinking from you." He turned to Seth. "You're a good teacher."

"I'll make a tactician of him yet," Seth said with a dark smile. "And the best strategist. When I asked him to plan an attack from the enemy's side, he came up with the sort of thing you could expect from a seasoned commander." He clapped Moses on the arm with rough affection. "What I can't understand is—"

"—why the enemy didn't do precisely that," Khafre said. "It was sheer madness—"

There was a voice behind him, muffled by the powerful roar of the river. Khafre turned and made room for a runner from the medical unit. "Yes?" he said.

"Beg to report, sir. Message from my lord Re-Harakht. The magus has found one with a little life left in him yet—if you hurry, sir."

The Nubian was sinking fast when they arrived at his side. He had taken a sword thrust in the belly and was in great pain. Seth knelt at the Nubian's side, while Geb hung back. "You've been badly hurt," he said in the black man's own tongue. "You may not last long."

"I know," the Nubian said. "You speak our language. You may know our customs. I would ask you not to dishonor our dead."

"Rest assured the proper rituals will be performed," Seth said. "I shall attend to the matter myself. I was sealed into the Lion Clan in Dodoth a dozen years ago. I am not a priest because I was not born of the blood, but what a member of your clan can do, I can do. I will sing your bones to sleep."

"Is this true?" The Nubian's voice was weakening. "If you are of the clan let me see your scars."

Seth reversed his left hand and displayed a curious scar in the middle of his palm. "I was sealed into the clan by a great chieftain called Lopore."

"He was the cousin of my father's wife," the Nubian said. "It is good." Pain contorted his features for a moment. When he spoke again his voice was a barely intelligible croak with little breath behind it. "What does my brother in the clan want of me?"

Seth looked him in the eyes. "We would know why the great warriors of Nubia fought like unfledged children today."

"Children?" the warrior said, genuinely puzzled. "I do

not understand." A cough, weak and painful, broke his last word into many pieces.

"I see," Seth said. "You do not remember." He looked up at the faces of the men standing above the two of them. "I don't know how much I'm going to get out of him," he said. "He may not even be aware of the fight today."

He switched back to the black man's native tongue. "Who was the commander of your unit?"

"Commander?" he echoed. "Who was the commander?" His eyes went blank. His lips moved but no sound came out. "Commander," he mouthed. "Commander of the unit. Of the . . . unit . . ."

And, still muttering words, he slipped into death. It was a very peaceful passing, and he did not seem to be in pain.

Seth looked up at Geb. "Did you understand his dialect?" he asked.

"I couldn't make any sense of it," Geb admitted.

Seth stood up and brushed off his knees. "Neither could he," he said sourly. "That's the terrible thing. He didn't seem to have any idea what was wrong with him. Re-Harakht, is there any way you have of testing these men for drug use?"

"Not when they're dead," the magus responded. "This one seemed to have been absolutely normal—within the parameters, of course, that he was dying and knew it."

Seth gave his companions a hard look. "You see?" he asked in an odd voice. "Some strange new element has entered here—something out of the ordinary." He frowned, perplexed. "I wish I had even the smallest idea what it was."

VI

Seth continued to puzzle over the problem as the men dragged the vessels slowly and steadily along the silt ramp past Mirgissa. He could make no sense at all of the curious phenomenon of an army detachment that had, for all practical purposes, committed mass suicide.

Five leagues beyond Mirgissa, the ramp ended, leading the ships back down to the water. The cataract was still crowded with islets of varying shapes and sizes, but now the straits between them and the soundings of the channel were safe for travel by water once more.

The men carefully eased the ships into the river. Geb stood atop a large rock supervising the matter. "Easy, there, boys! Remember these are the only ones we've got! If these get stove in by some ham-fisted idiot who can't be bothered with watching what he's doing, somebody's in trouble! We'll have to steal the whole Nubian navy to get home in!"

The soldiers laughed; they liked Geb, a man of the people who had risen through sheer ability from the ranks. Of all the little army that had come south, Geb was the acknowledged master of more soldiering arts, and they all respected this. To be sure, there might be a better bowman or swordsman, but no man's skills were greater in the aggregate, and he added to this an easy way with leadership.

Seth had been watching Geb with some interest. Now, standing in the stern of the last boat to be lowered into the water, he spoke to Moses about him. "Look how he jokes with them! Every jest is tailored to the idiosyncrasies of his listeners. He knows the strengths and weaknesses of everyone in the unit and keeps a good balance between complimenting them on their skills and twitting them on their failings. Geb won't go too far in his raillery unless someone's stepped well out of line."

Moses leaned his elbows on the rail and nodded. "They also know that he'd die for any one of them. Have you heard about the time when three of his men were surrounded in a Bedouin raid? Geb held up a general retreat, defying his superiors, until he and a small patrol could sneak into the Bedouin camp and recapture them. Six men against five hundred."

"There are great soldiers who are enshrined in the minds of their men," Seth mused, "although nothing gets written down about them. Unless some clever fellow makes up a song about their valor, their memory won't survive the last man in the unit they served with. But they're legends nonetheless."

Moses looked at him with a smile. "Baliniri says that his

men sang of your grandfather Hadad the Cripple when they besieged Mari, back in the great days of Hammurabi."

"This is true," Seth said. "Hold on!" Beneath them the ship shuddered, then plunged down the ramp into the water. Seth blew out a deep breath. "There, now. I was about to say that when I went to Babylon the songs of Hadad were there. Nowhere that I have traveled, save the dark lands south of here, is Hadad unknown. I don't know if Geb's fame will travel as far as that, but the army will not soon forget him. He will last as long as I, at any rate. I trust your observation of his tactics has suggested lessons to you?"

"I cannot act like him; I do not have quite the same common touch. Ideally I would be an officer who gave the order quietly and trusted a good subordinate like Geb to put it into the common speech and pass it on."

"I agree," Seth said. "I do see that in you. Something of the same could be said of me. I do not speak well in the familiar manner to the common man. But there is leadership and leadership. The main thing, as you seem to have grasped already, is to know what style you are suited for and stick to it."

As the maze of islets thinned out little by little it became possible again to put the ships under sail, and as the canvas billowed in the stiff wind, the scenery along the river moved past at a brisk clip. The ships passed two deserted villages at the water's edge; then, to their surprise, the men noticed a thick pillar of smoke in the distance. As they sailed closer they could make out the outlines of a river fort built roughly along the same pattern as Mirgissa, only smaller. The smoke appeared to be coming from inside this.

At Khafre's order the ships dropped anchor, and a small detachment went ashore. Seth and Moses watched from their boat as the patrol entered the great gate of the fort, which had been left wide open the same way Dorginarti's had been. "I have a feeling. . . ." Seth said. "Come along."

"I can't without informing Khafre," Moses said. "Not without a guard. I can't go back on my word once I've given it."

Seth clapped him appreciatively on the shoulder. "I

applaud you. A man has to be good to his bond. But *I've* promised nobody anything like that. I'm going ashore."

"What if he asks about you?" Moses inquired.

"Tell him the truth," Seth replied. "He knows what to expect of me already: independence. He'll understand. He'll swear at me, but he'll understand."

Seth dragged his little coracle a couple of body lengths up the beach and stalked up the steep slope toward the fort. On the way he passed the camouflaged opening of the water stairway, used during times of siege and covered over now to protect it.

Inside the gate, it was possible to get a good picture of the interior layout of the apparently deserted fort. Just inside the gate there was a small area where troops could be formed into units before marching out. From this square radiated the street system, with a main thoroughfare prominent in the middle. This wide avenue divided a series of military warehouses on the east side from the homes of soldiers and civilians, plus the splendid residence of the commandant.

Seth looked at the column of smoke. It seemed to be coming from an area inside the residential quarter. He moved down the main street toward this, only to be stopped by an Egyptian soldier. "Halt! Oh, excuse me, sir. I didn't know it was you."

"What have they found?" Seth asked.

"Come with me, sir. I'll show you. Very strange. Just like everything else about this trip so far, sir."

They rounded a corner and found themselves in a side street that ended in a little bazaar of some sort. Here the patrol had gathered, apparently to interrogate a single inhabitant of the fort. But as Seth neared the scene, he could sense that there had been a small, but fearful, slaughter here. Now that the wind had shifted, a terrible stench came to him.

"What's going on?" he demanded of the underofficer in charge.

But now he could see. He blinked and turned his head away for the moment. The smoke and the stench came from three stakes to which three men had been bound by chains.

Fagots had been heaped up at their feet and then set afire. The bodies had been burned beyond recognition.

But there was a fourth stake, with a fourth man bound to it. He was tall, thin to the point of emaciation, and clad in rags. The fagots heaped at his feet had been ignited, then somehow gone out. Perhaps they had been too green. The men cut him down, eased him to the ground, and were now giving him water from a leather bag someone had brought along.

"This one's alive, sir," one of the men reported unnecessarily. "He doesn't speak any of our languages, sir."

"Here, let me," Seth volunteered, hunkering down next to the emaciated prisoner and addressing him in three different languages before getting any response. "Who are you? What has happened here?"

As the man blinked, Seth recognized something akin to madness in his eyes—the look of a man who had peered into the darkest reaches of the Netherworld and had come back out again into the light, traumatized by his experience.

"You're only a few hours behind them," he gasped. A sudden fire blazed in his eyes. "*He* left us behind," he said in a voice saturated with hatred. "It was *his* idea, the bastard! Said we were traitors, spies, just because we had an Egyptian mother! He ordered us burned alive, just to make examples of us!"

"Easy, now," Seth soothed. "Water! Let him have a little more water, will you? There. Now don't drink it too fast." The soldier took the water bag back. "Now, my friend, who is this 'he' you're talking about? What kind of man burns his own soldiers at the stake? I assume you're a soldier, right?"

"No. The others were, but I was a smith. Please, sir, protect me from him!"

"I'll look after you," Seth promised. "I'm a smith myself. You're safe now. Just tell us about it."

"I wasn't doing anything, sir. I was as loyal as a man can be. But things have gone crazy around here. They've been taking people out of their houses and killing them for no reason. They say they did it because they're afraid of spies. We weren't spies, sir! They didn't even say spies for whom!"

"Are you talking about the local command, the one that

pulled out just before we came, then? And this 'he'—do you mean the commandant of the fortress?"

"That's right, sir. The army detachment moved the civilians out a week ago—all but me. They needed me. I was the only smith in the whole detachment. They always need a smith, so I thought I was safe. What kind of person tries to kill an armsmaker, sir? Even if I'm not very good, sir. I'm no Karkara. I'm no Teti."

"Ah!" Seth said. "You know these names, then?"

"Oh, yes, sir. All smiths know them. Great names in the craft, sir. Please, more water. My throat hurts. It's dry. I inhaled some of the smoke from my friend's fire, over there" —for the first time he looked at the closest of the three stakes and its horrid burden, and began to tremble—"just before the wind changed. And my wrists, sir. They're numb from the thongs they bound them with. I can't feel anything in my fingers. Oh, I hope I can still hold a hammer!" He wiggled his fingers awkwardly. "Oh, sir. The pain's coming back! Thank the gods! I can feel again! I was so afraid. . . ."

"We're getting off the subject," Seth said gently. "Your name, friend. What's your name?"

"It's Netek-amani, sir. Netek-amani of Kerma. Don't judge me too harshly, sir. I didn't finish my apprenticeship. I'm not a real smith, sir. Not like a fine gentleman like you would be. I know I haven't been approved by the craft, sir. But out here on the borderlands, they sometimes take whatever they can get. Until *he* came, nobody ever complained. Really they didn't."

"I'm sure you're right," Seth said softly. "But whom are you talking about? The man who did this to your friends and tried to kill you as well—who is he?"

"Oh, sir. I wish I didn't even have to say his name! The harshest, cruelest man I ever saw and hope never to see again. I hope a fine person like you, sir, never has to come into his presence."

"His name!" Seth said, finally impatient. "Please!"

"Oh, yes, sir." He made the sign against the evil eye as he spoke. "Apedemek!"

VII

"Sir," ventured the commander of the patrol, "don't you think we'd better get back to the boats, now? They'll be worrying about us."

Seth did not take his eyes off the tall, thin man seated before him. "It can wait a moment or two, I think. This is important. Netek-amani here is the first person I've spoken with who has actually *seen* Apedemek. Let me have a little more time with him, then we'll go."

"Oh, no, sir!" the skinny man quavered. "Please don't leave me here! He could come back! I can't face him!" He clutched at Seth's garment with numbed fingers and pulled at it clumsily. Seth saw a great fear and growing panic in his eyes. "Please take me with you! There's no place for me here anymore! I'll never be safe! If he finds out I've been spared . . . Oh, sir, you haven't any idea what a horrible man he is. I'll do any work you have. I'll work hard. I'll earn my keep!"

"Here, now," Seth said, getting to his feet. "Can you get up? I'll help you."

The tall man allowed himself to be helped up. He flexed his scrawny legs one at a time. "You have no idea what it's like to know you're to be burned alive, to see it happen to your companions, and then to be spared by a miracle. The gods must be merciful if they can save a man from death like that, at the hands of a heartless monster like Apedemek."

"You'll be safe with us. I'll want to talk to you some more, but we have to get back to the boats. People are waiting for us."

"Boats, sir? Please take me with you—just as far as Buhen, no more. If I can get to the rapids, I can work my way downriver on a fishing boat. Are you bodyguards for a merchant, sir? Because you're not safe here. Nobody's safe here."

Seth was beginning to find the man's hysteria draining. "We're part of a military expedition, come upriver to drive the Nubians back from lands and outposts that rightly belong to Egypt." He inspected the skinny man's wrists. "Come, I'll take you to our physician. He'll give you some salve for these and for the burns on your feet and ankles. You've had a very narrow escape."

"Soldiers, sir? An army? From Thebes?"

"Yes. Come along now. I'll ask the leaders of our expedition if I can bring you with me. If I explain, I won't have much trouble with Khafre or Prince Moses."

"Ah! A prince of the blood? Then you're serious, sir! You really mean to retake the captured territory. Oh, sir, if only you could! It's been such tyranny! Such oppression!" Netek-amani shuddered. "Oh, sir, if you could only talk them into taking me along . . . Surely I'd be safe with an army around me."

"Well, we're not much of an army, as to size," Seth said, "but yes, I think you'd be safe with us." Seth turned to the commander of the patrol. "Take him to Re-Harakht. Have the magus look at those burns and blisters. I'll stay here for a moment and examine the site. I'll look at these poor fellows they burned to death and see if there's anything that can tell me anything. I have the feeling that I need to know everything I can about this Apedemek fellow." He put a reassuring hand on Netek-amani's bony shoulder and tried to calm the panic he saw in the scarecrow's eyes. "They'll look after you. Perhaps we can even find something better than that to wear." He turned back to the patrol commander. "I'll be right along."

When the others had gone, Seth surveyed the scene of the carnage. In his years of wandering he had synthesized the medical learning of many countries and had by now a very good working knowledge of the pharmacopoeia. He had, however, never quite developed a magus's strong stomach, and inspecting the charred corpses made him gag more than once. He inspected the charred stakes and the chains that still bound the ghastly corpses to the uprights. Then he looked over the stake, set a bit apart, to which Netek-amani had been bound; took note of the wood that had been piled at the scarecrow's feet, examined the cords—not chains—that had bound him. They must have run out of links. He looked particularly closely at the curious knot in the rope; the soldiers, freeing Netek-amani, had sliced through the hemp with their knives rather than try to untie the strange, foreign-looking knot.

Interesting, he mused. This was not a common sailor's knot. In fact, he could not recall ever seeing one like it. Had Apedemek tied it himself, binding this poor scrawny devil to the stake? And if he had, what could be learned from the fact about Apedemek's country of origin? His background? His early training?

He stepped back. The wind changed and blew rancid smoke in his face from the charred bodies. He almost vomited. "Bah," he muttered. "I've got to get out of here." He started to leave; then he had a thought and cut the knot loose from the coiled cord and stuffed it into his pocket. It was a place to start. Maybe Geb, Khafre, or the skinny tinker himself would have some knowledge of it. The man's mind was nearly deranged from his trauma, but perhaps there was something to be learned from him.

Netek-amani, however, was belowdecks, being looked over by the magus when Seth returned to the ship. Seth joined Moses at the rail just as the sailors cast off. He briefly sketched in the events of the last half hour. "Did you see this chap Netek-amani?" he asked. "He's something of a familiar type: not worth much, cowardly, mendacious . . . but there's a chance I can pump him about Apedemek."

"By means of the same dark arts you used on the man who jumped off the wall?" Moses asked.

Seth's smile was cautious. "Not so loud, please. I don't want everyone to know about that." He lowered his own voice. "But the answer is yes. I can get a weak-minded and easily manipulated fellow like this under my spell little by little. Even though he won't realize what I'm doing, I'll get him blabbing, recounting things he doesn't know he knows—things his eye perceived, but his mind did not retain. When I let him out from under the spell, he will not remember having told me anything."

"Curious," Moses said. "If I hadn't seen it work with my own eyes I would be tempted not to believe it could be done at all. I hate thinking I'm weak-minded and easily manipulated, though."

Seth laughed. "You're not. But you trust me, so it was not difficult."

"Is there any chance that you could let me watch while you do this, just once?"

Seth thought for a moment, then shrugged. "I don't see why not. You might catch something I don't."

Khafre came up behind them. "Seth," he interrupted, "I understand you brought a prisoner aboard."

"Not a prisoner, really," Seth said, making room for him at the rail. "He's seen and talked to Apedemek. I have the strong feeling that this Apedemek is the key to Nehsi's highly uncharacteristic decision to invade Egypt. You know we seem to have just missed him?"

"Yes," Khafre said. "The patrol told me."

"This checks out," Seth said. "I examined the fire. I calculated how long it would have taken for the fagots at the dead men's feet to burn down. There was evidence of much quite recent activity: doors left open, bazaar items left in the stalls, goods the vendors hadn't had time to pack when they all left."

Khafre looked at Moses. "You are taking note of all this procedure?"

"If I didn't," Moses answered, "I'd never hear the last of it. Although it would help to know precisely what he was looking for."

Seth raised one eyebrow dramatically. "To tell you that would mean prematurely voicing certain suspicions I have regarding Apedemek—who he is, where he comes from, and what he's up to now. And I don't want to breathe a word of this until I've found out what's on the tinker's mind."

"Let me know what you find out," Khafre requested. "And what conclusions you're beginning to draw. We'll be coming up on the Semna straits soon, with twin forts—one on each side of the river. I've got to talk to Geb. I don't think we'll find deserted forts or incompetent soldiers there. I have the strong feeling, in fact, that there'll be a show of force."

A table had been set up beside the deckhouse, and here Geb had spread out a broad papyrus map. Khafre joined him, and the two looked down at the chart for a long moment. At last Geb pointed. "We're here, sir. The last fort was Askut. We're just coming up on Shelfak." He raised his eyes and inclined his head to starboard. "It's the one on the cliff. There'll be one more fort on the river before we get to Semna: Uronarti, on this island in the middle. It was a favorite of Akhilleus's; he preferred it to Semna. I suppose it was because he took the fort himself and distinguished himself by his bravery."

"Do you think it will be manned?"

"I don't know. This tinker chap Seth brought aboard—"

"No guarantee that he'd know, but it's worth a try. You know, Uronarti might make a good place to stop for the night, before we have to deal with Semna's twin forts. Attack in the morning, when we're fresh."

"Yes, sir. There's a fine view of the Semna strait from Uronarti, with both forts clearly in sight. There's supposed to be a treacherous bore coming through the gap. No way in the world that we can take the boats through it. If the Nubians stop us here, they'll stop us for good. We *have* to take the forts. Only way we can get the boats past there is to be able to portage around the Semna fort on the west side of the Nile. The east side's got rugged hills and is impassable. If we take Semna West, there's another silt ramp behind it. We'd be vulnerable to attack from the eastern fort, but at least it's possible. The other side's out altogether."

Khafre frowned, thinking. "All right. Drop anchor wherever you can. We'll scout the island. If it's unoccupied we'll use it to get a good look at the two forts. But then we'll take to the land and leave the boats here."

"Sir?"

"We're done with these boats. Either we take the Semna straits and the forts on either side, or we're dead. If we survive the battle, we'll have our choice of whatever vessels they have moored on the far side of the straits, and we'll sail to Kerma in those. If we don't, it won't matter. We stand or fall by the next fight."

Geb slowly nodded. Neither man was willing to articulate the implications, but each knew the other's mind. Semna! On it depended not only the future of the expedition, but that of Egypt as well.

VIII

The soldiers brought Netek-amani from below just as the crew dropped anchor in a quiet cove off Uronarti. The scarecrow's legs and feet were bandaged, and someone had found a uniform for him, worn and ragged but clean. It was much too short for his long, skinny legs and made him look even more gawky and ludicrous than before.

Seth looked into the tinker's eyes. The shock of what had happened to him had not ebbed, and his eyes darted back and forth, unable to focus. On the rare occasion when his eyes lighted on Seth's, the Child of the Lion could see abject fear in them. His face twitched, and his slack mouth bunched into a nervous smile.

"I see our good magus has treated you," Seth said. "I trust your wounds were not serious?"

"No, sir," the skinny man said in a voice that kept cracking. "The salve helps. Helps a lot. If only someone could help heal the wounds in my mind, sir. Oh, the horror of it. I'm not going to be able to sleep, sir. I haven't any idea what will happen when I close my eyes, sir, but I can guess—seeing my friends, right there before my eyes, sir, burning—hearing their screams—" He dissolved into tears.

Seth put a consoling hand on the scarecrow's shoulder. "There, now, my friend. Be of good cheer. I may be able to help you sleep."

"You mean you can give me some *shepenn,* sir? But *shepenn* makes you dream, sir, and I'd be afraid of what dreams I'd have now."

"Come now, my friend," Khafre consoled. "Soldiers see and hear worse in the normal course of an average month, and we learn to sleep like babies. Surely you can find in yourself the strength—"

"Oh, sir," Netek-amani sniffled, "I'm not a strong man. I couldn't begin to face what a soldier faces. I get the quaking horrors, sir." Indeed his hands trembled as he spoke. "If *shepenn* would make me live through it all again, I don't think I could take it. Isn't there some other way, sir?" He

looked beseechingly at Seth, who could not escape a certain
involuntary contempt for the man's weakness despite his
sympathy for what the man had witnessed.

"I think there is," Seth said. "When we're done talking
with the general here—oh, excuse me; Prince Moses, General Khafre, this is Netek-amani of Kerma, the only survivor
of that ugly affair back at Askut."

"P-Prince Moses?" the scarecrow echoed. "Oh, sir, I
didn't know. . . ." Awkwardly he tried to bow first to Moses,
then to Khafre. "Oh, sir—my lord—I don't know what to say.
I've never met anyone of such high rank before."

"Stand easy," Khafre advised, looking uncomfortable.
"We need to question you. I'll leave that to Seth. Prince
Moses and I have to supervise the landing of the patrol.
We're sending a detail ashore at Uronarti."

"Sir!" the tinker said in horror. "You're going ashore?
Oh, please don't, sir! It's much too dangerous!"

Khafre had already turned to go; now he swiveled, his
curiosity piqued. "Eh? What's this? Are we walking into a
trap? Come on, man. Tell us everything you know."

"Trap, sir? Only if you consider evil spirits a trap! Black
magic! Traffic with all the ten thousand demons! Terrifying
creatures come up from the Netherworld! Oh, General, please
don't go ashore there! The Nubian army won't even land
there. There hasn't been anyone there since Akhilleus died.
For some reason the demons wouldn't come out when he was
there; there was something about him, they said—he was
proof against the demons. But when he died, there was no
protection from them. The army had to be moved off the
island." He gulped and went on in that quavering voice,
"They say even Apedemek won't go there! Even he—the
master of evil—fears the things that walk in the night on
Uronarti!"

"Bosh!" Khafre snorted. "No soldier believes in that
twaddle. If you're telling the truth about its being uninhab-
ited, we land there and spend the night, after sending a
herald ahead to issue our ultimatum to the Nubian force at
Semna. And if you're lying to us, my friend—if there are
Nubians there, and they have any sort of ambush planned for

us—I will personally reward your lies in a worse coin than
Apedemek did. You will be the first to die. And the slowest."

"Oh, no, sir! I wouldn't lie about so serious a matter!"
Netek-amani vowed. "Please! Stay away from that horrible
place!" He turned to Seth now, and once again, for a fleeting
moment their eyes locked, and Seth could once more see the
shameless panic in his eyes. "Tell him, sir! Warn him!"

Seth smiled reassuringly. "Don't worry, Netek-amani,"
he said. "Nothing can harm you now. When we go ashore
there'll be guards with you at all times."

"Me, sir? Oh, please! Don't take *me* onto that terrible
island! I've suffered so much already!"

"Go ahead," Seth told Moses and Khafre. "I think I'll
have myself a conversation with our friend here and see if I
can calm his fears. He's had a bad time of it, haven't you, old
fellow? Well, I think I've got the cure for you. And it isn't
shepenn, or indeed any other drug."

"Oh, if only you could . . ." Netek-amani began. In his
eyes fear warred with the slenderest of hopes.

Since Moses and Khafre were landing with the scouting
group, three small boats full of soldiers accompanied them.
Geb was left in charge of the main fleet while Seth began
questioning Netek-amani.

On the landing vessel Moses took note of a curious,
distant roar barely audible in the dry desert air. "What's
that?" he asked. "Another stretch of rapids ahead?"

"You'll see when we get there, my lord," the general
said. The boat was skillfully steered to shore by the helms-
man. "Watch your step as you come ashore."

On dry land, Moses could feel nothing of the bizarre
atmosphere Netek-amani's panicky outburst had led him to
expect. "It feels, looks, and sounds just like any other island,"
he said. "Somehow I was expecting something. . . ."

"Don't pay any attention to that silly derelict," Khafre
urged. "No military man has much to do with any of this
spiritual business. After a lifetime spent at war, you come
eventually to believe only in the sword and the power of the
mind that guides it. If there's anybody lurking here, we'll

soon know it. And if they outnumber us fifty to one, well, then I'll consider entertaining a hint of fear. Maybe." He looked up the hill, where the advance guard had entered the fortress and now had sent a runner back.

The runner stopped within earshot. "Sir, from all we can tell, the place was abandoned quite a long time ago. It's cleaned out from wall to wall. From all we can tell, we'll be safe here."

"Good," Khafre responded. "We're coming up. You go down to the boats and tell everyone to come ashore. They can fire the big boats. And send another runner to me— preferably someone who has a good memory and can be trusted to deliver a message flawlessly. Do we have anyone who knows the Nubian tongue?"

"I do, sir. Takelot's the name, sir. Third Troop. Beg permission to volunteer."

Khafre looked the man over. "All right. You'll do. Once you've delivered the message to Geb to have everyone come ashore, report to me on the battlements. I'll be giving Prince Moses a view of the straits."

Moses and Khafre picked their way up the slope. "Then one can actually *see* the Semna forts from here?" he asked.

"Oh, yes," Khafre said, helping him onto the broad road that led through the open gate of the fortress. "We're only a league and a half away, at most. It's reputed to be quite a sight. Some say the finest on the entire river. But come, my lord. Have a look for yourself." They passed through the gate, turned, and walking past the soldiers who were still combing the premises, ascended the narrow staircase that led to the top of the towering walls. "Watch your step, my lord."

Atop the wall, they moved along the battlement until they faced upriver. At the highest part of the wall Khafre stopped and helped Moses up onto the rampart. "Now, my lord, doesn't that live up to the description?"

Moses looked some distance upstream, where the great Nile narrowed suddenly to the merest slit. A rocky islet split the rushing torrent into two channels, each so narrow that the swiftly falling current came roaring through the clefts, audible even at this distance and throwing tall plumes of spray heavenward. "Now I think you can see why I've decided not to bother about the portage. Just beyond the two forts, on either side of the central island, are moored quite enough boats to take us to Kerma." He grinned wolfishly. "All we have to do is take both forts. And believe me, my lord, I don't think we'll find that either of them has been deserted, be it early or late."

Seth had found a pair of large stones of like height facing each other, and he and Netek-amani had been in conversation for some minutes now. For some reason the tinker proved a difficult subject, resisting the crucial moment when he would at last come under Seth's spell. But Seth had patiently continued to speak to him in a low voice, one with an ever-decreasing pace.

Now, at last, it seemed Netek-amani was falling under his spell. Seth decided to test the matter. "Now," he said in that low, deliberate, unchallenging voice he always adopted for these affairs, "you will find that your wounds hurt you no more. You will find that you can touch that terrible burn on your leg and it no longer gives you pain."

Netek-amani did so, slowly. His face showed no fear or distress.

"Very well," Seth said, pleased. "From this moment your pain and fear will be lessened. You can look back on the terrible time you have been through, without distress." At this, Netek-amani smiled tranquilly. "Nod if this is true."

Netek-amani nodded.

"Very well," Seth said softly, slowly. "Now attend me carefully. The last face you looked into before the wicked people left you there, trussed to the stake with the burning wood at your feet—"

"It was Apedemek's."

"What did he say to you?"

There was a long pause. Netek-amani's bland, unintelligent face went totally blank for a moment. Then, by a series of startling changes, his face became someone else's. The slack quality disappeared and became another face. The softness became hard. The mouth firmed up. And suddenly the eyes became the fiery, staring, emotionless eyes of a great predatory bird!

And from this changed face came a new voice: cold, hard, powerful!

"Seth. At last the great Seth comes into my lands to meet me! He comes to match his paltry mind against mine! At last he sees my face and hears my voice through the worthless medium of this cowardly pawn I have left behind in order to make contact with him!"

Seth stared, shocked by the power in the voice, the hatred, the otherworldly coldness! He swallowed and said, in a voice that gave evidence of his surprise: "Y-you are Apedemek, then? But where do you come from? How do you speak through this man's voice? How is it that I can see your eyes in the face of this simpleton? Tell me!"

Ignoring his question, the lips moved instead at the command of the new and frightening spirit that now animated them. *"Turn back, Seth. You have met your master. Turn back or die."*

The alien presence disappeared from the blank, characterless face of the tinker, and Netek-amani was back again. Seth, too startled to continue, brought the scarecrow out of the trance.

"What were you saying, sir?" Then the dullard's expression changed once more. "Sir! The burns on my legs and feet! I can't feel them anymore! Are you a magician, sir? You've healed me, sir! Oh, thank you! You have my eternal gratitude. Just say the word, and Netek-amani's your man!"

IX

When Moses came down the hill from the fortress, he found Seth still sitting on the same rock, his mind obviously occupied. His face was set in a dour expression that mirrored the dark tension within him. "What's the matter?" Moses asked, concerned, taking a seat beside him and putting a comradely arm across his back.

Seth's long sigh spoke eloquently. He then told of his two meetings with the tinker and of each meeting's extraordinary events. "This puzzles and unsettles me," he admitted. knew my name and spoke directly to me, warning me to go terrible energy came from him—malignant, dangerous." He turned and looked Moses in the eye. "You've seen the tinker?"

"Yes. I understand he's a liar, a coward, and not very intelligent."

"Exactly. Yet he seemed possessed by a demon that knew my name and spoke directly to me, warning me to go away or die."

"Well, the Nubians have spies, and I suppose one of them could have informed the Nubians that you were coming."

"But there's more to it than that. The tinker was alive, while his three friends were dead. Moses, that whole thing seems to have been deliberately set up as some kind of warning to us. Apedemek left Netek-amani alive to tell us about him. He speaks through Netek-amani in more than one way."

"Through a harmless hand-to-mouth tinker?"

"Moses, the wood at the tinker's feet was green. It wouldn't burn. Moreover, the dead men were chained to the stakes. The tinker was tied with cord. He would have got loose, if perhaps with some injuries."

"That *is* interesting."

"There's more. The knot . . . I've got it here. Look. It's so fashioned as to spring free if you apply just the right pressure. See?" He untied it, his movements a blur, and then retied it. "If the fire didn't burn the rope, the tinker could still have got loose. He was meant to be alive when we arrived and to speak with me."

"Does he realize he was being used this way?"

"No." He got up and stretched. "Have you prepared your message for the herald yet?"

"Yes." There was a small smile on Moses's face. "I polished it the way Baliniri used to polish his public orations. He taught me that people will remember everything a man in power says, so it should always be the most perfectly stated thing he can produce."

"A potent and unanswerable maxim. So what did you tell the herald to say?"

Moses looked him in the eye and drove the smile from his face, albeit with some difficulty. "*Moses of Egypt to the usurper: Semna is mine. If the thing stolen is returned to me by sundown tomorrow, the thief may retain Kerma, his capital, and he may live as a vassal of Egypt. Otherwise he will learn what the foes of Sesostris III learned in our great-grandfathers' day—that no lord of Egypt is not also lord of Nubia!*"

Seth's eyes opened wide. "Strong stuff! What did Khafre have to say about that?"

Moses was grinning widely now. "He said, 'My lord, if I ever entertained any doubts about your kingly qualities—and I will admit I did at first—they are gone forever. I am proud to serve under such a leader.' " He chuckled. "What do *you* think, Seth?"

Seth embraced him. "The only way that I could possibly have improved on it would be to add something about Apedemek. But frankly, I think I shall have to deliver my own message to him. He has challenged me personally. Nehsi—or whoever is behind him—is your problem. Apedemek is mine."

"Is this sort of rivalry between magi a common thing? I've never known anyone like you, and I find it hard to believe that there may be others."

"Marduk-nasir told me of great battles of the minds that have taken place in the past. There are forces of darkness on which a man with the right training can draw, and it would appear this Apedemek is one of these. A man who has crossed over to the other side, you might say. Just what he has to do with me, I can't say. I have traveled much in my life, and I suppose I have offended many people. It may be that I have insulted this man somehow and not known it, many years ago. Or perhaps he sees me as a person he must somehow vanquish in order to prove himself in the world."

"And you are going to take up his challenge."

"I do not see how I can avoid it . . . that is, without turning tail and running. I can't go back to Thebes, of course, because of Amasis. To either side lies the desert. . . ." He threw up his hands in a dismissive gesture. "I will stay and meet this man. I will defy any threats he makes."

"All right. What next?"

"While we await the answer Nubia sends back by the herald, the men are making camp here by the river. I will spend the night in the fort."

Moses's brows shot up. "Alone?"

Seth grinned. "After what the tinker said about the place, could I get anyone to stay there with me?" He waved away Moses's impulsive protestation. "No, no. I know you would, and Geb, and particularly that unsuperstitious old fox Khafre. On the whole, I'm as little disposed to believe in the occult as Khafre is. I'm wondering whether this talk of evil spirits roaming the walls is just some suggestion Apedemek left in the mind of the tinker to frighten us off. By morning I think I'll know."

But as darkness fell and Seth prepared to go up the hill to the deserted fortress, the tinker, still looking absurdly awkward and ungainly in his ill-fitting clothing, ran stumbling up the slope after him. "Please, sir!" he pleaded, pulling at Seth's cloak. "Don't go in there! Not at night! Oh, sir! You don't know what you are doing! Listen to me!"

"Don't worry, Netek-amani," Seth said, speaking as one might speak to a child. "I'll be all right. I just want to see what happens. Nothing can harm me."

"Oh, you say that, sir, but you don't know. There are demons in the place. When darkness falls they come out. Men have been known to go mad there, to leap from the walls, to cut their own throats rather than face the monsters of the night."

Seth was growing mildly irritated. "Netek-amani," he said. "Go down to the magus and have him look at your bandages. I cured only the pain, not the burns. He'll give you some salve. If you calm down now, you should be able to sleep tonight. Get a night's rest, and don't worry about me. Now that's an order. You said you'd do whatever I asked. So do it."

And now it was night, and slivers of cloud drifted over

the face of the half-moon. Seth sat on top of the wall looking out over the river toward the mysterious, faraway shape of the narrow strait, with its twin forts on the two sides of the channels.

So far there had been no problems: nothing but the occasional sound of a night bird or the odd, human-produced sound that drifted up from the camp in the great cleft of the Nile. Otherwise there was nothing but the normal sound of the river below, and beyond it the distant roar of the furious progress of the current through the narrow straits.

Seth was thinking: *Apedemek, Apedemek . . .*

Who could the stranger be? And how could he do the things he did? Never before had he seen anything like the transferring of one's very voice and soul into the mind of an unwitting familiar.

There was a sudden flash. Seth turned, startled.

A figure, robed, hooded, garbed in an unholy light that was almost too bright to look at, stood in the center of the compound. He stood on air, at the height of the wall.

Behind him, in the darkness, other shapes dimly moved: great, misshapen things with the wings of bats and great, distorted limbs, which jerked violently and fell into postures no animal's legs ever assumed.

A cloud passed over the moon, and the figure of light stood out all the more distinctly against the nearly perfect darkness. The wind began to sigh, and the sigh became a moan. The area behind the burning figure began to grow more crowded. Figures writhed like a nest of snakes. They had the heads of humans and the bodies of great predatory cats. Other obscene creatures squatted, opening wide, toadlike mouths with great glowing teeth inside. Beings with eyes that burned into his . . .

He kept his eyes on these monsters to keep from looking at the being in the glowing robe. But now his eyes were drawn like a magnet to the figure standing before him.

It lifted the robed arms. There were no hands jutting out of the sleeves. Invisible fingers pulled back the hood, but there was no face, no head—nothing but the garment that was draped over the invisible body.

The wind began to howl. Below this was the low, deep

rumble of unknown creatures, muttering unintelligible syllables in voices pitched lower than any human throat.

The empty sleeves flourished, gestured, made mystical signs in the air. A voice spoke in a deadly whisper that was clearly audible.

"Seth. Seth of Thebes. Seth, whose father forswore him. Seth, who betrayed his king, his wife, and his friends for power and human vanity. Now hear me.

"You have come to the place where you will die. You will die a beaten man, a man who, for the first time in his life, has come before power too great for his puny strength to oppose.

"It is too late to turn back. You must face your destiny of defeat and humiliation and impotence. Nothing can save you now. You are in a domain ruled by a mind that makes yours seem like a child's. You have entered a world in which your power is nothing. You will end your days a shell emptied of hope and fortitude.

"It does not matter if you stay and fight, or if you turn and run. Your nemesis now surrounds you in the air you breathe, in the ground you walk upon. The moment you entered the domain of the Dark Kingdom, you were a man marked for obliteration and eternal damnation."

Seth's hands trembled. He searched his mind for a spell, a curse. He raised one hand, shouting half-forgotten words in a tongue he had learned far away. "Begone! Depart, creatures of darkness. . . ." But his voice was a hoarse croak.

The creature raised invisible hands, screamed something unintelligible above the now-howling winds, and rained fire from the sky: a great pillar of white-hot light, with flames that licked about on its fringes. The fire surrounded the figure, and yet the figure was not consumed.

There came, from the middle of the fire, from the unseen figure in the indestructible robe, a mad howl of unearthly, mirthless, hateful laughter such as Seth had never heard.

As the flames exploded into a great ball and the fire and the creatures inside it were sucked violently back up into the darkness that had spawned them, the voice roared.

"Death. Destruction. Annihilation. Obliteration. Devastation. Nothingness. The end of all things!"

*   *   *

In the morning Seth, looking like a man ravaged by a horrible disease, weak and hollow-eyed, stumbled down the slope to find a large gathering of soldiers clustered at the water's edge around a small boat that someone had retrieved and pulled up on shore.

He came up behind Geb, who was walking away from the boat and holding a bloodstained scroll. Geb's face was white. He blinked and looked at Seth. "Gods!" he gasped. "You look terrible!"

"So do you. What's that in your hand?"

Geb wordlessly handed over the scroll. He swallowed and said, "Watch out. That's blood on it."

"Blood?" Seth asked.

"Yes. The herald's. Takelot's. We've got our answer back from Semna. You don't look well, sir. Don't go look at the herald's body—or what's left of it, rather. You don't look as though you could take the sight just now."

CHAPTER EIGHT

Thebes

I

With the regular army gone southward and all external menace dealt with to Amasis's satisfaction, the Theban city guard now devoted its full attention to suppressing internal dissent and enforcing the new laws issued almost daily from the palace where Amasis reigned supreme.

No street was without its soldiers, marching by twos—or in the lower-class quarters, in detachments—shouldering citizens into the gutters. For the most part the guardsmen were foreigners, tough and battle-scarred veterans of many a war and back-alley brawl. They did not like the citizenry, and they showed it in virtually unmasked contempt.

For their own part, the citizens, unarmed and unused to this sort of treatment, restrained their indignation. It was not yet evident to the general public exactly what had happened. Their good king Kamose, who had driven the hated Hai from Egypt, was assumed to be ill—recuperating, perhaps, from battle wounds. Other voices had hazarded the guess that he had contracted a lingering disease. No one suspected that the king was a prisoner in the great country home of Amasis.

For the first few days of Amasis's unacknowledged supremacy, the ubiquitous guardsmen had restricted their suffocating omnipresence to the streets of Thebes proper and had ignored the port of Deir el-Bahari and the artisans' town on the hill behind it. No one expected this luck to continue for long, and daily the citizens of the little town across the river anxiously watched the Nile, expecting to see the boats bearing their hateful quota of officious and obtrusive guardsmen.

And finally the dreaded day came.

The ranking officer in the city guard by now was Demetrios of Rhodes, a burly mercenary who had won the command of his troop by beating his immediate superior to death in a drunken brawl shortly after the army's return to Egypt. He stood before Amasis, his long arms hanging down to the middle of his thighs, his great scarred hands splayed, insolence and hard-won respect at war within him.

"You're absolutely sure?" Amasis probed. "They can't still be hiding in some warehouse on this side of the river? Can there be some damned family hiding them out of misplaced sentiment?"

"Not that I can see. I had to break down a lot of doors to prove it, let me tell you."

"Huh," Amasis snorted, leaning back in his chair and regarding the captain of the guard with loathing and resentment. "I suppose it isn't too much to require you to observe the normal rules of courtesy in speaking to the head of state?"

Demetrios shrugged. "If you don't like the way I talk, fire me. If you want someone who can actually run this scurvy guard here and keep them in line, you'd better learn to live with me. We don't grovel where I come from. Kings aren't appointed, they get what they want by beating all comers to a pulp." He scowled and cleaned his fingernails with a dagger. "I know you think this is barbarism, but I don't give a curse what you think. If you want someone to lick your royal toes, go down to the whorehouse quarter and hire it done." He crossed his rugged arms over his chest in an attitude of defiance. "If you want someone kicked in the rear end and brought into line, I'm your man. But I come just the way I am."

Amasis's eyes narrowed. He looked at the Greek sourly, then he shrugged and smiled a hard, cynical smile. "All right. You'll do pretty much as you are."

"All right. Now what is it that you want?"

"The women. They can't have escaped up or down the river, then?" Amasis said.

"Unlikely. A boat would have been visible, and the princess has a reputation for being a weak swimmer. She'd have to be held up by somebody. The fishermen and ferryboatmen would have noticed that by day—and the women wouldn't have dared try it at night."

"So they've somehow managed to get across the river and eluded detection between here and Deir el-Bahari."

"That's about the size of it." The Greek never smiled. The scar running down from the corner of his left eye across his upper lip and down his chin was so large, so prominent, that Amasis often wondered if his face were not perhaps unable to assume that expression. "So we're left with the necessity of going over there and kicking around every householder, vassal, bondsman, and slave until we know for sure they're not there."

"Do it."

"Are you sure? That'll cost a lot of money. It means moving half the guard to the other side of the river—a damned nuisance. If I guarantee the men a free hand with the women, maybe I can lower their salaries. Pay them in kind, rather than in money. Of course, with the mainland Hellenes there'll be a boy or two raped as well. That's unavoidable. Those slobs will—"

"That's enough!"

"—anything that walks on two legs, and a lot of things that walk on four."

"Don't provoke me!" Amasis sat up straight now. "It's tiring, listening to your intolerable Rhodian bluster. If you think I can't find another braggart to whip that bunch of cutthroats into shape, you've got another think coming." His voice had been rising steadily, and now it was at tantrum pitch.

"All right. What has your viziership decided?"

"The western track, the one that leads to the oases, has been watched constantly, and no one has gone out onto it. If they're not in Thebes and they haven't escaped down the river, either they've gone eastward across the worst damned patch of desert in the whole region or they've managed to cross the river and are still in Deir el-Bahari."

The Greek shrugged insolently. "Deir el-Bahari it is. Do you want to pay for a really thorough search? It'll be expensive. Or you could give me a free hand. Under those fool rules you've got us enforcing over here on this side of the river, they can't touch any of the local women, and they're getting damned tired of the same old whores in the brothels. If you don't send down to the delta one of these days for some fresh stuff, male and female, I can't answer for the consequences. Well? What'll it be?"

Amasis's scowl could burn paint off a wall. "I don't know why I put up with you."

"Of course you do. I get the job done faster than anyone else. Well?"

"I'm thinking. The far side of the river has always enjoyed amnesty from harsh treatment. The tradition has been that you can't fool around too much with the artisans and architects. If you do, you find that an arch collapses on your head six months after the building goes up. Purely by accident, of course—"

"You're afraid of some oaf who carries a hod? Some gutless hind who lays bricks?"

Amasis's eyes flashed. "Of course not, you idiot!"

"You're afraid to break with tradition, then? Afraid of offending some glorified artist because he'll put your picture on a frieze with your eyes crossed? Or leave off your loincloth and expose your shortcomings?"

"Damn you! Go ahead! Do whatever it takes! Just find them for me! Do it now! And bring them to me alive if you can!"

"And if perchance the man in command of the patrol were to take a sudden fancy to the queen on the way home?

And suppose he decided to take an hour or two off for showing her how we do it in Rhodes? Teaching her a thing or two about obedience, and submissiveness, and how to please a man?" He chuckled nastily. "And the princess Thermutis, now. She's a bit younger, and a little less shopworn. Give us another hour to deliver her, perhaps. Maybe two. Who knows?"

"Damn you! Do it! Do it now!"

II

"See?" Onuris pointed out. "You wouldn't see them if you didn't know what to look for, but there they are, barely to the right of the shrub at the top of the hill."

Nemti nodded. "How many are there?"

"All I've ever seen were three. Apparently Amasis is on to us and figures that if the pass is left unwatched, we'll slip off onto the desert track and be at the oasis before he can stop us."

Nemti scowled. "Well, it's obvious we can't stay here. We're playing with fire living with the Habiru, poor souls, and I hate the idea of endangering them by our presence."

Onuris moved back from the height from which the two men had been observing the guards above the desert trail behind Deir el-Bahari and the artisans' village. "I wouldn't worry about them just yet. We've paid our way, after all. The food that has been smuggled through to us by your kinswoman Ti has been shared with them. Because of it, old Jochebed is up and around at last."

"Yes, but we're doing the Habiru no favor by making them well enough to go back to work," Nemti reminded as they slipped unobtrusively through the little valley that sheltered the wretched hovels of the Habiru.

"We've got to get out of here. Every day we're here the women are in ever greater danger."

Nemti smiled knowingly.

"Ah. You're finally getting around to admitting your attachment to the princess, then?"

Onuris held up his hands. "What am I to say? The whole thing is doomed. If we survive and things get back to normal, she won't want to stay with an ordinary soldier like me. But I can't help it. I love her." He looked at his friend. "You're in the same boat, you know. You don't think that she can carry on with you forever, with a husband still alive and a price on both your heads?"

"That's the worst part of it," Nemti admitted. The two moved back behind the row of hovels, safely out of sight. "I'm beginning to get some twinges of conscience about that, too. Things will never be tolerable around here until we have a king again. But Amasis is generally thought to be planning to kill Kamose—if indeed he hasn't already killed him."

"So what do you propose? What could we possibly do?"

"First promise that you'll keep your mouth shut about it," Nemti said.

"About what? What sort of crazy idea—?"

"Promise or I won't tell you anything."

"You know damned well I won't betray you. Now what is it?" Onuris asked.

"About an hour before the watch changes, in the first light of dawn, the guard will be tired. We're going to sneak up there and cut a few throats in that little eyrie where those three are watching the oasis route."

Onuris's eyes lit up. "And the women will be waiting with us, so we can slip off into the desert before the new shift comes on. Right?"

Nemti looked him hard in the eye before he went on. "Not quite. *You're* going to take the women to El-Kharga. I'm going back. And somehow, I'm going to get to Amasis's country place. That's where they're keeping the king. As much as I love Mara, I'm going to try to get Kamose out of there."

Onuris stared incredulously. "I don't believe what I'm hearing. Have you taken leave of your senses?"

"Listen," his friend said. "If it weren't so dangerous, I'd have rescued Kamose beforehand to bring him with us—even if that meant reuniting him and his wife. But we've got to save Kamose, or we'll be stuck with Amasis for the rest of our days. Him—or somebody worse. You know the moment he kills Kamose, he'll assume the throne."

"But with any luck, the army will be back from Nubia soon. Can't you wait for them to deal with this? What *if* Amasis kills the king? You'd be free to live with Mara without—"

Nemti shrugged. "I know. It sounds stupid."

Onuris let out a deep breath. "You idiot. You crazy fool." He shook his head unbelievingly. "You know, I saw something like this coming. You're the kind of maniac who goes around doing things on principle, where any man with half a brain would—"

"And you're the kind of maniac who'll help me. Oh, no, I don't mean you have to come with me. Somebody has to get the women to El-Kharga, after all. It's a long and dangerous trip."

"Can I talk you out of this folly?"

"Probably not. Don't think the worse of me, old man. For all I know, I *am* crazy. But I've been crazy before, and you covered for me." He grinned. "Remember the time we fought the Greeks back in the delta, over those street kids they'd kidnapped? I would have been a dead man if you hadn't bashed a couple of heads in." He grinned. "You tough old bastard. I can still see you giving that ugly one an elbow in the mouth, and him spitting out teeth."

"You kicked the tall one in the balls. I'll bet he walked all bent over for a month." He chuckled. "What a lot of fun we used to have, before the world came down on our heads." The smile was replaced by an expression of sadness. "Ah, the good days. Will they ever come again?"

"Not if we don't do what we can to bring them back. Escaping to the oasis isn't enough for me. I'd always have a bad conscience if I left the king here to die. Mara says he was a good man."

"I don't understand you. Why jeopardize your relationship with Mara?"

"Some people don't make you explain what principled behavior is all about. Some people understand what a conscience is. And you can't pretend you aren't one of 'em."

Onuris scowled. "I'd looked forward to a nice, peaceful little interlude before Khafre and the army came back."

"You can still have one. Just take the women to El-Kharga. I haven't even suggested that you come with me."

Onuris looked at Nemti sadly. He shook his head slowly back and forth a great many times, saying nothing.

The fist pounded on the door again.

"Quick!" Set-Nakht hissed. "Get dressed! Both of you! He reached for his own robe as he called out, "I'll be there in a moment!"

One of the young men yawned and reached for his tunic. "Where do you want us to go? Really, I can't see why you bother to hide anything from Neb-mertef. He certainly must know all about us by now. He pays our fee, after all."

"I don't care," the astrologer said. "The whole nature of my work for him requires that I retain some vestige of dignity. My personal life is none of his business!" Set-Nakht turned, tying his robe together in front as he did and stepping into his sandals, and saw the other boy, the blond one, was still naked, leaning seductively back against the drapery and smiling like a faun. "You! What do you think you're doing? Get something on!"

"Oh, darling," the boy teased, "you're such a prude. I'm comfortable. And let me remind you, sweetie, that only a moment ago you said it was a shame ever to put clothes on a body like mine. Well," he said with a pert little shrug, "I've decided to take your suggestion. I don't think I'll ever wear anything again. Oh, maybe a ring or a bracelet . . ."

"Curse you! Get out of sight, then, both of you! Into the other room!"

"Oh, baby, don't make me go. Not now. Let me stay with you while Neb-mertef is here. Seeing me like this will unnerve him. You know what an old woman he is about people like us."

Set-Nakht's balled fists gestured impotently. "You!" he whispered loudly to the clothed one. "Get him out of here!"

He turned, not waiting to see if his order was carried out, and went to unbar the door. "My lord!" he said. "I'm sorry. I was indisposed. I didn't mean to make you wait."

Neb-mertef glared at him, then looked past him into the room beyond. "Indisposed, eh?" he growled. "I can see the

source of your indisposition." His glare was cold as he brushed
past the magus and sat down. Set-Nakht wheeled and blushed
like a schoolgirl. The blond one was standing before the open
window, his naked body a picture of epicene grace, admiring
himself in a bronze hand mirror: turning the mirror this way
and that, striking the most flagrant sort of poses as if the two
of them were not there.

Set-Nakht found himself quivering with rage. "Y-you
wished to see me, my lord?" he said in a voice that sounded
half-strangled, trying to ignore the scene behind him.

Neb-mertef sneered. "When you've time," he replied,
his words dripping venom. "I wondered if you had cast a star
chart having to do with the issue we talked about earlier."

"Oh, yes, my lord," Set-Nakht said hastily. "I'll just get
the scroll—"

"Forget that," Neb-mertef cut in. "Just tell me the general picture." His eyes darted back to the naked satyr before
the window, now admiring his rear end, looking over his
shoulder through the little mirror. Neb-mertef frowned. "What
do the stars portend for me?"

Flustered, Set-Nakht stammered. "W-well, my lord, I
did a chart of the Nubian front. The aspects are mixed. The
fourth planet is in—"

"Never mind all that. Just give me the implications." He
shot another angry glance at the naked man in the far end of
the room and then looked back disgustedly at the magus.
"Come on, man, get it out!"

"M-my lord . . ." It was now impossible for the astrologer to maintain any pretense at all of the icy dignity he had
affected when the two had first met. "Things are quiescent
there for the time being. The menace of which I spoke is still
there but otherwise occupied. There is a deadly contest
between two mighty powers, both of which are highly dangerous to Amasis." He lowered his voice. "My lord, do you
really think I ought to be talking about this before a third
party?"

"In front of that thing?" His superior jerked his head at
the faun. "Don't worry about him. Speak."

Set-Nakht gulped at the easy dismissal of the boy across
the room. "Very well, my lord. Amasis is safe for now. The

two powers are almost evenly matched. But when either of them manages at last to break loose, Amasis will be in imminent peril."

"Ah. And the local scene?"

"Again mixed. Amasis has a problem he does not suspect." He sneaked a look at the slowly dancing form of the self-absorbed satyr outlined in the window and lowered his voice once more. "Other than yourself, my lord."

Neb-mertef smiled sourly. "Is there something I should be doing?"

"N-no, sir, other than remaining vigilant and consolidating your position as second in command in the, uh, cult, my lord. The stronger you are there—"

Neb-mertef suddenly stood. "Very well. I'll let you get back to your . . . meditations. Next time don't take so long answering. I'll view a repeat of this experience with severity." Throwing the door open, he stalked out and slammed it behind him.

Set-Nakht turned, his eyes blazing. "You idiot! If you do anything like that again—"

But the bacchant, as shameless as ever, was smiling and caressing his body sensuously. "Oh, don't be so serious," he said. "Come here and dance with me. There's a good boy."

III

The birdcall sounded again, but this time was longer than the first had been. A real bird's would have been just the same, fixed. Mara pressed her cheek to the door. "Yes? Who is it?"

"It's me, Nemti. Let me in, quickly."

She drew the bolt and ushered him into the abandoned warehouse where they had been hiding for the week. She closed the door behind him and locked it. Then she rushed into his arms. "I was worried about you."

"Don't be," he said, kissing her hungrily. "I'll always be all right. I lead a charmed life."

"I can't help it," she breathed. "I love you so." Her heart sank at the thought. *I'm so much older than he is. What's going to happen when he meets a younger woman who tickles his fancy?* She knew their present situation was exceptional—one that should never have happened. They had been thrown together by circumstance, and now they were bound together by common danger. There was a price on both their heads, as there was on Onuris's and Thermutis's. But what would become of them when they were safe at last? Would his eye roam? Would he start noticing her gray hairs, the little lines around her eyes?

"We almost got caught this afternoon," Nemti said. "We couldn't stop at my kinswoman's house. There were soldiers in the artisans' town! That's unheard of!"

"I know. One of the girls in the Habiru camp—one of Miriam's cousins, I think—said one of them tried to grab her as she walked past. Soldiers used to be disciplined for that sort of thing. There were rules, even regarding slaves."

"Yes. It's not the old army anymore; it's Amasis's army, full of the worst foreign scum." His face was full of concern.

"Where's Onuris?" Mara asked.

"He's going to slip into town and see what he can learn."

"Do you think that's safe?"

"If anyone can manage it, he will." There was the rough male pride of friendship in his voice. "If anything *were* to happen to Onuris—"

"Don't even think about it. Oh, my dear. My very dear. Hold me now. I've missed you so much."

"Mara," he said, stepping back to look at her upturned face. "Things are getting bad. We've got to get out of here. Every day we stay, the odds of getting away are lessened. And we're still endangering your friends Jochebed and Amram, even after moving out of their house."

"Yes, I know. Not all their kin recognize her debt to us. Some of them are resentful and, in the right mood, would turn us in."

"Those dirty, ungrateful—"

"No, no. I understand. I even sympathize. Their lot is so hard, and Thermutis has led such an easy life—I, also, by comparison, at least in recent years. I'd even understand if they blamed us for their misfortune. After all, we're members of the ruling class that ordered them moved up here, to work them half to death in a quarry—"

"Nonsense!"

"Yes, I know you disagree, but this is the way it must look to them. Jochebed and Miriam try to talk to them, to explain, but they can't really explain everything without revealing the truth about Moses. It would be fatal to let that out."

"I don't know why. Moses is marked for death, just as we are, the moment he comes back from Nubia. So is General Khafre—"

"True," she said. "But I swore to Baliniri—"

"He's dead. Oaths to dead men aren't binding."

"—and to Seth."

"Who's Seth? I don't remember any Seth going on the expedition."

"He was calling himself Nebo when he left."

"Nebo? The foreigner?"

"He's actually Seth of Thebes, the son of Ben-Hadad—a Child of the Lion, and very likely the wisest man of Egypt. Seth made the Sword of Glory, the one Kamose used to kill Apophis."

"Oh, *him*. I'd have thought he'd have died of old age long ago."

Mara's heart sank; Seth was younger than she was. "No. He looks much older than he is. He's suffered many tragedies. He and I and Baliniri were coconspirators against Amasis from the moment Kamose returned with the army from the Northlands. This expedition to Nubia was Seth's and Baliniri's idea. You can be sure that if Baliniri was killed by Amasis, a prince of the blood would also be in danger."

Nemti's face turned sober. "As is your husband."

"That's true," she said ruefully. "I've been expecting to hear the news of his death—'accidental,' of course—ever since Amasis installed him in his country house for 'treatment.' "

"Mara, what would happen if—"

"Yes, my darling?" She took his big hand in her small ones and held it to her cheek.

"What would happen if Kamose were free and well? Would there be a chance of reinstating him on the throne?"

"I don't know. Why?"

"Oh, I keep wondering. If he were all right again, maybe you wouldn't want me anymore. And even if you did, you wouldn't be able to stay with me."

"Oh, my darling." She kissed his hand. "There'll never be a day when I wouldn't want you and need you. I'm only afraid of—well, something happening the other way."

"Me leaving you? Don't you know yet how I feel about you? Have I left you in any doubt?"

"No, my darling, but—"

"Come over here where I can see you." He led her into a circle of dim light, which filtered in from the upper window that led to the roof. "I've never seen anyone so lovely." He kissed her passionately, on the lips, the eyes, the neck.

"Oh, Nemti—"

"Come over here. Come to bed."

Onuris, in the rough clothing of a sculptor's helper, his hands still dirty with the quarry dust he had rubbed into them before entering Deir el-Bahari, slipped through the doorway of the noisy inn and took a seat at one of the tables farthest from the front door.

He looked around. The soldiers had got off duty only a few minutes before, and already there were several of them at the front table, playing senet and arguing loudly in various accents about the rules. There was one Egyptian at the table, and the foreigners apparently resented his dominance in the ancient board game.

Onuris looked for the innkeeper but saw no one waiting on tables. He took a deep breath and stood. Affecting the tired shuffle of a manual laborer, he moved over to where he could watch the game, then sat down and motioned to the servant when she came back into the big room.

"Yes, sir?" the girl asked.

"What happened to the innkeeper?" he asked.

"Oh, sir, he's gone for help. With all the soldiers here, he'll need someone big and strong helping out. You know, throwing out anyone who gets out of line. Ordinarily I don't wait on tables."

"I didn't think so. You're the dancer, aren't you? And a good one. You're certainly pretty enough."

"Oh, you've a slick tongue on you. Can I bring you anything?"

"Well, under other circumstances, little one, I can think of a lot of things you could bring me. I might even be able to think of a thing or two that I could bring you. But things are hard these days, and I've just about enough money for a jug of wine. Could you be a sweetheart and bring me that?"

She winked. "I could bring some olives and flatbread while I was at it. I'll bet a big, strong, healthy man like you has worked up quite an appetite."

"You'd be right. But I couldn't pay for it."

"Oh, that's all right. I have a feeling you'll be in again. I'll dance just for your eyes alone."

"That'd be wonderful." He winked back. "I could feel at home in a nice place like this. Are there rooms upstairs?" As soon as the words left his mouth, he knew he had moved a trifle too fast.

"For rent, sir, by the month. We're not that kind of place."

"Oh, I meant nothing. But I haven't been able to find a place to live, and I wouldn't mind locating somewhere close to here."

"We'll keep you in mind." Her dignity had been restored. She was not a pay-by-the-night girl, but if the spirit moved her, she might make time in her life for a bit of adventure. "Where do you work?"

"At the temple of Amon. I work for a sculptor. I used to do this down in the Fayum, but times are tough there for any but the rich farmers. My boss just landed a nice commission, but the pay won't come in until we're done. Then I ought to be doing pretty well financially. I could show a girl a good time."

"I'm sure you could." Her smile was randy and familiar. "I'll bring your dinner."

He turned back to watch the senet game at the next table. The Egyptian had his opponent boxed in and wore a nasty, superior smile. The other player, a battle-scarred Elamite far from home, scowled. "The play was three spaces," he complained. "You moved four."

"The play was four," the Egyptian retorted. He appealed to the crowd. "Was it four, gentlemen? I ask you." He expected easy corroboration; that was clear from his relaxed attitude. But suddenly he realized he was among enemies.

"Dirty, cheating bastard," someone said with a Damascene accent. "The play was three. Move the counter back."

"Three? But sir, I assure you—" the Egyptian began.

"It was three," another man said. "You thieves from Deir el-Bahari think you lead such a charmed life. Well, those days are over. As of yesterday you're no better off than any damned Theban swine—"

"Yesterday?" the senet player said, puzzled. "What happened yesterday?"

His opponent reached over and moved the counter back one space. "Amasis," he replied with a sneer. "He cooked your goose. You people over here are hiding fugitives. Don't act so innocent; you know you're doing it. Well, we have orders to find 'em, using any means necessary to do it, including busting down any door in Deir el-Bahari. Including having fun with whatever women happen to be inside. Or grabbing anything that isn't glued to the floor. Or"—here he reached across the table and grabbed the Egyptian by his tunic and twisted it until the man was in pain—"busting the head of any dirty Egyptian bastard that tries to cheat at senet."

"I assure you, sir, I didn't—"

Onuris had had enough. Under any other circumstances, he would have stepped in and helped the Egyptian; but now that the Elamite had blurted out the news about the change in orders, he could not stay. He stood and headed for the door as unobtrusively as possible.

"Sir!" the waitress called after him. "Your wine! Your food!" But he kept on going, out into the night, not looking back.

IV

Onuris unobtrusively slipped through the back streets of the little riverside town, heading for the artisans' village in the foothills. Twice he had to duck back into the shadows to avoid patrols, and once he almost ran into a detachment of mercenaries—speaking a language he could not even identify—coming around a corner. On this occasion only an open doorway in a deserted building saved him; he moved inside and flattened himself against the wall, wishing he had armed himself before venturing out tonight.

Once inside the cool darkness, he pondered his options. Their situation had always been perilous, so the only thing that had changed for the four of them was the schedule. There was no time left for planning. He had to reach his friends, alert them, and get them into the hills, where they would at least be safe for the night. Otherwise there was no guarantee that the soldiers roaming the streets would not break in on them.

His mind suddenly flashed a visualization of it before his eyes: Barbarians grabbing Thermutis and Mara by the arm and—

No! he thought. *Over my dead body!*

But of course that might be what would happen. He would fight—so would Nemti—but they would be overwhelmed by superior numbers. Then, with the two of them dead, the two women would be fair game for these foreign pigs.

He forced the thought from his mind. *Gods!* he thought, feeling the sweat running down his sides. He had to do something right now.

He took a deep breath and slipped back out into the night. At the end of the street a patrol crossed the open space; he moved back into shadows and ran, crouching, for the deep cover of a warehouse. Once there, he peeked out from behind the wall and assured himself of a clear field. The long single street of the artisans' village stretched away up the hill. Toward the end of it, an unruly clot of five or six of Amasis's mercenaries were breaking down a door.

He gritted his teeth, moved into the space behind the houses, and made his way up the line of buildings. The soldiers were at the shop of the painter who did friezes for the temple. Poor man! He had a lame leg and did not look much like a fighter. He would have a hard time. And who was next door, next in the line of fire?

He stopped, gulped. Ti! Nemti's kinswoman. Worst of all, Ti had a niece visiting her, a delicate girl of fourteen. The idea of those filthy foreigners getting their hands on Ti or the girl filled him with black rage. Throwing caution to the winds he jogged up the hill to the back door of Ti's house and knocked softly on the heavy wood.

"Who's there?" called a frightened voice.

"It's Onuris. Open up, quickly!"

The door cracked. "Onuris! What brings you—"

"Is the girl here? Your niece?"

"Why, yes, but—"

"Get her now. Bring her with you. Amasis's soldiers are at your neighbor's. They'll be here in a moment."

"But, Onuris, they're not allowed to—"

"Get the girl! Now!"

In a moment she emerged with her niece in tow. Both were dressed for bed, in thin shifts. "Where can we go?" Onuris asked. "You know the area better than I do."

"The quarry," she answered. "It's uneven underfoot. The soldiers won't want to go there at night. If you can't see where you're stepping, you could break an ankle."

"Then come on."

"Wake up," Nemti whispered.

"*Mmmm?*" Mara said in a sleepy voice, burrowing closer to him under the coverlet. She tried to put one warm arm around him and hold him tightly, but he gently disentangled himself.

"Come on," he urged. "There must be trouble. There's a lot of noise in the village."

She sat up and rubbed her eyes. "But it's the middle of the night."

"Yes," he said. "Exactly the wrong time for anyone to be prowling around in the artisans' town."

She reached for her robes. "What can be going on?" she asked. "Surely the soldiers wouldn't—"

"I think they would. I wonder where Onuris is."

"He ought to be back. Check the loft. Thermutis is there."

He ran barefoot to the ladder and climbed to the loft. "Onuris?" he said. His whisper was insistent but did not carry far.

"Nemti?" Thermutis said. "He's not here. What's going on? Did you hear that noise out there?"

"Dress for travel. I think the soldiers are staging a midnight raid."

"And Onuris is out in the middle of it—"

"We don't know that. Don't worry about him. He knows what he's doing. Get dressed. Quickly!"

"I am!"

He jumped lightly down from the ladder onto the dirt floor of the warehouse. He grabbed the swords, his and Onuris's, from the wall and hung the belts around his neck as he put on his loincloth and stepped into his sandals. "Mara! Are you ready?"

"Almost. Is Thermutis coming with us?"

"Yes."

There was a knock on the door. Both of them froze, their hearts pounding wildly. Then the knock came again: a prearranged signal. Nemti unbarred the door.

"Come on," Onuris said, staying outside. "Get Thermutis. They're kicking down doors. At the far end of the street they're setting houses on fire. I took care of Ti and her niece, for now anyway."

"I'm grateful for that, old man. Here. Here's your sword."

"Thanks. Get the women. We've got only a couple of minutes. Amasis's men can do anything they want over here." He spat viciously into the darkness. "I caught one of them beating and raping the weaver's wife."

"No!"

"Yes. I brained him with a rock. But she was dead by the time I could get to her."

"Bastards."

"Yes. Hurry. Thermutis! Come along!"

"I'm here, darling."

Clouds drifted across the moon. "Now!" Onuris whispered loudly. The four, crouching low, scurried across the road and lost themselves in the darkness beside the trail. Mara was about to continue on when Nemti grabbed her arm. Onuris leaned over. "The women should stay here. Don't move a muscle, either of you. Nemti, here's our chance. Remember what we talked about? The night watch?"

"Yes."

"Let's do it."

"What are you two talking about?" Mara demanded.

Nemti's voice was tense. "We've been working on a plan. We'd hoped for better timing, but this has forced our hand."

"What plan?"

"Never mind. Too complicated to explain." He pulled Onuris well away from the women and lowered his voice. "The moment you hear a scuffle, grab the women and take off down the trail. The trick is to get past the big boulder before anyone can see you. After that your path is unobstructed. The only time you'll be vulnerable will be when you come up over the top of the rise and are silhouetted against the sky. With any luck, I'll have the situation in hand by that time."

Onuris scowled. "Three against one? You're crazy!"

"I haven't been drinking; they have. I slipped up this way after you went into town tonight and spied on them. They brought a couple of wineskins with them and are pouring it down their throats, commiserating over being stuck up there at the picket instead of on a rampage in the village like the rest of these barbarians."

"Ti and the girl are with the Habiru," Onuris said.

"Wise choice. The soldiers probably won't get to the Habiru huts until tomorrow at the earliest. You could break a leg getting there in the dark."

"Nemti, are you sure this is what you want to do?"

"It's what I *have* to do. Don't tell Mara my plans until dawn. Make sure you're some distance from here beforehand. And tell her that if there's any chance of getting back to her, I'll—"

"Of course." The two men embraced like brothers. "If you let anything happen to you, I'll . . . I don't know what I'll do to you."

"I love you too, you old bear. You're the best comrade a man ever had. If I can, I'll see you as soon as the king's free. And if not, well, live a good life. Be happy. Father some children. Name one of them after me."

"You'll get through, Nemti. I know you will."

"Sure." He took a deep breath. "Now give me a minute or two to get up there. I'll kick up a ruckus. The moment I do, grab them and get going."

"Nemti—"

"Hush. Get ready. I'm going."

"What are we doing?" Mara asked, her voice rising. "Where's Nemti?"

"Shhhh. He's covering our rear, just in case. There's going to be a lot of activity in a minute. When you hear hollering, we're to take off up this path. Can you see the road?"

"Yes. We're going to the desert?"

"It's the only thing to do."

Suddenly there was a bellow of rage on the heights, and a scuffle, and a string of curses.

"Go! Go now!" Onuris ordered, giving Mara a push from behind.

She lowered her head and ran.

V

The moon shining through the latticed window cast a patterned shadow on the floor. Kamose, the king of Egypt, sat in the corner, blinking at it, trying to get it into focus, to turn the swirling dots of light into sharp-edged patterns.

He shook his head, hoping to clear the cobwebs out. *I wonder if I can stand up. I'm not as dizzy as I was.* He put his heels down and rocked forward unsteadily until his feet were flat on the floor and he was crouched like an ape, his naked behind resting against his bare heels.

Then he rocked forward again, got his palms flat against the chill floor, tensed himself, and pushed. He was halfway erect; then, a bit at a time, he forced himself to a standing position.

His head swam. For a moment he had to steady himself with a supporting hand against the wall. Then he began to get his orientation.

He suffered a spasm of dizziness and would have vomited if there had been anything in his stomach. But he had been covertly ingesting only water for several days now—he wasn't certain how many—and disposing of everything else down the water-fed toilet. He wanted no more of the heavy dosage of *shepenn* they had been feeding him. The hunger had come to him very hard at first; now, with several days' fast behind him, he was not bothered by it.

He blinked. The lattice began a bit at a time to come into focus. Then he could see through it. He lurched forward heavily and suddenly came to the end of his tether. The manacle around his raw, sore right ankle pulled hard at the end of its chain and brought him up short.

"Bastards!" he growled in a hoarse voice, low and angry. "How dare they keep the king of Egypt, the hero of the people, chained to a wall like this? Like some condemned criminal!"

The realization that he was a prisoner suddenly came together with all its implications for the first time since he had been brought here—first to succumb greedily and wearily to the dangerous overdosage they had fed him, then to come slowly to his senses and begin to regain control over himself and mislead them into thinking he was still the burned-out hulk they had brought up from the delta.

He *was* a prisoner. And, like as not, a condemned one, awaiting a quick death at some specified time in the near future!

There was no other way to interpret the situation. He vaguely remembered having heard someone talking about him, back when he was under the influence of the drug.

There had been some reference to restraining him for his own good, of removing his clothing so that he could not fashion a rope with which to hang himself from tunic or loincloth when the craving for the drug grew too powerful.

But having presented himself for some time to his observers as a man totally addicted, totally passive, he could hardly see that restraints were still needed.

No, there was some other purpose to this, like keeping him trussed up and under lock and key while waiting for the order from Amasis to murder him.

He moved as close to the latticed window as he could and tried to look out. He could see a high wall and, in the predawn hush, a silent figure moving atop it, carrying something that looked like a pike.

Gods! he thought again. *I wish I'd been in condition to take some notice of this place when they brought me in!*

He sat again, the marble floor cold against his bare buttocks. The moonlight had been slowly giving way to the advancing pink flush of dawn. There was a distinct reddish tinge in the sky. That meant his room faced east.

His hands went to the manacle on his ankle. During a lucid spell some time back, he had pulled at the fetter long and hard and had managed to move the bronze just a bit. Now he tried again. The bronze gave a little, then sprang back into place. He cursed silently and crossed his legs, the manacled foot on top. He positioned his hands and pulled mightily. This time the bronze bent and did not return entirely to the original position.

He loosed a low snarl and attacked the fetter once more. *Ach! If only I had all my normal strength to draw upon now! How quickly this soft metal would give way!*

With a grunt he forced the manacle again. This time the two ends of the circle pulled a trifle farther apart.

He tried forcing his ankle through the gap but the opening was still too narrow.

Outside his door! Footsteps!

He rotated the manacle so that the widened gap was hidden from the person who would be entering the room. But surprisingly, no one ventured inside. Instead he heard voices, male and female. Nemaret's and the maid's.

". . . doesn't matter. I know he's been disposing of the food. He may even have withdrawn from the drug by now. That's none of your business, really. Your business is to follow your orders. I thought we had that straight."

"Oh, yes, sir. But if he's to die, and soon, why should it matter? If he wants to starve himself to death instead of—"

"Just follow your orders. Amasis has consolidated power now that Baliniri's dead."

Baliniri—dead! Could it be true?

". . . expect the queen and Princess Thermutis to be captured any moment now. The men are searching every building in Deir el-Bahari. The women should be located by noon today at the latest. With them gone, nobody is left to oppose us but the Temple of Amon, and we've got spies inside the priesthood already. When Amasis says the word, they'll move, and then it'll all be ours. Amasis says I'll be moving with him. And remember what I told you? If you continue to be nice to me—"

"Yes, yes. Don't remind me."

"Don't tell me what not to remind you of. You'd do well to remember who's the overseer of this household."

"Only when Amasis isn't here."

"It seems you need a lesson or two every so often to remind you. Get over here."

Kamose blocked the rest from his mind. He stood again and was thankful not to be dizzy this time. He tried furiously to get his thoughts together. Baliniri dead! Mara and Thermutis on the run—probably against some sort of phony charges Amasis had devised to make his actions seem legitimate.

Kamose dropped to one knee and pulled mightily against the bronze anklet that still restrained him. It gave a bit more, and after a painful interlude of tugging and scraping he was able to pull the metal away from his flesh and stand free of it.

But what to do now? The window was immobile. He was sure of that. And the door had a huge oak bar on the other side; he remembered that vividly. What to do? What to do?

Nemti tried to get up but could not. The wound in his side had begun to hurt viciously. He gingerly put one hand on it, as if to hold the pain in; in fact it seemed to feel a trifle better when he held on to it.

All three guards were dead, and his friends and his woman—the only woman he had ever loved in all his life—had got away. He looked around him at the dead soldiers and cursed the one who had caught him just below the ribs with that sword thrust.

Six months ago he wouldn't have got to me, he thought angrily. He looked around. It was dawn! The new watch would be coming on shortly! He had to get out of here!

He struggled to his feet, holding his belly as if his guts would fall out if he let go, and grimaced at the sudden pain.

I'm hurt bad, he thought. *I don't have much flight in me now. I'll have to run for somewhere close.* But where? It was no good going to Ti . . . or was it?

He looked down into the village. Ti's house was a shambles, like everyone else's. The villagers had managed to put out the fires the guards had set at the other end of her street, but the little backyards of each house were full of broken belongings the brigands had thrown from the buildings while conducting their brutal searches. In Ti's yard was what seemed like half of the furniture he had remembered seeing inside her little dwelling.

Well, if they had already searched her place and found nothing, perhaps that made it the safest place to go. Surely they wouldn't search it again. He would try to get down to her.

But now when he attempted to move down the hill—in full sight of the whole village, unfortunately—the pain was almost more than he could bear. He stumbled and nearly fell, and his progress down the rest of the trail was by lurches and blunders.

At the bottom he rested for a moment. The next thing he knew he was lying flat on his back in the road, blinking into the eyes of a stranger.

"W-who are you?" he asked.

The man's garments and pronounced Habiru accent gave him away. "Relax," he said. "I'm Aaron ben Amram. You're hurt. I'm going to take you somewhere safe."

"No," Nemti said. "Save yourself. Help me and you'll

get in terrible trouble. I killed three guards. One of them got me. The watch will be along in a moment or two. If they catch me, and you with me—"

"It's all right," the slave responded. "I know who you are. You've been bringing food to my mother, Jochebed. I'll take you wherever you want. Brace yourself—when I pick you up, it's going to hurt. Try not to cry out."

"Why isn't he here?" Mara fretted, looking back. "Something's happened to him, I know it! We've traveled three leagues by now. If nothing had happened, he would have caught up with us by now."

Onuris caught at her hand, trying to pull her farther down the trail, but she yanked her hand away. "You deliberately fooled me. You knew all the time he'd stayed behind."

"Mara, come along, please—"

"I'm not moving another step until you tell me what's happened to him."

So, looking nervously back down the path, he told her . . . and watched the stunned look wash over her face as she heard him out.

"Oh, no," she cried out. "I've lost him. I'll never see him again. How could he do this?"

"Mara," Thermutis said, "please, dear, we've got to go. They'll be along right after us. He'll be all right. I'm sure of it."

Sobbing like a child, Mara let herself be steered along the path. She stumbled blindly down the road, boxed in between them.

The path led up a steep rise to another narrow pass. The opening cut between two extrusions of a harder rock, which stood up like the erect, alert ears of some sort of great animal.

And from atop one of the twin sentinels, a great cheetah, invisible but for its luminous eyes, watched them pass.

CHAPTER NINE

Semna

I

From the topmost battlement of the great fortress of Semna West, young Princess Tharbis, daughter of the courtier Balaam, looked out over the straits. Below, on her side of the river, she could see the Nubian soldiers drilling, both on the flatland north of the fort and on the peninsula that jutted out to the east of it. This was not extraordinary; the soldiers always drilled, even in time of peace, at Semna West.

There was a difference now, however. The enemy Egyptian force was visible on the other bank of the Nile. They had burned their big boats and then crossed the river in smaller craft, to land on the drifted sand just north of the fortress of Kumma, across the strait from her own location.

Behind her, her father, Balaam, conferred with his chief adviser, Malenaken.

"They're thinking that Kumma will be the easier fort to take," Balaam said. "Well, ordinarily that would be true. This

271

place is well-nigh impregnable, while Kumma can be taken by any man who can handle the snakes in the southeast corner of the peninsula. The place is seething with them: the most deadly, poisonous vipers of all the lands beside the Nile."

"Interesting," Malenaken said. "Despite the apparently less formidable nature of the other fort, it will have a few surprises for the attackers?"

"Yes. Taking the fort will gain them nothing. The Egyptians' real problem is here, at Semna. They've quite wisely burned their own boats, having ascertained that they can't bring them through the straits. They've counted on being able to liberate our boats on this side of the strait, but they're going to have to fight for them. And they're going to have to fight us here at Semna, where the defending force—in an impregnable fortress, mind you—is much greater than theirs." Balaam chuckled.

"And when they come to fight Semna," Malenaken said, "they'll be exhausted from the effort expended in trying to take Kumma. That is, even if they do take Kumma, which isn't a sure thing in the first place." He smiled appreciatively. "You've done well. Our backers at Kerma will be proud of you. I have taken all precautions that none of the credit will be shared with Nehsi. Our people are busy at work at Kerma, blackening his name throughout the capital and exalting yours."

Balaam made a shushing noise, then he turned to Tharbis. "Don't you have something to do? Your devotions? Your studies?"

"I've finished everything, Father," the girl said mildly. "I wanted some fresh air. Please let me watch the battle from up here. It will be safe."

"Go below! This is no place for a woman!"

"That's the trouble," she protested. "Around here there is no place for a woman. Everywhere I go I'm unwanted. If I'm always in the way, why did you drag me into a war zone?"

Balaam glared at her. "I've been asking myself the same question," he said sourly. "It wasn't safe back at Kerma. Great things are about to happen, things that even you will come to appreciate."

"Such as?" the girl asked, tossing her dark hair. "You mean finding me a husband? I don't want a husband from around here. Women who aren't black aren't valued here. I don't want to be Wife Number Seven to some provincial chieftain whose other wives will stare at me as if I were a freak or a slave girl."

"Insolent! No respect! No grasp of the larger picture!"

"Well? What advantage will I derive from all this?" she asked. "And why would things be unsafe for me in Kerma now? I've always liked living at the court. There are civilized people in it, even women to talk to, not just a lot of sweaty soldiers who've been warned not to speak to me."

"You'll find out soon," he promised. "Just trust me." He leaned forward and whispered, "Within a matter of hours."

"Couldn't I have learned about it while I was in Kerma?"

"I have enemies there. You'd be in danger. I didn't want to leave you behind, because someone could break in and kidnap you."

"A fat lot you'd care," accused the girl. "All you care about is war and politics. Mother was lucky! She didn't live long enough to be moved into a war zone and bored to death."

"Curse you! Insolent little snip! Go back inside! Now!"

She flounced away. But the moment she was out of sight, she stopped and repositioned herself so that she could eavesdrop on the men; her curiosity was strong, and she wanted to hear more about the mysterious doings her father had almost blurted out to her.

". . . high-spirited but charming, my lord Balaam. The man who wins her will be fortunate, even if he has to do a bit of taming in the process."

"Taming!" Balaam exclaimed. "Good luck to anyone who tries! But nobody is going to 'win' her. Once the coup has taken place, she's going to be a very important part of my plan."

"Perhaps I understand. When you're king of Nubia, an advantageous marriage between the princess and another great power—"

"Precisely! An alliance between the new white regime in Nubia, freed of the yoke of the black rulers for the first time

in many years, and—well, I haven't made up my mind yet.
But Egypt itself is due for a change soon. Our spies tell us a
coup is impending. Baliniri will be out, and Kamose dead.
Amasis will be in charge. And once installed as king of Egypt,
he'll be starting to think of an heir."

"Amasis? At *his* age?"

Balaam nodded knowingly. "The moment he takes over
as king he'll be wanting a child of his own blood to hand the
throne over to. What an alliance *that* would make!"

"What does Apedemek think of this?"

"It was his idea."

Tharbis's dark eyes blazed. *So that's what Father is up
to! He's thinking of overthrowing Nehsi!* And of marrying her
off to a man three times her age! A dried-up, wrinkled old
prune, no doubt; a man whose reputation for cruelty was
known far and wide! What kind of father was he to consider
such a thing? How could he just toss his daughter away for
his own gain? Oh! If Mother were only here! She would know
what to do!

She sat and thought for a moment, then realized how
dangerous it would be for her if Balaam knew she had overheard his plans. She slipped down the stairs soundlessly and
went inside the great central hall of the castle, where she
leaned against an interior pillar and tried to think.

Nehsi! They were talking about deposing Nehsi, who
had been king for as long as she could remember. A kind
man! Depose, then kill? It would be necessary, of course.
Nehsi had been much loved in Nubia. There would be a
bloodbath if he were left alive. If they installed a new regime
composed of whites, the blacks would strike back. There'd be
civil war in Nubia! She had to do something. But what?

Perhaps I could get through to Nehsi and warn him.
Well, that sounded good. But what would the consequences
be? If it were known that her father was plotting to depose
the king, he himself would find his days numbered. And what
would happen to her then? She had not a friend here. Oh,
Nehsi would be grateful, but she would be the girl who
betrayed her father. She would be shunned. There would be
no place for her among either whites or blacks.

Oh, it was impossible. There was not anything she could

do without putting herself in a terrible position! If only she had a friend. If only there were someone to advise her. If only there were someone she could talk to!

Nehsi frowned. "You sent the Egyptians my answer to their challenge, and still they decided to do battle with us?"

General Aspelta shot a quick glance at his colleague, General Nataki, behind the king's back. "Yes, sire," he said. "We sent them your message of peace, asserting your right to occupy the twin forts on the straits as your father had done and declaring that you had no hostile intentions. But once again, the Egyptians have answered a friendly overture with aggression. See the answer? 'Moses of Egypt to the usurper. Semna is mine. If the thing stolen—' "

"Stolen! Imagine him saying such a thing!"

"Yes, sire. Such arrogance. 'If the thing stolen is returned to me by sundown tomorrow, the thief may retain Kerma, his capital, and may live as a vassal of Egypt. Otherwise he will learn that no lord of Egypt is not also lord of Nubia!' "

Nehsi's eyes were large and wide. "Who is this Moses person? I do not remember any Moses. Has there been a change in leadership in Egypt? What happened to my friend Baliniri? Where is Kamose?"

Again the surreptitious exchange of knowing glances behind the king's back. "We think there may have been a coup. There have been reports of plans in Thebes to kill Baliniri and Kamose and substitute someone new on the throne. Perhaps Moses is this usurper. The palace revolution might already have occurred."

"And this upstart chooses to insult me! What does Balaam say?"

"He says, sire, that this deadly insult must be answered in blood. Already the enemy prepares to assault Kumma, across the straits. Balaam proposes that we answer abuse with force."

"You mean war with Egypt, with whom we have been friends for a generation? Surely this Moses and I can sit down and talk."

Now the quick glance shared by the two generals communicated a sudden sense of alarm. "Talk, sire?" Nataki asked quickly. "It'd be too dangerous. You'd be risking your life."

"Oh, surely not. Would Moses attack under a flag of truce?" Nehsi looked up and almost caught Aspelta exchanging significant looks with Nataki. "Tell Balaam to arrange a meeting before the Egyptians attack Kumma. I want to talk with this fellow."

Aspelta's voice, when he finally answered after a long beat, had a strangled quality. "As you wish, sire. We will tell him." He saluted and left the room, Nataki in tow.

When the two were well down the long hall, out of earshot, Aspelta pulled Nataki aside. "That does it. If we don't do something, he'll foul everything up. The only thing to do is present as strong a case as possible to Balaam for doing the thing now."

"You mean assassinating Nehsi?"

"Whatever it takes. If we let him interfere, the whole plan is off. And you know what Apedemek will say about that."

"Gods! He'll have our heads!"

"Right. Come on. Back me up. I'm going to push Balaam hard."

"You can depend on me."

II

The two generals met Princess Tharbis in the hall. Aspelta made a courtly bow, barring her path. "My lady! What are you doing so far away from your customary haunts? Surely your father—"

"My father doesn't tell me where to go," she retorted. "I'm going to see the king. I haven't spoken with him in quite a long time."

"Oh, my lady," Aspelta said, "I'm afraid that will be quite impossible. The king gave the strictest orders not to be disturbed. If we were to let you through, it would go very hard with us."

Tharbis's eyes flashed. She looked past him to the towering guard standing watch over the king's door. "Very well. The king has always encouraged my visits, but I will believe you. If I find out, however, that the order not to let me through came from someone other than the king, Nehsi will be *very* angry."

To her surprise the thought of raising Nehsi's ire did not seem to bother them at all. And a sudden flash of insight came through to her: *They're in it too! They're my father's accomplices!* Thoughts rushed into her mind with bewildering speed. *If that is true, it is likely the king is already a prisoner in everything but name! The guard isn't there to keep people like me out; he is there to keep the king in!*

"Please, my lady," Nataki said. "We have our orders." He took her arm. She shook his hand off angrily, and he made a duplicate of the same little flourish Aspelta had done, half-deferent, half-insultingly officious. "We really must ask you to stay out of this corridor."

"Very well," she said, and turned on one heel, stamping angrily around the corner. She did not stop until she had reached the passage that led to her own rooms. When at last she had reached her apartment, she slammed the door behind her and flung herself down on her bed.

She was no more than a pawn in all this, a game piece to be bargained away. There was a war with Egypt now, it seemed, and apparently Prince Moses, whoever he was, represented King Kamose and his famous vizier, Baliniri. But both of them were targeted to be deposed or killed! Then Balaam would deal with Amasis, and she would be one of the bargaining counters when the negotiations began!

Who could have thought this up? Certainly not any of the staff officers; they did not have the power to implement schemes of this magnitude. Her father? She did not think so. She had no particular respect for her father's intelligence. Then who?

Only that frightening man Apedemek, who had appeared out of nowhere some months ago and wormed his way into Balaam's confidence so quickly. She shuddered, thinking of him: Apedemek was always turning up when and where you least expected him, frightening her until she was ready to jump out of her skin.

Yes. That had to be it. Behind any evil scheme that required brains and forethought there had to be Apedemek. He had the brains, the requisite ruthlessness, and the cold-bloodedness. Without the support—or even coercion—of a man like that, her father would never have been able to consider carrying out such a plan.

Where was he now? Down the hall scheming against Nehsi? Waiting for an unwary person like herself to cross his path, so he might move out of the shadows and scare her to death? Maybe he was over in Kumma, preparing the soldiers for the Egyptians' assault? Ah, if only she could be sure he was out of the fortress altogether.

What was it about him, anyhow? She had been frightened of him from the very first; so had virtually everyone else, including Balaam. They had all sensed that terrible power in him, only barely reined in for the sake of decorum. There was evil in him, immense and measureless evil.

She shivered and rubbed her arms. She was sure he had . . . plans for her. Plans that did not, like her father's, involve giving her away to some stranger for political reasons. Not, at least, before he had had his own way with her! Now she cringed, imagining herself in the hands—the claws—of a lustful Apedemek!

What a horrible thought! And it was made worse by the sure knowledge that he, of all the men in the fortress, was stronger and smarter than she was! None of her stratagems would work against him if he ever decided to go after her! She would be like a newborn child in the fierce jaws of a hungry lion!

She sat bolt upright, chilled by the thought. She had to do something! But what?

Aspelta and Nataki located Balaam and Malenaken watching the development of the enemy force below, on the peninsula just beyond the strait. "My lord!" Aspelta said. "There's something you ought to know!"

Swiftly he told what had happened in Nehsi's rooms.

"The guard is under strict orders to keep him where he is. And, quite incidentally, to keep anyone out. Most particularly your daughter."

Balaam wheeled, stared. "My daughter! What about my daughter?"

"She was trying to get through to see him."

Balaam looked Malenaken in the eye. "She must have heard us talking! If I don't do something, she'll find some way to tip him off about our plans!"

"Shall we put her under guard as well?"

Balaam thought a moment, brows knit, face contorted with anger and puzzlement. "Apedemek!" he said. "Never around when you need him!" He suddenly realized what he was saying. "Forget you heard that. I was just shooting off my mouth. I didn't mean to criticize him. I don't need Apedemek to make up my mind for me. I realize he has to be down there at Kumma, supervising everything personally. I'm sure he'll approve of what I'm about to do."

"My lord! You don't mean—"

"The time has come. Nehsi is in the way. We're going to need all the guards for the defense; I can't afford to have three shifts just watching the old fool to make sure he doesn't start meddling."

"My lord! You don't mean to kill him?"

Balaam considered. "Not without consulting with Apedemek. He may have some ideas of how Nehsi could be used. Our best field leaders are black like him. They may rebel against us when we stage a takeover. We'll hold Nehsi hostage to keep the blacks in line."

"I wondered why you had dismissed all those loyal black troops from the far south," Aspelta said. "I should have known you had a specific reason in mind. Now I see it's perfectly logical."

The others muttered assent. "My lord," Nataki said, "do you want to keep him under house arrest?"

Balaam thought for a moment. His face slowly took on a look of long-suppressed anger. "No," he said. "Throw him in the dungeon, with the common criminals."

"My lord!"

"You heard me. Why pamper him?"

"But who's in there now? Will they be dangerous to him? These riffraff tend to be vindictive. If you want to keep him alive as hostage—"

"Good point, but the worst that's likely to happen will be that he'll be roughed up a bit. And I don't mind that happening at all."

"My lord," Malenaken ventured, "we'll need a direct order, before witnesses, for so drastic a step as the deposition and imprisonment of the king. An order in writing."

"Get ink and papyrus." He glared at his assistant. "Well? What are you waiting for? Get them!"

In an upstairs chamber situated precisely above the king's window, Tharbis finished knotting a long rope of sheets she had stolen from the storage room, then fastened one end securely to the leg of the huge, heavy bed that stood before the window. Then, just to be sure, she piled all the furniture she could lift atop the bed. When the room's furniture was in place, she went out into the hall and took down, piece by piece, an ornamental display of captured weapons that had hung on the wall. When she had piled everything atop the bed that she could find, she went inside the room and barred the door.

She kicked off her sandals, went to the window, and looked out, then threw the free end of the knotted sheets out the window. She leaned far out to check on whether the sheets would reach all the way; satisfied, she impulsively stripped off her long, cumbersome robes and stood in her brief shift for a moment.

She climbed onto the window ledge, took hold of the sheet firmly in one strong little hand, and taking a deep breath, lowered herself carefully out above the yawning chasm. Far below, sunlight glinted on the half-filled moat.

III

Aspelta and Nataki, once again on the battlements, drew apart at the southern wall. The roar of the strait kept their words from carrying, and anyone who approached would be visible long before anything could be overheard.

Nataki snorted. "Imagine Balaam taking things into his own hands like that, without permission from Apedemek."

Aspelta nodded. "*And* talking loosely about him. Doesn't he know the walls have ears? That damned near everybody is reporting back to Apedemek?"

"Well, I'm glad he has to face Apedemek, not me. These are frightening times."

"Yes," Aspelta agreed. "On the other hand, being here is going to prove to be very beneficial to both our careers, don't you think? Anyone who's in on this with Apedemek from the first will rise fast."

"Think so?" Nataki asked. He shot a sharp glance at his friend. "I can't imagine him getting all soppy and sentimental about us just because we were with him at the battle of Kumma."

"Well, no." Aspelta looked across the citadel at the far wall, where Malenaken was watching the two of them with more than usual interest. "See that son of a bitch looking at us? I'll bet he knows pretty much what we're talking about. He's not as harmless as he looks."

"It won't help him any. He'll prove as expendable as Balaam in the end. Malenaken, at least, only acts dumb."

"No matter. When the time comes, he'll desert Balaam. He'll come over to our side the moment Apedemek declares himself."

"And when he does," Nataki vowed, "I'll cut his tripes out for him. I don't want any part of him. Sneaky bastard."

"Anyhow, Balaam's ordered Nehsi's arrest."

"But he won't kill him without Apedemek's say-so."

"I don't blame him for that. You won't catch me flouting the rules where Apedemek is concerned. I enjoy being alive. And I enjoy being one of the few people here who isn't either marked for disposal—like Balaam and Malenaken—or under Apedemek's spell, walking around like dumb beasts doing his bidding with no idea what they're up to."

"And a good thing, too; otherwise I wouldn't be talking to you, my friend, no matter how far we go back. You're just about the only person in the citadel I can be honest with—and then only when nobody's around, like now."

Aspelta's expression was bland. "And I'm glad you're not under his spell, either. You aren't, are you? But of course you're not." The doubt had been there, even if for no more than a heartbeat. "To be quite frank with you, he frightens the hell out of me. Those eyes. That voice. I haven't any idea when he's going to start manipulating my mind, the way he does with the weak-minded." He scowled. "Me, I'm not weak-minded as soldiers go, as I think you'll agree. But if he chose to work that spell of his on me . . . well, I'm not sure how long I could hold out."

"Let's change the subject. This one gives me the creeps. How long do you think Nehsi has left to live?"

"Not even as long as Balaam thinks. Balaam plans to lock Nehsi up only until Apedemek gets back from Kumma, but the dungeon is full of dissidents imprisoned under Nehsi's reign—people who blame him for the things we've been doing behind his back—as well as hardened criminals we've locked up and thrown away the key on."

"And you think that when they find out they've got the king with them they'll want revenge?"

"Wouldn't you?"

"Oh, I suppose so. He'll be paying a lot of back bills. Dungeons are filled with grudges." He grinned savagely. "Now there's Apedemek for you. When we started locking up dissenters, we were ordered to tell them that they were being thrown in jail because of some whim of Nehsi's."

"True. That's why I feel so uneasy." Aspelta shivered. "How do we know that Apedemek isn't right here between us, listening to every word we say?"

Nataki stared at him. "Gods! What a thought! But he could have both of us under his spell! He could have given us the suggestion that he's invisible and that we won't remember him coming here and telling us he was going to be invisible. Gives me the shakes just thinking about it."

Aspelta looked around him. Suddenly he took out his sword and swung it right and left, cutting the empty air. And then, sheepishly, he put it back in its scabbard. "Pardon me.

I'm getting a little sensitive to all this. But better safe than sorry."

"Who's there!" Nehsi called, stepping back and drawing the knife at his belt. "Stop right there where you are!"

The slim figure outlined in the open window stepped carefully down from the sill: a girl in her teens, dressed only in a shift. "Sire," she said softly, "it's me, Tharbis. Balaam's daughter."

Nehsi blinked at her and replaced the knife in its hanger. "Tharbis! Child, what are you doing trying a dangerous stunt like that? You could have been killed!"

"Yes, sire," she admitted, "but it was important that I get through to you. There wasn't any other way."

"No other way?" he asked, incredulous. "You know you're always welcome to come to me!"

"Not now, sire. The guard won't let me through. My guess is that he won't let you out, either."

A puzzled frown hung on the kind features. "How could that be? What guard would dare do such a thing to his king?"

"Sire, my father plans to depose you. You're to be put under arrest. He and Apedemek are going to replace you!"

Nehsi shook his head. "I can't believe what you're—"

"Then try to leave, sire. I'll hide behind the door. If I'm caught here trying to warn you, it'll go very badly for me. But try it. You'll see."

He stared at her, still frowning. As she slipped into shadow, he unbarred the door and looked out. Tharbis could hear the voices quite clearly.

"Here, now. I'm not supposed to let you out. I have strict orders."

"What are you saying? Do you realize I could have you flayed for speaking to me like this? Don't you know the rules of courtesy when speaking to your sovereign? Where's my regular guard?"

"I replaced him half an hour ago, under orders from Balaam. And as for that, he's in charge now. Back you go inside the door. I mean it."

From her hiding place, Tharbis could see Nehsi's knuck-

les tighten on the door. "Very well," he said slowly in a voice
full of controlled anger. "You've not heard the last of this."
He closed the door and turned to her. "I could have fought
him and won, I think, but then others would have come and
caught you here. Yes . . . apparently there's been some sort
of uprising. Why? What do they expect to accomplish?" He
sat down slowly on a chair by the door, a hurt and puzzled
look on his face. "This isn't like your father. It's that Apedemek
fellow, isn't it?"

"Yes, sire. I'm sure of it. You're in great danger."

"They'll know you came to warn me. The sheets will still
be dangling from the window, and here you'll be in your
shift. Nobody is going to assume from that that I've been
romancing a girl your age."

She grinned in spite of herself. "I've got to go. I don't
know what you can do. I'll try to help you when I can, sire.
Don't fight them. I don't want to see you get hurt."

"They won't kill me," he assured her. "I'd be worth
more to them alive than dead. Alive, they can use me for a
bargain with the men loyal to me in the army. If they kill me,
they've got a bloody uprising on their hands." He cursed and
pounded his fist on the stone wall. "What a fool I am! They've
been thinning out the ranks of the army for weeks! Why
didn't I realize why? The best units, who'd stand by me
through thick and thin, are in Kumma, with Apedemek!"

"I've got to go," she said. "I hear footsteps. I think
they're coming."

"Go, my dear. Be careful. I'll stall them until I can't see
you anymore. And thank you!"

Just once, poised on the sill of the great window, she
looked back. Then, taking a firm hold on her improvised
rope, she stepped out onto the rough stone of the wall, her
feet finding toeholds, her hands gripping the cloth. A half
step at a time, she edged her way upward. In a moment she
found a jutting projection to stand on and rest. She could
hear some of what the voices were saying above the faraway
roar of the falls.

". . . think you are doing?" Nehsi's booming bass. "You'll
hang for this!"

". . . matter to me. Your time is up, old man. I have my orders. It's the dungeons for you."

Dungeons! she thought. She had been sure they would only confine him to a house arrest. This was more serious than she realized.

She took a firmer grip on the twisted cloth and began to climb again, trying not to look down, trying not to see the rocks her body would hit if she lost her grasp, the jutting and jagged boulders exposed by the low water in the moat.

Six men with spears flanked him. The king glared at them but went quietly, head high, back straight. "You fools!" he said bitterly. "You don't know what you're doing. You don't know the type of man you're serving."

"Yes we do, old man," said one of the spearmen. "We're serving the winner. You're today's loser and tomorrow's forgotten man."

"We'll see about that," Nehsi shot back. "Meanwhile, I'll thank you to keep that spear out of my back."

"Shut up and march," the squad leader ordered. "Here we are. Open up, turnkey! I have another prisoner for you!" His voice rose. "Hey, you in there! You scum in the cells! I have a friend for you to play with! You may even recognize him! It's Nehsi, son of Akhilleus, formerly high king of Nubia, now just another sewer rat like the rest of you, locked away to die!"

Suddenly a dozen faces, angry-eyed, scarred, bearing the welts from recent beatings, appeared behind the bars, leering out. "By all the gods!" one of the prisoners rasped. "He's telling the truth! It *is* the king!"

There was a deranged roar from the inside of the great cells, and suddenly half a dozen more faces appeared behind the bars, one-eyed, gap-toothed, filthy. "Bring him inside!" one of them bellowed. "Let us at him!"

IV

Almost immediately after sealing the order for Nehsi's arrest with his own vizier's copy of the royal cartouche and dispatching Malenaken with it, Balaam, alone for the first time in days, found himself beset with doubts. Were his actions compatible with the plans he and Apedemek had discussed when the first reports had come upriver about the punitive expedition Egypt was mounting against them?

Nervously he climbed atop the battlement wall and looked out across the river at where the two camps, Nubian and Egyptian, had arrayed themselves in preparation for the battle that was sure to take place early the following morning. He scanned the ranks of the Nubians, trying to see if he could recognize Apedemek, but they were too far away. He could not distinguish one man from another.

He closed his eyes and pounded his fist on the rough stone of the battlement. *Curse* Apedemek! Why should he—he, Balaam, who was king now in all but name—have to worry about what any other man thought? Why should he have to tiptoe around Apedemek as if he and not Balaam were the most important man in Nubia now?

He glared across the straits at the unseen enemy. Resentment burned in his heart for the magus and his imperious ways, his diabolical powers, his gift of manipulation. Why should one man be given the power to control other men's minds?

Dark thoughts suddenly occurred to him: If Apedemek, instead of being able to guide the Kumma force to victory, were somehow to die in the attempt . . . if a stray arrow, from either side of the conflict, were somehow to strike him down . . .

He sat down atop the stone and considered these possibilities. The more he pondered them, the more he came to like them.

With Apedemek gone, it would be clear sailing. He could do virtually anything he wanted with Nubia, even restructure the whole of Nubian society. He could make his own deals with Egypt and the nations to the south—even with Punt, down the coast of the Red Sea. He could build a dynasty of his own, taking wives from other nations and fathering children upon them. He could build an empire! Who knew where it could lead?

And even as he thought this, there was a sudden chill on his heart. He closed his eyes, and a vision of Apedemek appeared in his mind. Those piercing eyes! That wooden, expressionless face! He opened his eyes and shuddered.

What if Apedemek really could get inside a man's mind? What if he knew, at this very moment, what he, Balaam, was thinking?

Suddenly he knew beyond the smallest shadow of a doubt in what terrible danger his actions and thoughts had placed him. He remembered, terrified, the Nubian officer back in Kerma, who had defied Apedemek just before they had left to come downriver. The officer was a chieftain in his own lands, splendidly fit and two handspans taller than Apedemek. From the look of him, he could have twisted Apedemek's head off with his bare hands.

Yet Apedemek had killed him slowly, horribly, one agonized gasp at a time, before a thousand witnesses, without ever laying a finger on him. The officer had perished after several minutes of excruciating pain, unable to breathe, his body twisted hideously out of shape as if he had fallen from a great height and broken every bone. And through it all, Apedemek had just stood there looking at him, speaking quietly in a voice only he could hear.

It had been a mind-boggling occurrence. Upon it had hung the entire success of their mission—to take Nehsi away from Kerma, where he was loved and revered, to the cataracts, where he could be deposed in relative safety, far from friends and bodyguards. The border war Apedemek, Balaam, and the generals had started against Egypt was a mere pretext for getting Nehsi where they had wanted him.

If the army had risen to defend that writhing, dying officer, Balaam was not sure even Apedemek could have controlled them. But the fact that Apedemek had used evil magic, pure and simple, convinced the blacks from the high country to stay out of Apedemek's way. Thus had the threat of rebellion passed.

From that moment Apedemek's moves had been gradual, perfectly timed, confident, and sure. He had demoted potentially dangerous leaders; he had separated military units, broken up long friendships between comrades, and created new units from men whose tribes had hated one another for many generations; and he had deliberately lessened the effectiveness of his own army, in order to weaken any resistance they might have gathered against his eventual takeover.

In all this, he, Balaam, had repeatedly tried to warn Apedemek about the advancing Egyptian punitive force, pointing out that the reputed leader, Khafre, was one of the most resourceful commanders in the entire Egyptian command. What if the Nubian force had been weakened so much that it could not now deal with the Egyptians?

Apedemek had told him: "Leave the Egyptians to me. When the time comes to fight them, it will not be your gelded army that has to engage them. It will be me, Apedemek."

He had sputtered against that, but Apedemek had broken in and said, "And it will not be a battle between the Egyptian invasion force and me. It will be a battle between Seth of Thebes and me."

Nehsi's eyes surveyed the half-circle of filthy faces arrayed against him. He edged back against the far wall, his body tense, his mind racing, as the criminals drew nearer. One prisoner had no right eye, just a gaping hole; another had lost his left hand—probably for thievery, as this was the common punishment—and had replaced it with a tarnished bronze hook. There were several smashed noses, and one face seemed to be almost entirely scar tissue.

"Get back," he warned. "I won't hurt anyone who leaves me alone." Since the king was so outnumbered, his bravado should have drawn laughter, but he saw several of them steal quick looks at his huge arms, the still-powerful hands, his towering height, and his great spread of shoulder.

Nevertheless, they did not draw back. The one-eyed man and the fellow with the hook exchanged glances, and he saw them separate toward the periphery of his vision. If both of them attacked from the flanks at the same time, they might keep him busy enough to allow the others to rush him. He assumed a crouch, which left him no taller than the rest of them, and readied himself for desperate battle.

Then, out of the shadows in the ill-lit dungeon stepped a young man, stocky, powerfully built, with huge, burly shoulders and great, rippling back muscles, which showed easily through his rough tunic.

"What is it there?" he asked in a sarcastic voice. "Nine against one? That's the sort of odds you cowards specialize in, isn't it? He's better than twice the age of most of you. I'd think that three of you to his one ought to be a little closer to fair. But you're not the type of scum to take chances, are you? What about that, One-Eye? Your style is more like beating up cripples, isn't it?" He spat at the one-eyed man's feet. "I'd hazard a month's pay, if I had any coming, that you're in here for something really slimy. Raping a corpse, perhaps, or molesting a child."

"You! Shut up!" the one-eyed man snarled.

"Hit close to home, did I?" asked the young man. "Well, you're going to have to prove your valor. The odds have changed. They're nine to two now. The king can sit this one out if he likes. Come on, you parasites! Who wants to be the first to die?"

The man with the hook lunged at him from the side. The hook swung in a wide arc, and Nehsi could see it glint with dim light. The hook had been sharpened to a razor edge some time before and could have cut off the young man's head. But the broad-shouldered youngster ducked and in one fluid movement dug a powerful fist into the one-handed man's ribs, with all his weight behind the blow. The criminal sank onto his knees, and the young man kneed him in the face viciously, just as One-Eye attacked.

The young man's reaction was almost too swift to be seen clearly in the dim light. He backhanded One-Eye in the face, sending him backwards into the bars. At the same time his foot lashed out and caught another attacker square in the face. That man staggered sideways, his face bleeding, his nose broken grotesquely.

The attack faltered. The young man laughed heartily, contemptuously. "Thank all the gods," he said, "that cowards and weaklings like you are here in jail and not out on the lines defending Nubia's good name. You would cut and run if a rabbit snarled at you."

The line moved back a step.

"Is nobody going to challenge me?" the young man taunted. "Are there only three of you brave enough to try to take my measure? Come on, now. Who among you wants his face smashed in? Who begs for a broken arm or leg? Who desires a kick in the balls?" He snorted. "I've got half a mind to turn you over to the king now. He could probably handle the rest of you while I lie back on the straw and watch. No takers?"

One by one the criminals slipped ignominiously back into the darkness in the far end of the room.

Nehsi blinked, almost unable to believe in the exhibition of bravery he had just witnessed. "Thank you, young man. But whom have I to thank for this act of valor?"

The young man turned, smiled, and showed Nehsi a face so round and friendly and likable that it was almost impossible to imagine it scaring off a mob of nine men. The young man respectfully fell to one knee. "Het, sire," he said. "Late of the Third Troop. I am at your command."

V

Balaam's face publicly bore a tense, worried expression. As the enormity of what he had done finally began to penetrate, he turned to action. He had summoned Nataki, Aspelta, and Malenaken to his sparely furnished apartment to puzzle out the problems his rash act had caused.

He turned first to generals Aspelta and Nataki. "Should I call a meeting of the field officers? Discuss it with them first, and then make a proclamation to the whole garrison?"

"A true leader does not discuss such matters," Nataki declared. "He acts, then informs everyone what he has done."

"Yes, my lord," Aspelta agreed. "But a certain amount of diplomacy will undoubtedly be necessary. Nehsi was well liked, so we'll have to accuse him of treason or something like that."

"Treason?" Malenaken echoed, raising one brow. He did

not elaborate upon this one interjection, choosing to sit at the far end of the table, frowning.

Aspelta thought about it a moment. "It does sound a bit extreme. After all, the man governed wisely for a long time, without any hint of any such behavior. On the other hand, everyone knows he's getting older, not the man he was. There may be something in that to work with."

"You don't throw a man in jail for being in his middle years," Nataki objected. "I thought at the time that the jail order was . . . well, you know. . . ." He massaged his temples. "It might have been better to confine him to his quarters, 'for his own sake,' as you might put it."

"Well, it's too late for that." Balaam sighed. "I've declared myself. The point is, what do I do to make my action palatable to the army? I don't have much time. The moment the shift changes, word will get down to the garrison outside the fort."

"That's two hours, at best," Nataki noted. "What if—" He stopped, pondering. "What if Nehsi was said to have proposed tactics that would have resulted in certain military defeat in the pending encounter?"

"Say, that's not bad," Aspelta complimented. "Not bad at all. After all, Apedemek had ordered us to abandon most of the forts and virtually to sacrifice the little garrison at Mirgissa. There's been grousing about that among the rank and file and the field commanders. I'm sure Apedemek had good reason for doing these things, but he hasn't bothered to share it with us, and we're the ones stuck with explaining the unexplainable to our critics. Perhaps we could blame these apparently bad decisions on Nehsi."

Balaam beamed. "I *knew* I could count on you," he said enthusiastically. "That's brilliant! That's exactly what we'll do! I want you to assemble the officers, and I'll make a speech. I'll do nothing but praise Nehsi and tell them how reluctant we were to take such a drastic step. I'll say the only reason I was finally forced into doing it was that I didn't want to endanger the lives of any more of our brave warriors."

"That's just the right tone to take, my lord," Nataki said. "We'll set up the conference. Would you like it at sunset, at the changing of the watch?"

"No, a little before. I want them to be able to explain it to their commands before the rumors have come down at the common-soldier level, from the troops getting off shift. Now go, all of you. I'll begin work on my speech."

Nehsi and Het, his young benefactor, sat on the filthy, cold stone with their backs to the bars. From the darkness at the rear of the cell they could feel eyes watching them.

"Don't worry, sire," Het soothed. "They won't be back. Not soon, anyhow. They're a cowardly lot." He scowled. "The most insulting thing about this is that Balaam would throw you into a place like this, with the dregs of Nubia, and not somewhere commensurate with your rank and dignity."

"No chance of that," Nehsi replied ruefully. "He's declared himself once and for all. No use wasting kindness or consideration on me—he knows full well that if I ever get free, he's a dead man. He and all those scum who have backed him in this. Aspelta! Nataki! That fawning toady Malenaken!"

"And, of course, Apedemek most of all. He's behind it, sire. You can count on that. Even Balaam probably knows he's no more than a tool in Apedemek's hands."

"I'm sure you're right." The king pondered for a moment. "You seem to know quite a lot for a—What was your rank, anyhow?"

"I'm a civilian, sire, attached to the Third for pay distribution and record keeping. That just means they have to feed me. I was originally sent here by the government officials in Kerma, to supervise the shoring-up of the forts' defenses. It was a good idea, but then I was ordered away first from Buhen, then Kor and Mirgissa and Dorginarti. In the end I realized there was something suspicious going on. When I complained, I was thrown in here."

"I see. That means that the commanders here countermanded the orders the court had given you back in Kerma."

"Yes. And that makes no sense. Look what's happened because of their idiotic policies: We've given up everything but Kumma. I do understand retreating for a strategic purpose, luring the enemy into a trap or an ambush. But this doesn't figure."

"No, it doesn't, does it?" Nehsi frowned, his mind working.

"And mind you, sire, the commanders aren't to blame for any of this. The order may have come from Balaam, but Apedemek spoke through him."

"I see," the king said, shaking his head slowly. "I obviously have not taken Apedemek seriously enough. Everyone seemed to be so afraid of him, manipulated by him—"

"I'm not surprised you were not similarly affected, sire. Akhilleus's son would not be easily bamboozled."

"Ah," Nehsi said, sighing sadly. "Your words flatter, but they skirt the truth. I did not see this coup coming. I neither recognized Balaam for the villain he turned out to be nor took Apedemek seriously. I did not take charge of my own army, and I left the decision making to others. I have been a fool—"

"No, sire! You wrong yourself!"

"It is the truth, my young friend. When I was younger, I would not have been such fair game for these wretches. There was a time when no one could have taken my throne from me."

Het gave the king a determined look. "Well, sire, they may not have possession of it forever. They're going to have to fight for it. And who knows? You and I may just take it back from them."

Nehsi turned his head to look at the young man. "You seem to forget we are in jail, both of us."

"That won't last, sire."

"But how? . . ."

"Shhh," the young man warned. "Too many ears. Later, when everyone's asleep. Too dangerous to talk about it just now."

Nehsi looked at him, taking note of the clear-eyed, fearless young face, at the decency in it. "Well," he said with a very slow smile, "I haven't got in trouble yet, trusting you." He chuckled. "I'll stick around that long, I guess."

"Father!" Tharbis said, her voice hard and angry. "How could you do it? Do you have any idea what you've committed yourself to? And what the penalty will be if you're unsuccessful?"

"Of course I do. How dare you use such a tone of voice speaking to me?"

"That *regal* attitude, Father, ill becomes you. Who gave you this idiotic idea? It couldn't have been Malenaken; he's not only too much of a coward, he has the intelligence of a sparrow. Whoever it was, you can be sure that when the reckoning comes, you'll be the one who takes the fall for it."

"Keep your tongue to yourself, young woman!"

"Aspelta? Nataki? No. Even they would have more sense than to depose the king of Nubia and throw him in prison!" She stood with hands on slim hips, and her color was high with righteous indignation. "No. It has to be Apedemek. That's it, isn't it? He's got you in his spell, then, just the way he's got all the generals."

"Nobody's got me under any—"

"Don't you for one moment assume that he's going to let you reign. Even if you do manage to avoid open revolt among the army and seize power, you won't last a month. He'll have you trussed up like a calf ready for the slaughter before the moon's changed phases."

"Tharbis, you're testing my patience beyond endurance!"

"You couldn't be satisfied with serving a kind man like Nehsi. He looked out for you. He made sure you rose much faster than your merits deserved. He interceded for you with the court and the army. The gods alone know why. There were men all around you who would have made better seconds in command."

"You ungrateful wretch! Get out of here! Get out before I forget myself and strike you!"

"That would be a fine thing, wouldn't it? Wait a moment, and I'll call some of your flunkies to witness it. Let them watch the great man show off his kingly qualities, beating up his only child. Let them see what kind of puppet Apedemek in his wisdom has chosen to put on the throne!"

Balaam slowly rose to his feet. His face flushed with fury, and his eyes bulged. His fists bunched at his sides, he advanced on her as his voice rose to a strangled scream. "Out!" he shrieked. *"Out!"*

She turned on one slim heel and stalked angrily to the

door before he lashed out. She stopped abruptly in the doorway and wheeled to face him. "You're going to be sorry you ever did this—this, and all the rest of it, including planning to sell me to that monster Amasis, just to seal some sort of grubby political maneuver of your own!"

"What are you talking about?"

"Peddling me off to a fanatic older than my own father, a man of such bad character that people make the sign of the evil eye when his name is mentioned! Well, you can forget it! I'd kill myself first."

"You'll do what I tell you to. Headstrong girl! You're just like your mother. If she were alive to see how you speak to you father . . . your *king*—"

"*King!*" She laughed loudly. "The army will have your pelt nailed to the wall within a week!"

Balaam went back to his chair and sank into it. "Tharbis," he said, drained. "I've never seen you like this. . . ."

"And I've never known you to do anything so outrageous," she shot back. Her voice softened. "You have to put things to right, Father. I can't watch you destroy yourself—and me—for someone else's gain."

He groped for a response. But by the time anything came to his lips, she had gone.

CHAPTER TEN

The Egyptian Camp

I

"Please, my lord," Geb urged. "Stay out of the first engagement. After one exchange we will know how things are going to go, and we'll better be able to protect you."

"I didn't come here to be protected," Moses responded simply as he looked out across the field in the pale light of dawn. He could see the enemy now: the Nubian ranks deployed out across the field, the bowmen arrayed to either side of the infantry units and awaiting the order to charge. "I came here with a commission to lead this army to victory. How do I lead if I stay behind the lines? No, my friend. I will not send any man into a danger I do not share."

Geb looked at him with new eyes. "Very well, my lord. I see the blood of Sekenenre flows strongly in your veins. I honor valor wherever I find it, and I am delighted to find it in a royal heir. Nevertheless, I hope you won't be insulted if I stay close to you once the battle starts."

"Not at all," said Moses with a grin. "Perhaps I can learn something from you in the process."

Seth came striding toward them. "Well, I suppose it can start at any time. Khafre says you intend to let them do the attacking this first time. That's wise. We'll get some idea how strong they are before we commit ourselves."

"Yes," Moses confirmed. "Are you going to be with this unit or Khafre's?"

"Neither," Seth answered. "I'm going up the heights. I want a look at the overall disposition of the enemy army. Besides, the tinker thinks I may get a look at Apedemek. He's said to be assuming direct command of the army on this side of the straits—or perhaps acting in some sort of advisory capacity. I'd hoped to capture one of their men last night to interrogate him. All we have are secondhand rumors to go on."

Geb smirked. "So you're going to take the tinker with you? I'm surprised you can get the big coward even within sight of bloodshed."

"It was easy," Seth explained, grinning. "I told him that either he comes with me and tries to help me identify his nemesis, or I put him in the front rank of the defenders in the field. It didn't take him long to figure out which option he feared most." He chuckled. "He still made me give him a sword to defend himself with, just in case, and I tampered with his mind for a few minutes, implanting suggestions that should allow him to look on without totally collapsing in fear."

"Well, good luck, all," Moses said. "I'll see you when the engagement's over, Seth. Take care!"

Impatient, Seth prodded the tinker as he lumbered awkwardly up the path in his ungainly gait. "Come along. If you don't hurry, we'll miss the attack."

"Oh, sir," the tinker said, "that talk we had did me so much good, I almost feel like going back with the soldiers and fighting. How dare Apedemek do those terrible things to my friends and me? I want to pay him back. I feel so strong, so confident! How could I have spent all those years being so timid?"

Seth prodded him again with the stout walking stick he held in his hand. "Don't get overconfident," he warned. "This is still war, Netek-amani. That bravery you feel may go away when you least expect it. And strength isn't enough; you also have to know how to use that sword I gave you. Those fellows down on the field are professionals who have been fighting for years."

As they reached the top of the little ridge, the tinker turned to Seth and drew himself up proudly. "I'll admit Apedemek had me frightened at first, sir. There's a tendency to be superstitious that runs in my family. I got it from my mother, may her poor soul find peace. But now that I've got my confidence, I could face him down, sir. Really I could."

Seth looked out over the field, where the two armies strained at the bit, ready for battle. "Could you now?" he said thoughtfully. "I'm not even sure *I* could face him without flinching, and I'm reckoned brave enough. Take a look down there, Netek-amani. Scan the Nubian command and see if you can locate him for me."

The tinker squinted into the distance. "I don't see him yet, sir."

"Very well," Seth said. "Keep looking."

But now, in the valley below, he saw the Nubian commander raise one hand high. The sunlight gleamed on the sword he held.

"There they go," Seth said.

The sword flashed down, and at last Seth heard the famous high-pitched, ululating Nubian war cry, which had struck terrible fear into the hearts of so many adversaries in the past. From the hundreds of throats on the southern side of the field came the terrible wail.

There was a hail of Nubian arrows, answered immediately from the Egyptian side. And then the two armies rushed together.

Seth looked over at the tinker. Indeed, the man's fear seemed mostly gone, but there was a residual look in his eyes that could turn into pure terror. Still, Netek-amani's face bore a wide-eyed smile, and his long, skinny fingers tightened on the hilt of his borrowed sword. *Wonder of wonders,* Seth thought. *The mouse may become a man yet, if he lives a dozen years longer or so!*

* * *

Moses, young and fit, with legs made hard and strong from hunting in the desert hills behind Thebes, found after ten strides that he had outstripped the line as the two armies rushed toward each other. He slowed, thus straightening the lines, and as he did he caught a quick glimpse of the men he had come to lead. Their faces bore expressions of workman-like concern, of professional commitment—anything but fear or apprehension. His heart sang. He was at last a man among men, a warrior among real warriors!

The first Nubian was suddenly upon him, and their outstretched blades clashed, then deflected, making twin cuts in the air. Moses rammed the man's body and nearly knocked him down.

The Nubian recovered, attacked, and gave ground, then fought back in a terrible frenzy. Moses kept his eyes on his enemy's eyes, not his blade—Baliniri had taught him that—and was able to anticipate most of his moves long enough to catch his wind. Moses counterattacked, disarming his man with a stroke he had learned from the soldiers in Thebes and, almost before he could think the matter out, ran the Nubian through.

His eyes caught a quick movement to his left. He spun around just in time to parry a thrust and, on the backswing, brain his opponent with the flat of his sword. Just beyond, Geb was battling two huge Nubian blacks, who towered over him. Moses came to his rescue and almost cut the first Nubian's hand off, putting him enough out of action to be nearly beheaded by a second stroke.

Moses looked around him. Where? Who next? The blood was up in him. His hands tingled with tense readiness. The mad thrill of battle was strong in his heart. A black soldier came at him; he met the onslaught with a wild cry, roared in a voice he could barely recognize.

Seth watched from the heights as the Nubians gave ground, battered back by the fury of the Egyptian counter-thrust. Moses was a startling surprise to him: The lad displayed a natural talent for battle and, now that he had been blooded, fought as if he had been a soldier for years. Seth watched, awed, as the young prince fended off a two-pronged attack by a pair of burly Nubian whites, simultaneously keeping both at bay. Seth, fascinated, followed the lad's progress as he skewered the one man and, without pause, turned to bludgeon the other to his knees. Such power! Such natural grace!

Seth was about to move into shadow, the better to see the fight in the valley through the morning glow, when the scarecrow to his left let out a shrill cry.

Seth turned. "What's the matter?"

"It's Apedemek! There!"

Seth followed where the tinker pointed. Near the left flank of the Nubian force, a figure in a dark, hooded robe moved into the battle. As Seth watched, the figure—he did not seem to be armed—pointed a finger, and the Egyptian before him, untouched, fell to the ground insensible.

"That's the dirty bastard!" the tinker shrilled in a voice full of anger. "The man who tried to kill me! The man who burned my friends alive!"

"Easy, now," Seth said. "You stay up here, Netek-amani, where it's safe. Remember what I told you."

He even put a hand on Netek-amani's skinny, stringy arm, hoping to soothe him. But the tinker, beside himself with a rage that overrode all fear, shook him off. "I'm going to kill him! Get out of my way! I'm going to give him a taste of what it feels like to have to beg for your life!"

And before Seth could stop him, Netek-amani, ignoring the path, had bolted down the slope, stumbling and bouncing off the rocks, headed for a battle he would, an hour before, have given ten years of his life to avoid.

Seth tried to run after him, but the tinker easily outdistanced him. He made his way awkwardly across the field, threading his way between the two sides, even ducking between duelists but always somehow managing to avoid being hit by the wild cuts and thrusts aimed his way.

And all the while he screamed, "Apedemek! Apedemek!"

Seth closed his eyes for a moment and breathed a silent prayer to the gods: *Please, let the poor fool make it back safely. Let him come to his senses. Don't let them kill him. He's not much, but he's harmless. . . .*

But his hopes were not to be realized. The tinker closed on the robed and hooded man, swinging his unaccustomed weapon wildly, awkwardly, ineffectually. He did not even seem to know that he was swinging with the flat of the blade. Six, eight, a dozen times he paused at the top of one of his idiot swings to gather strength, leaving himself wide open for the simplest sort of sword thrust. But, strangely, the robed figure refused to kill him.

Let him escape, Seth beseeched the gods. *Don't let him be killed. Make him remember where he is, so he'll run from the field.*

But even as he prayed, a Nubian came up from behind and struck the tinker a deft blow. It caught Netek-amani atop the head and drove him first to his knees, then to the ground. The robed figure gestured, and the Nubian lifted the unconscious tinker to his feet, got a shoulder under him, then easily carried him off into a grove just below the steep hill atop which the fortress of Kumma stood.

Seth shuddered, remembering the abject fear the tinker had shown every time he had thought of Apedemek. And now the tinker was in the bloodstained hands of the evil magus, and tonight when the false sense of security induced in Netek-amani had worn off, he would have to face the one man in the world he feared most. Seth could almost feel his fright and despair.

He shuddered again as cold self-loathing dug into his guts. *You did it to him, you and your irresponsible tampering with another man's mind. His blood will be on your hands. Yours! Yours alone!*

The battle raged for hours. When at last it broke up amid the long shadows of afternoon, Egypt had driven the enemy back to within fifty paces of the grove into which the tinker had disappeared. This position provided such poor protection against a night raid, however, that Khafre ordered the Egyptians to fall back to a place almost exactly in line with where they had started. Both sides had lost men and taken prisoners. There were a few deaths and many wounds. The day's work had been for nothing that the eye could see.

Dejected and plagued by guilt, Seth came to join the

encampment just as the evening food-fire was being ignited.
On the way he passed Moses but said nothing.

Moses sensed a problem instantly. "Seth!" he said, catching up with his friend. "What's wrong?"

But there was no answer, and Seth did not turn to speak
to him. Moses stopped and looked after him, puzzled. He
himself was tired but proud and happy. He had entered
manhood and expected some compliment from Seth regarding his performance.

What, then, was wrong?

II

At dusk Moses found Geb and Khafre sitting by the
campfire. Both men rose to salute him. "Greetings, my lord,"
Geb said. "A good blow was struck today, even though the
battle lines stand about where they did."

"Yes, I'm pleased," Moses said. "Are we going to interrogate our prisoners?"

"Yes, my lord," Khafre said, "right after dinner." He
looked around. "I expected to see Seth. Have you run into
him?"

"He walked right past me as though I weren't there,"
Moses answered. "Something's wrong."

"Yes," Geb said. "It probably has to do with the tinker
being dragged away unconscious, a prisoner, after attempting
to kill Apedemek."

"That's odd. Netek-amani is such a coward."

"Yes, but Seth fooled with his mind beforehand, to make
him brave. In retrospect this seems not to have been a good
thing. It's not enough to be fearless; one also has to be good
at defending oneself."

"I see I'm going to have to have a talk with Seth," Khafre
said. "He can't blame himself for that."

"Oh, yes he can," Moses disagreed. "Seth told me once
that in his youth he'd gone through a very irresponsible

period. Since then he's been acutely aware of the consequences of his actions. If anything happens to the tinker,
Seth will be devastated."

"I see. Well, I'll talk with him anyway. He's too valuable
a man to be put off his feed by a thing like this. Let's bring
him with us when we interrogate the prisoners. One has just
come across the strait from Semna, saying that there's been
some sort of palace revolution there."

Moses stared at Khafre. "Who's in charge now?"

"That I haven't heard, but I assume Nehsi has been
deposed. I won't know for a certainty until I've talked to the
prisoner." He smiled. "Changing the subject, my lord, your
valor today is being praised all over camp. It does much for
the men's morale when they've a fighting leader."

Moses hung his head, a little embarrassed. "I have to
admit, I did feel at home today. Things happened so quickly,
there wasn't time to be frightened. One seems to rise to the
occasion and delivers a blow or parries another almost before
thinking about it."

"However it may have worked, my lord, you were very
effective."

"I beg your pardon, my lord," Geb said, "but look who's
here."

Moses turned to see Seth trudging toward the campfire,
his steps slow and heavy. "Greetings," Moses said. "Join us."

Seth all but ignored him. "I understand there are prisoners," he said. "Will someone please take me to them?"

There were six prisoners at the edge of the camp, guarded
by two soldiers. The lot of them sat in a circle, each connected to the next by a leg chain. Their hands were bound in
front of them.

The senior of the two guards saluted Khafre. "Good
evening, sir. The prisoners are run-of-the-mill infantrymen
except this chap over here. I think you might get something
of interest out of him."

"Why?"

"He just came over from Semna. Last night some sort of
coup took place there."

Seth pushed past them with uncharacteristic haste. "This

one over here? Ah, yes." He hunkered down before the indicated soldier. "Good evening, my man. I'm Seth of Thebes. What's your name?"

"Islo, sir. I've heard of you."

"I suppose you have. Are you well?"

"Yes, sir. The magus tended to our wounds. Thank you, sir."

"Very well. You look fatigued. I won't keep you long." His voice was slow, measured, reassuring. "Just relax. Here, I'll loosen those knots on your hands."

Moses had been ready to join Seth and the prisoner, but Geb gently restrained him. "Not yet, sir. Do you see what he's doing? If we let him alone, he'll get more out of the fellow than all of us together."

"He did that to me once," Moses commented with a wry smile. "All right. Let's draw away a bit." He shook his head. "Seth's worse than I thought. He's a bundle of nerves. If you were to make a sharp noise, I think he'd fly at your throat like a hungry leopard."

"Yes. It's curious: I've met a number of people who knew him at different times in his life. Each draws a picture of a different man altogether. In his youth he was almost totally distracted. He wouldn't look where he was going, and he'd be likely to stumble and fall on his face."

Moses nodded. "Yes. Then there seems to have been a mellower period, when he paid attention to things around him. This would have been after that short while he spent in the army as a soldier. He was said to have been hopelessly incompetent."

Geb chuckled softly. "This is Seth, our genius, we're talking about. People from that period of his life remember him as hopeless an oaf as this tinker fellow."

Moses thought for a moment. "Maybe he sees himself in the tinker. Netek-amani is a bit of an innocent, too, in a lot of ways."

"There's something to that, my lord," Khafre began. But now Seth arose and came to join them. "Seth!" he said. "Have you found out anything we can use?"

"I've learned something interesting," Seth said. "I'm pondering the question of how to use it." His eyes focused on nothing in particular, and then he looked at Khafre with a puzzled expression. "Come away with me. I don't want to be overheard."

The four drew apart from soldiers and prisoners. Seth scanned the three faces one at a time, then looked at Khafre. "This prisoner was the messenger with the news about Nehsi. He was supposed to have gone to Apedemek directly but was intercepted by one of his own commanders instead. He evidently said something that the officer didn't like and was put in the front lines as a punishment. Another runner was sent to find Apedemek and give him the message. This chap thinks the thing he did wrong was to express support for Nehsi."

"What's happened with Nehsi?" Khafre asked.

Seth rubbed his nose. "Balaam deposed Nehsi yesterday. Islo thinks that when Apedemek hears about it, he'll be in a towering rage. Balaam was supposed to have waited for the go-ahead from Apedemek. It isn't wise or healthy to disobey Apedemek's orders."

Moses broke in. "But is Nehsi all right?"

Seth shrugged. "All this fellow knows is the message to Apedemek. The garrison is quartered outside the walls, and this revolt occurred inside Semna, where there's only a token guard." He looked at Moses. "But he thinks Nehsi was thrown into the dungeons with men condemned to die—men, most likely, who blame him for their sentence."

"That's not good," Khafre said.

"No," Seth agreed. "I think somebody has to get him out, to save him and to find out what he knows. Apedemek is too much of an enigma. I don't like going up against anyone who has that much power, without us knowing more than we do."

Khafre nodded slowly. "Good point. I have the feeling that you'll be able to handle him. But—"

Seth caught his hesitation and nodded agreement. "It'd be nice to know for sure. Someone has to get inside the fortress and rescue the king. I've been thinking about it: The interior layout of all of the river forts has been nearly identical. I suspect that the layout of Semna will be much like the others, only larger. I'll pump this fellow again. He seems to be a fit subject, and he knows the interior of the fort very well."

"Good. Meanwhile we'll think about a likely candidate to effect the rescue and—"

Seth shook his head. "I'll do it," he said. "I'm the only one who isn't vital to the battle. But I'll need another man who's fit and resourceful. We're going up the walls."

"Up the walls? That's very dangerous."

"So is facing Apedemek without more information. So is this whole expedition. So is the prospect of going back home and facing Amasis. Give me one man who can climb, fight, and move silently, and I'll do it."

"I'm your man," Geb offered.

"No," Seth said. "You're all three too valuable here. I want a man who can obey my orders or make up his own when mine aren't working. I want a soldier with every virtue and a subordinate nature."

"I think I've got a candidate," Geb said. "I'll go after him right now. His name is Ra-Hotpe. He used to lead a squad. He has the hardest head in his unit, but he's the best patrol leader you ever saw."

"Good. I want him immediately. We're going out tonight."

"Tonight?" Khafre echoed. "But—"

"The sooner the better. Nehsi's life is at stake, and he probably has some very valuable things to tell us. Maybe at the same time I can learn some other information about the revolt in Semna."

"Right you are, sir," Geb said, turning to go. By the fourth pace he took he had fallen into a jog, then a trot, then a dead run.

The moon was high when Seth stood on the bank of the Nile, ready for his perilous night swim and daring exploit. A dim figure appeared a few steps downstream. "Ra-Hotpe," he said, "is that you?"

There was a grunt of assent. Ra-Hotpe proved to be a surly fellow, a man of one-syllable answers, but he seemed a fit man for the job. "All right," Seth said, "here's a knife for you. We won't be able to carry anything else with us. Hang the belt around your neck, with the knife hanging down your back. But first strip down. We're going over the wall the same way the Black Wind did when it captured Dorginarti. Stark naked. Here, smear some of this dark grease on. It'll prove a better uniform than what you've been wearing to war, my friend. It'll keep us from being seen on the one hand and will keep us warm while we're swimming the Nile."

His companion grunted grudging assent again, and Seth saw the white cloth fall from his hand to the dark shore. "All right," Seth said. "Are you ready?"

Another grunt.

"Then walk into the water. Don't dive. It'll make a splash. Let's go."

Silently the two men slipped beneath the waters of the river and began swimming powerfully out into the current.

III

The dungeon was on more than one level. It sloped down and down, and the light grew ever dimmer as Het and Nehsi moved farther and farther away from the lanterns the guards had lit in the main room. At the second level down Nehsi could not see anything, and his hands groped along the wall as he blindly descended the crumbling stairs.

"Stop here," Het whispered. "If you go any farther, you wind up ankle-deep in Nile seepage. We're below the surface of the river now."

"I can't see," Nehsi complained. "Is there someplace to sit?"

Het guided him to a broad ledge. "Here, sire. Your eyes'll get used to the dark." Then he called out in a whisper: "Arnekh! Arnekh, are you there?"

There was no answer.

"You're calling out to someone down here?" Nehsi asked. "Who could possibly be—"

"A friend of mine," Het answered. "He's old and he's ill. I'll explain the rest later. I bring him food and drink. *Arnekh!*"

"Eh?" said a thin, reedy voice. "Het? Het, is that you?"

"Yes," the young man replied. "I've brought someone to meet you."

"To meet me? Have you gone mad? Take him away!"

Het patted Nehsi reassuringly on the shoulder. "Don't worry," he said. "Arnekh! Come over here. It's all right. It's a friend."

The old man muttered under his breath, but they could hear him approaching. When next he spoke, the voice was that of a very, very old man. "Het, what are you doing to me? Don't you know how dangerous this is?"

"Peace," Het said. "The person I've brought with me is also an enemy of Apedemek's. Arnekh of Kerkis, meet Nehsi, son of Akhilleus, high king of Nubia."

"Bah! Would you make sport of a sick old man?"

"Greetings," said Nehsi in the deep bass voice that all men in Nubia recognized. "If you come from Kerkis, you have been my subject, and from your voice you are a man of education and means. And yet I don't recognize your name."

Arnekh muttered unintelligibly to himself for a moment. "Het," he said at last, "is this true? This is really Nehsi? But what is he doing here?"

"He is a prisoner just as we are, old friend."

"A prisoner! You don't mean it! The king of Nubia! Then—" His tone changed. "A thousand pardons, sire. I am honored by your presence. But does this mean that Apedemek has taken over?"

"No," Nehsi answered. "It was Balaam who ordered my imprisonment."

"Balaam!" Arnekh snorted with disgust. "Balaam is nothing more than Apedemek's toy. I knew he'd be up to no good. When Apedemek returned to Nubia after many years' absence, I deserted my post and tried to find my way upriver to warn you. Apedemek had me captured and thrown in here before I reached your court." His voice took on a sad, fatalistic tone. "Apedemek wanted to keep me here forever—I know too much about him—so I managed to change clothing with a prisoner as old as myself, a man who had died. The guards hauled his body away thinking it was mine. Ever since then I have kept to myself on this lower level, where no one thinks to venture. This wonderful young man is the only person who discovered my hiding place and knows my true identity. The gods bless him, he brings me food."

"But you say you know Apedemek—and he knows you—from an earlier time?"

"Yes. I was a journeyman when he was an apprentice. He was a pupil of a friend of mine, a very great man. You may have heard the name: Karkara of Sado."

Nehsi's eyes went wide. "Karkara! Yes! My father knew him. Wanted him to work for the army. But Karkara would not make iron for us. Then Apedemek is an armorer by trade?"

"Among his many skills, yes. He turned to evil, however, when he was but an apprentice. Karkara suspected ill had befallen him, but his great love for the boy blinded the old man to the danger he was creating. By the time the lad had definitively enlisted in the army of darkness, it was too late—Sado could not unteach Apedemek the metalworking skills he had taught him. It would have then been Sado's responsibility to hunt his rogue apprentice down and kill him to prevent him from using the iron-making skills he had learned in the service of evil—but Apedemek had disappeared. No one knew where he had gone. I knew he would be back some day and that we would all suffer from the fact." He sighed regretfully. "If I had had the tenth part of his skills! If I had been a fraction as brilliant! But I was not."

"You were a metalworker, then?"

"Ah, yes. But Karkara would not accept me as an apprentice. By the time I came to him, I was too old. My meager skills were formed. Yet Karkara took pity on me and gave me a number of minor tips I could use in my craft. They helped me, though, and I like to think I was a useful man. I was no Child of the Lion, of course, but I armed the northern command for some years, and well enough, sire, if I say so myself."

"I honor your service and fidelity. So you have been here ever since Apedemek returned? In this darkness? In the damp, with the rats?"

"Yes. I feared even the other prisoners knowing I was still alive."

"I told him I would protect him," Het explained, "but he did not think it safe to take the chance to plead for his release."

"Yes," Nehsi agreed. "It is a sad commentary on how bad things have grown. If only we could escape . . ."

"That may not be impossible, sire. Arnekh knows things about the construction of the fortress not found in the official plans—things put in by the builders at the command of Sesostris III. There is a secret escape passage that connects with the outside. It was to have been his own escape route, in case of a siege or in case of a revolt against his reign like the one that has occurred here."

"Indeed! Why was I not told of this?"

Arnekh spoke up in his tired old voice. "Sire, I may be the only person who knows how to find it. I was here when your father conquered Nubia and made himself king. I was here when he marched through the front gate. I was here when the Black Wind, led by your mother, took Dorginarti."

"Incredible!" Nehsi said.

"Yes. Those were great days. Your parents were much loved. But we did not know that Akhilleus would prove to be a great leader. All we knew was that war had come to Semna. I came down into this level of the dungeon to hide and stumbled across the passage that led to the outside."

"How is it that no one has ever—"

"You will see when this young man shows it to you. I have shared my secret with him. But so far he has refused to escape without me, and I have grown too ill to travel. Convince him, sire. Make him save himself. I will die here soon. I can take comfort from knowing that, fortuitously, my discovery can save the king of Nubia from his enemies."

Nehsi's voice was somber and sympathetic. "How is it that I never knew of you, a true friend of the crown? I would have treasured knowing a good man like you was representing your country at this far outpost."

"Nubia has many good and loyal people who love you, sire. If you regain your throne, remember them, get to know them. It is too easy for a king to become isolated from the people."

"You are right, my friend. I will do as you say if the gods spare me."

"Then I will die in peace. Please command Het to save himself. Now's the time, before Apedemek returns to Kerma. If you are in prison when he returns, your life will be worth nothing. And Het will die with you."

Princess Tharbis quietly opened her door to the outer hall, then looked up and down the dimly lit passage. At one end, under a flickering torch placed high on the stone wall, a guardsman sat on a bench, his chin resting on his chest, dozing. Nobody seemed to be in the transverse passage at the far end.

She shrank back against the wall, took a deep breath before continuing, and then, summoning up all her courage, she moved out into the hall on bare feet. She was dressed in her dark robe and hood to escape detection. She closed the great door securely behind her and held her breath all the way down the hall. She did not dare take another breath until she was well beyond the somnolent guard. Once in the next passageway, the air in her lungs forced its way out.

It was one thing to defy her father; she had been doing that for years, ever since her mother's death and the subsequent realization that the self-centered Balaam never considered her welfare.

It was another thing, though, to do what she was about to do. Her father would undoubtedly consider it treason to set free, if she could, a deposed king. Not only would she be defying his wishes, she would be placing her father's own life in the direst jeopardy.

Nevertheless, it had to be done. Balaam had to be stopped; Nehsi had to be saved; Nubia had to be brought to its senses; and Apedemek's ruthless and relentless rise had to be opposed and brought to a halt. Otherwise no one's life was safe. The choice was not between danger or safety—it was between a cowardly retreat from danger or acting in accordance with her conscience. It was difficult to say which of the two held more peril, but only one of the alternatives held any honor at all.

*   *   *

Seth climbed out of the water, picked his way up the sandy shore, then wiped the water out of his eyes and looked around. What there was of the moon was behind a cloud, so he could see only vague outlines: a tree, and a fallen boulder, broken from the cliffs above.

Where was his companion? Had he found his way safely across the river, or had the swift current in midstream swept him downriver? Seth pursed his lips and let out a shrill night-bird cry, one generally recognized within the Egyptian command. Then he made the high-pitched sound again.

There was an answering cry close by, almost at his elbow. Seth was relieved. "Come along," he whispered. "We've got to skirt the Nubian camp. There's a path above them. Watch your step. Once we've passed the sentries, it's clear until we reach the wall itself. Our informant tells me the moat is only half-full of water, so we may be able to cross it without swimming and having to go up the wall with slippery fingers."

The moon suddenly came out from behind the cloud. The pale light of its quarter-orb fell on the darkened face of his companion.

Seth's eyes widened, and he let out an inadvertent curse. "You're not Ra-Hotpe! Who are you?" But after the initial shock had passed, he could make out the man's distinctive features under the grease: the cut of the jaw, the straight and prominent nose, and—now that the truth was out—the conspiratorial grin.

"Moses!" Seth sputtered.

"Of course," replied the young prince evenly. "You didn't think you were going to go into grave danger without me, did you?"

IV

"Guard!" Het called out of the main cell. "Where's the guard?"

There was no answer at first. Het, standing by the bars,

could see the night watchman's booted foot sticking out from behind the door. There was a sound that could have been a snore. "Hey! Guard! Wake up!"

Again no answer. The only sound was a rat scuttling along inside the dungeon. Het looked down and scowled and, as it ran past him, lashed out with his sandaled foot and sent the rat flying.

"That'll teach you, you filthy bastard," he growled. But then a thought struck him. Grinning, he went to pick up the dead rat and approached the bars again. Drawing back his elbow and taking aim, he hurled the little corpse into the adjoining room, where it struck the guard on the ankle.

"W-wha' . . ." The guard came awake. "Ugh! Who did that? You'll pay for this!" The boot hit the floor, and the guard, big-boned and broken-nosed, appeared in the doorway. "Which one of you—?" Then he saw Het, standing just behind the bars, watching him. "You! I should have known!"

"Come on," Het urged, "I've got a big surprise for you. If you act quickly, you'll earn some credit with the officers in charge."

"Why should you do anything to help me?"

"All right, see if I care. You might have earned a raise. You might even have earned a promotion." Het turned away. "If you want to be at the bottom rank the rest of your life—"

"Hey, wait. What do you want, anyhow?"

Het turned, stopped. "Well . . ." he began slowly. "Do you remember, some time ago, when . . ." He appeared to think better of it, though. "Oh, forget it. You wouldn't know what to do anyhow."

"Know what to do about what, curse you! Don't just drop something like that into the conversation and walk away."

"I changed my mind. I was going to give you the tip free, but now, well, there has to be something in it for me. I'm not just going to give it away."

"Give what away? Tell me, and I'll let you know what it might be worth to me."

"Not a chance. I have to get a guarantee. You'll just double-cross me."

The guard stepped close to the bars. "Look," he said, frustration beginning to creep across his face, "the other guard on my shift is asleep. You'll wake him up talking about this. And if I have to share anything with him, he'll steal the credit for the whole thing. He outranks me. Every time I do something, he gets the credit."

"Then I'll tell it only to you, and you can do what has to be done before he wakes up."

"Done about what? Tell me."

Het looked around cautiously, then he came very close to the bars.

The guard, alarmed, backed away.

"Don't make me speak up," Het said.

The guard hesitated.

"Come closer," Het urged.

The guard reluctantly came within arm's length, but no closer.

Het cursed inwardly; one more step and he could get the man by the throat.

But the guard maintained his distance. Het managed with great difficulty to keep his frustration and impatience from showing in his face. "Do you remember the old man that Apedemek asked about, only to learn the man had died?"

"Huh? Oh, him. Yes. It was Arn-something, wasn't it?"

"Arnekh of Kerkis. Apedemek was as mad as blazes that the man had died before Apedemek had had a chance to talk to him. He thought you should have known there was something special about the old goat."

"Yes. But how could I know? He didn't look special."

"Of course not. How would you like it if I could get you out of the hot water you got in then?"

"What would I have to do?"

"Not so loud. Come closer. I don't want to have to bellow like a fishwife."

"Say it from there."

Het sighed. "All right. What if the old man was still alive? What if you could deliver him to Apedemek?"

"But that's impossible." The guard took a step forward.

One more step, Het thought. *Just one more* . . .

"No, it isn't. I can show you."

"I'm going back to sleep. And if you disturb me again—"

"He's alive."

"I lugged him out by the heels myself. He'd already begun to stink."

"Wasn't him. It was somebody else. The old man exchanged clothes."

The guard had turned to go; now he lingered just beyond Het's reach. "Why would he do a dumb thing like that?"

"Because anyone Apedemek wanted that badly must know something important—something on Apedemek that the magus wanted no one else to know, or something the old man knew that Apedemek didn't. Maybe even information worth money."

"Good thinking. It'd be easy enough for a prisoner to hide. I don't have any idea how many there are in there now, come to think of it. Eighteen? Twenty?"

"Twenty-two, last time I counted." Het grinned conspiratorially.

"And you want to sell him to me, right? So I can tell Apedemek. But what do you want in return? You know I can't let you out."

"Not now. But when you've got your promotion? . . . Believe me, friend, you'll be getting one."

"Think so? Well, it does seem plausible. I could conceivably exert some influence. . . ."

"Quite a lot of it. And I'm plenty tired of jail."

"If he's alive like you say, then bring him here where I can see him."

"I can't—not without killing him. He's pretty weak. It'll take two people with a stretcher."

"Meaning you and me."

"Unless you want to count your friend in the other room into the picture."

"Not a chance. No, you're right. But you've got to promise not to try anything."

"You have my solemn word."

Het lied with great sincerity.

The footsteps of the watchman atop the Semna wall came closer. Seth, grasping his handholds, froze just a handspan below the wall's edge, hardly daring to breathe, until the moon once again slipped behind a cloud. Then, as darkness descended and the footsteps receded, he cautiously climbed the remaining arm's length and stuck his head above the edge. The coast was clear.

He carefully eased himself over the battlement's edge, then turned, reached over the side, and held down a hand to Moses, who quickly took it and allowed himself to be helped up onto the battlement.

Moses put his lips close to Seth's ear. "Now what?"

"Follow the guard," Seth advised. He crouched and padded silently along the long wall, with Moses only a step behind. As Seth approached the guard the Nubian started to turn. But Seth closed on him, his strong armorer's forearm locking around the man's neck and choking off his breath. With a mighty wrench, Seth broke the guard's neck, killing him instantly.

"Quick," he hissed, "get into this fellow's clothes, take his sword, then toss him over the wall. I'm going down to the dungeons. Clear a way for us down the hall. Keep an escape route open at all costs. Remember the layout, now?"

"Don't worry about me," Moses said. "Aren't you going to grab another of these boys and steal a uniform for yourself?"

"What for? Anybody I can look in the eye I can convince I'm a Nubian soldier. I can also convince him afterward that he's never seen me at all."

Moses nodded at the sense of that while he struggled into the guard's tunic. "I'll still look odd with this grease smeared all over me."

"The light'll be bad enough to fool anyone until you're right on top of him. Don't give anyone a chance to cry out. Get your knife out."

Moses shot a sharp look at him, then nodded gravely. "No mercy."

"Right. It's him or you."

The cell door was open, and the guard was almost within Het's grasp. But as luck would have it, the second guard woke up. "Hey!" he said, coming around the corner and seeing the door open. "What are you doing?"

The guard and Het cursed as if with one voice. "Uh . . . this prisoner says there's somebody down there that Apedemek wants," the guard with Het explained. "I was going to have a look."

"Then leave your weapon here. I don't want any prisoners taking it from you. I'll lock the door behind you." He laughed nastily. "When you've brought up this other prisoner and I can have a look at him, we'll see whether I let you back out again."

Het's fists opened and closed impotently. So close! So very close! And yet so far away!

Running down the circular staircase, Tharbis took the stairs two at a time. She abandoned caution in her haste to reach the landing, and as she came down the last flight she ran headlong into the arms of Malenaken.

"What's this?" her father's assistant asked. "Whom do we have here, so far out of her natural orbit? Why, it's Princess Tharbis." His smile was insolent. "What are you doing, my lady? Surely not trying again to talk to Nehsi!"

"Let go of me!" she demanded, struggling with the strong hands that had locked on her. "You're bruising me! If my father hears you've hurt me—"

The smile that answered this was ugly. "He'll probably reward me. Haven't you any idea how angry he is with you? Not half an hour ago 'damned insolent little slut' was the nicest thing he said about you. He was talking about marrying you off to a leprous, one-eyed, hunchbacked dwarf from Lydia."

"Sooner that than a toad like you!" she shot back. "Release me, and I'll forget this. Otherwise I'll tell my father that you tried to rape me."

For the first time Malenaken's smile broke. "You know, I think you might really try something like that. Spoiled little bitch! Where *were* you going just now?"

"I was going to free the king if I could!" she answered defiantly. "Just imagine how he'll treat the likes of you when he comes into power again—you and Balaam! My father might survive, with banishment thrown in and maybe seizure of his possessions. But you? A worthless insect like you? A parasite who lives on a lion's back and crawls into his mouth after every meal to lick the food off his teeth?"

"You little trollop! Your tongue's too sharp for your own good. The one-eyed dwarf will have to find his own whores; I'm asking Balaam for you myself. By the time I'm done with you, even the dwarf won't be interested!"

He tried to kiss her now. She turned her face away. When he held her so tightly, blowing his foul-smelling breath in her face, she had trouble breathing and went limp. He let her fall to the ground. Then he began loosening his garments. The violence had proved stimulating; he was breathing hard, and his hands were trembling with eagerness as he took his sword belt off and opened his tunic.

V

Suddenly Tharbis raised herself up and bit him hard on the calf. He let out a strangled howl and tried to kick her head away; when he did, she grabbed for the sword belt he had dropped, and rolled away until she was free of him. Then she sat, the naked sword in her hand, its sharp point aimed at him.

"Give me that, you little bitch," he demanded. "Don't do anything you'll be sorry for."

"The only thing I would be sorry for," she said through clenched teeth, "would be letting you go." She scrambled to her feet, holding the sword at ready in both hands. "Come at me," she taunted. "It'd be a great pleasure making even less a man of you than you already are."

He edged slowly toward her, hands outstretched. She backed down the hall at the same pace, her eyes blazing.

"Just put the thing down," he said, "and we'll forget this ever happened."

"*Forget?*" she sputtered. "Forget you putting your filthy hands on me? You, a worthless slug of low birth, trying to rape me?" She snorted with derision.

He suddenly lunged forward and grabbed for the blade; she pulled it back, then jabbed at his forearm, opening a cut. He cried out and pulled his hand back. "Curse you!" he said.

"Keep it up," she urged. "I'll cut it off at the wrist next time." But as she backed slowly into the darkness at the far end of the hall from the dancing torchlights, she blundered into a bench and knocked it over. It fell to the stone floor with a crash, and the shock startled her. As she lost her balance the sword clattered onto the floor.

In the blink of an eye, he was on her, grabbing her arm in an iron grip and picking up the weapon she had dropped, only to look up into a pair of eyes staring coldly out at him from a face as black as Nehsi's!

The figure stepped out into the hall. It was a man, wearing the uniform of a Nubian guard. But his face and arms were grotesquely smeared with something dark and dull.

"Let her go," the stranger commanded. "Your business is with me now."

Tharbis pulled free and rolled to the wall. From there she scuttled out of range of her attacker's grasping hands.

Malenaken looked back at the stranger. "Who are you? What are you doing here?"

The stranger did not waste words. He sprang forward, aiming a powerful blow at Malenaken's belly. The thrust was parried only at the last second, and Malenaken gave ground, trying to recover. The stranger beat Malenaken's sword aside and wounded him in the shoulder. Malenaken backed another step and transferred his sword to his other hand.

"All right, if it's a lesson in swordplay you want," Malenaken snarled, "I'll be happy to oblige." He advanced now, attacking with a powerful flurry of cuts and stabs. The stranger parried a little clumsily, gave up a step, then recovered with an unorthodox strategy that showed off the strength of his powerful wrists.

Now Malenaken retreated toward the light. But as he did, Tharbis, running toward him, raised her little bare foot and kicked him powerfully in the back of the kneecap of the leg she had bitten. He howled, bent over—and the stranger ran him through!

Tharbis stepped back and watched him fall.

The stranger stared at her.

"Don't just stand there," she ordered. "Finish him off! If you don't, I will."

He shrugged, then stabbed the fallen man again. "I promised no mercy. Not that this one deserved any. I heard some of your exchange. You were going to save the king?"

"Yes. What on earth is that stuff on your face?"

"It's—"

"I'm Tharbis. Balaam's daughter. Come on—we have to hide this fellow, then get out of here. There's a storeroom down this hall. Nobody will find him there before dawn, at least. By that time we can have the king back in power."

"Not the way I hear it. Nehsi has nobody but enemies here. We've got to get him to safety. Then maybe we can use him to stage a revolt of the black troops at Kumma. The white ones here are loyal to your father."

"How do you know so much?" she asked, eyeing the stranger. "Who are you, anyway?"

"I'm an Egyptian. I came to rescue Nehsi too. We might as well do it together. Come on."

But as she turned, the light of the torches fell full on her fair young face, and his expression changed. He stood thunderstruck for a moment, and then he smiled. "You're beautiful!" he said before the words could be considered. "Come on!"

There was a tiny noise behind the guard. He turned and looked, wide-eyed and openmouthed, at a naked man covered with dark grease. The man's face and beard were black; only white rings around his eyes betrayed his race.

His eyes . . .

The man was speaking. The words . . . somehow he could make them out, but then again he could not. . . .

He crumpled to the ground, lost in a deep sleep.

Seth looked down at the guard, shrugged, and bent to steal his keys. As an afterthought he also peeled off the guard's outer tunic and put it on. A loincloth could come later.

"Nehsi of Nubia!" Seth called out. "Where are you?"

Inside the locked cage there was the sound of a scuffle, and he heard something heavy—a body perhaps?—thudding on the floor. He rushed to the door and unlocked it. He heard footsteps. "Nehsi! Is that you?"

But the face that appeared out of the darkness was a white man's—a burly, round-faced, curly-haired, sharp-eyed young man in soiled clothing.

"Who are you?" the young man asked.

"I'm Seth of Thebes. Get Nehsi. If he's still in jail by morning he's a dead man."

"I suspected as much. Sire! Come along, please. It appears we've got help."

Now the face that appeared out of the darkness was indeed that of the old Nubian king. "Seth! I hardly recognized you. You've aged, my friend."

The two embraced quickly. "But you haven't," Seth said, laughing. "Let's get out of here; if we do, maybe we'll stand a chance of getting older still. Which way out?"

"I can help with that," the young man offered. "Shouldn't we take Arnekh, sire?"

Nehsi shook his head sadly. "While you were breaking that guard's neck, I tried to rouse the old man. He flatly refuses to leave. Oh, Seth of Thebes, this is Het. If we're getting out of here, he's coming with us."

Seth nodded assent. "Grab a sword off the wall by the guard's station. We'll likely have to fight our way out. A friend is guarding the hall for us."

"No! Go get him. There's another way out," Het said. "You can't get out that way. Not with this many of us, anyhow." He took a sword from the wall and tossed the king a second blade with his other hand. "We could create a diversion—we'll let the rest of these scum out when we go."

"I don't know how to swim, Het. My preference is to follow Seth's plan out of here," Nehsi said.

Het did not take the time to answer. He stepped back into the cell. "Hey, you! Get up, all of you! Up and about! Everybody gets out today. Door's open! Everybody out!"

"Back out of the light," Moses said to the girl. "From here we can guard the staircase and make certain nobody gets through. My friend is already down in the dungeons helping the king out."

Tharbis looked up at him, incredulous. "Your friend? And what might his name be? And you still haven't told me yours, either."

"I'm Moses of Thebes. My friend is—"

"Moses? Prince Moses?"

He nodded.

"I've heard my father talk about you. You know, if somebody were ever to scrub that grease off you, you'd be a pretty good-looking fellow."

"Oh, I never take it off," Moses said with great solemnity. "It's quite natural. Oozes out of my skin. Usually it's worse than this."

She giggled. "You've a ready tongue on you, too," she complimented. "Are all the young men in Thebes like you? Smart-mouthed? Handsome? Strong?"

"And do the girls always flatter and flirt like this in Nubia?" Moses asked, hardly believing he was bantering like this in the face of imminent danger. "Or is it only rich men's spoiled daughters?"

She laughed ruefully. "Spoiled? I hardly think so. Now if you'd said, 'insubordinate' or 'quarrelsome'—"

"All right," he conceded. "You know better than I."

"You were wonderful with that sword," she said, switching from the stick to the carrot. "Malenaken was said to be a master swordsman."

"By whom? Himself? Remember I had an unfair advantage. That was a timely kick you gave him. Thanks."

"I'd rather have hit him with something sharp and inflexible. But I looked around and couldn't find anything."

Moses's face grew serious. "When is the watch due? Are we in any danger of someone stumbling upon us while we pass the time like a couple of shoppers?"

She sighed. "I think it's due right about now. Perhaps a little later. I'm not sure how long all that business with Malenaken took." She looked at him again, trying to figure out just what he would look like with the grease off his face. "So you came over the wall? From the Egyptian side? You and your friend? Who is he? Are you with the Egyptian army?"

"Seth of Thebes. We're with the army, yes," he said. He

grinned. "Actually, I'm in charge of it. Nominally, anyhow. Egypt—"

Just then there was a loud noise from below, and footsteps pounding on the stairs. He and Tharbis slipped well back into shadow and watched as a wretched horde of filthy, bearded prisoners came clamoring up the round staircase, not caring about how much noise they were making. A dozen or so men passed, all ragged beyond description. Some still wore manacles on their wrists. Some had the eyes of madmen.

But on their heels came a figure familiar to Moses: Seth, face still besmeared like his own, now wearing the tunic of a guardsman. Moses stepped into the light.

"Come on!" Seth urged. "There's another way out! We've got the king!"

"We?" Moses said. "Who are 'we'?"

"I'll tell you later." But now he caught sight of Tharbis. "Who's she?"

"Balaam's daughter. She's with us. She was on her way here to try to do the same thing."

Seth looked her over; at last he smiled. "Good girl," he said. "Bring her along!"

VI

At the upper levels the prisoners blundered into the watch; the watch roused the guard; the guard roused Aspelta and Nataki; and Nataki, leaving the running of things to Aspelta, roused Balaam. "Sire!" he shouted, bursting into the new-made king's rooms. "The prisoners have escaped!"

"Wh-what?" Balaam sputtered, sitting up, rubbing his eyes. He stared into the sudden light that poured in from the hall. "Who escaped?"

"The prisoners! They just came pouring out of the dungeons! They're armed! Our men are fighting them at the top of the stairs!"

Balaam stumbled out of bed. "Call out the entire garrison! They mustn't be allowed to get away!"

"Yes, sire! Shall I bring in men from outside the walls?"

"No, you fool!" Balaam yelled, struggling into his clothing. "Don't open the gate for any reason! If we can stop them before they get out—"

"Right!" Nataki said. "Arm yourself, sire. They're dangerous."

"Yes, yes! You'd think my commanders would be able to protect me, but—"

"Sire, I would of course do my best, but—"

"Hand me that sword! Have any of them got past the guard post?"

"Not so far as we know."

"Is Nehsi among them?"

"He hasn't been seen, sire."

"Hasn't been seen! How could anyone miss him? He's a head and a half taller than anyone else in the fort! Surely he hasn't elected to remain in the dungeon, waiting patiently while I decide whether to have him poisoned or garroted!"

"We're looking for him, sire! We have men skirting the corridor where the fighting is, in an effort to head off the prisoners before they can escape the other way."

"Double the guard atop the walls and at the gate! Those are the only two ways they're ever going to get away." He buckled his sword belt with hands clumsy from nerves. "Gods! If Nehsi were to get away, I'd have a revolt on my hands. The army—the blacks, the Nuer, the Dinka—they're all still loyal to him. And—Apedemek! How would I face *him*?"

"I don't know, sire."

"Are you still here! Go! Double the guards! Bring up the bowmen!"

"Nehsi, reach up and grab down one of those torches, will you?" Seth asked. "You're the only one tall enough to reach it."

The deposed king pulled down two torches, one from each side of the hall, then handed one to Seth and held the other high.

"Now, sire," Het said, "you know the layout for this escape route. Lead us to the passage."

For the first time Seth and Moses could see the new-comer's face clearly. "Who's this?" Seth asked.

The king waved away Seth's concern. "Name's Het. He's as good a man as I've got in Nubia. You can trust him."

Seth and Het exchanged appraising glances. "Nehsi's word is good enough for me," Seth declared. He turned to the king. "Lead on, my friend. Het, Moses, you go on with the king; the princess and I will bring up the rear. We'll want the best fighters up front in case you run into trouble once we're outside the walls."

"That won't happen," Nehsi assured him. "This passage is known only to the royal family—never to soldiers. It allows escape in the event of an attempted military takeover. The opening's masked off by rocks. From the outside it's invisible."

"You're the guide," Moses said. "Lead the way."

Their path wound its way through the deepest subterranean storerooms, where ores and dried foodstuffs and sealed vats of wine stood in long rows. Balaam's thinning out of the main fortress command had left the interior of the citadel with only a token guard, so for half their route they encountered no one. Then, without warning, as they traversed a passage that ended in a staircase, they heard running feet, and down the steps came six of the fortress guards, two armed with bows.

The archers stopped as their comrades rushed ahead; with lightning speed the bowmen nocked arrows, drew a bead, and loosed shafts into the midst of the escapees, cutting their group in two. Seth and Princess Tharbis pulled back, and Seth thrust the girl safely behind him.

"Het! Nehsi! Seth's cut off!" Moses cried. The three turned to face the advancing enemy. As they did, one of the bowmen loosed another arrow, which narrowly missed Moses and clattered against the stone wall behind him.

There was only one thing to do. Moses let out a terrible yell and charged the advancing swordsmen, alone. His powerful young voice, echoing in the stone hallway, made a thunderous racket. Startled, the first soldier let himself be battered back as Moses piled into him and his mate, raining blows on both their bucklers with a terrible fury.

But even as he cut his way into the lot of them and they

seemed ready to close ranks around him, Het and Nehsi
attacked. But from above, on the stairs, the first bowman
nocked another arrow. He took careful aim on the black giant
Nehsi, who was fighting furiously with a broad-shouldered
white Nubian.

Tharbis still held the weapon Malenaken had dropped.
"Here! Give me that!" Seth shouted as he took the sword
from her. Just as the bowman had Nehsi targeted and was
about to shoot, Seth drew back and hurled the sword!

The weapon tumbled half a turn too many in midair, but
as luck would have it, even hitting broadside, it was enough
to spoil the bowman's aim. The arrow clattered against the
ceiling and rebounded harmlessly to the ground.

Now Moses was on the stairs, sword in hand, taking the
steps to the bowman's landing two at a time. The bowman
drew his own blade just in time to fend off Moses's powerful
attack.

Tharbis was enthralled with the young prince's overwhelming physical presence, boundless vitality, and power.
Now, however, new sounds came through to her, and she
wheeled to see six new guards coming after them from behind. "Look out!" she cried to Seth, who turned and reacted,
stooping to pick up a pike, which Moses's first whirlwind
attack had kicked out of the grasp of one of the guards.

Over the heads of the oncoming men, oil lamps, not
torches, lit the hallway. Seth reached up with the pike and
knocked both these out of their holders. They toppled to the
floor, casting burning oil in the path of the oncoming attackers. One of them could not stop in time and was splashed
with the deadly liquid. His legs were badly burned, and he
shrieked in pain.

On the stairs, more attackers came on. Moses and Het
were beaten back to the landing. "Come on!" yelled Nehsi,
dispatching his opponent with a well-placed sword thrust.
Seth grabbed Tharbis's arm and dragged her with him.
"Scream!" he ordered under his breath. "Don't let on that
you're coming voluntarily. Come on, scream!"

Tharbis blinked, then let out a shrill cry. "Let go of me!
Help! Help!"

Het, Nehsi, and Moses retreated until they caught up with Seth and the now-struggling princess.

"Come on, Seth!" Moses urged.

Seth stole a peek into the storeroom to his left. "Stay here with me!" he said. "Keep them at bay for a moment!" He turned the girl over to Het. "Hold on to her! It has to look at though we're kidnapping her!"

Het obeyed and looked down, for no more than a second, into the most fetching brown eyes he had ever seen. He blinked rapidly, then recovered. "You're coming with us!" he commanded roughly, dragging Tharbis away. "Go on, sire!" he called out to Nehsi, pushing him ahead down the passage with the flat of his sword.

Moses held off the first two attackers, then lunged forward, running one man through. With the backswing he brained the other and then had to fight off two more soldiers pushing through to him over the fallen bodies.

Out of the corner of his eyes he could see Seth rolling a big jar out into the hall. "Lamp oil," Seth called to him. "Watch!" Still fencing madly, Moses was aware only peripherally of Seth pushing the jar over and spilling its contents far down the hall.

Twenty steps down the hall the oil touched the still-burning fire. A wall of flame swept up the hall toward them! One of the men Moses was fighting jumped out of the way to keep from being burned, taking his eye off Moses just long enough to earn him Moses's quick sword in his belly.

"Now!" Seth bellowed. "Go! Go!"

Moses ran down the hall, through the mad shadows cast by the blaze behind him.

Seth turned to go but took a stone from a Nubian sling squarely on the side of the head. He dropped in his tracks.

Moses had sprinted many strides down the hall before noticing that Seth was no longer following. "Seth!" he called out. "Seth! Where are you?"

He would have gone back for his fallen friend if Nehsi had not grabbed his arm. "You can't help him," he said. "Not now. Come on! The entrance to the secret exit is just around the corner."

But Princess Tharbis took things into her own hands.

"They'll catch you," she warned. "They'll find out about the exit and close it off. And you'll need it when you come back to save Seth."

"What are you trying to say?" Het asked.

"Good-bye," she said, with a last longing look into Moses's eyes. "Good luck!"

Before he could stop her, she dashed back down the hall, barely skirting the flaming oil in her torn robe and bare feet, and disappeared beyond the wall of flame!

"Gods!" Het marveled. "That's the bravest thing I ever saw anybody do!"

"Yes," Moses agreed. "Now get along. She's bought us just enough time to escape."

"Close this door behind you. This is the hole we're looking for," Nehsi said.

"After you," Het said. "I'll pull it to." But when the others had disappeared down the narrow passage before him, Het looked back at the wall of fire, thinking of large, bold, brown eyes, the raven hair, the firm nose, the soft cheeks, and the slim, athletic body running lightly down the hall into captivity to save him and his companions. His heart was beating fast.

"Het!" Nehsi cried. And, heaving a sigh, Het complied, pulling the open door shut behind him.

Tharbis ran into the arms of one of the soldiers. "Oh!" she cried. "Thank heaven you've come! Those dreadful men grabbed me as I came down the stairs."

"Are you all right?" asked the soldier, awkwardly holding her close, not certain what to do. Balaam's orders regarding common soldiers speaking to his daughter were well-known and much feared. "Because if this old fellow on the floor here hurt you, I'll—"

"No! No! He *kept* them from hurting me! One of them was going to—to rape me! But this man stopped him! Oh, please! You have to spare him!"

"This one?" another soldier asked, toeing Seth lightly in the ribs with his booted foot. "Well, perhaps you're right, my lady. Your father would chain us up if we didn't bring him in one piece for questioning." He called over his shoulder. "Hey, there! Bring up that sand! We've got to stop this fire!"

Tharbis clung to the soldier in whose arms she had found refuge. But of course her thoughts were on the handsome young man who had fought for her honor, who had joked with her so wittily. Moses! A true prince of the blood, of the royal line of Egypt! And as brave and handsome as a god!

VII

The word reached Balaam very quickly. "What do you mean they got away?" he exploded. "Got away how? It couldn't have been over the wall. I had men all along the wall. They would have seen. They would have stopped them."

"Sire," the messenger said, "this is true, but—"

"The gate better not have been opened. I gave the strictest orders."

"True, sire. Nevertheless—"

Balaam's eyes blazed in the torchlight. So frustrated was he that his hand went to his sword, the intent to do the messenger physical harm. "Then where are they? How can they have escaped?"

"They appear to have come and gone over the top, sire."

"Incompetents! Fools! I am surrounded by idiots!"

"Quite possibly, sire."

"Well, we can't have Nehsi getting where anyone can protect him! Pass the word down! Alert the garrison!"

"I *have* taken that liberty, sire. But since the gate was not to be opened for any reason, the messenger I was going to send to the garrison cannot get out."

"Then open it up! Send him out!"

"Yes, sire. Your every wish is my command." He turned to go.

"Wait," Balaam said. "First tell me about the one that was captured."

"Yes, sire. An older man, with a gray beard."

"How did he get in?"

"Apparently over the wall. We found one of our sentries dead, stripped of his clothing and weapon."

"Double the guard atop the walls! Anything else?"

"They apparently tried to kidnap your daughter, sire. She says she was on her way to talk to Nehsi, but she was waylaid by these men. One of them is said to have threatened to molest her. The graybeard reportedly stopped him."

"Bring the prisoner to me."

"When he regains consciousness. He took quite a hard crack on the head."

"Then take good care of him. How did Tharbis get free?"

"A fire broke out, and during the confusion the princess seized the opportunity to escape to safety. The watch has her now, and the physicians have been summoned." He waited a beat, then added, "Did you wish to see her, sire?"

"Her? The interfering little bitch? Disobey my orders, will she! Talk back to me, will she!"

"But sire, she may have overheard things that could help us."

"Eh? That's an idea. Yes. Yes, bring her here. But first, open the gates! Alert the camp!"

High atop the wall a ram's-horn trumpet blared, and from their winding path above the river, Het, Moses, and Nehsi could see the torches as the great gate of the fortress slowly lowered and the lights of the citadel shone through.

"They've finally figured out that we're gone," Nehsi said. "I wonder if they found our escape route."

"No telling," Moses replied. "But we'd better make it to the river, before the garrison turns out."

"Here's an alternate path," said Het. "I was looking for it before, but there wasn't light. This will lead right past their sentry. If I can slip down there and deal with him quietly . . ."

Moses pressed the dagger he had brought with him into Het's hand. "Here, take this. Strike quickly."

Het's grin was briefly visible before a cloud drifted over the moon. He saluted and disappeared.

"Here she is, sire," the guardsman said, handing Tharbis

over. She stood proudly, head held high, obviously unafraid of her father.

"What have you got to say for yourself?" Balaam asked. "I trust you've learned your lesson, meddling with things that don't concern you."

"At least the king's free," she retorted. "That's enough to satisfy me, even if I wasn't the one to do it."

Balaam glared. "You don't mean to tell me you had notions of—?"

"I would have tried. I'm glad the deed is done. You would have killed the king tomorrow, wouldn't you?"

Balaam looked around at the guards standing by. "You!" he bellowed at them. "Get back to your posts!" They blinked and went away on the double.

"It's no good hollering at anyone," she said. "Nothing could possibly alter the facts. Have you considered what impact it will have on the fighting in Kumma when the Nubian king suddenly appears on the Egyptian side? Do you think his loyal Nuer and Dinka will lift so much as a single sword against him? They'll probably throw down their arms and go over to the Egyptian side."

This thought had not previously occurred to Balaam. "Gods!" he said, thunderstruck. "Whether I like it or not, I have to get the word to Apedemek before dawn tomorrow. Otherwise—"

"Apedemek! Always Apedemek! Consider this instead: When Nehsi is back on the throne, you'll be food for the crows. But instead you're afraid of what Apedemek will think of you!" She threw up her hands. "Men! Idiots!"

But even as she said it, she knew she didn't mean it. The part about her father, yes. But the part about men in general? No. How could she say that about the man they had captured, Seth? How could she even think that about the king? Or, least of all, Prince Moses?

Just the thought of him sent a thrill through her. How strong he was! How independent and fearless! How witty and handsome! When all of this was over . . . when order had been restored, and there was peace with Egypt once more, perhaps . . .

What was he like? Seth seemed to know him very well.

They appeared to be the closest of friends. If she could talk to Seth alone . . .

Ah, but how to do that? One thing was obvious: Balaam and the others must never be allowed to learn who Seth was. They must not know that the young man who had come over the wall with Seth was Prince Moses, the leader of the entire Egyptian expedition! She had to curb that wayward tongue of hers!

The runners who had first come through the encampment had already roused the garrison, and the entire area blazed with light. But now the special runner bound across the river to Apedemek's camp—a lean, long-legged boy of sixteen, wearing only a loincloth—jogged surefootedly along the trail toward the Nile. He was a familiar figure to all, so he passed without challenge.

He skirted the cliffs above the river and looked for the path down to the shore where he could walk out into the water and begin swimming. But just as he turned off the main path and made his way down the beach, a muscular form tackled him, threw him to the ground, and clapped a rough hand over his mouth as hard-callused hands grabbed his arms and legs.

A face, indistinct in the dim light, loomed near to his. "You won't be hurt if you don't cry out. All we want to know is where you're bound." The runner broke out in a cold sweat, suddenly feeling a knife's blade at his throat. The hand over his mouth relaxed for a moment. "Try it and you're fish bait," the voice warned softly. "I don't want to have to kill you, but I will."

The hand came away from his mouth. For the blink of an eye the boy thought of screaming anyhow, but he knew it would mean a wasted effort and senseless death. "To Kumma," he croaked.

"And your message?"

"T-to Apedemek."

"Precisely what were you going to tell him?"

"The prisoners escaped. Nehsi escaped."

There was a chuckle from the darkness. "I see Balaam

has recognized the dangers," said a deep voice the runner recognized as the ex-king's.

"Very well," said the voice close by. "Shall I let this one go?"

"Not awake."

And before the runner could get a hand free to shield his head, he felt a crushing blow in the temple.

Balaam inspected the area where the fire had broken out and Tharbis had made her escape. "I don't understand," he muttered. "There isn't a way out of the fort within two floors of here— Unless they went back down into the dungeons, where can they have gone? My men control the landings of every staircase. Could there be some sort of secret passage?"

"Not that I know of, sire," Aspelta replied. "Of course, there are lower levels in the dungeons themselves that nobody has gone down to in years. Might one of the prisoners know something we do not, sire? The bottom levels are actually below the level of the Nile itself. There's seepage, and the bottom level is flooded. If there were a way to swim through the flooded areas to some hidden opening and come up out in the river itself—"

"If there were such a thing, the prisoners would have gone out that way in the first place, and not had to rouse the whole damned fort. Idiot!"

"Sorry, sire."

"There has to be something. One minute they were right here, just on the other side of the fire, and the next they were gone, without a trace. Keep searching! A reward to the man who finds a secret passageway here!"

The three escapees stripped at the riverbank and walked into the water. Nehsi went in with Het, who brought the king across the Nile by swimming with long, powerful strokes of his right arm, while the left was hooked around the king's shoulder and under his armpit. And now Moses moved out behind them and began swimming.

Yet he himself hesitated for a moment.

What if I were to go back for her? he wondered. When he closed his eyes, he could still see her dashing back into the flames, her long bare limbs flashing under her gown. He could see the fine-boned symmetry of her face, bright-eyed, intelligent, spirited.

He shook his head, came back to reality, and trying to keep his wandering mind firmly on the task at hand, swam vigorously out into the broad Nile, arms and legs churning furiously.

VIII

"What do you mean the runner didn't get through?" Balaam groaned, bleary-eyed and out of sorts after a worried and sleepless night. "What could have stopped him?"

"The escapees evidently waylaid him and knocked him cold," Nataki explained. "The physicians are treating the boy now. Shall I dispatch another messenger?"

"Yes!" Balaam ordered. But another idea struck him. "Wait! No! No! Bring the messenger to me. I've got to figure out some way to handle this. Apedemek will never believe that I sent a messenger who didn't get through. How can I explain it to him?"

"I don't know, sire. This *is* a lot of bad news to be sending him at one time."

"If only there were some good news to pass along with it."

Footsteps sounded on the stairs, and Aspelta came into the room. "Sire," he said with a broad smile, "there may be just that. I'm pleased to be the bearer of good tidings."

"What do you mean?" Balaam asked, running thick fingers through unruly hair.

"Well, sire, it's your daughter. The princess felt grateful to the old man who helped her last night, the one we captured. She paid a visit to him early this morning, to see if he was badly hurt. He was awake, and the two had a pleasant conversation . . . which I overheard." Self-satisfied, he waited for a moment, and then went on. "They spoke very candidly."

"And you learned? . . ."

"The names of the men who came over the wall last night to rescue the king."

"The ex-king, curse you!"

"A thousand pardons. Slip of the tongue. But imagine, sire: The younger of the two was Prince Moses, commander of the entire expedition."

"But of course. Egypt can't send an army out without a prince of the blood in charge. But—Moses? I don't know the name. Don't tell me Kamose had a son!"

"Oh, no, sire. This is the son of Princess Thermutis, daughter of Sekenenre. Moses is being groomed for the throne. He is the nominal leader of a resistance movement against Amasis. Just think what the implications of that may be, sire."

"Eh? What? Oh, yes: If he were captured or killed . . . but, damn it, he wasn't."

"The battle isn't over, sire. Anything can happen. I also learned the identity of the man we captured last night. He happens to be the one man on the Egyptian side whom Apedemek said he could conceivably fear—the one man brilliant enough to oppose him in a contest of wills. Sire, this is an opportunity sent by the gods! Seth of Thebes is the one man Apedemek would most like to have in his hands."

Balaam did not say anything for quite a long pause; nor did he visibly move. Then he blinked and said, "You're right. This was brilliant of you! Tharbis spoke freely, under the impression that she and Seth were alone?"

"Yes, sire. She appeared to be very much under the spell of Prince Moses. She could talk of nothing else. She asked Seth one question after the other about Moses—Seth is, among other things, the adviser to the boy, as well as being one of the conspirators who hope to put him on the throne when Amasis is deposed—about his likes and dislikes."

"This could mean a real change in our fortunes! Thank the gods the first runner didn't get through. The one who goes this time will bear quite a different message. We've got a standoff! They've got Nehsi, but we've got Seth! We could hold him for ransom. We could arrange an exchange."

"More, sir. Without Seth—a magus like Apedemek and

a man of great powers—our enemy has no defenses against Apedemek's magic and illusions."

"Yes! Yes!"

"Furthermore, sire, imagine what Apedemek could do with Seth as his prisoner. His food could be drugged. Apedemek once spoke of Seth as a man who could be brought around to his way of thinking. He looked forward to meeting Seth. He—"

"Yes! Yes! Get the news to Apedemek! Bring him here!"

"Permit me, sire," Nataki broke in. He had been so thoroughly upstaged by Aspelta's coup that he had remained silent. But now he saw an opening. "There is one problem, sire."

"Yes?"

"Apedemek must be in Kumma when Nehsi reveals himself to our soldiers. Only Apedemek would be capable of countering the powerful effect Nehsi will have on them."

"You're right. Apedemek must know anyhow. We must get the word to him. It will lift his spirits."

Nataki muttered below his breath, "Imagine Apedemek needing one of us to lift his spirits."

"What was that?"

"Nothing, sire. Just thinking out loud."

"Bring me a runner! Bring him to me now!"

Tharbis, on Seth's advice, had haunted the hall outside her father's rooms ever since leaving the physician's rooms in which he was being held prisoner. Now, as the new runner came jogging down the hall, her eyes went wide and she smiled. What luck! It was the young soldier into whose arms she had run the night before, the one who had held her so tenderly. She impulsively stepped out into his path. "Hello! I wanted to thank you for last night!"

The runner stopped, then smiled nervously. "My lady! W-what an honor! I have to go to see the k—"

"Can't it wait? Please? I did so want—"

"My lady, I'm summoned urgently by the king. I'll be at your command in just a moment, after I've spoken with him. You know how he is when he—"

"Oh, yes," she agreed sweetly, her eyes large and liquid.

Her voice was its most seductive, and her very stance was that of a woman deferring to a big, strong male. "Your business must be very important. I wouldn't dream of detaining you. But please, before you go in, I must know the name of the man who saved me last night. You were so brave!"

"W-why, it's Tanwet, my lady. I'm attached to the—"

"Tanwet. I'll be sure to remember a fine name like that. Well, Tanwet, go in and see my father. I'll be waiting right here when you come out."

He gulped, smiled uncomfortably, and went in. She stepped away while the door was open, then moved close to it after it closed behind him. Try as she might, she could hear only the runner's voice. Her father's, from the far side of the room, was muffled. She caught a word here and there.

But then suddenly a name caught her ear: Prince Moses.

Prince Moses! How had they learned that name? She pressed her ear to the crack of the door and strained to listen. The words came only in spurts: ". . . him that we have Seth in captivity. . . ."

Seth! But how—?

". . . await instructions. That is all. Now repeat it for me."

"Very well, sire: To the honored Apedemek, greeting. The former king of Nubia, Nehsi, escaped in the company of Prince Moses and—"

Tharbis's heart almost stopped as she heard him out. When her father expressed satisfaction and dismissed the runner, she scampered back down the hall to prevent anyone from seeing her near the door. She affected a casual stance as Tanwet approached. "That didn't take long," she said in the same soft, seductive voice. "Perhaps now we can talk for a moment. I was hoping that you and I could—"

"I'm sorry, my lady. I've just been given a most important message. If I'm caught dawdling—"

"Oh, surely you can—" But even grabbing him by the tunic could not hold him.

"I'm sorry, my lady! Duty first! I do hope you'll understand." He saluted and was gone.

She stood looking after him. *Oh, yes,* she thought. *I understand all too well.* Even a low-level soldier like this one would grasp the importance of getting this particular message to Apedemek. Seth had told her only this morning of the strange duel that seemed to be under way between him and Apedemek for reasons even he could not fathom: a duel to the death, one in which stakes were of the highest imaginable.

Of course! That was it! Someone had listened in on them! That was the only possible explanation.

Seth was in terrible danger. From what he had said, it was certain death for him if Apedemek were to learn that he, Seth, his enemy, was under lock and key in Semna! And with Seth gone, the lives of the whole Egyptian party were in equal danger!

This was horrible! What could she do?

She hurried down the hallway, into the shadowed area at the head of the stairs. It would not do for Balaam or any of his flunkies to find her here. She had to go somewhere and think this all out.

She found her way to her own rooms and threw herself across the bed. How could she have done this? What could she do? How could she have failed to check the physician's room? How could she not have looked under every chair, under the bed, behind every piece of furniture?

Well, that was spilt milk. The thing to do now was see if the situation could be mended.

What if she could find their secret passage, the one they had used for the escape? She knew for a fact that Balaam's soldiers had yet to find it. If she could decoy the guards away somehow, then find it to escape herself and make her way over to the Egyptian camp and tell them about this new and disturbing development . . .

Yes! She would do it! She would do it tonight!

IX

A dawn raid by the Nubians had driven the Egyptians back another two hundred yards after spirited fighting. During a lull in the battle Nehsi and the Egyptian leaders took the opportunity to confer.

"I'm sorry I wasn't awake for first muster," Nehsi said. "I am not as young as I was, and the night was an eventful one. Being brought across the river was emotionally almost too much for me at this stage."

"It's quite all right, Your Highness," Moses said graciously. "If we could have spared you the crossing, we would have done so. We're just happy to have you safe with us at last—you and Het."

"I suppose it's time I showed myself to my army," Nehsi said. "Few among their ranks will be moved to shoot arrows at me, even if Apedemek tells them to do so."

"Eventually, my lord," Khafre said, "that is an idea worth testing. But first we need to know everything you and Het can tell us about Apedemek." Little by little Nehsi and Het pieced together everything they knew from their own experience with what Arnekh of Kerkis had told them.

At the end Moses looked up from the ground he had been pensively staring at. "I don't even know what Apedemek looks like. He's never appeared in the field without that hood. All I know is that he's tall."

"You don't want to look into his eyes," Nehsi cautioned. "There's a burning, piercing quality about them. His eyes dominate his face. One you've looked into the eyes, you can't quite remember what the rest of the face looks like."

"This sounds like that trick Seth has. He can make you forget anything. All he has to do is look into your eyes and speak to you. Sometimes it takes no more than a word of command."

"It would appear that Apedemek is capable of more than that. Remember the magic he did to Seth from far away: the visions Seth had in the deserted fort."

"Yes," Moses admitted. "I can't explain that, and neither could Seth. It appeared to be an entirely different process, one beyond any powers Seth ever laid claim to."

"My lords," Geb said in a serious voice, "if Apedemek's powers exceed Seth's, then Seth is in the direst trouble. If Apedemek learns that the prisoner they captured last night is his enemy Seth of Thebes—"

"That kept me awake all night," Moses confessed. "I

don't know what to do. If we only had a spy inside the fortress—"

"We may have just that," Het broke in. "The princess Tharbis."

Moses looked at him. "I hadn't thought of her," he said. "She's rebellious and spirited, to be sure."

"She risked her life to warn me of the coup," Nehsi put in. "She can be trusted, if anyone can."

"I agree, sire," Het said. "What if we could establish contact with her? What if one of us could reach through to her via the secret passageway, and get her to pass information out to us?"

"Sounds like a splendid idea," Moses approved. "Geb, can you find us a good, reliable volun—"

"You have one," Het interrupted. "Me." He grinned. "I'd take any excuse to see her again."

Moses looked at the others. "Does anyone object?" he asked, smiling. "Het distinguished himself last night by extreme bravery, and Nehsi swears by him." No one dissented. "Very well. See if you can find your way inside tonight. Find out what she knows. We'll maintain a regular liaison with her if we can."

"Right you are!" Het said, grinning hugely.

"Very well," Moses continued. "You know the layout of the fortress. If we learn where they are holding Seth, a rescue attempt can be mounted. Get some breakfast and draw your gear first. You're a soldier of Egypt now."

"Yes, sir!" Het said. "I'd venture into the Netherworld if it meant seeing her again!"

When he had gone, Moses turned to the others and grinned. "If I ever saw a man smitten, there he stands. He talked about her all the way back last night. And frankly, if you'd seen her, you'd understand. Of course he's a commoner— but whether that or her father's current status will have any effect after all this is over is quite another matter. Stranger matches have been made. I wish him well."

"Yes," Nehsi agreed. "As of yesterday, he is my brave and resourceful friend and commands my complete loyalty. But . . . Moses, there is something I was thinking about after we discussed Apedemek. Tell me what you think of this, will you?"

"Yes?"

"Arnekh said Apedemek was an apprentice of Karkara of Sado's." Nehsi looked at Geb and Khafre. "I assume you two are privy to certain privileged information about Seth's secret society."

"We know something about it. Go on," Khafre encouraged.

"Karkara would accept only apprentices who qualified as candidates for membership in the Order of Chalybia. This was the only way one could learn from Karkara."

"You mean—Apedemek is a Chalybian?" Moses asked, thunderstruck.

"In all but fidelity to the oath he took. We see no sign in him whatsoever of the high principles and lofty ideals of the Chalybian Order. The order was—is—very hard to get into. Harder even than poor Arnekh imagined. Arnekh thought the thing that kept him from being accepted as a pupil of Karkara's was his age."

"It wasn't?" Geb asked.

"No. It was the absence of a certain birthmark on the lower back."

All three men stared, aghast.

Moses was the first to speak. "What you're saying is that Apedemek is—No! That can't be!"

"It cannot be otherwise," Nehsi said slowly in that deep voice of his. "Apedemek is a Child of the Lion. One gone over to evil, taking all the vast knowledge and power of the order with him."

There was a long, horrible moment of shocked silence. Moses was the first to break it. "And Seth is his prisoner."

There was no reply. All were thinking of the consequences.

The first person to speak at last was Geb. "This birthmark, would it resemble the one that Seth bears on his lower back? The one resembling the paw print of the lion?"

"Yes," Nehsi answered, "although Seth's is less distinct than most. Usually the resemblance is rather exact. Why?"

"It's just that—" He shook his head. "When the three of

you came into camp last night, you were all naked from the swim across the Nile."

"And?"

"One of you bore a birthmark so placed, and looking much as you describe it." He searched the faces of his companions. "The new man. Het." He took a deep breath. "Is Het a Child of the Lion? And if so, by which line? We don't know anything about him. We only know he's a white man raised in Kerma. Could he be . . . I hesitate even to suggest it. . . ."

"Go on!"

"Could he be Apedemek's son?"

Tanwet, Balaam's messenger, beached his little coracle and stepped onto land. As he did, a soldier of Nubia came forward. "Halt!" the soldier ordered. "Who goes there?"

"Oh, shut up," Tanwet said. "You know me, you ninny. Get me a bodyguard, and be quick about it. I have a message for Apedemek, an important one."

"Nobody gets through without a pass. You have to have signed orders, or know the secret password."

"If you slow me down, he'll have your head. I can guarantee you that."

"Well . . ."

Tanwet sat patiently while the soldier went for help. As he did, his thoughts went to the princess Tharbis's unexpected interest in him. What a pity not to have been able to spend time with her! All too obviously she was taken with him. What a fortuitous event last night! She had just run into his arms, and he had held her for quite a long time. And now? Now she wanted to get to know him better!

The soldier came back. "Pass," he ordered. "You'll pick up your bodyguards just over the rise. And don't you go telling Apedemek I gave you a bad time."

"Yes, yes. I'll see you on the return trip."

A soft night wind had come up since the moon had risen; it was just enough to bring shivers to Het, naked and wet from the waters of the Nile, as he crept over the ridge and past the sentries who marked the edge of the camp in the plains below Semna.

The moon was scarcely more than a sliver as he moved carefully across the barren space between the last of the large rocks of the plain and the rockslide that hid the opening to the secret passage in the side of the fortress. The knife belt around his neck banged against his back, and now he took it off and buckled it around his waist. It was good to have a weapon with him; he could soon clothe himself by surprising a sentry and killing him to rob him of his uniform. He could hardly go inside the fortress naked.

The patrols in the halls would surely have been doubled in the wake of their escape, but a man who knew his way around, who knew the ways of the garrison, could find his way to the princess's apartments without much problem.

There was a noise up ahead.

He froze, hand on his knife. The moon immediately went behind a cloud and left him in darkness. Yet even in the darkness he fancied he could see a glow up ahead. Yes! It was at the opening to the secret passage itself! Someone had a covered lantern! He moved behind a large rock that had come down with the slide and listened as soft footsteps drew nearer.

He drew the knife. Now he could see the faint leak from the covered lantern, and the dark robe of the person carrying it. A guard? Had they found the entrance?

He tensed, then launched himself out into the darkness.

One hand went to the walker's mouth; and the walker's arms were pinned by the position of Het's body. "Don't move a muscle," he threatened. "And don't drop the lantern."

But it was immediately evident that the trembling body inside the robe was not that of a man. He stepped back, aghast.

The covered lantern opened a mere slit. "P-Princess Tharbis!" he said. "Don't run! It's me!"

"You scared me half to death!" she scolded in a whisper. "Who is that? Moses? Is that you, Moses?"

"Cover the lantern!" he said hastily. "I don't have any clothes on. Come inside the passage! Someone might see you!"

"Answer me!" she demanded in the same loud whisper. "I warn you, I have a knife. And I'm not afraid of using it. If you're not Moses, who are you?"

"It's Het," he answered miserably. "Now come along. I have to talk to you."

"Het?" she said. "I don't know any Het."

His hopes were dashed, and his heart sank to the depths. She did not even remember him!

X

"For Isis's sake," he complained, "I'm the fellow who escaped with the king last night. You'd know me with this grease off my face. Now come on inside."

She joined him inside the passage, and the moment the inner door had been closed behind him, she opened the lantern and had a look at him. Hastily he covered himself with his hands.

"Well, you do look familiar at that. I see why I thought it was Moses. You're built a lot like him. He has big shoulders, and—"

"Please, cover the light up, will you? You're embarrassing me."

"You're funny." She caught his eyes now and smiled. He almost forgot his discomfiture in the dazzling radiance of her smile. "What are you doing here?"

"Actually, I'm trying to get through to you. The king asked me to."

"Like that?" she said with a giggle, giving him an appraising look up and down.

"No, confound it. I was going to find something to wear before I reached you. What kind of idiot do you take me for?"

"A naked, funny one. If someone had told me I'd be standing here talking to a fellow conspirator who wasn't wearing a stitch—"

"If you don't cover that light, I'm going to smash it," he said, annoyed.

"Oh, you're no fun," she said, but she half covered the lantern. It was not enough. He remained fully in view, and she kept throwing him malicious little smiles and looking him up and down. "What did the king want from me?"

"We need a spy inside the fortress to help us rescue Seth."

"Oh!" she said, forgetting her teasing behavior for a moment. "That was why I was trying to get out—to get a message to you. They know who Seth is. My father learned about Seth and Prince Moses and all of it. He's already sent a messenger to Apedemek. Seth's in the gravest danger."

"So he is," Het said, worried. "I'll have to get this information back to Moses. He'll have to do something that will keep Apedemek in Kumma tomorrow morning."

"What?"

"A major attack. If Nehsi can let the Nubians know he's escaped, and that Apedemek was the one who ordered him jailed—"

"But he wasn't. My father was."

"Doesn't matter. Anything to cause dissension—maybe even a revolt—within their ranks. That's the only thing I can think of that's likely to tie Apedemek's hands and keep him from coming to Semna."

"If he does come, what then?"

"I don't know. I have only the word of the others regarding Seth's supposed powers. He's said to be Apedemek's peer as a magus, but if he's here? Under lock and key? Wounded? That's no contest between equals."

"Oh, he isn't hurt badly. I saw him this morning. He doesn't look too great with that bandage over his head, but he's okay."

"Is he heavily guarded?"

"More than you and the king were. You won't be getting him out this time with only two men. It'll take more, and some kind of diversion as well."

"You think like a man." He paused. "You sure don't look like a man."

"I take it that comes as a kind of compliment," she said. "Well, one good compliment deserves another. You may not have a silver tongue in your mouth, but you're pretty good-looking, really, particularly dressed like that—"

"Come on now!"

"—or you would be if somebody gave you a bath."

"Why did I come? Why did I volunteer for this?"

"Good question. You seem brave enough." The teasing tone was back, along with a little malicious flirtation. "Was it because you wanted to see me again?" This struck home; she pressed on. "Or was it because you wanted me to see you?" Now she opened the lantern again and this time really gave him an inspection from head to toe as he squirmed and tried to cover himself. "Not bad at all," she said in the appraising voice of a slave auctioneer. "Nice thighs. Now turn around and let me have a look at your bottom."

"Curse you! Curse you, anyhow!"

"Oh, all right, take all the fun out of everything. Do you want me to meet you every night about this time, so we can maintain contact between the two camps? Oh, I hope it's you. If it can't be Moses I hope it's you. We'll have such fun."

"You have a really malicious sense of humor!"

"But I won't come if you don't dress like that every time. Tell you what: Next time leave off the grease. I want to see what you look like without it."

"Little vixen."

"I'm serious. You show up here out of uniform and I won't even talk to you. I'm having the time of my life teasing you. If I'm going to risk life and limb disobeying my father's orders like this, I have to be paid off in some kind of coin. Well, you've heard my conditions. Either comply with them or find yourself another spy inside the fortress."

Het gritted his teeth and growled assent. "I've got to go. I'll see you about this time tomorrow."

"Oh, yes," she said, her smile at once mean and coquettish and full of wicked fun. "And I'll see *you*."

He turned and went to the door, feeling her eyes all over him and feeling like the world's greatest idiot. When he carried his message back to Moses, he would leave this part out of it.

How annoying she could be!

Yet how adorable!

In the afternoon Balaam had had Seth transferred to the same dungeons in which Nehsi and Het had been held. The guard had been doubled, and the soldiers in charge had been ordered not to speak with Seth or get close to him. By evening Seth had explored the lower levels, all the way down to the flooded portion, and had found Arnekh of Kerkis, still forgotten, and abandoned now even by Het, his only companion.

Seth had taken him down to the lowest level, where their whispers could not be heard by the guards above, and had by now learned Apedemek's background. "Tell me, Arnekh. When you knew Apedemek, did he have a certain red birthmark on his lower back, just above the buttocks?"

"Yes. Just as Karkara had. I often wondered if this had something to do with Karkara's decision to train him and not me."

"Anything is possible. I've been trying to piece things together a bit at a time. Karkara and Apedemek and I . . . I think we're all distantly related. We also are—or perhaps *were* would be a better word—members of the same secret order."

"Yes. The Chalybians."

Seth gave an appreciative grunt. "You kept your ears open in the company of Karkara, I see."

"Yes. I wish Karkara had been equally astute. He was too close to Apedemek, too fond of him, to see the lad had taken a fall. He had such high hopes for the boy. He was, after all, the most talented apprentice Karkara had ever taken. The old man never encouraged me to become close to them. From my more distant perspective, I could see the rift between them as inevitable. I could see the telltale signs even as they developed. I was older than Apedemek, you remember, and watched the boy, little by little, give in to temptation."

"If only Karkara had listened to you!"

"I was too timid to press the issue. You know that a man does not turn to evil in one great irrevocable step. More often he simply makes bad choices one at a time. We march through life and make fifty, a hundred small choices every day. Each one of them moves us toward the light or toward the darkness. How many steps toward the darkness does it take before a man finds himself committed to evil? We slide imperceptibly into a shape distorted, ugly, unrecognizable, and we do not think we have changed. . . ."

"All this is true. This is how my own mistakes came to be made."

"Yes. There comes a time when a man befriends the darkness and starts calling it light. Apedemek had the potential for greatness. But he became dominated by a lust for power over all things, over all people."

Seth nodded, silently thoughtful.

Arnekh shook his head, lost in memories. At last he said, "Seth, this man could become an emperor!"

Seth let out a long breath. "I know. I have already had a taste of his power. And while I am reckoned a man of great resources, I have my doubts as to whether my own power is equal to such a challenge. You see, Arnekh, as arrogant and conceited as this may sound, I have lived a full and varied life across many lands without meeting my master. Nor yet my equal. It is, I suppose, time for me to meet him. But I ask myself in all honesty: Am I up to such a confrontation? Will I be able to handle him when at last we meet?"

"Do you have to meet him?"

"That's just it. Somehow I feel that he knows me and will recognize me. And here I sit, a prisoner in the dungeon of a fortress under his control. Can I avoid meeting him? And when he finds out that I am here and comes down to find me, what will happen? Will I meet my master on earth, once and for all? One thing I do know: When the battle is joined, one or the other of us will be destroyed. But who, Arnekh? Who?"

CHAPTER ELEVEN

In the Fourth Nome

I

At the end of his long and punishing workday, Aaron ben Amram sent his sons home with a message for his wife, Elisheba. "Tell her that I have gone into the desert. She will understand. I will be back when the moon is high."

"Yes, Father," said Nadab, his eldest. "Don't you want to take some food with you?"

"I will find my own supper," Aaron replied. "Tell her not to worry. Now run along. I want all of you in bed early tonight."

He watched them go. They had all been born in slavery, and this tore at his heart every time he thought of it. *When, O Lord? When will You send us the promised Deliverer? How long must we wait, ground underfoot by these monsters?*

The hint of impatience was all but blasphemous, and quickly he breathed a prayer to erase all trace of bitterness in his heart. The God whose name could not be spoken had him and all the Habiru in the palm of His mighty hand, and it was unseemly to question His will.

This did not stop Aaron from asking the question fifty times a day, however, as he and all his kin—women, children, the infirm—struggled to get through each day, cutting building blocks out of the living rock in the quarries west of the great Nile. And all for the blasphemous glorification of unbelievers. Not only were they forced to labor all the daylight hours under the blazing Egyptian sun, but their efforts produced the raw material to build temples to false gods and iniquitous kings, their own oppressors! Surely there was some convoluted reason for this hateful curse, but try as he might, Aaron could not find it.

Wearily, he turned his steps toward the hills behind the quarry area. Tonight, he thought, he would pray for the unknown and unknowable God to instruct him. There had to be meaning in this wretched life they led. There had to be justice. Sometime, there had to be an end to it all. Perhaps the God would tell him, if he could restrain himself from this unceasing questioning and complaining.

He followed the path around the hill and came down into a narrow arroyo cut centuries before, when the rain patterns in this part of the world had been different.

And from the high hill above him, the great yellow eyes of a cheetah followed his every step as he proceeded deeper and deeper into the narrow canyon.

Elisheba opened the door of her hut. The apelike, broadshouldered Demetrios of Rhodes stood in the doorway, fists on hips, feet spread.

"Yes?" she asked.

"Woman!" he said in his rasping voice. "Where is your husband?"

Elisheba thought quickly. "Why, sir, didn't he find you? He went looking for you. You must have crossed paths. I'm sure that if you retrace your steps—"

"You know he didn't go looking for me."

"Well, sir, that's just what he did. But you keep on the move, sir, and—"

"Curse you!" he said. "Tell him to report to me at first light!"

"Oh, yes, sir. I'll tell him as soon as he gets back. He'll be sorry to have missed you."

He cursed and stalked away. She allowed herself to shudder now. Of all the soldiers who had ever had charge of the western bank of the river, the Greek was the worst. He alone had Amasis's permission to take whatever sanctions he liked against his helpless charges.

His brief reign over the slaves had been without mercy. After that first night, when he had raided the artisans' town, an outright revolt broke out when the men of the town had found out what had happened. But Demetrios had been ready for them; six artisans had died, and others had been severely beaten. If their work had not been needed for the new villa that Amasis's second in command, Neb-mertef, was building in Thebes, Demetrios would probably have given the order to destroy the whole village.

Well, we remain alive as long as they need our inexpensive labor, she thought. But what would happen to them when all the work was done?

What could Demetrios want Aaron for, now? She hoped it was nothing serious, and that, if questioned, Aaron could hold his temper. He did have a way with words, quick and cutting, and was often beaten by the guards for speaking out of turn.

Ah, when would it all end? How long would this cruel servitude go on? Would they ever know freedom again?

Slowly the cheetah crept along the ridge, checking each step carefully before committing to it, its nose testing the wind, its eyes on the arroyo into which the man had disappeared.

Behind it, the woman moved slowly, carefully, crouched to make a small silhouette against the dusk sky. As the animal now moved down to a ledge and walked easily along it, the woman stepped into the animal's footprints and kept pace with it, entirely at ease on the narrow path.

There, now! The man below had turned and moved into a narrow defile invisible from the main road. The woman smiled; she was glad she had come this way, where his movements could be traced in safety.

She made a soft noise to the animal, and the cheetah doubled back to join her. Now she poised and leapt out across the narrow gap separating her from the next ridge, landing softly on bare feet, then creeping forward stealthily as the great cat padded along patiently behind her.

To the west the sun, no more than a copper ball, began its last, quickening descent toward the horizon. The woman paused. Down below she could hear voices.

She turned her head and made a gesture at the cheetah to stay where it was. Then she crept closer to the edge and, unobserved, looked down.

"I told you," Aaron said. "You must rest. Your wound is not yet healed. You will hurt yourself."

Nemti nodded and sat carefully. "You're right, I know. But I keep thinking that every day I delay, sitting here mending, Kamose comes closer to death."

"That may be true," Aaron conceded, "but you cannot change that by reopening your wound. If it is meant for the king to die at the hands of Amasis, this is the will of God. All your efforts can do little to stop this from happening."

Nemti snorted. "You're a good man, Aaron, but your point of view is too fatalistic for me. I'm used to having control over my life. When I know that that son of a bitch Amasis is planning to murder Kamose and install himself on the throne, I see red."

"I am not made happier by it myself. Amasis has singled my people out for special savagery ever since he came to Egypt. He is one man we can thank for the difficult times we have had to live through." He sighed. "But I bow to the will of God. I am sure He has plans for us that He will unveil when the time comes."

"I'll bet you haven't eaten, have you?" Nemti said. "And after working like an ox all afternoon in the sun for those bastards—" He passed over a sack. "Here. Olives. Your sister, Miriam, brought them to me yesterday. They're pretty good. I wonder where she got them."

"A woman brings them to us. A woman of the village, named Ti."

Nemti laughed. "Ah! My kinswoman! I should have known. Well, help yourself. There's plenty more where they came from."

"I appreciate it."

Nemti passed over a wineskin as well.

"Thank you," said Aaron. "The thirst is terrible after a day in the sun."

Nemti watched him. "Your people are very close, aren't they? Yet they know how to keep a secret. That's unusual."

"Do they?" Aaron asked noncommittally, sitting at last on a rock opposite Nemti and sampling the ripe olives. "What secrets do slaves have to keep? But of course: You're talking about yourself. Well, you need have no fear of that. Only I, my wife, my sister, and my mother know."

"Thank you for your discretion. I wonder somehow that they have not shared the other secret with you, just to give you hope."

Aaron looked up. "What other secret?"

"You expect a Deliverer, one sent by your God. You despair of living long enough to see this happen. Yet you keep the faith. I don't know if I would have had the patience to continue doing that in your place. I'd need occasional reassurance."

Aaron shook his head slowly and sadly. "I do, my friend, I do. There are times when it is very difficult to believe, to hope, to keep faith with God."

"Well, can I trust you to keep a secret? Even from your mother and sister? It's a dangerous secret to share—dangerous for everyone concerned. Dangerous for your people, dangerous for Egypt."

"You have my word."

Nemti took a deep breath, then plunged onward. "There *is* a Deliverer. He's being trained for the job."

Aaron stared at him. The olive in his hand rolled to the ground. "If this is some kind of jest—"

"No," Nemti promised. "The problem is in keeping him alive and healthy. If he can be saved from Amasis long enough to learn the things he has to learn, he'll come back to crush Amasis and liberate Egypt, and when he does, he will liberate your people." He coughed softly, and the cough brought pain to the wound in his side. He winced and doubled over, then recovered.

"Don't lead me on with false hopes," Aaron warned. "It would be too cruel." He paused, then said in a steadier voice, "But if it were true . . . if I could know for sure that there lives the man Levi spoke of, the man who will lead us out of bondage and take us back to the land of Jacob—"

"Well, I don't know about that. I don't know the whole story, you see. I just know what, uh, certain people told me. This person is supposed to come to Thebes and take the crown away from Amasis and set your people free."

Aaron's eyes searched Nemti's face.

"That's why I came back," Nemti explained. "If this Deliverer returns and finds Amasis in sole command of the throne, it'll be very hard for him. But if the king could be saved, it would be easier when this fellow came back, because Amasis would already have his hands full of problems."

"You are a brave man, especially with what you have to lose if you free Kamose. You will lose the queen, yet you follow the path of honor and what your conscience tells you."

He was about to say more, but suddenly they were no longer alone.

A slender figure stepped out of the shadow, into clear visibility in the sunset's afterglow. She wore golden bracelets and anklets and a quiver of arrows, and she held an unstrung bow in her left hand. Unlike the warriors of the Black Wind and the Desert Legion, she wore also a brief tunic of leather.

She nodded to Aaron, but her eyes were for Nemti alone.

Nemti stood up so fast it brought a stabbing pain to his wounded side. He winced, but managed to get one strangled word out.

"*Mara!*" he breathed.

II

She came forward and embraced him. "I went along with your plans at first, knowing you'd want me to," she said, "knowing you'd done this to keep me safe. But when I reached the oasis I asked myself, safe for what? If Kamose is dead, I'll be nobody. I'll just be another oppressed victim of Amasis's." She kissed him and stepped back. "Oh, my dear. You're hurt. Let me look at—"

"Never mind," he said, putting a gentle hand to her cheek and enjoying the nearness of her. "I'm going to be all right. The question is, am I going to have my strength back in time to save the king? For all I know, he may be dead already." He put his other hand to his side, where a spot of blood showed through the linen bandages.

"That's why I came back," Mara explained. "He's my responsibility, too. I can't live the rest of my life among the women at El-Kharga, knowing I'd abandoned him to Amasis. Even if we haven't meant much to each other for a long time, my conscience won't allow me to leave him in this kind of predicament."

She turned now to the third party, barely visible as night came on. "Who's this?"

"Oh, it's Aaron," Nemti said. "Miriam's brother. He's been caring for me ever since he found me, right after I got hurt."

"Then you're a brave man, Aaron," Mara said. "I'm in your debt, as I am in the debt of your mother and sister."

"You have always been a good friend of our people, my lady."

Mara reached out in the gloom and patted his arm. "We will dispense with titles and honorifics, my friend; we are fellow conspirators now. Could we have a small fire? We need to talk."

"Certainly," Aaron said, and moved away into the cool darkness. She saw one spark, then another, and after a few moments the dry twigs he had gathered caught fire. Soon a small fire was burning, and they sat beside it, warming their hands and eating the olives and figs Miriam had brought to the hideout earlier.

Aaron spoke first. "Nemti was about to tell me about someone who is being trained to defeat Amasis."

"I've got an oath of secrecy out of him," Nemti cut in. "He's promised not even to discuss the matter with Jochebed or Miriam."

Mara looked at Aaron and smiled. She sat with her knee touching Nemti's, and now she reached over and put an arm around his broad back. "It's true, Aaron. I don't know exactly how the facts dovetail with the prophecy you heard from Levi, but there is somebody on whom the hopes of Egypt depend. Thermutis, Baliniri, Seth, and I have been raising ourselves a king. When it became obvious that Kamose wasn't going to be strong enough to throw off the terrible hold Amasis has on him, we started grooming someone for the job."

Aaron was clearly perplexed. "But how could you do that? The only reason Kamose was accepted by the nobles and priests in the first place was that there wasn't a legitimate claimant with the proper bloodlines. There wasn't anybody but Prince Moses, and he was a baby—"

Then he began to understand, however dimly. "Oh," he said. "And Moses has been sent away, with an army to guard him. I wondered why that happened just when it did. It didn't seem worth it, sending a punitive expedition to Nubia over a few forts that haven't been used in a generation."

"It wasn't. But Baliniri knew that Moses's life was in danger, so he acted to preserve it. He's not only being saved, he's being trained by Khafre and Geb, two of the best men in the army, and by Seth."

"I thought Seth was out of the country."

"He was, but he came back for this. A king must be a great leader of men. Seth is providing Moses's advanced education."

"But what has he to do with Levi's prophecy?"

Mara squeezed his hand. "I'm not sure just how it will work out," she admitted. "The prophecy has some aspects I frankly can't reconcile with our plans. But his destiny is as closely tied to that of your people as it is to mine." She paused for a moment and then said, in a gentler voice, "Aaron, Moses is your brother."

There was a long moment of shocked, incredulous silence. Then Aaron vigorously shook his head. "I don't know what you're talking about. Moses, my brother? He's a prince of Egypt, and I'm a slave and the son of a slave."

"And the great-grandson of an uncrowned king of Canaan," Mara pointed out. "Don't sell your own bloodlines short. Jacob was a great man, the founder of what will come to be a great nation. Moses draws his nobility from quite as prestigious a line as he would have if he were really the child of Thermutis and Zer."

"What happened to their son?"

"Thermutis bore a damaged and sickly child the same night your mother bore Moses. Her child died within the day and was spirited out of the palace for a quiet interment before the princess had fully awakened from the *shepenn*. We kept her in seclusion while she recovered from the birthing and dealt with her grief, then arranged for her to find Moses. All who were with her at the time were loyal handmaidens, sworn to secrecy and transferred to new duties and noble households in outlying nomes. One, a weak link, was quietly killed. Everyone outside the immediate circle thought she had borne a healthy boy. Amasis, in the meantime, had left orders that all Habiru male infants born under those stars mentioned in the prophecies as being auspicious be put to death. Having Thermutis adopt Moses was the only way your mother could preserve her baby."

"I can't believe this!" Aaron said.

"You must. I was there. I swear it."

"But Mother never—"

"You can't let her know you know. She never even told your father or grandfather. Levi went to his grave thinking that either your God had spoken falsely or he had misunderstood the prophecy."

"I suppose he knows better now, God rest his soul."

"I hope so. The rest of his prophecy is, I assume, also accurate, although I do not understand the part about Moses leading your people back to Canaan. Perhaps when Moses becomes king of Egypt he will lead an expedition to Canaan and return your people to the land they forsook for so long. But from what Kamose told me, his defeat of the remaining Hai overlords left Canaan in political chaos. The Canaanites won't give up the land they hold without a fight, so the Egyptian army will probably be needed to help the Habiru carve out a place for themselves in Canaan."

"This is amazing!"

"I know. You expect your God to do it all by miracles, but I suspect that when and if He makes His move, it'll be through the efforts of ordinary people like the three of us. It seems to me—as it seemed to Nemti—that our next step is to save Kamose. If we can create dissension or civil revolt here, we can lessen Amasis's power. That could pave the way for Moses, when he returns from Nubia at the head of a trained and blooded army, knowing at last the mission we've been training him for."

"This is a lot to take in at one time," Aaron remarked. "I need to sit and think about all this."

"I understand," she said, and watched him draw apart to the edge of the little circle of light beyond the fire. Now she turned to Nemti. "My dearest, you thought that saving Kamose would cause you to lose me. Yet you came back to save him."

He threw up his hands. "I brooded over it. But my conscience—"

"I know. That's why I love you. My darling, I'm done with Thebes. If I survive all this business, I'm going back to El-Kharga. I've seen the life there, and it suits me. Kamose can find another woman. If you will go with me to the oasis—"

"Oh, Mara! I've thought about nothing else since I've been alone here, resting and thinking. I was lovesick from our first night together, but I couldn't believe things would ever work out between us."

"Yes. Yes, I understand." She looked at him with a wry smile. "I should keep you away from El-Kharga! Have you seen how the Desert Legion women go around out there? And they're all so lean and young and beautiful."

"But they're not you."

"Oh, Nemti, if we were alone here just now!"

"We will be. And soon we'll have all the time in the world."

"Then you'll let me help you? I'm not new to this kind of thing, and I'm a good shot with a bow and arrow. I know you won't regret it."

"You're sure of that, eh? Well, I don't have any money to bet with, and as a matter of fact I'm out of a job and not in line to get one. But if I had any, I'd bet you—"

"There's other currency to bet with." She pulled him close and kissed him, then, laughing low in her throat, licked his ear.

"A fine bet that'd be, when I wouldn't know whether it would be more fun to win or to lose."

"Oh, Nemti, if we get out of this alive, we're going to have such a good time together."

She was about to kiss him again when they heard Aaron coming back to the fireside. They drew apart and looked at him.

"I'm with you," he said firmly. "Tell me what I can do."

Amasis made a practice of meeting with his underlings one at a time; he preferred to keep them in the dark about what the others were up to and to play them off each other. But tonight was something special: a dinner party at Amasis's apartment in the Theban palace, attended by his inner circle of trusted assistants.

Amasis sat at the head of the table, attended by slaves who had been permanently silenced by sure and summary means: Their tongues had been cut out. He waved them to and fro, and it was some time into the dinner before his guests realized that the slaves were deaf as well.

Now, at the end of the feast, he gestured away all of them except one silent sentinel whose duty it was to bring wine. When the last of them was gone, Amasis looked about him at the small group he had called together: Neb-mertef at his right, the brutal Demetrios of Rhodes at his left, and beyond them Mont, the physician, and Nemaret, the custodian of his country villa.

"I've called you here together," he began, "to let you

know what I've decided to do. The last of Baliniri's party is gone: The queen and Thermutis have vanished into the desert and have been given shelter by the Desert Legion. Demetrios?"

"This is true," the Greek confirmed. "One of the soldiers who helped them escape was seen limping down the hill after his fight with the guards. I think he's still in the area. The last word was that he was given shelter by a man who, I think, is a member of the Habiru community. I can't prove that yet, but I'm getting close. It's down to a dozen candidates."

"Good," Amasis said. "Keep the pressure on. The point I wanted to make is that everybody knows we drove the queen and the princess Thermutis out of the city, but there has been no protest from the priesthood of Amon. There has been no protest from even the nobles of the upriver nomes. Most surprisingly, among the mute have been Thermutis's kin. I was expecting trouble from them."

Neb-mertef leaned forward, a small, guarded smile on his lips. "Then the time has come," he intoned.

"Yes," Amasis confirmed. "Tomorrow evening I would have you all meet with me at my country place. Nemaret will lead us to our . . . prisoner. Then, under the supervision of Mont, we will all stain our hands with royal blood."

"My lord!" Neb-mertef breathed.

"The killing of a king is serious business," Amasis retorted. "Should this matter ever come to an accounting, I want no innocent and passive witnesses. All of us must be equally guilty, so that no one—*no one*—will be able to point the finger at anyone else."

He looked around the table. Mont was pale, his face drained of blood. Nemaret was nervous, unable to make eye contact with anyone. Neb-mertef had recovered his equanimity and sat placidly, nodding once in agreement. But on the brutish face of Demetrios of Rhodes there was the slow smile of a man eagerly anticipating participation in unbridled revels.

III

By noon of the next day Neb-mertef was back at his own country estate, riding through the open gate, past the silent guards on either side. He dismounted and a slave took control of the chariot as Neb-mertef strode away past the gate-keeper's lodge and the little temple to Amon—neglected these many years—into the inner courtyard and up the shallow staircase to the front door of his villa.

As he entered his house he looked up with pride at his own name staring down at him from the lintel above the doorway. Servants materialized seemingly from nowhere to remove his outer robe and sandals and offer him various refreshments.

He looked about him with satisfaction as he entered the great central hall of his house. Years earlier he had tired of domestic life, and, having no son to pass his name to, he had put away wives, concubines, and daughters, settling them in a villa in the distant Fayum, and committed himself to a bachelor's existence. He preferred a life given over to political intrigue, power-brokering, and the accumulation of money to the placid routine of domesticity.

Now he was surrounded by chattels and servants whose only pleasure was to serve him. In anticipation of his arrival, the servants had arranged the central hall's table tops with fresh fruit and flowers, while musicians played flute and harp, and a lone dancer, voluptuous and big-breasted after his preference, circled slowly in the middle of the room. Her brown body showed through her transparent garment, and she tapped a tambourine softly, keeping time to the music with the little bells on her toes.

Neb-mertef sat down in the great master's chair on the raised dais opposite the dancer. Immediately a slim maidservant, tanned and wearing only a wig and circlet, a ring of beads around her neck, and a faience waistband, knelt at his feet to bathe them in scented water and dry them with a spotless white linen towel.

The girl looked adoringly up at him, with large and luminous eyes. "My lord wishes anything?" she asked in a

smooth and soothing voice. He looked her up and down, at
firm breasts and smooth thighs and flat belly, and for a
fleeting moment a twinge of desire came over him. She had
been trained well. He knew the look of adulation she was
giving him now to be an expedient sham, but that fact did not
matter; as long as she consistently kept up the ruse, he did
not care what she really thought of him.

For a heartbeat or two he thought of taking her right
then and there, with all the slaves looking on. There was a
certain pleasure in knowing that his control of everyone's life
was so complete that no one would dare interfere. He had
done so before, and the memory of what had happened to a
slave who had taken notice was still fresh.

But now his top priority was to rid himself of the dust of
the road he had taken from Thebes. He clapped his hands
three times; two naked girls appeared. "Bathe me," he commanded, and without further ado retired to the place of
ablutions. Here, in a room to the east of the great hall, he
allowed the girls to strip him, while a male slave brought
containers of scented water. He lay on a marble slab and let
the women pour warmed water over him and then massage
his muscles, tired from his ride. Then he stepped into a soft
robe and dismissed the pair.

Slowly he walked upstairs. The usual pleasures of his
home life did not satisfy him today. There was something
unsettling and exciting about knowing that great things were
to happen tonight. He smiled and thought of the power that
would now shift into Amasis's hands with the impending
murder of Kamose. The same power would in time shift into
his own hands. But when?

On impulse he steered his steps to the suite of rooms in
which the magus Set-Nakht was being held a virtual prisoner.
In return for providing Neb-mertef, his master, with the fruit
of his astrological speculations, Set-Nakht had at last found
himself provided with unrestrained debauchery, which, in his
more restrained days, he had not the imagination to dream
of.

A virtually endless stream of male whores and catamites
had been provided to minister to Set-Nakht's every fleeting
lust. He had tasted every pleasure that a male partner—or

two, or several—could provide. And with every broadening of his sexual education, with every further step down the road toward complete and unbridled license that he took, he became more and more Neb-mertef's slave.

By now he could hardly relate to the life of self-restraint and self-denial that he had lived in the years before he had had access to Neb-mertef's wealth and the pleasures it could buy. By now he hardly even bothered to conceal the flagrant, guilt-free pleasure he took in having at arm's length, any time of the day or night, a partner, or partners, ready and willing to do anything he commanded.

Yet when Neb-mertef would appear, the guilt resurfaced, and the shame, and the furtiveness. Of all the people he associated with now, only his master had ever known him when he had been a man of dignity out in the world. For some reason he could not fathom, he still wanted to impress Neb-mertef, to maintain a properly respectable front.

It was for this reason that Neb-mertef could and did manipulate him cruelly and shamelessly. Neb-mertef, glorying in the man's now complete subjection to him, chose to play with the astrologer the way a bored cat might play with a crippled mouse.

Thinking of this now, Neb-mertef smiled to himself. Since he had discovered the power he held over the magus, he had ordered all the locks to be removed from the doors in this wing of the villa, thus destroying all possibility of privacy. His arrival was never announced in this part of the estate, thus keeping his visits a surprise to Set-Nakht. Any servant or slave who spoke of Neb-mertef's arrival to Set-Nahkt would be whipped and exiled to the stables or the care of the compost heap.

Therefore, as he padded softly and silently down the upstairs hall, he paused for a moment of delighted contemplation before Set-Nakht's door and then, suppressing a vicious smile and replacing it immediately with a dark frown, threw the door open!

It was perfect! His strategy caught Set-Nakht in a position of extreme and embarrassing degradation, on hands and knees between two towering, brutal-looking Nubian slaves bought a week earlier at the pederasts' brothel. At the mo-

ment the door burst open, the magus was giving intimate
attention to the man in front of him and being mounted like
an animal by the man behind him.

The threesome fell apart. *"Well!"* Neb-mertef bellowed
in the voice of a roaring lion. *"What is going on here?"*

The two slaves jumped back with unseemly haste, and
the mortified astrologer was frozen to the spot with sheer
shock. Neb-mertef, his face wooden, chose this moment to sit
on the pile of garments Set-Nakht and the slaves had shed
before beginning their orgy. The magus, all dignity utterly
destroyed, stood up, shielding his insignificant manhood with
his hand. "M-my lord!" he sputtered. "I . . . I did not
expect . . ."

"Apparently not," his master said coldly. "I need your
services. Now! What do the stars say about tonight? I need to
know. Well?"

"Please, my lord, if you would only let me . . ." In vain
he gestured ineffectually at the pile of clothing Neb-mertef
was sitting on. Neb-mertef took the greatest pains not to
notice or to understand.

"Do I have to ask again? Or do I have to find another
and better magus to advise me?"

Neb-mertef could see the man shrivel. "My lord, I do
not have the charts in this room. They are in a cabinet on the
main floor."

"Get them."

"Like this?"

"Get them! How many times must I say it?" Smiling with
perverse delight, Neb-mertef sat on the pile of clothing and
awaited the magus's return.

This was a happy inspiration. Forcing the issue meant
that the magus, who prided himself on staying aloof from the
house servants and slaves, had to slink down stark naked into
the great hall under the eyes of the lowest of the low. He
would hardly be able to face any of the staff again without a
sense of absolute shame. In this household only girl slaves
went naked in front of others, while male servants wore a
loincloth while performing their duties.

When Set-Nakht returned, he had somewhere found a
dirty loincloth to put on. It only made him look, if anything,

even less dignified than before. He spread his papyri on the table in the center of the room and would not meet his master's eye.

"Here," he began in a weakling's voice that cracked and broke. "I did this yesterday. If you'll only step over here, my lord. The, uh, moon is here, and the evening star is aligned so, and, uh, you will perhaps notice this configuration."

"I don't care about the mechanics of it!" Neb-mertef bellowed. "Just tell me what's going to happen tonight! Tell it to me in plain words!"

The magus blinked and dissembled, all self-possession deserting him altogether. He fumbled with the scrolls, dropping two of them on the floor, where they rolled in opposite directions. Neb-mertef, of course, made no move to help, and the magus stumbled clumsily after them, looking and feeling a fool. When he picked them up and tried to put them on the table, he dropped them again. The whole thing had to be done again under the disapproving and impatient eyes of Neb-mertef.

"Get on with it!" Neb-mertef commanded. "Can't you do anything right?"

"M-my lord, it's just that—"

"Tonight, man! What's in the stars for tonight?"

"My lord, what is it exactly that you wish to see?"

"If you're competent, the chart will show great things happening tonight. Something that'll affect my future for the better. Something to make me richer and more powerful than I've ever dreamed of being."

"That's just it, my lord."

"What do you mean?" Neb-mertef's angry impatience was no longer feigned.

"My lord, I don't see any sign that anything even remotely like that will happen. I see a setback. I see nothing but mixed signals."

Now Neb-mertef's rage was real. With one angry sweep of his hand he dashed the scrolls to the floor and stalked to the door. There he turned and fixed the unhappy magus with a burning scowl. "Do it again! And do it right this time!"

IV

The magus repeated every step of the process, but the stars still said what they had said before. Next, other means of divination were tried; regardless of which process was used, the portents remained much the same.

Although Neb-mertef felt sympathy for Set-Nakht's predicament, he knew better than to show any. After three hours of grueling labor he gruffly dismissed the harried and haggard Set-Nakht. Still not satisfied with the complete subjection of the magus to his will, Neb-mertef waited in the hallway for the count of fifty, then threw the magus's door open and screamed threats at him. This caught the magus seeking tender consolation in the arms of one of the burly Nubians, and Neb-mertef was pleased at the terrified leap into the air his bellowing provoked.

When he shut the door again with a tremendous slam he debated waiting another ten counts and repeating the action. Instead, he shrugged and walked down the hall to his own rooms.

He lay on his bed and shooed away the maidservant, not even bothering to look at her as she walked briskly out of the room, bare buttocks waggling invitingly. His thoughts were on the night. . . .

He was convinced that the magus's reading was no error. Watching Set-Nakht work, he had learned a bit about the configurations of the bones as well as those of the stars, and the basic outlines of his divinations checked out. But if this meant that Amasis would not become king tonight, it had to mean that the king would somehow survive!

He sat up. How could this be? Kamose had been a prisoner in Amasis's villa; Amasis kept the king's room guarded; and Nemaret, the man in charge of the household at the country home, had the strictest orders to—

But Nemaret had been absent from the house last night. Who knew what might have happened in the meantime?

What had Demetrios said last night? One of the soldiers who had helped Mara and Thermutis get away was still in the area? Being hidden by someone?

What if there was a plot to free the king?

But who could possibly be a member of such a thing? It seemed that with the departure of the queen and the princess, all dissent had been effectively silenced. Even the priesthood of Amon had held its collective tongue after the queen's escape, despite the high-handed way in which Amasis had been treated at the time.

Despite all evidence to the contrary, his skepticism persisted. What if the king did escape now? Would the country rise under his banner and depose Amasis? Would Kamose be able to organize the citizenry for a new civil war?

It did not seem likely. Not without the return of the army from Nubia. Now if the army were back from Nubia and had retained its autonomy, that would be another matter. If the king was himself again, the loyalty he had enjoyed all these years from his soldiers would be enough to win them over to his side. The army Baliniri had sent to Nubia was large and disciplined enough to pose a formidable threat to the command Amasis had brought back with him from the delta.

Ah! This was getting interesting! If the king was free, hidden by someone, he could become the focus of a whispering campaign all around Thebes, his name rallying support for rebellion. The whole city could be mobilized against the cult, with the king as a symbolic figure at their head.

What if he, Neb-mertef, could step in at this point and covertly throw his weight behind the movement? What if he could engineer the death of the king and plant evidence to show that Amasis had ordered the murder?

The more he thought about it, the more certain he was that he had discovered the true meaning behind the magus's puzzling prediction: Something would happen tonight to foil Amasis's plans and delay his coronation as king of Egypt.

That interference need not have a direct effect on his own future unless he took steps to make it so.

He smiled. Tonight he would do as little as possible. He would go to the villa as planned and keep up the appearance of compliance. He would keep his eyes open and attend to his own hidden agendas the whole time.

*   *   *

Nemaret was the first of the five to arrive at the villa. He strode into the central hall, looked around him, and bellowed for the slaves. Six appeared immediately, one at each door that led off the hall.

"This place is filthy!" he roared. "Our sovereign lord will be here in a little while! Look at the dust on the top of this table. Look at the leaves on the floor."

"But, my lord, the leaves fall when they like. There's no sense picking them up now when they will fall again," the steward in charge of the main floor said. "We'll do the area a bit closer to when our patron arrives—"

"Do it now!" the overseer shouted. "I want everything spotless! He'll have important guests tonight, who will be arriving before sundown. See to your work—all of you!"

With that he strode away, turning his back on the lot of them and taking the stairs two steps at a time. When he reached the landing he saw the little upstairs maid crossing the hall from one guest room to another, fresh linens in her hands. "There you are! Have you got the guest facilities in order?"

The girl looked up at him with the seductive look she had learned to give him whenever no higher-ups were present. "The rooms will be ready when the guests arrive. Everything is at their disposal. As," she said significantly, "I am at my lord's disposal."

His lip curled in a look of savage triumph. How nice to have her trained at last! He approached her and held out his hand for her to kiss.

As she did so, a flash of hot desire came over him; he would have had her right there on the spot, Amasis or no Amasis. But the urge passed as quickly as it had come. He caressed her rump with an indulgent hand and smiled, his eyes mere slits. "Have you looked in on our prisoner today?"

"No, my lord. If my lord will remember, he told me to leave the prisoner alone except for pushing his food and drink through the slot in the wall. The dishes disappear, and they come back an hour later. I assume everything is all right."

"Good girl," he said, his hand exploring her breast and feeling the nipple rise. If there were only time . . . but there wasn't; Amasis might arrive early. It had happened before.

"Very well. I'll look in on him. You supervise the finishing touches of the cleanup downstairs. You've done well. You will be rewarded when our master has departed for the city."

"Thank you, my lord," she said, bowing again.

He smiled as she withdrew. Then he made his own way to the next higher level, where the prisoner's room was the only enclosed space otherwise devoted to a rooftop garden.

He thought about the night's coming events. He alone of the household staff had been singled out for the honor of being allowed to shed the king's sacred blood.

Sacred blood? Kamose was an upstart of half-Hai blood; the other half was as common as dirt. He had risen to power by the sword; tonight he would fall as far as he had risen, again by the sword.

He yawned and, one hand checking the sword in his belt, drew the bolt of the heavy door behind which the prisoner had been kept since his arrival at the villa.

The room was empty!

He blinked, stuck his head inside, and was knocked violently to the floor by a powerful blow from an unseen fist! For a moment he saw stars, then he saw the naked, heavily muscled prisoner lunge toward him. Worst of all, Kamose was totally alert and in control as he had not been since the first day of his arrival.

Nemaret curled into a tight ball to protect his face. It was not enough. The prisoner's hard bare foot lashed out and caught him in the face. He tried to cry out, but the hard heel of the same foot smashed him in the mouth. Powerful hands lifted him by the bunched fiber of his tunic and smashed him against the wall. His head struck the stone with a hard crack and brought a jolt of blinding pain.

"P-please . . ." he begged, but the fists pounded into his gut and took his breath away. As consciousness faded he wondered what had happened. The dead had come to life!

Kamose let him fall, crumpled into a shapeless mess. He looked down with disgust at the inert form at his feet. Imagine, this—*this!*—had kept him prisoner for months! His foot poised over the slack face, ready to smash the unconscious man's nose flat. But he thought better of it and instead began to strip Nemaret and put on his clothing.

The tunic barely covered him; his shoulders were much more massive than Nemaret's. He fastened it together with the sword belt. He considered taking Nemaret's sandals, but bare feet were quieter. He went to the door and looked out cautiously. No one was in the rooftop garden. Keeping an eye on the silent guard at the rooftop's far edge, he slipped behind a row of potted palms and bided his time; then, as the guard routinely turned, he leapt forward, grasping the guard's neck. One swift and powerful twist, and he heard a telltale crack and dropped the guard, instantly dead.

Kamose paused, looked out over the gap between this rooftop and the roof of the slave quarters, opposite, then moved back ten paces. He dashed forward and leapt far out into the air, landing atop the brick dwelling. He broke into a run and vaulted to the wall of the enclosure just as a guard let out a bellow. An arrow whizzed past the king's head as he leapt down from the wall, hit, rolled, and was on his feet again, a fierce grin of triumph on his face.

He turned, sword in hand, at a noise behind him. There stood a man in the rich clothing of a successful merchant, in a chariot, staring at him.

"Give me the chariot," he commanded, "or I will kill you."

"Take it and use it in good health," the man offered, dismounting with alacrity and handing him the reins and a sword. "Good luck, sire. You will need it."

Kamose stared at the weapon, then his benefactor, and finally he climbed into the chariot. But before turning the horse away from the villa, he stopped and looked down. "I do not know if we have met," he said. "I would hope I would remember my friends, if that is what you are."

"I aspire to that honor," the man said smoothly. He did not bow but looked Kamose directly in the eye. "My name is Neb-mertef."

Kamose nodded. Then he turned the horse around and made way across the barren hills at a gallop.

V

As Kamose neared the city's edge it became obvious that the magnificent chariot and horse made him too conspicuous. They were obviously the possessions of a very rich man and someone like himself would draw suspicious stares.

So at the fringe of town he dismounted, loosed the horse from the chariot, then slapped the animal on the rear and set it free. Afoot, Kamose found his way through the outlying areas, getting his first good look at what Thebes had become in the nearly two decades he had been gone. It looked vaguely familiar. He wondered if anyone would know his face after all this time. After he had passed several large clots of people walking home after a day's shopping in the city's marketplaces, he wondered why Neb-mertef, whom he did not think he had ever met, could have recognized him at sight. But he dismissed the thought in the general interest of exploring the fringe of Thebes.

There was a chance that someone else might recognize him, though, so as he passed a long row of mud-brick houses he stole someone's hooded robe off a clothesline. With this on and the hood up he could enter the city gate with confidence.

He was famished, having starved himself for the last three days when it had become obvious that his food was drugged. He had thanked his lucky stars that they had not thought to drug his water as well.

He needed food and drink, but he had no money. He headed directly for the thieves' quarter, determined to find the price of dinner, drink, and a night's lodging before nightfall. As darkness began to settle on the city, he made his way through the streets where he had fought against his father, Apophis, so many years before. His eyes were alert under the hood that hid his face.

But just as the sun sank below the horizon and the eerie afterglow set in, he rounded a corner and ran into a pair of swaggering off-duty guardsmen, already drunk enough to be belligerent. "Pardon me," he said, making way for them.

"You damned dirty beggar," the taller of the two said in

a vile Cretan accent, "what are you doing wandering here after curfew?"

Kamose's eyes flashed, but he held his temper. "Curfew? I'm just in from the country. Nobody told me about any curfew."

But even as he spoke he looked right and left. They were well down the street from the nearest street lantern, and nobody seemed to be looking on. Thus, when the first guardsman moved one hand nearer his sword, Kamose did not hesitate but drew his own, lightning-fast, and buried it in the man's gut, stabbing upward into the heart.

The guardsman sank to the ground as the other man cursed and grabbed for his weapon. But, being inebriated, the guardsman's hands proved clumsy, and he could not get the sword out of its scabbard before Kamose had skewered him.

Kamose again looked right and left, thanking the gods for his good luck. He dragged the men into a transverse alley, then covered the blood in the street with dust. Lastly, he went back into the shadows of the alley and picked their pockets, coming up with two purses that jingled pleasantly. *Now to get out of this neighborhood,* he thought.

Kamose doubled back through familiar back alleys and side streets. His feet seemed to know all the paths across town by feel alone. The moment he crossed into the middle-class quarter, he took refuge in a crowded, dimly lit inn.

No sooner had he sat down, called for wine, and looked about him than he noticed two burly Greek guards, armed to the teeth, sitting next to him. Kamose kept his hood up, called for food, then turned to his meal, trying not to betray his extreme hunger and thirst.

As he ate he became aware of the conversation:

". . . something big about to happen. Nobody's sure what. But there's a big parade in the offing any day now. I'm betting end of the week. The shifts are being adjusted to put as many men as possible in the city at the same time. Amasis has something planned that involves everybody."

"You ask me, he's probably gone and strangled the king."

"You know, I'll bet you're right. So that's the way the wind is blowing—to put himself in charge of everything. I knew when he killed Baliniri and drove the queen out of town, he'd committed himself all the way."

Kamose kept his eyes on his food, devouring the fresh fruit and warm flatbread and washing it down with gulps of raw wine. No one noticed the almost imperceptible jolt that whipped through him. What sort of place had Thebes become? Baliniri *was* dead! Murdered at Amasis's command, from the sound of it! And Mara driven out of town? How could this have happened? He would have to learn later.

He stood, called a servant, and paid his bill out of one of the two stolen purses. Then he slipped into the darkness, never having taken down the hood he wore.

Once in the street, he pondered his next move. From what the Greeks had said, the streets would soon be full of soldiers, all called into Thebes for Amasis's planned coronation. Kamose snorted. Coronation! Well, Amasis would have to come up with the body of the former king before a new one could be installed. Without a corpse confirmed as Kamose's by the priesthood and physicians, Amasis would not be able to assume the crown legally.

The shocked thought came now, however: What if legality was already a thing of the past?

It was plausible. As the two in the inn had said, Amasis had irrevocably committed himself the moment he had killed Baliniri. If low-level soldiers like those Greeks knew it, it wouldn't be much of a secret anywhere!

Kamose felt saddened by the seemingly complete absence in Thebes of the old army cadre. Had they been mustered out, like his old comrades back in the delta, to be replaced by those whose only loyalty was to Amasis?

One thing was certain: Without the protection of his old, loyal army, he was a dead man. There was nothing for him to do but to hope to get out of Thebes alive and try to organize some kind of resistance. He would have to go either farther upriver or across the Nile.

Reaching into a stolen purse for a coin, he tossed it into the air. The thing spun in the air and landed in his palm. He quickly moved under a lantern and stood in the pool of light. The stamped side was up.

He would cross the river—tonight, before someone found the two dead guards and closed the city.

VI

Nemti and Mara had picked Aaron up at his house a few minutes after darkness fell. He had come along quietly. But now as the queen and her lover led the way through the back streets of Deir el-Bahari, they passed under a lantern and saw his face: the lines of worry, the haggard and exhausted look.

Mara stopped and turned to him in the soft light. "Aaron! What's the matter? You look as if you've aged twenty years since the last time we saw you. Are you ill?"

"No, I'm all right," Aaron replied morosely. "But when I came home last night, I found out that Demetrios had been asking about me. He told Elisheba that he had his eye on me. He suspects something. I went looking for him then, to corroborate the excuse Elisheba gave him for my absence, but he wasn't to be found. His aide let it slip that he had a meeting this evening with Amasis, at his country home."

Mara and Nemti exchanged shocked looks.

"We'd better get moving," Nemti said. "If we can rescue the king, we'll take him with us to the oasis. Aaron, this is getting too dangerous for you. I can't let you take any more chances."

"I am not afraid for myself," Aaron assured him. "I am as strong as Demetrios, and my people are good fighters—we have had to be. But my wife is frightened."

"Do you want to go back?"

"No. Our mission tonight must be accomplished. Three of us will be better than two."

"Take my sword, then," Nemti offered. "I'll use Mara's dagger. She doesn't need anything but her bow for covering us."

"No," Aaron said, brandishing his tall, stout staff. "This will do. It's the traditional weapon of my people. With such a staff, anyone of my clan could break every bone in your body without breaking the skin. In Canaan we sometimes killed lions with these."

Nemti smiled. "Then come along. And perhaps we can deal with this Demetrios in the morning, before we go."

Moving into deep shadow, they hurried down the hill toward the quays and the row of beached ferryboats.

Now, however, on the far side of the river, in Thebes, the two slain guards had been found and the garrison roused to comb the streets and alleys. Demetrios of Rhodes, meanwhile, galloping on horseback along the high road from Amasis's country estate, despite the poor light, pulled up and leapt from the horse before the assembled officers of the city guard. "Quick!" he panted. "There's a prisoner escaped! He's armed and dangerous! A hundred *outnou* to the man who brings him to me, dead or alive!"

"A prisoner, sir?" said his adjutant. "Could you describe him?"

"Damn your eyes," Demetrios hissed malevolently. "It's the king! If he gets loose—"

"I understand, sir. He may already have been here. Someone killed two of our men in an alley. We thought it was a robber; their money was missing. But what robber could deal with two of our toughest men? Kamose, I know, is a master with the sword. He could have killed them easily."

Demetrios scowled. "You're probably right. Well, he has better sense than to stay in town. Close the roads and station men on the quays. No—I'll do that myself. You and you! Come along. If he gets away, we're in deep trouble."

Kamose stood on the quay, frantically looking around. The regular ferryboats had been pulled well up onto land, so to drag them down to the Nile would attract attention. He was beginning to wonder whether he should risk it anyway when he saw a slender boat making its way toward him across the dark waters. He waved his arms but did not dare cry out.

He heard a noise behind him. He wheeled to see three guardsmen jogging toward him. The first one had broken into a run. "There he is!" he bellowed, drawing the bow from the quiver on his back. "Stop him!"

Kamose looked back at the Nile, calculating. If he dashed out and dived into the river, could he make it far enough out into the current to be beyond the reach of an arrow?

He almost dived into the water, but at the last moment he thought better of it and elected to stand and fight. He hoped the people in the approaching boat were not guards as well. He thought he might handle three of them, but with further reinforcements the outcome might well go against him.

"You!" one soldier cried out in a raucous voice. "Stop where you are and explain what you're doing here!"

Kamose took a deep breath. Then his hand went to his scabbard and came up with his stolen sword. "Cutting your tripes out," he answered in a flat voice, and attacked.

The sheer violence of the rain of blows aimed at the soldier drove the man back. Then the other two caught up with the first and joined him. Kamose knocked the sword out of one man's hand, then immediately turned his attention to the other two. The first soldier lunged forward and almost caught him in the guts. Kamose turned the blade aside, though, and stabbed at his attacker; his blade hit the breastbone and thus did not go deep. The soldier recovered but collapsed to his knees, winded.

Kamose, hacking like a woodcutter, went after the man's companion until he had beaten the sword out of his opponent's hands by sheer strength. He ran the soldier through, then turned to parry a furious attack by the first man he had disarmed, giving ground as the leader recovered and joined the fight.

"No!" Mara cried out, putting a hand on Aaron's strong arm. "Don't steer to shore just yet! Look there on the quay!"

"We'll steer a bit downstream," Nemti decided. He and Aaron had shipped their oars, but now he made as if to dip the blade into the water again.

"No! No! Can't you see? The men fighting there?"

"Yes," Aaron answered, puzzled. "Can't we help? Two soldiers against a civilian—"

"Gods!" she gasped. "I think I know who it is. Oh, Nemti, only one man in the world fights like that!"

"Why can't we help him?" Aaron asked.

"Stay out in the current. When he's done, he'll swim to us."

Aaron peered into the darkness. "I think one of them is Demetrios. Yes, that's his voice."

"How did Kamose get free? How did he get this far? But that's he, all right! Kamose! *Kamose!*"

The sudden and unexpected sound of his wife's voice threw Kamose off his stride, and the second soldier lunged forward and stabbed him in the upper arm. Kamose deftly switched hands, gave up a step or two, then counterattacked. His blade caught the second soldier in the throat, and the man dropped his weapon and clutched at his neck, staggering back.

Kamose barely avoided being skewered as the first soldier attacked once more, raining blows on him that were deflected with great difficulty.

Having aimed a good dozen cuts at Kamose without hitting him, the soldier stepped back and saluted.

"The compliments of Demetrios of Rhodes, sir. You should know at whose hands you are going to die. You're good with the sword, but not good enough."

Just as Demetrios assumed the fighting stance, there was a dull *thunk* and he fell flat on the quay, headfirst, out cold. Yet there was no one near him. Kamose looked down, puzzled. Far away across the broad quay, men were running toward him.

Out on the water there came the cry again, from that unmistakable voice. "Kamose! This way! Swim!"

He could see her standing up in the shallow-draft vessel, beckoning. He grinned. She had always had good timing. "I'm coming," he called, and headed for the edge of the quay on a dead run to dive far out into the river.

"Where did you learn to do that?" Nemti asked, incredulous. "That's amazing." He watched as Aaron again reached inside his garment, withdrew a pebble, loaded it in the sling he had made from the belt of his robe, and twirled it around his head. The small projectile hurled at the guards on the quay flew with deadly accuracy and felled an archer. Nevertheless, many arrows were launched from the shore at the swimmer and the boat, several narrowly missing Kamose. One landed upright on the crossbeam next to where Mara stood.

"This is the *other* native weapon of my people," Aaron announced calmly, withdrawing another pebble. "This is the way shepherds drive predators from their flocks." He twirled the sling around his head and brained yet another guardsman, who stood so far away that Nemti could not even make out his features. "One advantage of this weapon is that it doesn't look like one."

Now the swimmer was getting nearer—but so were the arrows from the shore. Mara steadied herself and leaned out over the water. "Here!" she offered. "Take my hand!"

The others in the boat braced themselves as Kamose climbed over the side. When he was safely aboard, Mara sat down beside him and reached for her shipped oars. "Let's get out of here before they can get another boat in the water!"

"Here, give me those," Kamose said. "These long-idle hands will welcome the touch of oars." He took over from her and joined the others in rowing the boat powerfully out into the current. "How is it that you're here, Mara? And who are these men? I understand you're a wanted person like me these days."

"Yes. You'll have many questions and answers tonight, Kamose. I'm sure we'll have some of our own, as well. This is Nemti, late of the city guards, and Aaron ben Amram."

"Ah, a Habiru. But why should a Habiru help me? I'm the titular head of a country that has abused your people terribly."

"The mere fact that you recognize this injustice is significant," Aaron replied, not missing a stroke. "Besides, I am told you are no friend of Amasis's and would not approve of what he has been doing in your absence."

"Probably not," Kamose admitted. "What *has* he been doing? They've kept me totally incommunicado."

"They poisoned Baliniri. I have Nemti to thank that they didn't murder me too." Mara looked over Kamose's head, and her smile was visible in the moonlight. "For that and many other things. His friend Onuris took Thermutis and me to the oasis for safety's sake, while Nemti stood off the enemy to cover our escape. He was hurt in the process. He shouldn't be manning an oar now."

Kamose shot a curious glance at her and missed a beat rowing. "Ah, so that's the way it is, eh? Well, however it worked out, I'm in the debt of all of you. Now what do we do?"

"The only place where we'll be safe now is at El-Kharga," Mara answered. "From there we can work out plans for your return. Amasis can't be crowned without showing everyone your dead body, and we won't give him that."

"The oasis it is," Kamose agreed, pulling mightily on the oars. "By the way, who killed that soldier on the quay? It was a sling that did it, wasn't it?"

"That was my work," Aaron replied. "I thought I recognized him, but I wasn't sure."

"He gave his name. Demetrios of Rhodes. He thought I should be impressed with the fact."

"Demetrios!" Aaron grinned and pulled even more lustily on his oars. "God be praised! Once again He has delivered us from our oppressor!"

CHAPTER TWELVE

At the Semna Straits

I

There were distinct advantages to being a princess, Tharbis thought, looking herself over in the tall, bronze mirror in her room. Oh, to be sure, there were problems, and the constant lack of privacy was one of the worst of them. But when you wanted to look your best, there was the wherewithal to do so.

It was a time, she had decided, to go for subtlety. The rings of black kohl painted around her large, warm-brown eyes were understated, and the beads around her neck were not rubies or emeralds but simpler fare: amethysts, turquoises, and carnelians. Their purpose was to draw attention not to her wealth but to her pert young bosom, its prominent nipples clearly visible through the nearly transparent cloth.

Similarly, her other jewelry was kept simple: two gold rings on her fingers, a single toe ring on one foot, and a slim, gold stomacher clearly visible through her dress, to draw attention to the fact that she wore nothing underneath it.

The effect would not have been considered daring at a court function, but it was designed to have a startling impact when worn—as she intended to wear it—on a visit to the dungeons, to visit Seth.

She twirled before the mirror, admiring the way the stomacher, drooping fetchingly like a slave-girl's beaded belt, drew attention to her hard little bottom. She faced the mirror again, posed prettily, and winked at her reflection. Then she went out the door into the hall.

Guards were everywhere. Now, an hour or two before sundown, the obligatory soldier stood watch by her door. She decided to test her effect and batted her eyes, smiling seductively, while she fiddled with her beads and thrust out her breasts so they strained at the cloth. She watched his eyes dilate, blink, and travel from her head to her toes. Then she made sure, as she walked away from him, that he once again broke rules by letting his gaze follow the round globes of her rump, which undulated like a dancer's.

Well, she thought, *so far so good*. Provided the evening shift in the dungeons was not a pair of boy lovers, she ought to be able to get through to chat with Seth.

It had been an interesting day. Judging by the reports to her father from the constant stream of messengers from Kumma, Moses and his men had managed to delay Apedemek's arrival at Semna by launching a powerful attack early in the morning, one that won a great deal of ground and seemed on the verge of driving the Nubian force all the way back to the walls of the fortress of Kumma.

Then, in the early afternoon, Nehsi himself had made an appearance in the field, towering over the shorter Egyptians, unmistakable in his imperial grandeur. It should have been a powerful suit to play at this point, but the evil genius Apedemek had come to the fore once more, using his uncanny means of persuasion and casting a spell over his entire army. He convinced them that they were seeing a sorcerer's illusion and not the beloved king they had served so long.

The result had been a standoff, so the morning's gains and afternoon's losses had left the battle lines about where they had begun the day. As she moved quickly and efficiently down the stairs, Tharbis pondered the effect of this on Moses. It must be terribly frustrating for him!

She could not get him out of her mind. He had been so powerful, so strong, so exciting! What a great pity they could not have met under other circumstances; by now she was confident she would have been able to cast a little spell of her own. No doubt Moses was well worth the trouble. A prince of the blood of Egypt? A young, virile one, handsome and vital? Any woman would kill for such a prize.

What a shame it could not be Moses who would be her nightly liaison, instead of Het! But the leader of the expedition would not be doing such things; he would leave the work to a subordinate.

Admittedly, it was fun to flirt with and tease Het. He was a nice boy, really, and would make a fit husband for an ordinary woman. But she had her heart set on a prince, a general—someone of consequence. Moses of course was both, and—she sighed now, thinking about it—as handsome as a god.

Het was a lot of fun. Imagine finding a boy his age who blushed! Who could be teased with such ease!

She passed a pair of guards and rolled her hips with half-innocent seductiveness. She knew that they would talk about her in the most provocative terms the moment she was out of earshot and that they would not share these thoughts with any superior.

Now, however, came the tricky part. She did not know the men on this shift on the enclosed staircase. It was always easier to use her womanly charm on one man at a time, but now she would probably be dealing with two guards.

She took a deep breath and moved silently down the stairs on her soft leather sandals.

Seth, dozing just beyond the circle of light that filtered, broken into stripes, through the bars, was awakened by voices in the corridor. Both guards were talking at once, but there was a third voice as well—softer, higher-pitched.

He sat, then got to his feet. As he did, he saw a guard come to the bars. "You! Somebody to see you! The lady wants to thank you for a favor the other night. Now don't try anything. I'll be watching."

From the expression on his face it was obvious *what* he was watching. Seth nodded silently and observed the princess Tharbis as she walked slowly across the room, her movements no longer utilitarian and efficient as on the occasion of their earlier meeting. He smiled. She had it, he thought, amused, and already at this young age she knew exactly how to use it. "Good evening, my lady."

She moved close to the bars, her face serious. Seth peeked over her shoulder and watched the guard staring intensely at her little bottom. "Don't mind that," she said. "I had to do something to divert their attention."

"You are doing that admirably," Seth commended. "You have news for me?"

"Yes. Moses is doing everything he can to keep Apedemek busy in Kumma. Moses doesn't want him coming over here and finding you in the dungeon. Apedemek knows who you are. You're in danger."

"Let him come," Seth said. "I'm looking forward to meeting him."

"But everyone fears him so," she said, "and for you to be facing him at such a disadvantage . . ."

Seth smiled. "I am not sure about that. If I wanted to get out of here, these bars and those guards could not stop me. But there is a thing I must learn here, and I can learn it only from Apedemek. I might as well let him come to me." He grinned. "This is the lazy man's solution."

"Aren't you afraid?"

"I was briefly. Apedemek's powers are awesome, and he has some tricks that I cannot explain. Others are familiar to me, if his particular way of invoking them is not. It is almost as though we were rival senet players, feeling each other out, sparring, if you will."

"I admire your spirit," Tharbis said. "Look." She drew closer to the bars and lowered her voice. "I'm supposed to meet with someone from the Egyptian camp in an hour or so. I'm to tell him what I've found out during the day. He'll need to know if you want his people to storm this place and get you out." She paused, all concern. "Please don't face Apedemek if you don't have to. Not like this. Not in an unequal situation."

Seth waved away her plea. "Tell them not to worry about me, but to apply themselves to defeating the Nubians. I take it Nehsi is safe."

She nodded, then swiftly sketched in the day's activities, including Apedemek's response to Nehsi's surprise appearance in the field.

Seth smiled tranquilly. "I wonder how he does those things. I can fool a crowd into thinking a thing has happened when it has not. But I have to be there. He can create mass illusions without even being present while they are happening." A thoughtful look crossed his face. "I wonder . . ."

"I have to be able to tell Het something," Tharbis said nervously. "What do you want me to tell him to pass along to Moses?"

There was a change in her voice when she spoke Moses's name. Seth caught it. "You're quite taken with Moses, aren't you, my dear?"

"Does it show that much?"

"To me. I doubt if he'd notice. He's not experienced with girls." He changed the subject. "You mentioned Het. That is the young man who was in jail with Nehsi when the rescue took place."

"Yes. You'd like him." She started. "You know, this is really strange, my telling you what's on my mind. I mean, I hardly know you, but I'm baring my soul as if you were my father."

"Perhaps that's why," Seth said. "You and your father don't get along, I gather."

"I'm nasty to him even when I don't want to be. It's almost as though I weren't in control. It's like the way I find myself teasing Het. And really, Het's a nice boy. It's just that I find that I can tease him, so I do."

"Ah," Seth said. There was much meaning in the one syllable. "I get the feeling that you don't understand all of your feelings all of the time." He smiled winningly. "Don't mind me being an old busybody. It's my way."

"I don't mind. There is something about you that makes me want to trust you. I was raised around men after my mother died. I know how to manipulate them a little—"

"As you are doing with those poor guards. They will dream about you for days."

"Yes. But I don't know very much about how to be a girl."

"It's all right. You'll learn. Do you want to know why you're so comfortable with me?"

"Why?"

"Because you realize that you can't manipulate me at all." His smile turned into a conspiratorial grin. She found herself returning it. "Now go, and give my best to my friends. Keep an eye on young Het for me, will you? I want you to report to me about him. He seemed like an interesting fellow . . . even if he doesn't know much about girls. Even if you can manipulate him." He chuckled. "I'll bet you can't manipulate Moses, and that's one of the reasons you're so taken with him."

She stared. She had never considered this.

"Now, go," he repeated. "Thank you for coming to see me. You're a brave girl. You're going to make some lucky young man very, very happy one of these days."

She blinked, smiled nervously, and beat a hasty retreat. All the way out the door she could feel the guards' hungry eyes watching her; but all she could see in her mind's eye was the look of affectionate amusement on Seth's face.

II

After the musty closeness of the long tunnel from the fortress, the cool, clear air of the nearby Nile was a welcome relief. A light breeze was blowing, and the wind's soft and balmy touch felt delightful on her skin. Tharbis checked the covered lantern to make sure that no light leaked out, then stepped into the night air.

Immediately there was a night bird's soft cry nearby. She tried to repeat it but botched the attempt. She pursed her lips to try again but an unseen finger reached out and touched her lips.

"*Shhhh!* What are you doing wearing white out here?" a familiar voice admonished in a penetrating whisper. "Come inside before someone sees you."

His hand took the lantern away, and his other hand guided her gently back into the tunnel. Only when they were standing in complete darkness did he take his hand away from her back and reach down to uncover the lantern.

They stared wordlessly at each other for a long moment.

She was the first to speak. "You cheated! You're dressed!"

"Oh, come on," he protested. "Don't start on that nonsense now. This is serious." He looked her up and down, and while the expression on his face did not change otherwise, his eyes said a great deal. "It looks as though you made up for my putting on a tunic. What is that outfit made of? Spider webs?"

"Don't tease me," she chided, embarrassed for the first time. "I had to do something to distract the guards so I could get down to see Seth."

"You're going to have quite a reputation."

"I already do," she responded defensively. "I'm a palace brat. I can usually get by with murder. The other side of the coin is that nobody ever says a kind word. It's very lonely. I'm forced to do something outrageous every so often to stir people up just to keep myself from dying of boredom."

When he snorted, she found herself annoyed beyond belief. How had things got off on the wrong foot all of a sudden? The last time she had seen him, she had been able to do anything she wanted with him. "You don't look as nice this way," she said petulantly. "You look like a country bumpkin."

"And you look like a whore about to do a bawdy dance at a tavern," he retorted gruffly. "Where's your tambourine?"

"Stop it!" she said, hurt. "I have to tell you. I saw Seth."

"All right," Het responded, glad to be back on course. "What did he say?"

"He said don't worry about him. He isn't afraid of Apedemek. How can he not be afraid of Apedemek?"

"I don't know. According to your friend Moses, that's the way Seth is." There was heaviness in his voice as he said this. "Nobody understands him. He does as he likes. He was somebody really important once, married to the daughter of the king of Babylon, just before the Hittites burned the city. Moses says that technically he was king of Babylon for about an hour, between the death of his father-in-law and the fall of the city. King of Babylon! Imagine! And yet he looks like just any other old man."

"A fat lot you know about it," she said, hating the resentment in her voice. "You know, he asked me to ask about you. He sees something in you that the rest of the world doesn't."

"You're quite sarcastic tonight. Huh! Just because I wouldn't play your silly games."

"Maybe Seth isn't as smart as everybody says he is. Imagine anyone being interested in the likes of you!"

"Look, if you're finished . . . is there anything more?"

"Only to keep hammering away at Kumma. I can't understand. He says he's actually looking forward to meeting Apedemek. I suppose *you* think *you're* smarter than anybody. I suppose *you* think Apedemek wouldn't have any power over you."

He shook his head. "I wouldn't make any claim like that. Apedemek seems to have cast a spell over Seth himself, when he—Apedemek, I mean—wasn't even there. Moses tells me that Seth is the last man in the world that anyone should ever be able to fool. He says that all Thebans acknowledge the superiority of Seth's intelligence."

"Yes," she agreed, her mood gentling. "I could believe that, having talked to him. Why, I hadn't exchanged ten words with him before I was blabbing away as if I'd known him all my life. I felt as if he were an uncle who had bounced me on his knee when I was a little girl."

He looked her up and down again. "If you continue to dress like that," he said, "some soldier is going to forget who your father is and take you up on *his* knee. Whatever possessed you to dress up like that?"

For some reason she felt like crying. "I don't know why you have to be so mean," she complained. "Just because I teased you last time we were together, you don't have to take it out on me now."

"You're so used to having your way. And you were hard

on me, letting me know how disappointed you were that I wasn't Moses. You made me feel like a nobody."

"I'm sorry," she said. "Something just gets into me sometimes. It's like the way I get when I'm around my father. He's such a pawn. My mother used to be mean to him, calling him names. Now I find myself doing the same thing, even when I'm not mad at him."

"Well, I'm not your father. There's no reason for you to give me the same treatment."

"I am sorry."

"Your mother and father must have got along at some time back there," he consoled. "At one time you loved your father and respected him, I'll bet."

"I don't want him to go wrong," she said, tearing up, "as he seems to be doing. I'd like to be able to stop him. If I could do it by just talking to him, I'd do that. But we haven't been able to talk to each other for a long time. It goes all the way back to when my mother died."

He felt more at ease because of her vulnerable mood. "I like you better when you're not being sarcastic. When I first saw you I thought—" He gulped and stopped; he wasn't ready for that deep a confidence. "You're very pretty. You don't really look like a tavern slut. I shouldn't have said that."

She smiled. "But I do," she admitted. "Anyhow, it worked—I did get through to Seth. I'm going to do it tomorrow night, too. Are you going to be back?"

He looked her in the eyes. "If you'll promise not to tease me. I'm sorry I have my back up tonight. I was still steamed up over your behavior from last night."

"Then we can start over? Are we friends?"

"Sure."

He held out his hand, and she took it, and it was as if a strong jolt of electricity passed between them. They drew their hands away at the same moment. Their eyes met, and both blinked. He stood like a statue for a long moment, then a sudden change came over his face. "Gods!" he said. "I almost forgot what I was going to say. We had a defector come over to our side today. Just threw down his weapons and ran away, and asked if he could join us. It was even before the business about Nehsi."

"What did he say?"

"He told us that Apedemek isn't in the Nubian encampment. That he took off this morning to come here to Semna. That was the dumbest thing I ever heard. In the first place, not an hour later, Apedemek cast that spell over his army to convince them that Nehsi was a fake. Besides, we could see him, just standing on a hillock directing the course of the battle. Their runners would go back and consult him."

"But then what could the man have been talking about?"

"I don't know. A man can't be in two places at the same time, can he?"

Arnekh had finally drifted off to sleep, his breathing labored and difficult. Seth had begged a filthy, ragged blanket from one of the guards to cover the old man. He was just preparing for sleep himself when he heard a clatter on the stairs of hurried footsteps, those of several men. As they grew closer, the guard went out into the hall. A number of voices, loud and forceful, overrode one another in the anteroom beyond his field of vision.

The inner guard came in. "You! Seth! You've got more company! Get up!"

Seth sat and looked at the guard, now fumbling with the lock. "I'm being let out?" he asked affably. "Well, this is a pleasant surprise. I thought you people were going to keep me in here forever."

"None of your damned sarcasm," the guard growled. "Now come out here."

Seth stood. He had taken the opportunity to bathe in the brackish water of the flooded sector of the dungeon, so most of the dark grease was gone; he wore only the torn uniform of the guardsman he had killed. "Well," he said, "I'm not exactly in parade gear, but it'll have to do. Who is kind enough to visit me this time?"

But as the guard opened the door of his cell, the visitors moved into view.

Seth's face went blank. *"You!"* he gasped.

III

There were four men standing there. Two were guards in bloodstained uniforms, brutal and big-boned men whose battered faces Seth had never seen. Behind them stood a tall, broad-shouldered man in a hooded robe, which concealed most of his face. Between them, looking as emaciated and frightened and disorganized as ever, was the tinker Netek-amani, whose eyes darted back and forth between Seth and the guardsman who stood behind him.

"Greetings!" Seth said. "I can't say that I'm happy to see you being led off to jail like this, my friend, but it's a pleasant surprise to see you've survived that mad rush you made down into the Nubian camp. They haven't harmed you, have they?"

He did not wait for a response but addressed the man in the hood. "And you," he said, making a mock flourish, one that looked ridiculous in the context of his soiled and stolen clothing. "My compliments, sir. I've been waiting for you. I'm sure that we will find quite a lot of things to talk about."

There was no response. Seth pursed his lips in thought. "Perhaps I've made a mistake. I am speaking to Apedemek, am I not?"

There was still no verbal response from the man in the hood, but his powerful, long-fingered hands slowly began to remove his hood. Now the face was visible. It did not match the expectations: The eyes were quite ordinary, set in the bruised and scarred face of a professional soldier. The expression was that of a man with no more than average intelligence. The nose was broken. A white scar ran from the corner of one eye to the jawline. When he opened his mouth, he bared broken and missing teeth.

Netek-amani gave a nervous, high-pitched laugh. "Oh, no, sir. This gentleman here is Ergamenes. He's the general, sir, in charge of the Kumma force."

Seth stared as the tinker's shoulders slowly squared. The foolish smile slowly disappeared from the no-longer-foolish face. He seemed to grow a good handspan in one amazing moment. The slack jaw firmed. And the eyes—the eyes—

"A near miss," the "tinker" said in a new voice, deeper,

silkier, sinister. He laughed humorlessly, ominously. "My compliments indeed. I expected to find a peer, but instead I found only a fool—a weak, sentimental fool. One who lets his heart mislead him."

Seth finally caught his breath. "Apedemek—*you?*" he said.

Again the dark laughter. "At your service," the magus replied, making a mock bow. He turned to the men behind him. "Leave us," he ordered.

The two men were alone in the outer room of the dungeon. Seth shook his head slowly. "I . . . I can't believe it," he said softly.

But now Apedemek's voice rolled out, and it was the terrible voice Seth had heard in his vision of the invisible man in the hood, speaking from the flames in the deserted fort downriver. There was great power in it. It was a voice that could kill with a word, or even a whisper. "Listen to you," he said scornfully. "Puzzled. Confused. Speaking of 'belief.' If you were the man I had hoped to confront, you would not speak of 'belief.' A true magus either knows or knows not. He does not speak of 'belief,' except to describe a process by which idiots and hinds talk themselves into swallowing the delusion a stronger mind has thrown at them."

"I was fooled completely." Seth's voice had suddenly become small and weak. "I thought you a harmless half-wit. I felt sorry for you."

"Sorry!" Apedemek exploded. "*Sorry!*" His laughter reached a great crescendo, then grew to a proportion that hurt the ears. "He felt sorry for me! He *pitied* me!"

"There was so much that I could not understand," Seth confessed, puzzled. "The visions. The strange way the defenders of the first fort rushed to their deaths. But that means you killed them yourself! You planted the suicide orders in their minds! You murdered your own men!"

The awful laughter grew.

Seth put his hands over his ears. "And the men burned alive! You killed your friends! I *wondered* why they were lashed to the stakes with chains, while you were tied with hemp. It was so you could get loose and they couldn't! You burned them to death!"

But his voice, his words, his pain and indignation were buried under the great rolling cascade of that hideous and deafening laughter!

Tharbis closed the door behind her. She felt humiliated by the leers of all the guards she had had to pass on the way up to her room. Why, she wondered, did this bother her so now? They surely had not taken any more interest in her on her way back from the dungeons than they had on the way down. What had caused her change of mood? Why did she feel so vulnerable? Something had obviously happened to make her feel so uncomfortable.

Uncomfortable? Too weak a word! She felt stupid, shallow, and irresponsible. Why?

Responding to her discomfort, she threw off the transparent gown and put on a heavy robe, clutching it around herself as if she were chilled to the bone, despite the balminess of the evening. She hugged herself close and, lifting her eyes, suddenly caught a glimpse of her image in the mirror.

The person looking back at her seemed a stranger. It was a very odd sensation. Who was this person in the reflection?

Well, she was tallish for a white girl, however tiny she might seem among the towering black Nubians, whose women stood a head taller than her father. The face was narrow with high cheekbones and dominated entirely by the large brown eyes.

The body—here she opened the robe to look at herself— was strong and athletic. Her belly was flat, her thighs long and strong, her bosom small and pert and provocative. Her hips could be wider, perhaps, if one favored the court standard.

But look at the expression on her face! Had she always looked like that? No! She looked stunned and insecure, years younger. She looked like a confused and frightened girl.

Was this why the guards had taken no pains to mask their desires? As a self-confident, spoiled princess, she could provoke men, and no one dared to say or do anything about it to her face. But the moment she showed herself to be vulnerable and lacking in confidence, the smirks would now be shown to her face.

This was understandable; men were men, and they responded to power and to the loss of it. But the real question now was how and why had she lost the power?

Was it the conversation with Het? He had been much different this time, independent, spunky, strong. He had been a man, not a bumbling, manipulable boy.

But part of her transformation was owed to her time with Seth. What was it about him that had allowed and encouraged her to open up so to him? He had seemed like family. And although Seth was quite manly, she had felt free to talk with him, a feeling lost to her since her father had brought her to Semna, leaving Irenas, her longtime maidservant and confidante, behind at the capital. The thought tugged hurtfully at her heart. *Oh, Irenas! If only I'd been able to bring you along! How I miss you now! I don't understand anything at all—either about my own feelings or about those of others!*

"But you're one of *us*," Seth said. "How could you have gone over to the other side? Don't you have any concept whatsoever of what a Child of the Lion is supposed to be?"

Apedemek's smile was chillingly malevolent. " 'Supposed to be?' " he mocked. "Don't tell me you let yourself be hemmed in by standards set down by others. At whose knee did you get your training? Did your mother take away your spunk and spirit, or did your father perhaps give you a lecture at puberty, all stern and disapproving? No wonder you turned out to be such a weakling, so powerless."

"Leave my parents out of it. My mother didn't even tell me who I was for years. My father wasn't around. He never acknowledged me as his own while he lived. Because the birthmark was blurred on my body, he thought I was not a true Child of the Lion."

Apedemek stepped forward and pulled aside Seth's stolen uniform. "If I were your father, I'd wonder too. But it's a perfect indication of what is missing in you generally. By contrast, look at *my* birthmark." He pulled aside his coat. Low on his back, on one side, the paw print of a lion fairly glowed, a dark and angry red, its outline distinct. "From the look of things I'd say your part of the line is all played out. You are of which branch of the family?"

Seth drew himself up with some pride. "My grandfather was Hadad of Haran. His father was—"

"Hadad of Haran! *That* fool! No wonder you'll never amount to anything! If I had an ancestor like that, I'd disown him. I'd make up new ancestors, so nobody would be tempted to laugh at me. Let's see, now . . . *his* father would have been Kirta, the idiot who abandoned his wife and children. I heard he died a beggar. Is that true?"

"He died a hero."

"And Ahuni. He drowned, I think. And his father, Belsunu . . . well, there was a man with a bit of talent. I've seen a few swords he made that weren't too contemptible. But a lunger. Limped around coughing all the time. Your line is comprised of idiots and weaklings, always giving in to the nonexistent bugaboo they call conscience."

"This is tedious," Seth retorted. "Do you think you can provoke me by descending to cheap insults and loose-tongued drivel?"

Apedemek finally turned to look at him. The eyes—hot, burning, intense—bored into his. "Drivel, is it?" His hand went inside his garment and pulled out a huge emerald, suspended from his neck by a leather cord. He held it high. "Drivel? Test *this* for drivel!"

Suddenly, out of the stone blazed a green fire, painful to look at. It glowed like a nimbus around Apedemek's outstretched hand for a moment, then shot a powerful beam of green light at Seth. It touched his head, enveloped it like a halo, then suddenly exploded in a huge ball of light, blinding and powerful.

Wordlessly, without a sound, Seth collapsed to the floor and lay still.

IV

In the day's fighting, Prince Moses had taken a sword cut in the upper arm, and the army physician had cleaned the wound and bandaged it. Moses had refused *shepenn*, preferring the pain in order to take part in the postbattle analysis with a clear mind. Now, as the officers and advisers rehashed the matter, the pain returned with a vengeance, and he gritted his teeth to keep from crying out. He sat on a flat stone, his back leaning against an abutment on the limestone wall.

Halfway through the discussion Geb noticed Moses's discomfort. "My lord! What is wrong? Can I help you?"

"No, no," Moses assured him. "I'll be all right. Just continue."

"But there's no need to suffer when there's a plentiful supply of *shepenn*, my lord. Please let me bring the surgeon back."

"No, I'll just rest. I want to be fresh for the morning. If I need a painkiller later to help me get a night's sleep, I'll call for you."

"All right, my lord, if you're quite sure . . . but I don't think you should take part in the fighting tomorrow."

"Nonsense. It's only a scratch. Baliniri taught me to use my left hand as well as the right. I'm just tired. It's been a long day."

"It certainly has, my lord," Khafre agreed. "What a pity their afternoon rally canceled out our morning's gains. If only Apedemek hadn't been there! What a difference it would have made!"

"Precisely," Nehsi said. "Somehow he must have managed to convince my soldiers that I was an impostor."

Moses spoke with his back teeth locked together against the pain. "It doesn't matter," he said. "We have to hit them again tomorrow, even harder."

Khafre's expression turned serious. "My lord, we cannot afford a war of attrition. They have more men than we have. Even if they lose two men to our one, as they have done so far, they will outlast us."

A new voice spoke up. "Perhaps not, sir," Het said, stepping into the circle of firelight. His brief tunic was wet from his swim across the Nile, and his face and limbs were obscured by the dark camouflage grease. "I have news that may affect your plans."

"Report, then!" Moses ordered, sitting up suddenly and wincing. "We can use some good news."

"Very well," Het said. "Is there any wine here?" Someone passed him a wineskin, and he drank deeply, then back-handed his mouth. "As I was skirting the camp below Semna, I passed close to the Nubian sentries while the watch was changing. You know how all the camp rumors and informa-tion get traded just then."

"Yes," said Geb impatiently. "Go on."

"Apedemek's in Semna," Het reported.

While the others exchanged concerned glances, Nehsi was the first to speak. "This is a mixed blessing. On the one hand, it means we will not have to deal with Apedemek at Kumma in the morning. We'll have a good chance to take back that lost ground. If we had more men to throw at them, we could even break the enemy and send him packing."

"True," Khafre said thoughtfully. "On the other hand—"

"On the other hand, Seth's life is in great danger," Nehsi finished.

"Yes, sire," Het said. "More than Seth realizes. The princess Tharbis told me she'd just got back from visiting him, and he claimed to be looking forward to the meeting."

"That sounds like Seth," Moses pointed out. "Treating everything, even the matter of his own life or death, as an educational experience. We have to do something."

Khafre frowned as he considered the options. "If we attack before dawn and do damage to the lines at Kumma, it'll force Apedemek to come back. The spell that convinced his men that the king isn't who he claims to be probably won't work when Apedemek isn't there. We'll hit them quite hard; then, during a lull, the king can—"

"That's not enough," Moses interrupted, standing up with some difficulty and facing them. "Apedemek will kill Seth. We have to create a diversion so someone can get inside and rescue him. Het, how heavily guarded is the fortress interior?"

"I don't know. The princess will, though. If our people can break in and open the gate for us, once we're inside—"

"Too risky," Geb objected. "There's still a large, tough garrison outside the walls."

"True," Khafre said. "If only there were more of us."

"If only the Black Wind were here!" Nehsi said. "If only we had a runner who could get through to my sister, Naldamak!"

One moment they were alone. The next moment there was a new presence in the circle of firelight. The newcomer was as tall as Nehsi, and so black that even the dancing flames of the fire did not create highlights on her skin. She wore golden jewelry and nothing else. Her hair was gray, but her body was that of a woman half her age. "No need for a runner," she said. "I am here, my brother."

From out of the darkness behind her, a golden cheetah moved up now to rub against her leg.

"Naldamak!" Nehsi gasped and rushed forward to embrace her.

They had thrown Seth, unconscious, onto a pile of straw in the cell and abandoned him. Now, with the visitors gone, the guard inside the large room dozed lightly in his chair, the keys to the cell in his lap.

Cautiously, silently, Arnekh of Kerkis crept out of the deep shadows to Seth's side. "Seth!" he whispered. "Seth, are you all right?"

For a moment he thought his friend was dead. But then he held his old hand close to Seth's open mouth and felt the escaping breath. "Seth, speak to me. Awake, my friend."

A slanting shaft of light streamed into the room from the lantern outside the cell and lay across Seth's face. Suddenly, as Arnekh watched anxiously, Seth's right eye opened and looked at him.

"Seth! I thought—"

But Seth waved away further discussion. "Help me back from the door," he requested in a barely audible voice. "If you can, drag me as if I were still unconscious."

Arnekh looked around cautiously. The guards thought he was long dead, and he did not want to disprove that notion; first Het, then Seth, had fed him out of their own rations and helped him lie low. Now he complied, straining to lug Seth's spare body into the far shadows.

Seth sat up. "Did you hear any of the exchange between Apedemek and me?"

"Some, but I could not always understand what was going on. Whenever I would steal a peek in your direction, I could make no sense of what was happening."

"Did you see the flash? I would have thought it would have been visible all the way down to the lowest levels. I was blinded by it for a long time."

"I don't know what you're talking about," Arnekh admitted, puzzled. "There was no flash."

"What about the loud sound?"

"There was no loud sound. He raised his hand, and you fell down."

"No green glow?"

"I thought you had fainted."

Seth was silent for a long, long moment. "Is there something wrong with your eyes? Might your vision have been impaired from living so long in the dark?"

"Not that I know of." He laughed mirthlessly. "I am a wreck otherwise, but my senses all seem to function properly. Why?"

"I don't know. I think I'm beginning to figure a few things out for the first time." He thought a moment more. Then he said, "He isn't going to kill me—not yet, anyhow. If only I could get that word to the princess! My friends in Kumma must know; otherwise they're likely to do something rash and try to rescue me, when they ought to be attending to the business of defeating the Nubians."

"But how can you be sure he won't kill you?"

"Because he took the trouble of trying to impress me. If he were going to kill me, he wouldn't have bothered to do that. No, he's as vulnerable as I am, in a way."

Arnekh snorted. "Indeed. And what is Apedemek's vulnerability?"

Seth let the matter rest for a moment, seeking the right words. Then he said, "He needs disciples. It's not enough to eliminate me; he desperately needs to convert me. He wants me to come over to the other side with him."

"Why? I don't see what he gains from that."

"I do," Seth said. "And I can even understand it. He's lonely."

"Lonely? Apedemek? Nonsense!"

"Not at all. When you knew him as a youth, what was he like?"

"Well, he wasn't vicious then, you know. Vain, but—"

"Exactly," Seth declared, triumphant. "Vain. Did he show off a lot? Did he always need an audience? Was he always posturing, striking poses?"

"Well . . . yes."

"Then watch. The next time he comes, it will not be to impress me—it will be to woo me. He can't stand being the only Chalybian—the only Child of the Lion—ever to go over to the side of iniquity, betray the craft, and turn his immense powers to the cause of evil." He shook his head. "I must say I don't blame him. I don't know if I could live alone with that knowledge, either, if I had done what he has done."

"Is he really as powerful as they say?"

"I have no idea what the limits of his powers may be. He has gone further in the craft than I, but I do not know by how many degrees."

"Does that mean his power is greater than yours?"

"I do not know that, either," Seth said slowly. He waited a moment, then added, "But I have the feeling that I am about to find out."

"Ah, my friend," Arnekh said cautiously, "I would not be so eager to learn this, of all things. I am convinced that the power he throws around so rashly does not come from within himself."

"Oh, no. It comes from tapping the secret sources of—"

"Wait," Arnekh pleaded. "Observe. Test him. Then and only then, make up your mind whence comes his strength. Seth, I do not care what your philosophical prejudices tell you. There *are* demons, many of them. And not a few of them are loose inside Nubia. Inside this province. Inside this fortress."

V

"How did you get past our pickets?" Khafre asked. "Some guard is going to wind up on report for this."

"Please don't," Naldamak requested. "This is a trick the Black Wind is famous for. Besides, you'd have to put everyone in the army on report. We are camped in force just north of here, and nobody has seen us."

"In force?" Nehsi echoed. "How many? Can you help us here?"

Naldamak smiled. "All in good time. First you, Prince Moses, and the general here must visit our camp." She focused on Moses's wound. "Oh, you're hurt!"

"It's nothing," Moses dismissed, but his face was drawn, and he was visibly working to hide the pain he felt.

"You will come to our camp anyway. We have healing methods not known to outsiders. Besides, there is a special reason for bringing you to us." She turned to Nehsi once again. "Come, my brother. This young man is in pain. We must do something about him."

"No," Moses said. "Not necessary . . ."

She ignored his protestations. "While the prince is being treated, you and I, my brother, and General Khafre will plan the day's strategy."

But as she looked across the fire, she saw Het removing his wet tunic to dry it by the fire. He stood, lean and strong and broad-shouldered, in his loincloth. Naldamak's eyes narrowed. "Who is this young man?" she asked Nehsi in their own tongue.

"His name is Het. He helped me to escape from prison the night Seth was captured. He is very valiant."

"I have no doubt," she said, still in the Nubian tongue. "Bring him along."

"But—"

"Bring him. Don't ask questions. Trust me. I know what I am doing."

There was a knock on Tharbis's door. Cautiously she called out, "Who's there?"

"Your father," a familiar voice said. "Let me in."

She unbolted the door. She had just dressed for bed and was barefoot, in her shift, a comb in her hand. Balaam strode inside and slammed the door behind him. "I've been hearing reports about you," he said angrily.

"They're probably all true," she retorted flippantly, before she had even had time to think about it. "Which reports? The one about my opening a soldiers' brothel? Or the one about my eloping with a wall-eyed leper from the Sudd? The second one isn't true. At least, he hasn't got here yet."

"None of your damned insolence! You know perfectly well what I mean! Prancing about here in front of the soldiers improperly attired!"

"Oh, that," she said, relieved. She had been worried right up to that moment that he had learned about her recent political activities. "I was getting bored. Don't worry, I'll dress like a Bedouin tomorrow. Today a tavern drab, tomorrow covered up to the eyes and sweating like a pig under all those robes. It's the only way I can get any amusement. That and vamping these dull soldiers of yours."

"That irresponsible behavior must come to an end. You know they've no women here. Provoking them like that—"

"No harm will come of it. They wouldn't dare touch me."

"When I think of the hopes I had for you when you were a child! You were so beautiful, so loving. And now—"

"If you wanted a loving child, you might have tried being a loving father."

"That isn't fair! You haven't any idea how demanding it's been, rising as fast as I have in a court where no white courtier has climbed to the top levels in four generations!"

"I'd rather you had stayed where you were. We were happy. But you were so ambitious, I never saw you for days. You didn't care about me anymore. If it hadn't been for Irenas, I'd have been the loneliest person in the world."

"Now don't bring her up again! I told you why we had to leave her in the capital."

"You could have left me there, too."

"My enemies would have kidnapped you and held you hostage."

"That would have been less dull than coming here has been. Have you any idea how boring this is? Stupefyingly, staggeringly boring! If I have to sit around another day with absolutely nothing to do, I'm going to go berserk."

Balaam threw up his hands. "Why do we have to fight all the time? Why do you always have to make a major confrontation out of everything? Can't we ever sit down and talk rationally? You're the only child I have. You're all I have left."

This really set her off. "Don't you *dare* try that one on me! I know what you've planned for me! Giving me away to some horrible old man for political gain! And you have the nerve to act as though I'm supposed to accept blindly everything you do because you're my dear father and you love me!"

"Tharbis—"

"No, thank you! I'm not *that* stupid!"

"I thought we could talk it out."

"Go away!" she shrieked. "Get out!" She went to the door and threw it open. "Either you're going to leave or I am!"

He cursed under his breath. "I'll go, but you'd better start showing some common sense about the way you act, or I'll—"

"You'll what? Huff and puff?"

He sputtered unintelligibly for a moment, then left her chambers, slamming the door behind him.

Tharbis sank into a chair, drained. *Why did I do that? I didn't want to fight with him. We might have really communicated for a change. . . .*

In the night Seth lay back, having settled Arnekh down to sleep and covered the old man against the damp cold. And after a period of pure and soothing emptiness, a dream came to Seth, in which he found himself standing alone in a large field.

The empty field was featureless and seemed to stretch away to all infinity. The sky was no particular color; there was nothing unusual about the air around him. He stood and turned but saw no break anywhere in the dull sameness.

Where am I? Why am I here?

No sooner had he let the thought into his mind than he felt a great, all-enveloping presence—heavy, threatening, almost suffocating in its enormity. A great, booming voice rang out, resonating not only inside his mind but echoing through and around and beyond all the air around him.

"*Prepare,*" the voice warned.

The loudness, the hugeness of the voice rocked Seth. His knees buckled. It was only with difficulty that he managed to hold himself erect.

"P-prepare for what?" he asked in a voice that seemed puny and weak by comparison.

Again the great voice boomed forth: "*Prepare to choose— and be chosen. Prepare to judge—and be judged.*"

"I don't understand," Seth protested, feeling like a child again, the child his father had rejected. The child whom not even his mother had known. The child who had not known how to ask for love and so had not received it.

"*Life is an infinite succession of forking paths,*" the voice said. "*Every moment is a choice. We choose to breathe or to smother. To grow or to wither. To live or to die.*"

"Y-yes," Seth said, "that is true. But—"

"*In your youth you chose to become learned and wise. When you did, all else in your life suffered for it. You cleaved to the world of thoughts and forsook the world of feelings.*"

"I know," Seth agreed, "but—"

"*And there came a time when you took pains to repair the lacks in your life. You explored the world of friendship, the world of love. You found not one father but two, and they conferred upon you the validation of your manhood.*"

"Yes," Seth said, the thought tugging strongly at his heart. "I met Marduk-nasir, who confirmed me in the craft. I met Samsi-ditana, that great and good man who took me to his heart and gave me limitless power over all of Babylon. He gave me his daughter to wed, and his kingdom. He made me happy for the first time in my life. I knew friendship, both with him and with Criton the Greek."

"*And what did you do to these people you loved? What did you do with the power you were given?*"

Seth's breast heaved now, almost a sob. "Samsi-ditana is

dead. My wife is dead. Criton is dead—Criton and my other companions. Babylon is in ruins. The forking paths lay before me in Babylon, and I chose the wrong path, misled by ambition."

"Then you destroyed all that you had been given and killed all who loved you."

"Yes," Seth admitted ruefully, "because of my self-absorption. But there is more: When I left Thebes to seek out the masters of the craft, I left a woman pregnant. She bore my son alone—unmarried and a pariah for the fact. When my son was born, the woman was living with my mother, who would not believe the child was mine and threw her and my son out. When I returned from the death of Babylon, I learned all this for the first time. I have looked for my son and his mother for many years, but I have not found them. The dead, I can do nothing about. But these, if they live, I could ask for their forgiveness."

"What if you could find them?"

"What do you mean?" he asked in anguish.

"What if you could restore Babylon? What if you could bring back your wife, your king, your friends and companions, alive and well? What if you could cleanse yourself of guilt and suffering? What if the passing of time could be annulled for these things, these people? What would you give for this power?"

"How can you torture me like this?" Seth cried, holding his hands over his ears. "What are you that you can offer these things? Are you a god or—?"

But now he dropped his hands at his sides. The presence was gone. He was alone in the empty field.

Then, in the blink of an eye, he was sitting up in his cell on a straw bed, his sweat-drenched skin covered with goose-flesh, his hands shaking, his heart pounding wildly. The voice had been that of no god. It had been Apedemek's—or that of some being who spoke through Apedemek. That of a demon, perhaps, as Arnekh had said. A demon who knew his every weakness. Who knew where he was vulnerable. Who knew with shocking exactitude the only things in the world that would tempt him.

VI

The moon was bright and clear, and their progress along the drifted sand was easy and painless. To their right, as they marched northward, a high ridge dominated the flatland below it, stretching long and straight. "We will climb to the top here," said Naldamak suddenly.

At this, Prince Moses tried to struggle out of the litter in which he was borne by Naldamak and Nehsi. "You can't climb that slope carrying me."

Naldamak paid him no mind at all, shouldering the supports and trudging up the steep slope surefootedly, as if he weighed nothing. Nehsi was surprised to find steps underfoot, well spaced, easy to surmount, and swept clean of drifted sand.

At the top they found a road—wide enough for one cart and clearly visible in the moonlight. On the far side was a deep valley, and ahead of them the road stretched to the horizon.

"How could I have missed this?" Khafre wondered aloud. "I should have sent a man to reconnoiter here."

Naldamak did not answer. At her heels the great cheetah moved along, the epitome of power and grace. Het lagged behind a bit; he kept one eye on the big animal. Not used to wild animals acting like household pets, he did not trust the beast.

In due time Naldamak spoke. "This road was built by the men who built Kumma," she explained. "It leads to the quarries from which came the stone used in the fort." She turned right, then said, "We will descend here."

They slowly made their way down another set of steps on the far side of the slope. And as they came out from behind a great rock projection, they could see a vast network of small campfires, all burnt down to white coals. It was the encampment of an army of considerable size.

At the bottom Naldamak paused. "Weret!" she called out.

Instantly they were surrounded by warriors, white and black, all women, all wearing only the distinctive gold jewelry and the belts from which hung their now-unsheathed swords. From their ranks stepped a lean figure, no longer young but dauntingly fit, her face severe in the slanting light.

"I am here," Weret declared. "Bring them this way."

Food and drink were waiting for them. Het, hungry after his long swim against the current, accepted flatbread and roasted ox fresh from the spit and slung a wineskin over his shoulder as he sought out a space by one of the fires. As he did, a simply dressed man in a homespun tunic, round-faced and with curly hair, came forward. He had a slight limp. "Do you mind if I join you?"

Het shrugged. "Be my guest," he answered as he unslung the wineskin and passed it over. He watched the man seat himself and drink sparingly, then pass the bottle back. "Are you with the army? The, uh, Desert Legion, I mean? I thought they were all women."

"I'm attached to them," his companion said with a child's guileless smile. "By that I mean they tolerate me."

"Hunh," Het said, biting into the meat on the flatbread. "They make me uncomfortable, going around like that."

"When they're on the march or at war," his companion countered, "there's no fooling around. But just you wait until the battle's over. A good-looking young fellow like you will have to fight them off."

"They make me uneasy." He stood up, stretched, rubbed his aching neck. "Ugh! I'm stiff all over! I just got finished swimming the river—twice."

"Hard work," the round-faced man commented. "If you like, I could massage your back. The women say I have a healer's touch."

"Well, now that you mention it, if you've got good hands at that sort of thing, my neck's as stiff as a board."

"Fine. Come sit over here, with your back to me. I'll start with your neck. Then maybe you can lie down, and I can get the shoulders and the muscles of the upper and lower back."

"That's very kind of you." Het grinned. "I can see why the women 'tolerate' you. Tell me, how long have they been here?"

His companion massaged his neck with powerful fingers.

He had not looked that strong, and it came as a surprise, given his gentle demeanor, that his hands were not at all soft; they were the hard, calloused hands of a laborer. "They arrived last night. Weret and Naldamak watched the battle from the heights. I joined them after noon. Too bad about that rally the Nubians mounted in the waning hours."

"Yes. Apedemek has them under a spell. But he's in Semna now. We don't think he'll be able to control them that way at a distance."

"Who knows? He is a man of great power. I fear for Seth. I think this is the reason Naldamak decided to intervene. Seth is much loved among the people of the oases." He chuckled. "He's my cousin, you know. My name is Neku-re. I am Teti's son. Seth and I had the same great-grandparents."

"Pleased to meet you. I'm Het. I met Seth during the king's escape from Semna."

"We are well met," the masseur said. His hands clamped down on Het's neck and kneaded the flesh like bread. "Where are you from?"

"My mother raised me in the capital. My father died when I was a baby. I was trained as an engineer and was sent here to help supervise the shoring up of the fortifications in the cataract forts. But Apedemek wouldn't let me do my work, and I have a hot temper, and—well, I wound up in the dungeons, where just about every Nubian with spirit winds up these days."

"Apedemek is a very dangerous man."

"Do you think Seth can handle him? Seth has some powers of his own, but—*ouch!*"

"Sorry. It'll feel better in a moment. There, I'm done. In the morning you'll be a new man." He cracked his knuckles. "As for your question—I don't know. Weret's been studying the situation. Someone has to go in there and open the gate."

"I'm your man. I know that part of the fortress very well." Het grinned. "Besides, there's a lady I would do anything at all to see."

"Ah! The princess Tharbis!"

"How do you know that?"

"I'm also good at knowing things I'm not supposed to know. Then you're taken with her?"

"I don't know what I am. She's annoying. She teases me mercilessly. I get the feeling she's terribly spoiled. She's got a nasty wit, and . . ." He stopped, and when he resumed speaking there was a different, softer tone to his voice. "She's got spirit. I don't like timid girls with the downcast eyes and subservient attitudes. They're like food with no salt. Even when she's giving me a bad time, she's exciting. And even though she's a princess and I'm a nobody, I think she likes me. If only it weren't for Prince Moses! She has a crush on him!"

"So she talks about Moses, and it hurts your feelings. You want her to think about you, and she thinks about him instead."

"That's it in a nutshell, Neku-re."

"Would you feel better if I told you that her attraction to him is entirely one-sided? That he hardly knows she's alive? That his destiny lies along quite another path?"

Het paused and stared at Neku-re. "You do seem to know about things. I suppose you know the outcome of the battle."

"Perhaps. But it's no good telling people about it; they never listen. Suffice it to say I understand some things about destiny, while my friend Tchabu knows the rest." He paused. "Moses is with Tchabu now. Tchabu will heal him . . . and will be letting Moses know a thing or two about his destiny."

Het looked sharply at him. "And you've been doing the same thing with me that this Tchabu fellow is doing with Moses, eh? Well, my neck sure feels wonderful. Thank you. But how about my destiny? Do you have any insights for me? Am I going to wind up rich and famous despite my low birth? Will the princess take pity on me and—"

"She won't pity you," Neku-re stated, grinning. "Not if you keep her busy. I'm going to recommend you be one of the party to go into Semna to save Seth. But when you are there, keep Tharbis off balance. You may do better with her than you think. Bloodlines aren't everything." But now he closed his eyes for a moment and frowned. "I shouldn't have said that. Blood counts for a lot. As a matter of fact, bloodlines will assume an enormous importance in her life. She's going to give birth to a king."

"I was afraid of that. Are you sure?"

"Absolutely. She'll become the wife of a king—"

"Curse the luck!"

"—a king who is in turn the son of a king, a man rich and famous."

"Stop! You're breaking my heart!"

"I'm sorry. I didn't mean to hurt you. I have to learn to keep my mouth shut. Tchabu is always telling me to hold my peace, but I never seem to listen."

"I wish I'd never met you! I wish I'd never come here!"

"Then you don't want to go along with the party to rescue Seth?"

"Of course I do. I'd do anything to keep a good man out of Apedemek's hands. And it'd mean a chance to see her again, even if—"

"Ah, poor Het. What a blundering, insensitive fool I am."

Khafre conferred with Weret and Naldamak, pausing every so often to glance over at the little grove where they had taken Prince Moses. "You're sure he's all right? This healer fellow is competent?"

"Very much so," Nehsi said from over his shoulder. "But I appreciate your concern. You are fond of Moses, then?"

"I'd love to have a son just like him—honest and true and without a mean streak anywhere. And as brave as a lion. With any army of some size behind him, a lad like that could conquer the world."

Weret and Naldamak exchanged glances. "What would you think," Weret said in an odd voice, "if I told you that the time will come when he will lay down his weapons and fight no more?"

"No!" Khafre said. "You're not going to tell me he's going to die!"

"No," Naldamak answered gently. "But he will lay down the sword and become a man from whom violence will have fallen away, as one's youth falls away to be replaced by something entirely different."

Khafre stared, anguish in his eyes. "A soldier like him?

How do you know these things? How can this possibly be
true?"

The woman did not answer but looked at him silently
with solemn eyes.

VII

Tchabu the dwarf looked particularly grotesque, his knobby
face and great, misshapen head distorted by the dramatic
shadows cast by the leaping flames of his little campfire. The
hump on his back seemed larger, and the tiny arms and legs
appeared shorter.

Nevertheless, now that Moses was alone with the little
man, he perceived little but the dwarf's sympathetic qualities: his extreme gentleness, his eagerness to please, his
solicitude over any possible pain Moses's wound might be
causing. When the bandage had been removed and Tchabu
finally had examined the stab wound, the little man said, "Is
not deep. Will heal. But much pain, no? Much pain. Why
you not cry out?"

"It wouldn't do any good," Moses responded. "It would
hardly stop the pain. And Baliniri taught me that it isn't a
good policy to let the ranks know how bad you feel."

"Ah!" said the little man, busying himself with the crushing of herbs in a bowl. "Baliniri! Is good friend to Tchabu.
Tchabu love Baliniri."

Moses winced. "I hate to be the one to tell you, but
Baliniri's dead. I just heard from Weret."

"Not worry," Tchabu said blithely. "Tchabu talk to
Neku-re. Baliniri happier now. Not old. Always young now.
Baliniri want to be young again."

"You don't understand," Moses protested. "Baliniri's
dead."

"Dead not mean what you think," the little man explained. "Neku-re speak with dead now and then. Speak with
his mother. Speak with Baliniri."

"You mean he's a seer? And you're an extraordinary healer. That's why they brought me here. Look, if you do something to the wound, make it look as though you hadn't changed the bandage. I don't want to hurt the feelings of the army physician."

Tchabu's smile was benign and loving. "You good boy. Not want hurt feeling of friend. Here. Tchabu put this on wound." He gently put on the poultice and bound it with the same bandage again, as Moses had wished. "There."

His hands lingered on Moses's arm. He closed his eyes and stood quietly for quite a long time, until Moses began to fear he had had some sort of seizure. "Tchabu?" the prince ventured. "Tchabu, are you all right?"

After another long moment, though, the little man opened his eyes and released Moses's arm. "Is all right," he said, and moved back to look at the young soldier. "Yes, Tchabu see you not know. Time you learn."

He sat down atop a fallen log, his tiny, crooked legs stretched out in front of him. It was a curious thing, Moses thought: After a few minutes Tchabu did not look grotesque at all; he looked beautiful in a way. There was such kindness, such intelligence in the great brown eyes and the sensitive mouth. "You are prince of royal blood of Egypt? You are boy Baliniri train to become king? Baliniri need someone with better bloodline than Kamose. You are this person. Tchabu get this right, no?"

"Well . . . yes. What did you do to my arm? The pain seems to have gone away." He flexed it, made a fist, moved it this way and that.

"Not exercise it. Not tonight. Wait till morning. Morning you go back to duty with army."

"Good. Then it was only a scratch. I'd been afraid it was worse."

Tchabu shrugged. "Reason not matter. But, Moses, you not fight anymore."

"Not fight? There's work to be done. Tomorrow, with the Black Wind filling out our ranks—"

"Not matter. You, Moses, never fight again with sword. Fight with *mind*. Maybe with hands, but not sword or arrow."

"I don't understand. I came here to fight. I'm nominal

commander of the expedition. How can I just stand by and not fight?"

"Plenty else to do. Rescue Seth from bad man. This you do. You go with other young man you bring along."

Moses stared. "Het? Well, he's a good man and a fine fighter and does know the palace. But how could I get inside there and not fight? That doesn't make sense."

"You find way," Tchabu answered cheerfully. "Is good reason. Trust Tchabu."

"I *do* trust you, but for the life of me I can't think why. It isn't a habit with me to trust strangers."

The little man smiled. "You sit and listen. Please. Tchabu tell story. You have hear of prophecy? About Deliverer who will save people from oppression?"

"I've heard something like that, but I suspected that Seth had made it up to convince me to unseat Amasis and take his place. He's capable of that sort of thing, you know."

"Seth good man. You be not mad at Seth. Not at Baliniri either, or Princess Thermutis either. All mean well by you. Work to make prophecy come true."

"But I don't want to be king of Egypt."

"Not *be* king of Egypt!"

The flat statement, bald-faced and straightforward, was so shocking that Moses felt as if he had been slapped. "What do you mean? Are you telling me that Baliniri's prophecy was a fake?"

"Not fake. Wrong prophecy. Speak of prophecy made by slave."

"What slave?"

"Great-grandfather of Moses. Was slave. Just like grandfather and father."

"What are you talking about?" Moses demanded, in some agitation. "My grandfather was Sekenenre, king of Egypt. My father—"

"Was slave," Tchabu said simply. "Is still slave. Good man but slave." He put his stubby-fingered hands together palm to palm. "Moses was born slave."

Moses sat for a long, long moment, looking at him. Then, when he spoke, his voice was calm and thoughtful. "Something tells me to listen to what you have to say. Please tell me. All of it."

Unhurriedly, at a measured pace, Tchabu told the story: the terrible order that had come down from Amasis that all the Habiru boy-children were to be killed; the ruses one Habiru woman after another had used to conceal the existence of her son; Baliniri's plan to create a fake heir to the throne; the birth of Thermutis's damaged child and his death soon after; the plan, suddenly and brilliantly conceived, to kill two birds with one stone and substitute Jochebed's child for Thermutis's, the little boat made of rushes, hidden in the bulrushes . . .

At the end Moses shook his head very slowly. "My old nurse, Jochebed!" he whispered. "Why, that means Miriam would be my sister, and—"

"Yes," Tchabu said. "You have also a brother, cousins, large family. All slave, trapped here far from homeland. Moses begin to see destiny, no?"

"You mean the prophecy about a promised Deliverer who would take these people—"

"*Your* people."

"My people, then. Who would take them out of the terrible bondage they've suffered ever since Joseph's day, and lead them back to their homeland in the North."

"Yes. Oh, prophecy real! Tchabu *know*. Time you know all of it. Now you know more than Baliniri. More even than Seth, who think they train you for become king. You become instead slave, like others in family. Instead of king, you become more important than king. Whole world change because of what you become. Because of what you do. Whole world, Moses! King not important. People in time forget all kings, forget more than man can count. People not forget Moses. World never forget."

"A slave more important than any king?" Moses inquired. "It sounds absurd."

"Think," Tchabu urged. "Has Moses ever felt at home in castle? In court? Always feel strange. No? Tchabu tell truth."

Moses thought for a moment. "It's true," he confessed. "I never believed in this bright future everyone thought I was going to have. I always knew something was wrong with it. Oh, I went along with it, doing everything everyone expected of me. I learned to fight, I—"

"Yes?"

"Tchabu, I murdered a man in hot blood, back in Thebes. He was oppressing a Habiru. One of my family, I suppose."

"Tchabu know. Somehow Moses know, too. Yes? Yes?"

"I did feel a kinship with him. Just as I felt a great love and kinship with Jochebed—*Mother*—and her family. But the prophecy. Does this mean—" He frowned. "How am I going to get them out of Egypt? You know Amasis hates them and is not just going to let them go. They'll have to fight. I'll have to teach them. But you said I was going to give up fighting."

"Moses has already give up fighting. No?"

"Somehow I know you're right."

"Not fear. Not be impatient. Something will tell you. You will know."

"When will all this happen?"

"In own time. Tchabu know, but Tchabu not tell. Not good know too much of future."

Moses threw up his hands and felt no pain in the wounded arm, when he should have winced in agony. "Why am I listening to this? Am I going mad? Have you slipped me some drug?"

Tchabu smiled the angelic smile. "Tchabu tell truth. Truth good for mind and body. Truth heal wound. Truth no drug. Lie is drug. Even kind lie like one about royal blood."

The two came back out into the firelight where the others were gathered; Moses's hand was on Tchabu's crooked little shoulder as they walked slowly out to face the officers of the two armies and the deposed king of Nubia. There was something different about Moses's demeanor, and Weret was quick to pick up on it. "You've told him."

"Yes," Tchabu answered. "Not good for young man not to know destiny. Time for change."

"You mean he won't be at the battle tomorrow?" Khafre asked.

"Moses go to Semna," Tchabu replied. His eyes sought

out Het. "He go with *this* young man. This young man be bodyguard. See Moses not come to harm."

Het's eyes went wide. This wasn't fair. He had wanted to be the big hero of the rescue, but instead he would be playing bodyguard to his rival! Moses would get all the glory! Just when he was beginning to make an impression on Tharbis!

"You don't want the job?" Khafre asked.

Het kept his eyes on the ground. "You know I'll do it."

"But?"

"Never mind. You can count on me. I'll do it."

The next hour was spent in planning. But just as the group was about to disperse, a runner, lean and beautiful in her proud nakedness, came up to salute Weret and Naldamak. She addressed Weret. "My lady, important news from the battle site."

"Yes, Satre?" Weret said. "What's happened?"

"It's the Nubians," the young woman said. "Under the cover of darkness they've taken to the boats over on the south side of the fort and crossed the Nile. They're at Semna now. They're going to make their stand there, not at Kumma."

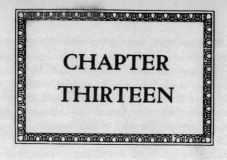

CHAPTER

THIRTEEN

Thebes

I

The candles had burned down almost to the ends. Two mute servants came out and replaced them, not waiting to be told. All the time they were present, Amasis remained silent, but when they had gone out and closed the door, the words fairly burst out of him. "I don't care if the official wisdom is that the oasis is impregnable. Something has to be done. I can't have him out there, laughing at me, scheming, biding his time, waiting for the day when he can come back."

Neb-mertef let him finish, waited a beat, and then inquired mildly, "What do your generals advise you?"

"Generals!" Amasis exploded. "What do they know? They're foreigners. They all talk nonsense and don't know a thing about the desert. Apophis used to send patrols out along the old trade routes, hoping to surprise the Black Wind and that army of bitches Weret and Teti put together out there. The patrols were never heard from again. And they were men who knew their way in the desert. What are a lot of Greeks and Lydians and Cretans going to know about it?"

"I have no idea, my lord," Neb-mertef said. His voice and his face were neutral. Inside him was a feeling of great exultation. He had slowly been discovering that there were few joys to match that of watching one of one's superiors slowly coming unraveled for lack of information one held secret and had no intention of revealing.

He had bullied the latest out of the astrologer only this afternoon, after humiliating him and threatening to throw him out into the street. How easily a man could be entrapped by his vices and shamed into utter servility and dependency!

Set-Nakht was his now, body and soul, veritably spewing up-to-date predictions.

It was worth a king's ransom to sit here in Amasis's palace apartments and listen to him fret and worry and toss about for solutions—all of them extremely unrealistic—to the problem occasioned by Kamose's escape. To watch this, and know better, and do nothing about it was a real delight. For a moment—just a moment—his heart softened, and he thought of rewarding the magus for having cast the charts accurately.

He ignored Amasis, pacing back and forth, thinking out loud. Neb-mertef smiled and thought about Set-Nakht instead. What had the magus said? Something about the alignment of the planets being in perfect balance but badly aspected. He had waved his charts about, and Neb-mertef had pretended to understand; somewhere, far from here, a great battle was taking place between balanced forces, and on the outcome would depend the fortunes of many, not least of all Amasis himself. But whatever the outcome, Amasis would suffer.

This was very satisfying. All Neb-mertef had to do was sit and watch and feign concern. What was he saying now? ". . . could have managed to let Kamose get away? How could they not have known he hadn't been taking the drug? I wish Nemaret had survived, if only to ask him the question. Nemaret had deliberately kept the others away, the better to keep that part of the household under his own thumb."

"My lord," Neb-mertef said, "didn't I hear something about his having trusted one of the household sluts? Given some of the duties of feeding the king and checking up on him over to her?"

"Yes, yes! The little bitch was sleeping with him. Thought she'd rise higher in my service by playing up to him. Let me warn you about that sort of thing, my friend. Don't let your subordinates create any little fiefdom within your household. Keep them all worried. Don't ever let anyone get comfortable or secure."

It was, Neb-mertef had to agree, good advice. "I gratefully drink from the fountain of your wisdom, my lord," he said. "I shall henceforth take the greatest of pains to follow any advice you are pleased to give me."

And all the time he was thinking: *The man's a fool. A fool. He thinks the king is still thin and weak from the drugs. Well, that description may have been fine when he first came south from the delta, but it doesn't work now. The Kamose I saw looked strong, focused, and mean.*

How delightful it all was! It did not matter which faction was in the ascendancy, Neb-mertef would profit by the fact. He was kept safe on the one hand by the misplaced trust Amasis had in him—and on the other hand from Kamose himself, who now thought him an ally against Amasis.

And for all he knew, this great event the magus had told him about, the one that would diminish Amasis regardless of which faction were to win, would help him grow in power. He would have to ask the magus about that.

"Why couldn't you have told me?" Aaron asked, pretending to be outraged. "Or Father? Or Grandfather, or Levi while he lived?"

"We had sworn not to," his mother replied. "Now tell me true: Do you think your father could have kept a secret? Amram is the last man in the world to dissemble. He is open and straightforward and honest, and he has fifty virtues to another man's one. But he could never have kept a thing like this to himself."

"How did Miriam keep it secret? How did you?"

"There exists an essential difference between men and women. Women are natural conspirators, while men solve problems among themselves by physical force. We solve disputes by biding our time and undermining our enemies. And when we're done, our enemies have suffered more damage than any man could do with his fists."

"You make me feel like a half-wit." He could never let his mother know that Nemti and Mara had already revealed to him the truth about his brother, Moses.

"Not at all! An honest man. This is a virtue, and women respect it. But a woman with your simple heart would be thought a fool because it is not necessarily a virtue in a woman. Not in a woman's eyes anyhow."

"Do you mean to tell me that my Elisheba—?"

"Elisheba is a very smart woman, and I have applauded your father's choice of her ever since he arranged your marriage. She hides her brains from the men, but no woman is fooled by her. Not for long, anyway."

"Such revelations! I'd better sit down."

"Listen to him! He can go off and risk his life trying to save the king without giving a second thought—"

"That's not true! I agonized over it! After all, if I'd been killed, what would have happened to Elisheba—"

"And I am proud of you, my darling. But listen to yourself. You can deal with terrible physical danger, but when someone tells you your wife is smarter than you are, you have to sit down and catch your breath."

He stared at her. "Mother, I didn't tell Elisheba, but that Greek who came to her door and frightened her—"

"He didn't show up next morning . . ."

"No. I killed him the night the king escaped."

"You killed him!"

"Yes. With a stone from my sling. It was the best shot I have ever made, even though the light was bad."

"All praise to God, who guided your hand! Once more He has delivered us from the hand of our enemy!"

"Then you don't think I have to pray for forgiveness?"

"Pray all you like, my son. There is no such thing as praying too much. If you do not daily place yourself in His hands and resign yourself to His will, how do you ever expect to become wise?"

"I thought you just got finished telling me I was stupid!"

"Not stupid, just a man. You are by no means stupid for a man. It's just that when one tries to weigh your brains on a female scale, well . . ." Her shrug was eloquent.

She watched his face in the candlelight. Aaron was easily hurt, sensitive. She wondered if Moses shared these qualities. She supposed not, from her memories of him when she was a servant in the household of Princess Thermutis. She had last seen Moses when he was just moving from childhood to manhood, when a boy was old enough for confirmation into the faith. How it had hurt her for him to have been passed by in this, due to the tragic ruse they had adopted to save his life! He was basically the person he would be for the rest of his life, unless he deliberately opted to flout God's will.

Moses! When would she finally see him again? When could they all drop the pretense that had protected him all these years? When would he finally learn who he was, and who his people were, and what his destiny in life would be?

What if he knew already? What if someone had already told him? What if, at this very moment, he was sitting somewhere far up the Nile, thinking of her and wondering the same things?

Oh, my son! she thought. *My son!*

CHAPTER FOURTEEN

At the Semna Straits

I

Dawn of the day following the Nubians' mass exodus across the river found Moses sitting on a flat rock overlooking the Nile, thinking, unable to sleep. From time to time he touched the bandage on his upper arm, as if to reassure himself that he had actually been wounded the day before. There was no pain or stiffness to remind him.

Yesterday's meeting with Tchabu had been totally unsettling. Never had he encountered a healer of this sort before, who had only to lay hands on the patient to make him feel better. Even now, the absence of pain perplexed him. Evidently the dwarf had special powers, above and beyond anything normal people had.

But did these powers include clairvoyance, as Tchabu and the others would have him believe? And was the surpassingly strange story he had been told true?

It was a lot to take in at one gulp. Imagine coming this

far in life thinking he was one thing, only to find out suddenly that he was another! That his whole life had been a lie! That his destiny lay in refusing a pleasant and protected life in which he was a person of great consequence! That the thing he must now do was to become less than nothing!

Yet he knew this was not an accurate picture of what Tchabu had told him. If Tchabu were to be believed, his destiny was to become more important than any king's!

That was the incredible part. That, and the fact that everyone here seemed to treat Tchabu as a well-nigh infallible vessel for truth. No one seemed to regard him as unreliable.

Well, now, he thought. *And even if Tchabu is reliable . . . does that mean I must do as he says?*

He did have a choice, did he not? He could refuse this destiny others had picked out for him.

What if he were to tell them he was not going to go along with it? After all, look at what they were trying to get him to do: to lay down the sword, and never pick it up again.

That was insane! Why would they want him to become weak? To put aside the fighting skills Baliniri had been at such pains to teach him? Never again to count on the protection accorded a member of the royal family? Why, he would be a slave, with none of the rights of a human being!

Why should he believe the word of a crazy, funny-looking little dwarf?

Ah, but that was the problem. He *did* believe. There was something about Tchabu, something he trusted. He was sure the little man was everything he said he was, that the deference everyone seemed to show him was well deserved.

No! he thought stubbornly. *I won't do it! I won't go along with it!*

But then some perverse impulse in him forced his mind into other channels. *Miriam . . . Jochebed . . .*

The strangest thing about all of it was how completely he accepted that he, Moses, was not the son of a princess of the realm but the son of the dear old nurse who had watched over his childhood, the brother of the playmate of his youth.

I have never known who I was, he thought, wondering at the strangeness of the idea. *Why should I curse the man who finally tells me?*

He reached down for the sword at his feet and with his left hand pulled it from its scabbard. He held it up and looked at it.

Baliniri had insisted that a good fighter be prepared for all eventualities and as much a master with one hand as with the other. It tended to put one's opponent off balance to fight deliberately with the left hand anyhow, even if the right were not incapacitated. It would be little trouble for him to use his left hand, but just to test the severity of his injury, he transferred the sword back to his right hand and turned the blade this way and that. There was no pain, even though his arm ought to be hurting like fire.

He stood and flourished the weapon, saluted with it, assumed the ready position, parried an imaginary thrust, fended off an imaginary cut at his legs, turned his wrist deftly and dealt his invisible enemy a fierce hack at the hams, battered a ghostly defense down, and ran the specter through!

He let his sword arm fall to his side and touched the supposedly injured upper arm. There was no pain. The arm felt as healthy as if nothing had ever happened to it.

What is happening to me? Am I going mad?

Het had not slept well, either, and had arisen to walk off the stiffness that still dogged him after his night swims. Now he stood near the water's edge, a hundred paces upstream from Moses, watching the young prince do battle with an enemy he could not see.

Look at him! Het thought. *That arm was supposed to have been badly hurt yesterday! Had Moses been malingering?*

He scowled and looked away and, for lack of something better to do, leaned over and filled his left hand with pebbles from the river's edge. He picked one of these out with his right hand and idly threw it far out into the Nile.

The physical action seemed to satisfy some uneasiness he could not define. He threw another pebble after the first; then another. Then he tried skipping them along the top of the waves.

Listen to you, he thought, disgusted. *Desperately trying to find something discreditable about the prince just because you're jealous of him!*

This was so petty and hateful, he was immediately ashamed of himself. He had by now heard accounts from both Nehsi and Geb of Moses's heroism the day before: his exemplary bravery in rushing to the aid of a fallen comrade and single-handedly standing off an attack by three huge Nubian warriors until help could arrive and the wounded man could be carried to safety. Moses, Geb had said, had fought like a lion all day and had only begun to tire toward sunset. Only then had anyone noticed the gaping wound in his upper arm.

Gaping wound? he thought now. *But look at him. He is using the sword as if there were nothing wrong with him. What kind of man is this, who can rebound so quickly from a serious wound? Is he some sort of demigod? Is he more than human?*

He sighed long and hard. This was the sort of rival that he, Het, would have to deal with in his assault on the princess's affections!

Oh, if only his rival were an ordinary fellow, so that the odds would not be so heavily weighted in Moses's favor!

The sounds of the troops coming to life drifted to him. He turned from the river and wandered back toward camp. He and his companions had spent the night in the camp of the Desert Legion, the better to confer in the morning at first light.

Teti, founder of the Legion, had retired into the desert to live by herself, but her fame as an armsmaker and as the only female practitioner of the trade in all the long history of the Children of the Lion had slowly begun to draw other women to her, women who rejected the traditional subservient role of women in Theban society.

Thus, little by little, he knew, a women's army had begun to develop. In keeping with the cleanness and purity of the desert in which they lived, Teti had decreed that their uniform would be nudity, like that of the famed Black Wind, the Nubian women's army founded so many years ago by Nehsi's mother, Ebana. To the nakedness of her women, though, Teti had allowed one addition: the golden ornaments that she—and, later, her son, Neku-re—would make for them.

In those years, Weret had told Het, Neku-re had been

the only male allowed to live in the oasis with the women. So it had been for many years, although Baliniri had made several clandestine visits to train the women's army, which guarded the desert trade routes from invasion.

Teti eventually left the oasis forever for a new life in Thebes as wife to Riki, general of the Egyptian army, eventually to die there of the plague. By all rights the women's army should have died, also, except for Weret's fierce pride and stubborn determination that the unit Teti had worked so hard to build would stay together and continue to guard the western borders of the upriver nomes.

Now, it appeared, the Desert Legion was a permanent fixture in the scheme of things, as was the Black Wind. For many years no man had laid eyes on any legion members, unless it was Weret herself, accompanied by a retainer or two and the ever-present cheetah, making one of her infrequent visits to Thebes to confer with Baliniri.

And here he was in the middle of them! Idly, discreetly, he let his eyes rove over the lean, naked bodies, and as he did he wondered why his mind went not to their nakedness but to the clothed form of Tharbis, which was all he could see in his mind. When he closed his eyes to blot the women out for a moment, there was Tharbis standing before him, fire in her brown eyes, a mocking smile on that adorable mouth.

What a girl she was! How he loved her! How desolate he would be if she were to choose another!

II

The two great facing peninsulas that jutted into the Nile channel to form the straits of Semna had, with Gindikol Island in the middle of the channel, been extended by a combination of masonry and landfill into a dam that had blocked the flow of the Nile and formed a great lake behind it.

The dam had been eroded from over a hundred years of

neglect, and the battering waters of the river had swept the last traces of the impediment away. Now the Nile flowed freely through two channels that flanked Gindikol, but a narrow fjordlike harbor remained between the Kumma peninsula and Gindikol.

This harbor was cut off from the channel by a long peninsula made of obdurate rock, and it was from here, masked from view by the dark of night and the high ground on which the Kumma fortress stood, that the boats had transported the entire garrison of Kumma across the channel to the far side of the river.

Now, in the soft light of dawn, their tents were arranged side by side in long files. The preparations for siege had begun as soon as the first pink shafts had appeared above the horizon. The Kumma force, largely formed of black Nubians, had set up on the plain downstream from the towering stronghold. The northern garrison, composed mainly of white soldiers, was still deployed on the drifted sands upstream from the fort. This gave Semna two distinct ranks of defenders to the north and south, and only the exposed areas facing the peninsula and the river were without heavy concentrations of troops.

The move had been a considerable coup for Apedemek. Before deserting Kumma, his men, having used virtually all the boats in the little harbor to move across the stream, had burned the rest. This would occasion considerable inconvenience for the combined forces of the Egyptian command, the Desert Legion, and the Black Wind, who would have to cross the river by other means.

The resulting delay would give the defenders additional time to dig in and to choose their positions with great care. As the Egyptians made their way across the river, they would face the entrenched forces of both commands, firing upon them from high ground and selling every handspan of land very dearly.

Thus, in the Nubian camps, north and south, the soldiers prepared for a major confrontation, sharpening their swords, while the fletchers hurriedly made new arrows for rank upon rank of archers on the heights. All were ready for the Eygptian attack. And all settled down to wait.

*   *   *

Atop the wall Princess Tharbis looked down on the preparations with concern. The situation had changed radically, and with the dense concentration of troops everywhere, she wondered how Het would ever find his way through to rendezvous with her tonight. There seemed to be no way to avoid being spotted by the Nubian pickets.

Yet something within her said that despite all the odds, Het would succeed. He struck her as being utterly reliable, in a world full of people who disappointed you at every turn.

That was in his favor; a woman wanted a man she could count on. Oh, why couldn't he have been born rich and aristocratic and dashing and—well, *exciting*.

That, after all, was the thing about Moses. You could not escape the fact that he was special—a man chosen by the gods for great things. Everyone thought so: Seth, Het, just everyone. She had heard Apedemek talking about him with her father, sharing that general impression, even though her father had not met the boy. Apedemek had, of course, when he was among the Egyptians and impersonating the tinker. Having formed a firm impression of Moses, Apedemek apparently had begun to make his own plans for the prince. These involved using him, manipulating him, taking him under that uncanny spell.

She hoped the opportunity never arose; she had seen the way men were when they were in thrall to Apedemek—her father, for example. Balaam was not a strong personality in the first place, and when he was around Apedemek, he lost what little backbone he did have and became subservient in a way that pained her terribly.

Why, she wondered now, did this bother her so much? Did she still love her father and want him to stand up for himself? Did she believe there was still some dignity and manhood left in him to assert, before he was no more than Apedemek's slave?

Perhaps. Although she felt contempt for her father for failing to resist Apedemek's spell, she also felt great empathy for him; after all, how did she know that she would do better against the magus?

He was, she knew, not unaware of her: On the few

occasions when she had been in his presence—she had taken pains to make these as brief as possible—she had felt his eyes on her, and she had felt her flesh burn. Although Apedemek had no one woman around him, and although he had not openly consorted with women while in Kerma, he was known to be strongly sexed; rumors had leaked out of the orgies he had held at his lavish quarters in the capital—orgies in which the women outnumbered the men by three or four to one.

Thus it was unsettling every time she felt his eyes upon her, and she had steered away from him as often as she could. She had never known a man yet, for all her second-hand knowledge from Irenas, her maid, whose experience had been considerable. And although Irenas tended to a certain cynicism in matters concerning men, she had still explained to Tharbis that the way of a man with a woman could be beautiful and moving.

She would never let her father give her away as a diplomatic gift. More than this, she had decided that the likes of Apedemek would never touch her. She would die first!

There was a sudden sound behind her. She whirled and looked suddenly into the hard, unearthly eyes of Apedemek!

Seth sat cross-legged in the middle of the cell, his eyes on an invisible presence. Slowly he raised his hands and began to mold the empty air. As Arnekh watched, the presence took shape: It was the form of a human being, robed in brown, wearing a hood. And slowly the figure—it was about a quarter the size of a real human being, and proportionate in every way—began to glow softly with a warm light.

"Seth!" Arnekh gasped. "What magic is this? What are you doing?"

Seth did not answer. His mind was concentrating on the task at hand. The little figure now glowed with an unearthly white light, a diabolical glow that hurt Arnekh's eyes.

Seth's voice, when it came at last, was full of strain. "I am calling forth demons to do my bidding." The tension in the cell was palpable. "This one is hard to control." And indeed, even as he spoke, the glow faded, and with a flash the figure disappeared!

Seth blinked. "I have much to learn about the control of

demons, it appears," he admitted. "This one was in the image of Apedemek, and its mind was strong. I could not hold it, but I will learn to do so in time. I will ask Apedemek when next I see him."

"Seth! What's the matter with you? Are you embracing corruption?"

"I seek wisdom," Seth explained. "My mind has been inactive too long. I have grown soft. Apedemek is right. There is a streak of weakness in my family. We stop short of the final revelations. But it is not too late to learn something new."

"Seth! This sort of trick can doom your soul to eternal horrors! Please! Come to your senses!"

"Stop now," Seth asked, "when I'm just beginning to learn something? Look, my friend, I've come this far in no more than a day, just by paying attention to what Apedemek does. I haven't even had a chance to question him. I'm sure that when I do talk to him tonight, he will be impressed with my progress. If I can learn so much without a master, what more can I learn with one?"

"Seth! You're not thinking of—"

"I have decided to learn the arcane mysteries. I am going to go the whole way. Only by committing myself can I undo the horrid things I have done."

"Seth! I beg of you!"

"Guard!" Seth called. "Guard, come here!" The guard cursed, rose from his chair, and wandered over to the bars to look inside.

"See what a mere beginner can do!" he said. His hands waved, and a green ball of light suddenly appeared in midair. Slowly he got to his feet, the motions of his hands subtly molding the ball of light. "Observe. I shall call up a face from my youth, a ghost to speak to me."

The guard shrank back. "I'm going for help," he said in a strangled voice.

"Stay," Seth commanded. "See my father, Ben-Hadad, who never recognized me as his son, who rejected me!" The ball of light became the head of a man in his thirties, curly-haired, round-faced. The face bore a puzzled, tortured expression. The face blinked uncomprehendingly.

"Father! Wherever you are now, hear me! This is Seth of Thebes, your son! Seth, whom you treated as if he were a bastard sired by a beggar! Seth, who withdrew so far from the world in which he felt your hatred that he barely spoke for the first ten years of his life!"

"S-Seth," the head answered. "I can hear you, but I can't see you! Where are you? How can you speak to me now? What is happening to me? Are you real?"

"Father! Surely you must know how things stand now. Surely you must know how wrong you were. What have you to say to me? Tell me whom you've wronged?"

"Seth! My son! Forgive! Please forgive!"

"It's too late, Father! You waited too long. By the time you died alone and deserted, it was too late to acknowledge me! The only way you could have done that would be to do as I am doing, to make a bargain—at whatever price—with whomever you could find to help you reach the person you wronged! But this you did not do!"

"Seth! Please! Forgiveness! You can't imagine the pain—"

"Oh, but I can, Father! I too have wronged many people—nearly everyone who was dear to me. But I am not going to wait until it is too late to save my conscience. I have carried this burden around with me long enough, and my back is bowed under the weight."

"My son!" The light was fading. The voice was weakening every second. "Just forgive me!"

"I forgive you!" he said with a shudder just as the head disappeared, leaving not so much as an afterglow. Seth bowed his head. "May others forgive me as I have forgiven you."

Wordlessly the guard stumbled to the door and rushed outside in a clatter of falling furniture.

"No, Seth!" Arnekh of Kerkis begged in a broken voice. "Tell me you won't cooperate with Apedemek! Tell me you jest. Seth, please!"

But Seth's answer was silence.

III

Tharbis lay spread-eagle on a great slab of marble, the stone cold against her naked back and buttocks and legs. Her hands and feet seemed fettered, although as she turned her head to look, there were no restraining ropes or chains. She could raise her head and turn it from side to side only a bit. When she did, she could see that the slab on which she lay was surrounded by a circle of fires, beyond which was darkness.

But no! There were people in the darkness. She could see their eyes, looking at her, staring at her nakedness, watching . . . waiting.

She tried to call out: *Help! Please!* But although her mouth worked, there was no sound.

She heard a sound directly in front of her, past her widespread feet. She raised her head in alarm. *Who's there?* But again there came no sound.

Suddenly there was a great flash and a puff of evil-smelling smoke choked with sulphur. She craned her neck, straining against the invisible bonds. Out of the smoke walked something huge, grotesque, naked. It was not human, for all that it bore a horrid resemblance to man. It was powerfully muscled, and its skin was covered with leathery scales. Its hands ended in cruel claws. Its bald head was horned, and it had the glowing, slit eyes of a cat.

Her eyes traveled fearfully down its body to the scaly waist, then to the horribly engorged penis—and turned her head away in terror. Her heart almost stopped with fear. It was horribly, animalistically *ready* for her, and the realization of what was going to happen next was too brutal, too frightening to imagine!

The catlike pupils widened. The ugly mouth opened to show hideous, bloodstained teeth between leathery lips. It was getting closer. She could smell its foul breath now.

No! Please! she screamed silently.

The faces in the darkness leaned forward in eager anticipation. Inhuman animal cries were loosed from the unseen world beyond the ring of fire.

The thing leaned over her. Its foul breath was hot and

reeked of sulphur. It raised a great, scaly hand and flexed those horrible claws, covered with dark, dried blood.

No! Leave me alone!

One of the claws touched her naked little breast. She closed her eyes, hoping to shut it all out, but she could feel that hard, scaly hand on her flesh, caressing her roughly. Her skin crawled. He was above her now. She kept her eyes tightly closed.

He mounted her, and a terrible stabbing pain ripped across her body.

Please make him stop! Somebody! Please help me!

And then the pain *really* began.

Silently, slowly, Het climbed out of the water. The night wind was cool on his naked skin, and he bit his lip to control his shivers. He slipped behind a rock and watched the water, looking for Moses.

They had chosen the most difficult—if the shortest—swim of all. This was the strait itself, the narrow space between Gindikol Island and the headland, the spot least defended because of the rocky terrain. Here he and Moses, also naked and smeared with dark grease, would find their way across the rocky barrier, climb the earthen rampart before the fortress, slink down into the shallow moat, and circumnavigate the northeastern and northern faces of the stronghold wall until they came to the secret passage, camouflaged by shrubbery and an ancient rockfall. At least this was the plan.

Het fretted, his eyes searching the dark waters for a sign of the prince. The timing was very crucial; in a short while the Black Wind would swim the strait behind them and follow the path to the moat. From there, after implementation of the planned diversion, they would scale the walls. As they did so, the diversion would become a full-scale attack on the two Nubian garrisons outside the walls. But the timing was exact, and it was very important that there be no deviation from the schedule.

Het leaned forward, peering through the gloom, his hand on the knife in the belt that was all he wore. Presently he heard a splash, and a dark arm rose out of the waves. He moved forward, grabbed the outstretched hand, to drag the prince from the water.

The Nile pulled hard against Het's efforts, but he worked his muscles powerfully and hauled the dark hand toward him. Moses emerged from the water, got his feet firmly under him, and whispered, "Thanks. Where are we?"

A beam of moonlight broke through the clouds and illuminated them. Het ducked and pulled Moses down. "Careful! Where's your knife?" he whispered.

"I threw it away," Moses answered. "I don't want a knife."

"What are you talking about?" Het erupted. "Have they sent me here to my death, with a man who doesn't want to fight? How are you going to cover my back?"

"When there's trouble, I'll be there," Moses assured him. "Don't worry. You'll be exposed to no sudden danger because of me."

Het blew out an angry breath. "We'll talk about this later. Come along."

They crept up the rocky hillside, keeping the larger boulders between them and the Nubians whenever possible. Once Het's heart almost stopped as a Nubian picket hove into view and came within twenty steps of them; but the two young Egyptians froze and were not detected.

The hardest part was scaling the rampart that held in the shallow waters of the Nile, which had been diverted into the moat. Here they were exposed to view from all sides. Het waited for a cloud to drift over the moon's face, then he dug a hand into Moses's ribs and scuttled up the slope and over, to fall heavily onto a natural ledge on the far side.

"Quick!" he urged. "Down into the moat!"

Moses scrambled down behind him, and the two men began to make their way slowly along the shallow shoreline of the half-empty moat, in the view only of the guards high atop the walls; Het breathed silent prayers to all the gods that no one would look down.

As he moved slowly forward, he stifled the rage burning in him. What sort of fool was Moses that he would throw away the only weapon he had? How could they have saddled him with an accomplice who would be a liability? Had the prince turned coward?

A hopeful thought interrupted his angry ruminations: If

he had, did this mean that there was the opportunity to outshine Moses and win Tharbis's heart?

Tharbis awoke in darkness, feeling bruised, filthy, and ill. She lay atop a rumpled bed. On the far side of the room was the tiny, guttering flame of a candle. She half stumbled, half fell out of bed and limped on leaden legs toward the light source. She managed to locate a second, longer candle next to it, and she lit this with the stub just before it went out.

She straightened and held the candle high.

The room was her own. The bed sheets were ripped to shreds. She walked toward the bed, her whole body aching, and caught a sudden glimpse of her own image in the full-length, gleaming bronze mirror: She was naked, her hair tousled.

There was a great dark stain near the top of her thighs, a stain that spread down the inside of her legs.

She cried out. "It wasn't a dream!" she choked with horror. "It was real! Real!"

"Here we are," Het said. "But where is she? Here, get behind this rock. You'll have to squeeze through."

"Was she on time yesterday?" Moses asked.

"She was here waiting for me. Something's wrong. They've caught her. I just know it."

"Relax," Moses said. "She might just have got delayed. It must be difficult for her, making her way down here without anyone knowing where she's going."

"You're right," Het admitted, feeling a little foolish. "We'll give her another couple of minutes. I wonder if the Black Wind has started up the walls yet."

"Probably," Moses responded evenly. "Calm down, will you? No one will see them. The Nubians are expecting the trouble to come from in front of them, not from the rear."

"You're right, I know. The Black Wind's fire arrows ought to keep the Nubians hopping. The army quarters below the walls have thatched roofs. Six lucky hits and the Nubians will have their hands full fighting the fires. Then when the Black Wind comes down from the walls . . . damn it, why isn't she here?"

"Perhaps you're right," Moses said. "Maybe something has gone wrong. But the moment the Black Wind are on the walls, it's time for us to get inside the fortress. I'll wait until the arrows start lobbing over the walls and the Black Wind are in command of the heights, then I'll make my way to the gatehouse."

"Alone?" Het asked. "Unarmed?"

"I'll be all right. I guarantee I'll survive the night. The dwarf told me that much, although he won't tell me any more. You go see what's happened to the princess."

"But I was supposed to—"

Moses's teeth showed in a smile. "Don't argue. It's an order. The girl's important—she's risked her life for us and deserves a loyal defender."

Het nodded in assent. "Let me give you my knife. You're a brave man, but you're not going to make it all the way to the gatehouse without having to fight like a tiger. Besides, there's Ben-Azen."

"Who's he?"

"Ben-Azen is the gatekeeper and happens to be the finest sword in all of Semna. You'll have to kill him to get past him. Here, take the knife. Don't be stubborn. I wish it were a Hittite sword."

"I'm done with swords and knives," said Moses, unbelievably calm, considering his circumstances and the predictable events to come. "The dwarf was right. I've decided to accept my destiny."

"You're mad!" seethed Het in a fervent whisper. He paused, then grinned wolfishly. "But you're my kind of mad. Here's my hand. May we both come out of this alive and victorious."

Moses pressed his hand in a gesture of comradeship; then he moved up the narrow stairwell, silent and surefooted in the darkness.

IV

Trailing two guards behind him, Apedemek moved rapidly down the curving stairs, his long robe swirling on the stone floor. The guards had to exert themselves to keep up with him; it was as if all the usually buried energy, never expended until necessity demanded it, was being unleashed now. The air fairly crackled around him.

At the landing to the dungeons, he called in to the guards manning the cells. "You! Come out here! Both of you!"

The guards recognized that tone. They hurried out, one man rubbing sleep from his eyes, the other trying to comb his hair into some order with his fingers. "Yes, my lord?" said the senior man.

"Take a break," Apedemek said. "My men here will cover your duties. I'll send someone after you when I want you back."

"Yes, my lord." The two saluted and went out.

Apedemek turned to his personal guards. "Stay out here. I'll bar this door so no one but me can get in. You'll be able to see through the bars, so you can keep an eye on things. But let no one past you."

"Yes, my lord." The first burly guard saluted.

Apedemek turned and went in. "Seth! I have come for you."

Across the room, behind the bars of the inner cage, Seth peered out at him. "I am here," he answered calmly. "I have been waiting for you."

Atop the wall the captain of the Nubian guard paced to the corner of the wall, the end of his territory, paused a moment, then smartly turned on one heel and reversed his direction, the spear at his side keeping perfect dress all the while. He started to march back his thirty paces but found himself suddenly looking into the blazing eyes of a seven-foot-tall, naked Nubian woman armed fearfully with a long knife!

He tried to cry out, but the knife flashed, beheading him on the spot.

The woman waved to her companions, waiting below her. She reached down and pulled one of her comrades, who was almost at the wall's edge, up to the top.

Meanwhile a second guard, farther down the wall, spotted her and brought his spear to the ready. But even as he did, a huge shadow materialized at his back, and a silky cord went around his throat and was drawn tight by the only man to scale the walls. The Nubian guard dropped his spear to clutch at the cord around his neck. In a moment his body fell senseless.

Six more women warriors climbed agilely to the top of the walls. The warrior who had strangled the guard stood watching them as he drew a long sword from the scabbard that hung over his back.

Two more women scaled the walls to stand behind him. "Come," said Nehsi, high king of Nubia. "Let's win back my fortress."

On the ground level far below, Aspelta looked up just then, expecting to see the captain of the guard walking slowly along the ramp. There was no sign of him.

He stepped back, trying to get a better view. But he could see nothing until his eye picked out one dark form, then another hurrying along the ramp.

"Ho!" he called out. "The guards! Guards, to me!"

But even as he summoned them, the first flaming arrow arched its way high into the sky and cleared the top of the fortress. It fell soundlessly into the center of the compound, stuck upright into the thatched roof of the officers' quarters, and ignited the tinder. Three more arrows soared high into the air, their pitch-dipped tips ablaze.

"Call out the alarm!" he ordered in a loud voice. "We're under attack!"

Moving silently on bare feet, Het took the last flight of stairs to the landing three at a time, pausing just a moment before sticking his head cautiously around the corner. Down the hall, the guard before Tharbis's door stood with his back to Het.

Het moved slowly out into the hall and tiptoed up behind him, knife in hand.

At the last possible moment the guard sensed something was wrong and began to pivot. Het's dagger caught him low in the back, in the kidney, and sank home.

The guard let out a gasp and fell to one knee. The movement almost pulled the knife out of Het's hand, but Het held on, drawing the blade from his victim's back, and with his free hand yanked the man's head back so he could cut his throat.

This done, he turned to the door. He tested it first, hoping the bolt inside was not drawn. The door opened easily.

The room was in near darkness. The single candle picked out the form of a young woman, her eyes wide with stark terror, kneeling on the bloodstained bed, gripping a torn and befouled sheet to her chest.

It was a moment before he understood the terror in her eyes. And here he was, naked, stained black, bearing a bloody dagger, his stance that of a man who had just committed violence.

"No!" she begged in a broken voice. "Not again! Stay away from me, please!"

"Princess," he said gently. "It's Het! I'm here to rescue you!"

On the two fronts flanking the stronghold, the second rank of bowmen opened fire on new targets: the tent cities of the Nubian army encamped both northeast and southeast of the fortress. Nearly half the flaming arrows landed in the tents, and fires ignited immediately and spread quickly.

Khafre, standing on a high point on the rocky peninsula, the better to supervise the two fronts, looked up at the Semna walls. They were now commanded by Black Wind sentries, each armed with the long bow of the Upper Nile tribes. Their lean figures, as tall as cranes, were outlined against the leaping flames that were now visible above the citadel walls.

An arrow whizzed by him and spent itself on the rocks behind him. Geb turned and said, "Sir, don't you think you'd better get out of range?"

"They'll be too busy to bother with me shortly," Khafre answered phlegmatically. "Look! Weret's charging the southern garrison! Gods, what a woman! I tell you, my friend, if I were ten years younger—"

Geb shrugged. "She'd probably eat you alive like a mantis, sir. But I know what you mean: Even at her age she's quite a sight, particularly in action."

"Well, let's give her some help. Signal the northern army to charge. If they can turn the western flank, we can drive them into the Nile."

"If that happens, sir, you and I had better find some other vantage point. We'll be right in their path."

"Oh, have no doubt about it, my friend—if they want this place, they can have it. Issue the command. And let's give the fortress itself another volley or two. A big enough fire inside the walls will drive them out the gate."

"We may not have to wait that long, sir. If Moses and Nehsi can get through—"

"But that's a long shot. Believe me, I wouldn't have let Moses try if I hadn't had Tchabu's solemn word that the prince will survive this battle."

"And you're normally the least superstitious of men."

"It isn't superstition at all. I played senet last night with Maat, Weret's second in command. Tchabu wrote down the final disposition of the board beforehand and sealed the papyrus with wax. When the game was done, we opened it. He had accurately predicted the entire course of the game, even down to the serious error I made in the penultimate move and the desperate expedient I went to, bailing myself out. I came away a true believer."

"And did he predict the events of this battle?"

"I asked him not to. A man shouldn't know his own destiny. If I were to die today . . . well, I'd rather remain unaware of the fact right up to the moment it happened."

"You're wise in this, sir. I'll go signal for the advance."

She stood pressed closely to him, holding on for dear life, trembling with fear and shame. He was uncomfortably aware that both of them were naked. "There, now," he soothed, stroking her back. "You're safe now. Nothing will happen to you again. I promise. Anyone who comes near you, I'll kill him."

"Oh, Het," she sobbed, "I'm so ashamed. I was so helpless against him. He brutalized me, shamed me. Putting those hideous pictures in my mind! Assuming the form of a demon!"

"It will be all right. It's over now."

She cried all the harder. "It's not over for me! Don't let go of me! Don't leave me! I couldn't bear to—"

"Leave you? Wherever I go, you'll go with me."

"Oh, Het, Het . . . I can't look anybody in the eye again. To be raped by a monster like Apedemek—"

"You don't have to feel ashamed with me. It was against your will. I'll stay with you, and I'll try to help you forget, if it takes me the rest of my life."

She hugged him harder, and he became more aware of how very, very dear she was to him. Calming, Tharbis burrowed her face into his neck and laid her hand against his strong, young chest.

"Gods!" he said. "I've got to get you out of here. And I've got to save Seth. The attack is going on right now!"

"Attack?"

He gently extricated himself but, still holding her hand, pulled her over to the window and looked out. As they watched, a dozen arrows arched high into the air, aiming at the flame-engulfed interior court. Beyond the moat they could see the fires already blazing in the northern camp, and flaming arrows hurtling through the air to start new ones.

"It has already begun!" he confirmed. "Quick! Get dressed! I've got to get you out of here!"

She looked at him with hurt, stricken eyes. Then she nodded and tried to smile. His eyes took her in hungrily, and his heart ached with love. He watched as she went to her trunk at the bed's foot and opened it. Gone now was the robust independence she had shown before. She seemed a vulnerable little girl, in need of protection. His eyes lingered on her slim legs, her adorable flanks. . . .

What am I doing? he wondered, then went to the door and threw it open. He looked both ways, then grabbed the dead guard by the heels and dragged him inside to strip him of his loincloth, don it himself, and steal his sword.

Apedemek hesitated. Seth could, after all, be planning a trick. "It is unusual for a man to arrive at the frame of mind necessary for true commitment so quickly."

"I have had ample time to think," Seth declared. "And I have decided to make my move. I have been a fool too long. I

look back on the benighted years and feel disgust and shame."
He looked Apedemek in the eyes. "But are *you* sure you can
promise what I ask? Can I bring my dear ones back? Can I
make my peace with them? Can I undo the course of history?"

"Seth!" Arnekh cried out from the rear of the cell. "Don't
do it!"

"Silence," Seth commanded. "This is none of your affair.
I have carried this burden of guilt for far too long. Anything
that can rid me of it has to be a good thing."

"Seth! For the love of all that's good and beautiful! It's
not too late!"

"I can do all you ask," said Apedemek, his voice ending
on a rising note of triumph.

Seth watched him turn the key in the lock. "Then let us
begin. I am ready."

V

To the south of the fortress the Desert Legion had
attacked in force and been thrown back by the fierce defense
put up by the Nubians from the Kumma garrison. Now,
dust-covered and bloodied by a shallow sword-cut near the
hairline, Weret backhanded a trickle of red from her face
and, scowling, turned her back to the enemy to exhort her
troops.

Her warriors stood panting from exertion, looking at her,
trying to catch their breath. No one moved at first.

"All right!" Weret bellowed in a piercing voice that
carried to the whole command. "*I'm* going to charge them,
with or without you! Either I'll fight with an army at my side,
or I'll fight with cowards at my back! Which will it be?"

Not even waiting for an answer, she turned to face the
foe, her lean body illuminated by the flames leaping above
the walls of Semna. She began walking slowly and deliberately toward the Nubian lines, while arrows fell spent to her
right and left.

"Wait!" Maat called from behind her. "Who said we weren't coming? Wait for us!"

And with her the women's army spoke in force, in the wild, high-pitched battle cry of the Legion!

Inside the Semna stronghold, it was almost as bright as day because of the roaring fire consuming the roofs of the soldiers' quarters. One level below the wall, the Black Wind battled the elite fortress guards, who fought with the strength and zeal of madmen. As the great fire raged out of control, the men on the lower levels abandoned attempts to put it out and, weapons flashing, pounded their way up the stairs all around the enclosure to join the fight against the towering black women.

Just in the nick of time, Moses noticed a squad of guards coming and ducked back behind an abutment, flattening himself against the wall. His hands itched for a weapon now, and he wondered if his oath to forswear the use of the sword was not the first sign of insanity. And here he was, naked and unprotected, with the armed might of a major river fortress surrounding him on all sides!

It looked as though he might escape notice entirely, but the last soldier in the file turned his head just as his foot touched the first step and spotted Moses! "You!" the soldier said, turning to face him, holding his sword poised for action. "What are you doing here?"

Moses looked around desperately. The other soldiers, not noticing the confrontation, had continued down the passageway. Above the landing stood a wooden structure topped by a canopy, which was propped up on one side by wooden poles. He leapt up and grabbed one of the support poles, a stout stick about the length of his body, and pulled it down. The canopy collapsed atop the soldier's head, giving Moses the chance to back away and test the heft of the staff in his hands.

It was odd; the staff seemed *right* somehow. He balanced it in his hands and faced the soldier as the man struggled out from under the canopy. The guardsman blinked, growled under his breath, and attacked with his sword!

Moses was surprised at how easy it was to parry the blow

with the improvised weapon, which seemed as light as a feather. He beat the blade aside and lightly touched the soldier in the middle of the chest with the stick's tip; then he shoved the soldier back hard enough to send him sprawling over the collapsed canvas.

Now! he thought. Now was the time to catch him off guard and smash his head to pulp with the staff. *Now!*

But he did not. As the soldier rose to stand again, a flame shot out from the point of Moses's staff, like one of the flames in the courtyard, picked the sword out of the soldier's hands, and tossed it with a deft flip over the side of the passage into the fire below!

The soldier stared at Moses, then he stared at the stick. Finally he blinked, cursed, and took off up the stairs at a dead run.

The corridor ran as straight as an arrow shot all the way to the end, then turned a ninety-degree corner. Around this corner Nehsi, the long sword of a Nubian warrior in his huge hand, ran an opponent through, then stopped to look around him.

Up ahead, he could see Moses, armed only with a stick, disarm his enemy and drive him away, and Nehsi's old heart beat strongly with admiration. How lucky the Egyptians were to have such an heir! He, king of Nubia these many years, had no son to survive him once he had won his kingdom back again. The injustice of it pained him.

As his eyes roved beyond the young man, he saw what Moses could not: Between the young prince and the lower floors, three full squads of Nubian soldiers blocked the way! He had to help! Left to his own devices, the boy would walk into a trap and be killed!

"Moses!" he roared at the top of his considerable lungs. But the noise of the fire and the fighting overwhelmed the sound of his warning.

Gritting his teeth, Nehsi set out down the corridor toward the corner, cursing his legs for not going any faster.

Outside, on the northern flank of the castle, Khafre's powerful attack had driven the Semna branch of the Nubian

army back to within fifty strides of the moat. Leading the
attack with Geb at his side, Khafre rushed forward at the
head of a handpicked unit of seasoned fighters and cut a deep
hole in the enemy's front ranks. Quickly the men on his flank
drove forward to wipe out the salient and pulled the line
straight.

Grinning madly with the sheer physical exhilaration of it
all, Khafre skewered the man facing him and watched him
fall; then he glanced upward. The gate! If only the gate would
fall! If only Moses had found his way to it! Where was he?
What was he doing? *Open the gate, Moses!*

Slipping as silently as possible down the great curving
staircase that led to the dungeons, Het and Tharbis bumped
into three guardsmen running in the opposite direction.

Het was almost bowled over by their forward rush and
barely brought his sword up in time to keep from getting his
throat cut. He fell back, stumbling on the stairs, and felt
Tharbis's strong little hands supporting him, pushing him
forward. He parried a thrust, beat the probing sword aside,
and punched the guard in the face with his free fist; the
soldier blundered back down the steps and knocked over one
of the other two coming up quickly behind him.

The third man was not so easily dispensed with. He
came on, sword weaving, dipping, cutting. His blade grazed
Het's wrist and drew blood. Het came back with a raging
counterattack that was all power and no science, swinging as
if he were beating a recalcitrant beast of burden. The soldier
fell back, only to turn Het's wrist and nearly disarm him, but
he suddenly staggered, his throat spouting blood from a
knife, thrown with all Tharbis's might, that had buried itself
up to the hilt in his neck!

The soldier's sword clattered to the ground, and he
stumbled back and down. Knees buckling, he toppled off the
side of the staircase to the floor far below!

Het emitted a triumphant cry and charged the other
two, hacking, stabbing, cutting, driving them down to the
landing with sheer unleashed fury. With a single stroke, he
gutted the first soldier! The second man's halfhearted attack
ended equally quickly in a pair of passes by Het, the second

of which caught the guard just below where the ribs came together. He fell like a stone.

Het let out the breath he had been holding, looked around him, and only when he was satisfied that no fourth soldier lay hidden behind a pillar, turned to Tharbis, her fine features radiant in the light of the overhead torch. "And where did you learn to throw a knife like that, my delicate flower?" he inquired.

"There isn't anything else to do around here," she replied. "I was bored. Where did you learn to fight like that?"

He took a deep breath. "Just now, I guess." How could he tell her that he was in love for the first time in his young life, and his fear for her had brought a strength to his right arm that he had never known before!

There he was, at the bottom of the last staircase. Moses looked up; the great gate of the castle loomed above him, with the mechanism for lowering it. . . .

He lowered his eyes and blinked. Standing before the mechanism, sword in hand, was a powerful man with piercing eyes that seemed almost to glow in the light of the fire. He smiled a reptile's smile and showed pointed, gold teeth. "From the look of you," he snarled in a metallic baritone, "you'd be wanting to let this thing down and let the Egyptians in." He chuckled nastily. "Did you think I would allow you to get through to cut the rope? And did you come naked and covered with slime to contest my right to be here? Bearing only a stick?"

Moses did not know what to say.

"I am Ben-Azen, guardian of the gate. There is no man in the world able to take this job from me. Never have I met my better with the sword, and I think, looking at the naked and bedraggled likes of you, tonight is not going to change that fact at all."

Moses still could not find his tongue.

Ben-Azen's smile became even more unpleasant. "It does nothing for my reputation when I'm forced to kill a bare-bottomed imp coated with goo and bearing only a stick like some sheep-loving herdsman from Moab or Midian. Get yourself a sword. Get yourself properly armed so that I can kill you."

Moses's hands were sweaty. How could he face this man with only the staff? He had been able to best the previous soldier only through the advantage of surprise and a miracle. He had no such benefit with this man.

His eyes sought out the gatekeeper's large, competent-looking hands. One of them held the sword parallel to the stone floor; the other lightly tested the razor-sharp blade with an idle finger.

His vow seemed so foolish now! And yet he knew that he had taken it quite seriously when he had made it. Backing down would mean a loss of honor, even if no one ever knew about the fact but himself.

What could he do?

Seth and Apedemek faced each other in the dungeon anteroom. Behind Seth, Arnekh had painfully pulled himself to his feet and now stood unsteadily, clutching the bars of the cell for support, watching, his face contorted by an expression of utter despair.

"Seth," Arnekh pleaded, "you don't know what you're doing. The decision, once made, can never—"

"Tell the old fool to shut up," Apedemek said, not recognizing his one-time acquaintance, "or I'll kill him. Shall I show you how masters of the higher craft kill people without laying a finger on them? It's very simple. It'll make a good first lesson."

"Never mind," Seth said in a changed voice. "I'll do it myself." He turned, looked at Arnekh, and waved one hand. A puff of bright smoke, acrid, sulphur-scented, erupted not an arm's length from Arnekh's face, and the old man's eyes slowly rolled back into his head and closed, and his knees buckled, and he sank limply onto the straw at his feet.

"Admirable!" Apedemek commended. "You will make a prize pupil! You learned that on your own?"

"From watching you, my master," Seth intoned. "Once I decided to apprentice myself to you and learn the higher calling, I closely observed everything you did here and tried to remember what I had seen earlier, when I thought you were Netek-amani the Tinker."

"Splendid!" said Apedemek. "Now observe: I shall draw

the pentagram on the floor. We will stand inside it, you and I, and prepare to receive the spirit. It will not be long in coming, I assure you—not when summoned by such as I, with an apt and dedicated apprentice like you working with me. We will accept you into the craft tonight, without delay. You will receive the power. And when you do, you will not believe the paltry fool you were before you made your choice and decided to go . . . beyond."

"Proceed, my master," Seth urged. "I am in your hands."

VI

"Come on!" Ben-Azen taunted, the same mocking, hateful smile on his square, coarse-featured face. "This is what you came all this way for, isn't it, boy? You came to open the gate so your friends could come inside. Well, it isn't going to be easy. I'm disinclined to stand aside and wave you onward. It's a matter of pride, boy. I'll surrender the management of this machine that raises and lowers gate and drawbridge over to my master with the sword and to no other."

Moses, fretting, stood shifting the weight of his stick from hand to hand.

"Come, now," Ben-Azen said. "Under that grease must be a boy of some mettle, or you wouldn't have got this far. I was born of Syrian parentage, and I'm proud of the fact. Who whelped you? Have you a name? Did your mother crawl under a bush and drop you on the ground like a brood sow making little piggies? Have you a father somewhere who will mourn you when I've finished with you?"

Moses glared. He tried to speak but found his throat dry. He cleared it and stammered, "M-my name is—"

"Get it out, bastard!" Ben-Azen ordered harshly. "Who do you imagine your father to be? Or were there too many soldiers calling on your mother that night for her to be sure?"

Moses was seething now. "You overstep yourself," he said at last. "I could say I was the son of Thermutis of Egypt, daughter of Sekenenre, king of kings—"

"Ah! A princess's offspring! But look at him now!"

"But I don't think I will say that. You speak to Moses ben-Amram, of the tribe of Levi, born a slave but of a line of uncrowned kings in Canaan. Heir to Jacob, called Israel. Heir to Abraham of Ur, who led the great army that defeated the Four Kings, who humbled the rulers of Shinar and Elam alike in the great days of the Twelfth Dynasty of Kings."

"Ah, now this is more like the kind of talk I—"

"A moment ago I would have claimed the finest blood-lines an Egyptian could have." Moses's voice grew stronger. "But now I am not so proud of an alleged lineage among the people of the Nile as I might be. You say you're a foreigner, just as I belatedly find myself to be. And you say you're proud of the fact. Well, I understand that. A man should be proud of what he is and where he comes from."

"I've wronged you, boy! You're more than you look to be."

Moses ignored him. "I'll never know whether I might have been your match with the sword. I've vowed never to pick up a sword again. But this stick is not unlike the basic weapon of my people, and although I am not instructed in its use, let us see how well I do with it. My stick against your sword."

Strangely, a little thrill went through him, and for a moment he felt for the first time in his life the powerful and disturbing suspicion that some higher power had spoken through him. A stick against a sword. The weapon of a weaker vessel against the weapon of a stronger. It was as though the heavens had opened before him, and he had seen the most fleeting glimpse of his own destiny.

"Be ready," he advised.

For answer Ben-Azen's mocking smile came back. "Indeed. The stick against the sword. You have spirit. I like that. For that I'll improve the odds in your favor a trifle, Habiru. I'll switch hands."

But as he did, Moses saw his chance. Almost too swiftly for the eye to follow, the tip of the stick lashed out and deflected the sword. It flew from Ben-Azen's hand and clattered on the stones. As Ben-Azen stooped to reach for it, Moses's deft hands moved as rapidly as before. The stick's tip caught Ben-Azen on the side of the neck and battered him erect, then withdrew only to shove him back against the very gate he guarded. Again the tip of the stick flashed, coming to rest on Ben-Azen's nose.

"Move so much as a muscle," Moses threatened, "and you'll die in a particularly ugly way. They'll have to bury you with a bag over your head to keep from offending your family and friends."

But even as he said this, he saw Ben-Azen's eyes dart to his right and he heard footfalls on the stones. He pulled the stick away just in time to wheel and parry a pike aimed at his guts by a newly arrived soldier. Moses fell back one step and to his chagrin saw Ben-Azen retrieve his sword. It was two against one now—a swordsman and pikeman against his staff— and he had to move quickly. He swung the staff in an attempt to disarm Ben-Azen again; but this time the gatekeeper was ready for him, and his grip survived the clash.

Moses kept his two adversaries in sight as he backed away. The pikeman again thrust at him, and he routinely parried. But as he did, Ben-Azen's blade lashed out. The near edge of Moses's stick barely managed to deflect the cut.

"Move farther to your right," Ben-Azen told the pikeman. "Let's get him between us."

Moses's eyes swung from one man to the other as they moved apart a step at a time. His mind was racing madly.

Het paused, looked furtively around the corner and into the guards' area outside the dungeon's anteroom, then jerked his head back. He put a restraining hand on Tharbis's shoulder. "They're there," he whispered. "Two of them." He sneaked another peek, then flattened himself against the wall beside her. "I don't like this. I know those two. They're personal bodyguards to Apedemek. Apedemek must be with Seth."

"We've got to do something."

"If you can create a diversion here, maybe I can go around the other side and hit them from the rear. Give me a minute, then do something. Scream. Faint."

"I'm not the fainting type," she told him. "Nobody would believe it for a moment."

"I don't care what you do, so long as it isn't dangerous. And it won't be if you give me enough time to come up behind them."

"I'll distract them," she promised. "Never fear about that. But don't you do anything dangerous, either." She was going to leave it at that, but she looked into his eyes and saw something there. She impulsively reached up and kissed him, quick and hard, and followed this up with a caress as soft as down, her fingertips brushing his cheek. She smiled. Het blinked and grinned foolishly. "Now go," she said. "I'll count to a hundred, then I'll do what I have to do." She pressed his hands warmly between her own, and then released them.

Het blinked again, smiled, and went to the transverse hallway, pausing at the corner to look around cautiously. There was only one corner separating him from the two bodyguards, so he stopped, caught his breath, and paused to compose himself.

She had kissed him! She cared about him! She was worried about him!

The thought was almost enough to blunt his purpose; but he stifled the rejoicing, straightened his shoulders, and took a firm grip on the sword in his right hand.

He heard her scream! Loud and piercing, it echoed in the stone halls like the agonized howl of a damned soul in the Netherworld.

It addled him, as he was sure it must have startled the guards. He peeked out into the middle of the hall, where the two guards stood side by side, looking toward the brightly lit corner beyond.

Under the torches Tharbis stood, naked, her hands shielding various parts of her body in a way that only drew attention to them. Her posture spoke of vulnerability, helplessness, submissiveness. *Help me!* her stance said. But it all too obviously said something else, to which the men were responding.

He took all of this in in the blink of an eye, then he attacked!

As he raced down the corridor, he let out a ferocious bellow of his own, made deafeningly loud by the echo. One of the guards half turned, and the wild slash of Het's sword cut his throat wide open, spewing blood right and left!

Het turned immediately to the dead man's companion, who drew swiftly and assumed the ready position just as Het lunged. The Nubian deftly parried and disarmed him!

Het fell back, empty-handed, his eyes large and wide. "Tharbis! Run!"

But just as the soldier drew back for a mighty cut, something hit the man hard from behind.

Het looked down. A bloody sword point was protruding from the soldier's stomach!

The soldier dropped to his knees. His sword fell to the floor. Het picked it up and prepared to finish him off, but that was not necessary. The soldier pitched forward on his face.

Het looked up. There stood the naked Tharbis, dusting off the two slim hands that had held the sword dropped by the first guard Het had killed.

He swept her into his arms and hugged the breath out of her. But she pushed him away after kissing him quickly and said, "Seth! We've got to save Seth!"

He nodded and hurried toward the door while she ran back after her discarded clothing.

But when he reached the door to the dungeon's anteroom and pulled at the large ring handle, it would not budge. As Tharbis came up behind him, pulling her robe around her hastily, he reached through the small aperture that allowed the guards to identify whoever stood at the other side and tried to reach the handle. His arm was too large at the bicep, however, to allow it to reach all the way.

"What's the matter?" she asked.

"It's locked. I can't get my arm through."

"Give me a boost up and let me try."

He knelt before the door as she stepped into his laced fingers. But when her face was near the window in the door, she looked in and saw Seth and Apedemek standing inside a five-pointed star drawn on the floor. Seth's wrists were crossed over his chest, and Apedemek was mumbling an incantation in a tongue she could not understand.

"What's the matter?" Het asked. "Just reach inside."

"Het, there's something wrong. Apedemek's doing some sort of ritual, and Seth is doing it with him—voluntarily."

"Stop him! We can't let that happen!"

She cried out at the very considerable top of her healthy young lungs. "Seth! No! Don't do it! Seth!"

There was no interruption in the ritual. Both Seth and Apedemek had closed their eyes, as if by doing so they could shut out both sight and sound. Now Apedemek raised his arms and cried out in a voice that echoed and reechoed: "Now come, spirit of darkness! Enter the two of us now! Come, father of evil!"

"*No!*" Tharbis shrieked. "*Please, no!*"

VII

The pikeman lunged again, but Moses's stick turned the thrust to one side. The parry left him open to attack from the other side, and Ben-Azen came forward one steady, purposeful step at a time, stabbing and lunging. Moses barely escaped being skewered only by ducking to one side and then unexpectedly moving toward the swordsman. He stood broadside now to Ben-Azen's advance and returned the stick to its ready position. The staff caught Ben-Azen in the ribs and knocked the wind out of him; he seemed to fold in on himself, coughing and wheezing.

The pikeman drew back his weapon and aimed it at Moses's unprotected side but suddenly looked up to see a towering—and instantly familiar—figure standing before him, sword hand upraised in a mighty backswing!

It was the last thing he ever saw. The mighty blow that decapitated him bore testimony to the great strength that still lay in Nehsi's right arm. And now Nehsi stepped forward, saluted the faltering Ben-Azen, and shot a quick smile at Moses.

"This is *my* work," Nehsi declared. "This man has betrayed my trust in him by going over to the enemy. He is mine, Prince. Your job is over, except for cutting the rope that holds the gate and the drawbridge. As soon as I have killed him, I want you to sever the rope."

Ben-Azen scowled up at him, one hand on his chest. His eyes narrowed. "Well. Comes the reckoning. I did not hope for so much. The black bum himself comes to me and begs to be killed."

"Kill me if you can, renegade," Nehsi challenged, slowly circling, his blade outstretched. "If you want to call this begging, so be it." His sword tip pointed at Ben-Azen's eyes. "Unlike the men of the Kumma garrison, you were not under any spell when you conspired to depose your king and murder him in his cell."

"It is a fond wish yet to be fulfilled," Ben-Azen said. "Now die, tyrant!" With this he lunged powerfully forward.

But while his feint and thrust were expert, he had not reckoned with Nehsi's's superior reach. Halfway through the long thrust, his parry missed Nehsi's long blade. And the king's razor-sharp sword found its way deep into Ben-Azen's gut.

Nehsi stepped back and watched Ben-Azen fall. He saluted, then cried out through gritted teeth: "Now, Moses! The gate!"

"Oh, Het!" Tharbis moaned. "I can't reach it! My arm's too short!"

She stepped down, and he scrambled to his feet beside her. They pressed their faces to the narrow opening. Through it they could see the two men. An unearthly glow had begun to appear in the area surrounding the pentagram in which they stood. "He's corrupted Seth," Tharbis breathed. "Seth's going over to the other side."

"No, Seth!" Het bellowed. "Resist it! Fight it! Don't go along with him!"

At this Apedemek opened his eyes and smiled coldly. The spell broke for a moment. The glow disappeared.

Seth opened his eyes. He looked around and noticed the two at the little window in the door.

"Pay no attention to them!" Apedemek commanded.

But Seth looked solemnly at the two faces in the little window . . . and winked!

Suddenly Seth and Apedemek were no longer alone. Instead, the cell was full of tall, lean, hard-muscled female warriors, naked, their arms and ankles gleaming with gold ornaments, and formidable swords of glowing bronze in their hands!

The Desert Legion, en masse! They . . . or their ghostly images!

Apedemek, his eyes giving expression to his horror, fell back. He cursed aloud and waved his hands at the figures before him!

As a result the room filled with monsters of every description—hideous demons from the darkest depths of the Netherworld; six-legged dragons with gleaming jaws dripping gore; creatures with scaly tails and bat wings; chimerical creations with wolves' heads and lions' bodies; horrid mutants with tentacles, and the claws of eagles at the ends of those tentacles!

Seth's hand arose to gesture. From his outstretched finger shot a bolt of white-hot fire, a fearful lightning bolt that focused on each of the demonic creatures one by one, blasting them to bits, leaving only their quickbroiled, drying husks wriggling feebly on the floor!

Apedemek cursed, then erased the women warriors with a single wave of his hand!

"You were shamming all the time!" he raged at Seth. "You never had the smallest intention—"

"Not for so much as a moment," Seth agreed. "Join the likes of you? To become what you have become? I'd sooner stick my head in a crocodile's mouth."

"Then why—"

"I had to test you," Seth said airily. "I had to know how strong you are. My conscience will punish me later, I suppose. It was pure vanity. I had to know if you were, as you claimed to be, more powerful than I." His smile was gentle, unassuming, and absolutely intolerable.

Apedemek cursed. "I *am* more powerful than you!" he hissed. "More powerful by far! You shall see! I will destroy you! I will obliterate you as if you were no more than a grease spot on the floor!"

Seth smiled placidly. "Destroy, then," he invited. "I want to know the full extent of your strength. Do not be timid. Use everything you have."

"Timid!" Apedemek roared.

"That's it," Seth said, an island of calm.

Apedemek's eyes blazed with rage, and his voice shook. "*So be it!*" He backed away two steps until he could see Seth from head to foot in one glance. "*Die, then!*" Apedemek screamed.

Through the wall, as if the piled and mortared stones were as insubstantial as a thick fog, crashed an enormous hand, a sickly yellow, its knobby and clawlike fingers tipped with cruel and ugly talons. It grasped Seth around the chest and squeezed with an awesome power!

Seth struggled in the grip of this monstrous hand, trying in vain to get enough breath to speak. The two watching through the window could see the desperation in his face. His hands pried at the thing that was squeezing the life from him, but with less effect than the bite of a desert ant.

"Stop it!" Tharbis cried out. "You're murdering him!"

Apedemek looked at her with a vulture's icy eyes. "Not I, my little plaything. It is the lord of darkness, the prince of evil, whom I serve."

"You demon! You monster!"

His smile was chilling. "He will not only die, he will be destroyed, annihilated by degrees, in this life *and* the next. Death will be no escape for him into peace and calm; it will be a passage through blistering flames into burning acid. When the body has been obliterated, the spirit will undergo a slow and agonizing destruction. His thoughts and memories will be burned away one by one until there is nothing left of them, and each loss will be a fresh agony."

"Het!" she screamed. "Try the door again!"

Het pushed her aside and thrust his arm through the little window, shoving it downward, downward. The pain in his arm was sharp and paralyzing, but he pushed ever harder. Finally his fingers brushed the closed bolt. He gasped and tried again, pushing fiercely in spite of the pain.

"This will avail you nothing," Apedemek said triumphantly. "Even now life seeps away from him. Even now his mind fails. Even now his mental powers are being carved away, burned by the flames of hatred! Even now the lord of darkness is gutting his memories! Soon there will be nothing left of him. He will be an idiot, a broken hulk of a man, while he yet lives!"

Behind him Het could hear Tharbis's sobs. He shoved harder and felt his fingers close around the bolt. He cursed and tried to get some purchase on it.

Miraculously, the bolt slid back!

He fell forward with the opening door, which almost tore his arm out of its socket. He gasped and tried to get his feet under him. The door swung and tore at his arm.

But then Tharbis was beside him, holding the door still. He pulled himself loose, and the sudden pain of being free of the door was worse than the pain he had suffered before!

He tried to pick up the sword he had dropped, but his hand would not hold it. Desperately he grasped it with his left hand and straightened, ready for combat. But Apedemek was nowhere to be found!

"Where is he?" Het asked in a strangled voice. Wildly, desperately, he swung his weapon clumsily where Apedemek had been. The sword cleft empty air.

He looked at the huge hand, at the man still struggling feebly inside it. Seth's eyes were full of bitter tears—of rage, of impotence, of physical and mental agony.

Het raised the sword and hacked at the gigantic hand. Instantly it disappeared. Seth sank heavily to the floor and lay still. And in the far corner, there was Apedemek, his eyes blazing with hatred.

"Very well, then!" Apedemek snarled. "Suffer with him! Both of you."

When he raised his hand and the bolt of power flicked forth, it was not Het that it struck—it was Tharbis. A powerful, invisible force hurled her back against the wall and pinned her there!

Apedemek's hand gestured again, and a narrow beam of light went from his outstretched forefinger to her head. She screamed and continued to scream.

"She is reliving her experience of today," Apedemek told Het. "She is remembering how I enjoyed her, in the guise of a denizen of the dark world! The experience will be burned into her brain forever. You will never be able to erase it. It will corrode her, eating into her soul until the memory of it dominates her life. She will—"

Het came at him in a rush, the sword waving in his left hand!

Apedemek did not have time to react. He tried to make the same gesture he had done at Tharbis, but Het's blundering sword knocked his arm down, numbing it with a clumsy blow to the forearm with the flat of the blade.

Behind him Het heard Tharbis crash to the ground.

"You bastard!" Het said in a contorted voice. "You son of a whore!" And he pulled the sword back, prepared to run Apedemek through, but the white-hot bolt of light again spat out from Apedemek's free hand and hit him in the middle of the chest. Suddenly a great invisible fist inside him crushed his heart within its grasp. He fell to the ground, clutching his chest.

Apedemek looked at the door. Sounds of commotion came in from the hall: the clash of sword against sword, the screams of pain, the curses, the crackle of fire.

He looked quickly at his victims: Tharbis, cowering against the wall, eyes wide with fear and hurt; Het on the floor, gasping, trying to catch his breath, looking at him with eyes that could barely focus; Seth in a heap, unconscious, his chest rising and falling irregularly.

"No," he told himself. "No time. Later. Some other time."

In a great, mad rush he swept past them and out the door just as the first trickle of smoke found its way through the opening from the hall and began to filter its way into the cell.

VIII

Nehsi had found a stout Nuer shield that was nearly as tall as he was, and he was using this now to protect Moses from the occasional arrow that came their way. "What's the matter? Why isn't the gate coming down?"

"It's stuck," Moses answered. "Ben-Azen probably did something to it. He knew good and well the moment our people came over the wall that we'd be heading here, so he probably gummed things up deliberately."

"Cut the rope," Nehsi told him. "The weight of the gate will pull it down the moment the rope is cut."

"All right." Moses took the sword from near where Ben-Azen lay.

But as he did, Nehsi was rushed by two enemy warriors from outside the passage, and he barely managed to prevent one of them from getting past him and attacking Moses's unprotected back. He rammed the huge shield into the man's face, shoving him back, as his free hand parried a stroke at his own neck.

And as the shield pulled away from his face, the two men saw him and recognized him. They were tall blacks from the upper Nile, nearly his own height; they fell back a step and stared at him. "Majesty!" one said. "I didn't know."

The other lay down his sword and fell to one knee. "Sire, forgive me! They told us you were dead!"

Nehsi set the shield against the wall. "Rise," he commanded. "We have all been betrayed. Come with me into the yard. We'll show our people whom they have been mistakenly fighting."

"Yes, sire!" the two men said as with one voice, just as Moses's last blow with the sword severed the heavy rope that held up the gate, and door and drawbridge came plunging down with a resounding crash!

Tharbis bent over Het. "Get up. Oh, please, Het, get up!"

"Here, give me a hand." He let her haul him heavily to his feet, and he stood dizzily. "Seth," he said, rubbing his eyes with the heels of his hands. "Where is Seth?"

But when he finally managed to focus on Seth, he saw a figure bending over him. He closed his eyes and opened them again. "Arnekh! I thought you were dead!"

"Not quite," responded the old man. "And neither is our friend here, although he's the worse for wear. We have to get him out of here."

Tharbis had already gone to the door, only to be driven back by a wall of flames. "Both ends of the hall are on fire!"

"That may be a blessing," the old man said. "There is the possibility that Apedemek got caught in the fire. But we're in some trouble. If we can't get out through the hall—"

"Wait," Het said. "You said once that the flooded part of the dungeon went under the wall and connected with the moat outside. Is there a chance—?"

Arnekh thought a moment. "I don't know. You're a strong swimmer. You could make it. But the lady—"

"I can swim too," she said gamely.

"Good. That leaves me—I'm sure that I haven't got it in me—and Seth, who's still unconscious."

"There has to be a way," Het said.

"I'm . . . not unconscious," said a weak voice at their feet.

"Seth!" Het knelt beside him. "I've come to—"

Seth weakly struggled to sit up. "I know just who you are," he said. "My friend the princess had told me about you." He sat erect and tried to clear his head. "What an ordeal! And what a letdown to realize that so far, at least, he's stronger than I am."

"I couldn't tell what was happening," Arnekh said. "You two just seemed to be standing there gesturing at each other. One would gesture, the other would wince or fall back as if he had been struck in the face."

Seth stared. "You mean—"

"He wasn't affected!" Het said. "That means the spells don't work on bystanders whom the magus doesn't specifically include in the conjurings."

"Arnekh," Seth said, "Can you tell us what words Apedemek used for his incantations?" He allowed himself to be helped to his feet.

"There were no incantations," Arnekh answered. "He simply told you what you were to perceive and allowed your own imagination to do the rest—just as you were doing to him."

Het looked puzzled. "You mean—all the flashes of fire, the monsters I saw, the women of the Legion . . ."

"I saw nothing like that at all," Arnekh confessed. "I

heard them speak of these things, but I saw nothing." He looked alarmed. "Seth! What's the matter?"

Het and Tharbis held Seth up from both sides. His knees had buckled, and there was a perplexed look on his face.

"Something's happened," he quavered. "My memory. There are blanks. I—"

Het and Tharbis exchanged shocked glances. And as they did, the first flames reached the door and ate away at the wooden frames as more and thicker smoke began to billow into the room.

Two ranks of stragglers were all that separated the Egyptian force from the lowered drawbridge. Khafre, his face set in a savage battle grin, hacked his way through the lines of defenders and became the first Egyptian to stand on the bridge. "Come on!" he ordered his men as they charged the ragged lines. "Follow me!"

Throwing a glance at the black smoke that billowed from the open gate, he dived blindly through it, sword in hand, trusting to luck. He knew this was foolish—a commander should not be out of the field of vision of his men—but he was in a reckless mood. With a chuckle he mortally wounded a defender with a single curving stroke and jogged belligerently into the compound.

As he did he saw Nehsi put down the big shield he had been carrying and step out before the massed defenders, his long arms held high. "No, Nehsi!" he bellowed. "Don't do it!"

But the king, magnificently tall and erect, cried out in a rich voice that carried over the compound despite the roaring flames and din of the fighting: "Men of Nubia! Behold your true king!"

There was a moment of hesitation; then it was evident that everyone knew him. To Khafre's great relief, the rebellious soldiers of Nubia, deprived now of the illusion that had set them at odds with their king, threw down their arms. And from a thousand throats came a great cry of triumph at the return of the king to Semna!

As the joyous cry went out, Moses, exulting in the

victory, came forward, weaponless, to stand beside Nehsi. As he did, however, he did not see Ben-Azen staggering forward, one protective hand to his gut. His face was a mask of pain. Twice he came close to blacking out. He worked his way agonizingly toward the king, holding a short dagger by its point. He conquered his weakness and aimed the knife at the middle of the king's back.

Just as he was ready to release it, Moses turned to see him. "Sire!" he cried out, and tried to push Nehsi away.

But the knife thrower was giddy and ill and had thrown wide of the mark. Moses's push moved Nehsi precisely into the path of the knife.

Nehsi half turned and took the knife square in the side.

"Go! All of you!" Arnekh urged. "You can all make it! An old man like me will only cause the death of one or more of you! I've had my time in this world."

"No," said Seth. "We'll not leave without you."

"Think of the young ones," Arnekh pleaded. "They're just starting out in the world."

Het wiped his smoke-irritated, tear-streaming eyes and looked at the two men. The four of them squatted against the cell wall, away from the fire and under the smoke. Long flames shot inside from the guards' room. Tharbis had her arms around Het.

"Come on," Seth told Arnekh. "We're all getting out of here, if I have to swim the whole way dragging you under one arm! Het! Tharbis! Follow me!" And, helping the old man by the arm, he led them down the dark staircase toward the flooded lowest level of the dungeon.

Moses eased Nehsi to the ground. "Sire! Are you—" But he could see the agony on the old king's face and the terrible wound in his side. A mortal wound, one from which he could not even remove the blade for fear that life would flow out with it!

Moses cradled the man's head in his arms. His heart was breaking; he had grown to admire Nehsi. He looked around helplessly at the fifty anxious Nubian and Egyptian faces looking down.

"M-Moses!" the king said in a voice from which the lion's roar had been removed forever.

Moses leaned closer to the king's mouth.

Nehsi's words were hardly above a whisper. "Moses. The succession. I have no son."

"Don't think of that now, sire."

"I must. Moses, listen to me . . ."

Moses smiled gently and leaned to listen at Nehsi's lips. When the instructions were complete, Nehsi smiled beatifically up at him, nodded, then closed his eyes and died, an expression of great peace and calm on his face.

"You've got to leave me," Arnekh said. "Or we'll all die."

"None of us is going to die," Seth insisted. "We're all going to come out of this alive and be happier than ever before."

"Where is it, Arnekh?" Het asked. "I don't remember." He held the torch they had made from a fallen beam and looked around him at the flooded area of the dungeon.

"The corner," the old man said. "You go first. That way you'll be waiting when the princess comes through, and you can help her."

"Good," Seth said. "You can help us, too, Het. I think we're both going to need it."

Het handed the torch to Seth. He looked at them for a moment, then turned his back and eased himself into the watery depths.

IX

"Where's Apedemek?" Balaam asked, panicky. "He's supposed to be leading the defense! Why isn't he here?"

General Aspelta would not look him in the eye. "Someone saw him heading for the dungeons. The lower levels were cut off by fire, so he's probably dead down there." He sneaked a sidelong glance at Balaam now; they stood atop the battlement wall, and only a thin line of defenders protected them from the Egyptian soldiers—and Nubian ones too, who had gone over to the enemy—who were swarming up the stairs in search of the last holdouts. His hand fingered his sword hilt.

"Our men went over to Nehsi! They would never have done that if Apedemek had been here!" Balaam looked right and left. "I'll bet he escaped somehow. Or made a deal with them! Perhaps he sold me out too!"

Aspelta moved slowly around behind him, keeping an eye on the soldiers on the stairs. "Could be, my lord. But perhaps it might be the more prudent thing, right about now, for us to consider changing our status. If we were to surrender now, perhaps they wouldn't kill us. After all, we let Nehsi live, didn't we?"

"No! Didn't you see? Some fool struck him down!"

"Nehsi—dead?" Aspelta said. His hand did not leave his sword hilt now. His face held a sober expression. "That puts a new aspect on things."

"Of course it does!" Balaam exploded. "Now they're going to exact a terrible vengeance against us! They'll kill us all!"

On the stairs another defender fell to the besiegers' swords. The rest of the guards fell back a step, and as they did, new reinforcements surged up the stairs.

Aspelta frowned and looked the other way. Here the second staircase lay undefended, and a squad of Egyptian soldiers rushed up it, led by a naked young warrior, his body covered with grease, a stout staff in his hand. "My lord—look!" Aspelta said, pointing.

"He's the one with Nehsi when the king died. He must be P-Prince Moses!" Balaam said. He held one hand over his heart as if it were going to stop; then he reached for his sword, preparing to surrender it.

Aspelta saw his chance. He drew his sword and attacked Balaam from the rear.

"No!" Moses cried out, rushing forward. "Spare him!"

But it was too late. Aspelta had committed himself. *"Die, tyrant!"* he screamed, and thrust!

Balaam half turned. "Y-you?"

It was his last word. The sword caught him below the rib cage and buried itself. Aspelta could see the incredulous look on his face, as if the stroke and defeat and death all came as a surprise. The light left his eyes immediately, and he slowly pitched forward.

Aspelta turned to face the oncoming enemy. He threw his sword down, put out his hands, rolled his eyes toward heaven. "*I* killed him! *I* rid our nation of the despot, the usurper! I claim sanctuary! Sanctuary!"

Geb, standing beside Moses, made a sour face. He turned to his subordinates. "Dispose of him," he said simply.

A towering black Nubian stepped forward. His mighty arm rose; in his hand was an axe already stained with the blood of many men.

"No!" Aspelta cried out. "Please!"

Seth was the last to go. The cells in the upper levels were choked with smoke now, and he was having trouble breathing. He leaned out over the water, his eyes searching its depths, the guttering torch held high.

He hoped Het had got the others to safety. It was by no means a sure thing that Arnekh would survive the underwater swim, even with a powerful young man like Het helping him. And he?

He was not so sure of his own ability. The blackouts were lasting longer and occurring more frequently. There were holes in his mind, and not only his thoughts but his physical capabilities were failing him. What had Apedemek done to him? Could the damage to his mind be mended?

The prospect of mental impairment was even more frightening a notion than that of dying. If he were to die now, it would be an honorable death. Apedemek had escaped, but he, Seth, had done the best he could. But the idea of surviving as a mental cripple? Of coming through this physically whole but mentally maimed? It was almost too much to bear.

This time the blackout came in midthought. The torch fell from his lifeless hands and splashed into the water, leaving him in complete darkness.

And when he came back to himself again, he stood in a

coal-black limbo, full of panic. "Het! Het, where are you? I'm blind! I can't see! Help me, Het! Help me, please!"

There was an answering splash nearby, and a familiar voice spoke up. "Hang on, Seth!" said the young man. "I'm right here!"

Seth let himself be guided into the water. "Now just hold onto me," Het told him. "Hold on tight. We're going to dive. Hold your breath."

Het, swimming powerfully, pulled him under. He could feel the young man's powerful strokes, and the strong pumping of his muscular legs.

In the end the last Nubians threw down their arms and let themselves be taken out across the drawbridge and into the plain, where the women of the Black Wind and the Desert Legion ordered them to assume their regular formations.

The Nubians chose two representatives from among their number, a broad-shouldered young white named Kark and a towering black warrior named Tekeride. As Moses and Khafre marched out to meet them, the two came forward to bow deeply before the young prince.

Tekeride was the first to speak. "We have dishonored our nation, our families, and ourselves. Under the evil spell cast by the false Apedemek, we have risen in unjust revolt against our king and father, who now lies dead by a Nubian hand. It is yours to dispose of us as you will, mighty Prince. Any death you decree we will deserve."

Moses glanced at Khafre. Then he took the two Nubians by the shoulder and turned them so that they and he faced the assembled captives. "Egypt is understanding!" he proclaimed in a strong young voice. "Egypt is merciful! Let no man blame himself for falling under the spell of the wicked Apedemek! Let us now work to heal the breach between your people and mine!"

There was a startled murmur from the crowd. Clemency was rare. Moses waved them to silence. "Nehsi, the great king, is dead. Who will now lead you?"

"My lord," Kark said, "do you not intend to name a regent? To leave a conquering force among us?"

"Before he died, Nehsi spoke to me!" Moses said. "Now

hear me! Dawn breaks in the east. A new day is upon us. When the sun is high, I will come back to you and tell you what Nehsi planned. Until then, think upon the loss of honor you have sustained, and think on how best to regain it in the days to come."

A warrior of the Desert Legion had found the escapees shivering on the moat's edge and sent for Weret. Now the tall commander called for animal hides to throw over them and sent a runner to her own camp for additional aid.

Geb intercepted the runner and after hearing the news, went to find Weret. "Are they all right?" he asked her. "Did Seth escape?"

"Seth is safe, and Het and the princess, and there is an old man with them. Seth's mind has been affected by a duel with Apedemek. His memory is partly gone. How long this may last, we do not know. I have him resting in our camp. I have sent for Neku-re and Tchabu. Between them there should be some chance of his being able to heal, in time."

"Good. And the others?"

"They're with him."

"Keep them there, if you please. I'll bring Prince Moses. He'll be with you by the time the sun's all the way up."

"Splendid. I'll wait for him there."

Dawn found the besiegers inspecting the lower level of the burnt-out fortress. As they passed through the dungeons, Geb found Moses and informed him that Seth and the others had been found, safe and sound.

"All of them?" asked Moses eagerly.

"Yes. Young Het distinguished himself, saving the others. They found their way out through a tunnel below the walls, through the water. He swam with them one by one to safety."

"Excellent. His bravery will be rewarded handsomely." Moses, now wearing a general's uniform, borrowed from Khafre's wardrobe, beckoned to a runner. "Go tell Khafre that Geb and I are going to the legion camp. He can meet us there."

"Yes, sir!"

Moses turned back to Geb. "There's something special about this fellow Het, I think. I see great things for him in the future. Don't you?"

"Yes, sir!" Geb agreed smartly. "And, sir, if you don't mind my saying something personal? . . ."

"Go ahead. Speak."

"Freely, sir?"

"As from a friend to a friend."

"Very well, sir. I feel as if I'd aged twenty years since this expedition began."

"What do you mean?"

"Watching you, sir. Watching you grow up. When we began, you were a beginner, brave but untried. Now there's an air about you, sir. An air of command. You'll make an incredible general, sir. You'll make an even better king of Egypt."

"Thank you," Moses said thoughtfully. "Coming from a seasoned soldier like you, that is high praise, and I will treasure it." He sighed. "How strange finally to find a profession, just at the moment when one must leave it."

Geb stared.

"This battle was my farewell to my military career, Geb. I have put aside the weapons of war forever."

Geb's eyes popped open. "But, sir! Our work has only just begun! You must remember Baliniri's plan! We are to go back to Thebes and scour the country clean! Smoke out the cult and destroy it, depose Amasis and—"

"I know. But the bulk of that work must fall to someone else. I spoke with Tchabu—".

"No, sir! Don't pay any attention to him!"

"I have to, because something in me tells me that he tells the truth. I must speak with him again, but I am certain that my feet are set on a different path."

Geb looked at the prince with astonishment and dismay. "Sir!" he said. "We have just gained a victory! And here I feel as if I'd suffered a personal defeat!"

Moses put a comradely hand on his shoulder. "Don't," he soothed. "There is the hand of destiny in all this, which none of us can refuse. Come with me to the legion camp. The story is not yet played out."

X

"For heaven's sake, young man," Arnekh said, "please sit down and relax. You must be exhausted after what you've done. You're a great hero! But even heroes must rest before they collapse."

Het turned back to the others, his drawn face etched with fatigue. "I have to know," he said impatiently. He hailed one of Weret's warriors, who evidently liked what she saw and gave him a provocative smile. "Please," Het said, "I heard a rumor that Nehsi was dead. Is this true?"

"Yes," she said, "struck down from behind by a traitor. And Balaam is dead—"

"No!" Tharbis cried out.

"I'm sorry," the woman said. "One of his own men killed him trying to win favors from us."

Het put his arm around Tharbis but that did not seem to lessen the naked warrior's interest in him. "Then Nubia has no king. What disposition will be made of the country? I have to know; I have friends in Kerma."

The woman smiled. "Nehsi made his wishes known to Prince Moses, and the prince told the captured Nubians he would announce the decision at noon." She watched his face. "But I did overhear Moses saying he was coming here to have a conversation with Princess Tharbis."

Het's face fell. "Oh. Ah, yes. I see. She's the only one left with the proper bloodlines, and Nubian law prohibits her from ruling alone." He swallowed hard. "And her consort must be a man of equal rank."

"Not necessarily," the woman said. "Remember that Nehsi's own father usurped the throne. There *is* precedent for the introduction of new blood. But obviously, for the sake of stability, it would be better—"

"Yes. Better if Egypt and Nubia were united. Yes. I can see that."

"What are you saying?" Tharbis asked. "You're talking like my father. He wanted me to marry Amasis." She stopped, her face suddenly somber and pale. "I—can't get used to the idea of Father being dead."

The woman warrior reached out to her and squeezed her arm. "There, now, girl. Go ahead. Give way to your feelings. Even a man like Balaam deserves to be cried over. I'm sure there was some good in him, despite everything. He was just under Apedemek's spell. That could happen to anyone."

Tharbis's face changed once again. She remembered her own gruesome experience and pressed her face into Het's broad chest.

"Is that Seth?" the woman asked. She kneeled before him and put a hand on his shoulder. "Do you remember me? It's Satre. I used to be a runner for the—"

"Yes, yes," Seth said. His voice was an old man's now, weak and confused. "That much I can remember, although I don't guarantee much else right now. So we have a great victory, then?"

She regarded him, lying back against the bole of a tree, looking pale and drained. "Ah, Seth. Yes, we do. But we lost twenty or thirty of our best fighters."

"I'm a wreck, Satre. Bring Neku-re and Tchabu to me, please. I've never felt so ill." Seth dragged a hand across his forehead.

"I'll get them right now." As she patted his shoulder, a second Desert Legion warrior approached. "Satre," she said, "Prince Moses sent me to bring Princess Tharbis to the council fire immediately."

"All right," Satre said. "Meanwhile, I'll get Tchabu and Neku-re."

As the princess left with the messenger, Satre turned to Het and looked him up and down again. "You should get some rest. You look tired, and you've earned all the rest a man could ask for."

When the women were out of sight, Het's broad shoulders slumped. "Well, that's it. I can see what's coming."

"I doubt that, young man," Arnekh said, "for all your intelligence. But since nobody is listening to me this morning, I think I'll go over to the campfires and see if anyone will give me anything to eat. I haven't had anything but prison food in so long, I'm not sure what proper food tastes like. Even army rations will be an improvement."

He ambled slowly away, leaving Seth and Het alone. "Come, sit by me," Seth said. "Keep me company. You've saved my life. It's time we got to know each other."

"I don't know if I'll be good company for you," Het said. "To be sure, I *am* tired. But I'm so tense I can't relax."

"If my mind were in better shape I could fix that," Seth said. "But that last fight with Apedemek has sapped my strength for a while." He shuddered. "I *hope* it's temporary," he added. "But sit down."

Het did so, and as he did, he turned his back to Seth, who shot a sharp glance at him as he sank to the ground. "You'll be all right soon," Het said. "They tell me Tchabu has healing powers."

"Yes. And when the powers of Tchabu and Neku-re are joined, there is little they can't do. But even they have never met the likes of Apedemek." Seth sounded defeated as he added, "But then neither had I. . . ." He shuddered again and changed the subject. "I'd like to know about you. You're from Kerma?"

"I was raised there. Mother told me I was born downriver. But you can understand that having raised me as a bastard by herself, she wasn't eager to talk about the early years." At the word *bastard* his voice wavered a moment; it was obviously a painful thing for him to admit.

"You did not know your father?" Seth spoke in a compassionate voice.

"No. And to tell you the truth, I know almost nothing about Mother either. She was very closemouthed about herself. She loved me very much and did her best for me. I did manage to get some education, despite all the odds, and that took a heroic effort on her part—the castes are fixed in Kerma, and a bastard encounters barriers every step of the way. But the work of raising me must have exhausted her, taken away her strength. Remember when the plague swept up the river? We didn't suffer much of it, compared to the reports I heard of the devastation in the delta and in Thebes. But even a mild case of it was enough to carry her away."

"Ah!" Seth said, his voice tight with sympathy. "A painful story, my friend. But did you ever find out where your mother came from?"

"No," Het said. He drew up his knees and wrapped his arms around them. "There was no one to ask. She did not make friends. She did not invite confidences." He turned and looked at Seth, reacting belatedly to the older man's tone. "Why? What's it to you? Pardon me if I'm being rude, but—"

"But you question my need to know these things. And well you might. What was your mother's name?"

"Why, Isis. At least that was what she called herself here in Nubia. Her real name was something else, because they pronounced it differently down the Nile, she said. Let's see, what was it? It was—"

Seth dabbed at his eyes, and there was a catch in his voice as he completed the sentence. "Her name was Aset. She was a great heroine in the war against the Hai." Het stared. "And once upon a time she had an affair with a young man who went away and left her, not knowing she had conceived a child by him." His voice broke, and he stifled a sob. He covered his face with his hands.

"Seth! What's the matter? How do you know all this?"

Seth took his hands away and let one of them fall heavily on Het's shoulder. "Last night I saw by the light of the torch the red birthmark on your back. All the men in your family have it. Today I saw it even more clearly. Het—you're my son."

When Satre returned with Tchabu and Neku-re, they found Seth and Het sitting opposite each other, cross-legged, Het eagerly asking questions and Seth answering them. Both the sages instantly understood what had happened. "Look Neku-re!" Tchabu said. "Seth find son! Not have to look more."

"Yes," Neku-re confirmed happily. "I'm delighted for both of them. But Seth has been much hurt, and even this will not cure him."

"Bring to oasis," Tchabu said. "Seth come to El-Dakhla. We fix mind."

"Yes, of course, but it will take time. He has fought a terrible fight, which he has neither won nor lost."

Seth looked up at that. "I lost," he confessed. "He

defeated me. Oh, it may have looked like a draw, but when the duel was done, I was wounded and he was not."

Het frowned. "Not wounded? What do you mean? He's dead, isn't he? Didn't he die in the fire? Hasn't someone found his body? Nobody could get out of there alive. Why, the flames—"

"Bad man not dead," Tchabu verified, putting a stubby hand on his tiny chest. "Tchabu feel bad man *here*."

Seth blew out a great sigh. "I suppose I ought to feel relieved. After all, it means I'll have another shot at him. But with things the way they are? With part of my mind gone? I could never face him now. He reached inside me and started *breaking* things. I'll never be the same again."

"Seth not say never!" the dwarf scolded. "Come. We go home to El-Dakhla. No interruption, no distraction. We make all new again."

Seth shook his head. "You don't understand. At least some of what he said, about the prince of evil and whatever, was true. I felt it. If any more time had been allowed to pass, I could have been taken over by another intelligence, another spirit, as Apedemek has been."

Neku-re smiled. "Is that so?" he challenged. "Or are these just suggestions he placed in your mind when the two of you were struggling for dominance? Seth, you had been starved. You were tired beyond endurance. He found you in a vulnerable frame of mind. Who knows what a confrontation would be like if the two of you were to meet again on more equal terms?"

"I don't know. He's so much farther along than I am at this."

"But will he still be when you have rested and healed and regained your strength? Seth, one thing I know as sure as I'm standing here: You and Apedemek will meet again."

"And the outcome?"

"That I cannot tell you. No man should know such things. But the game is not yet done. He has made his move, and the time will come when you will have yours. And when that times comes, the odds will be different than they were today."

There was a noise behind him. He turned to see Satre,

standing slim and straight, a serious look on her face. "Prince Moses presents his compliments," she said. "It is time for the disposition of the affairs of Nubia. He would appreciate having all of you in attendance."

XI

The plain below the still-smoking fortress was now covered with orderly ranks of soldiers: The Nubians, white and black alike, were in the center, unarmed and unguarded but flanked by the Black Wind and the Desert Legion, with the Egyptian army in the rear. A natural rock outcropping formed a rough platform before them, and on this stood Khafre and Prince Moses. Beside them stood Princess Tharbis, wearing a clean robe salvaged from the ruins of the Semna stronghold.

Seth moved up to the front rank to stand beside Het, and Weret made room for him. They looked up at the platform, and Het tried to catch Tharbis's eye but could not. He sighed—long and loud enough to catch Seth's attention. "What's the matter?" Seth asked. "Oh, you think you've lost her, eh?"

Het tried to be philosophical. "I suppose it doesn't matter all that much. I was a fool to imagine that she and I . . ." He shook his head.

"You are not a fool. I'm sure you have never been a fool."

"Perhaps not, but I feel like one now." He tried to smile as he patted Seth's arm. "Look at it this way: I may have lost a woman, but I have gained a father." The smile became real. "I still can't believe it. A Child of the Lion! I've heard of them for years but never had the faintest idea—"

"It's incontrovertible. The things you've told me about your mother in the past hour make it a matter beyond dispute. I hope you know that I loved her very much. We had a dispute at the worst possible time, just as I was preparing to leave. If I had known—"

"I know, I know. Nobody has to convince me you're a

man of honor. Ah, Seth, we have some lost time to make up for, don't we? I understand you're going to the oasis with Tchabu for a while. Do you think they would let me come along? We could get to know each other."

"I'll ask Weret." Seth turned and spoke rapidly to the Legion general on his left, in a low voice Het could not make out. After a moment or two she nodded, and Het's heart soared. Then, after another sentence or two from Seth, she shook her head emphatically, and his heart sank to the depths. Seth turned back to him. "I'm sorry. Weret doesn't think that would be a good idea just now."

"But—"

"Maybe later. You have to realize, I'll be staying at the farther of the two oases: El-Dakhla. Since Teti originally set up El-Dakhla as the heart of her stronghold years ago, very few men have ever been allowed there—myself, Riki, Baliniri, and Neku-re and Tchabu. It will take a bit of time before this number can be increased. Perhaps we can meet in El-Kharga when Tchabu is done with me. I will try to prevail upon Weret."

He turned to speak to her again, but the tall warrior general had turned and smartly marched away, climbing the platform and conferring for a moment with Khafre and Prince Moses. After a moment both men nodded, and Moses turned to speak to Tharbis, standing beside him. Weret signaled to the Black Wind command standing opposite, and Naldamak detached herself from her elite corps and joined them on the platform.

And now Khafre raised both hands, calling for silence, and slowly the murmuring stopped, leaving only the sound of the river.

"We have been at war," Khafre called out, "and now we are at peace. Nubia and Egypt alike have rid themselves of an enemy, the usurper Apedemek, and of the false leaders he appointed to do his bidding. It is time for peace and brotherhood to return to our two nations."

A great cheer answered this. He waited until it had died down before continuing. "Nubia must choose a ruler today. Apedemek has gone; the noble Nehsi is dead without issue; Balaam has passed on to his fathers. There remains among us for consideration only the princess Tharbis, whose bloodlines are the finest in Nubia."

After the initial cheers, however, to which Tharbis responded at Khafre's urging, a voice rang out from the ranks of the Black Wind: "Naldamak! Naldamak!"

This time the response was mixed: wild cheers from the black ranks and confusion among the women warriors. Again Khafre called for silence. "We have asked her," he called out, "and she has cast her lot with the Black Wind and with the women of the desert." Naldamak nodded solemnly, and this time there was a resounding cheer from the women's ranks.

"In fact," Khafre said, "Naldamak herself suggested Princess Tharbis to rule in Nubia. But then we were reminded that Nubian law does not allow a princess, even a princess of the blood, to rule alone. So we put the question to her, and she has chosen a consort. The man who will reign beside Tharbis will bring to the Nubian succession the blood royal of one of the greatest nations in the world, and a family tradition of noble accomplishment second to none in any dynasty of any country anywhere, any time."

Het's heart fell. He wished now that he were a million leagues away. Seth leaned over and nudged him. "Steady, there, Son. Don't let them see how it affects you. Courage!"

"Thus," Khafre said, "if the princess and her chosen consort meet with the approval of the army of Nubia, Egypt is pleased to announce its provisional decision as to who will rule in Nubia."

Het's mind reeled. He looked at the two of them standing beside each other: Moses and Tharbis! He sighed, and the sigh was almost a sob.

"But you, the people of Nubia," Khafre continued, "must confirm her choice, and he himself must tell us if this union is his will."

Het's eyes were abrim with tears. He saw the smile on Tharbis's face, and the one on Prince Moses's, and his heart felt as if it were going to break.

"He is a man," Khafre continued, "who had no idea of his real lineage. A natural nobility of mind was united, in him, to the blood of a great race. He thinks of himself not as a hero but as a man who was doing the job assigned him. Let me tell you, my friends, there are worse qualities to have in a king."

The Nubian ranks were quiet. Of whom was Khafre speaking?

Now Khafre beckoned to Tharbis. "The princess herself shall name her choice," he said, "and present her proposed consort for your approval."

Tharbis stepped forward. Het's wet eyes drank in her fresh beauty and happy smile, and his fists clenched impotently.

"I choose with my mind," she said, "the man whom my heart had already chosen for me. And I ask him to stand with me before you. People of Nubia, I choose—"

Het's hands trembled. He was in a cold sweat. *I'm losing her forever!*

"—Het of Kerma: Child of the Lion and son of Seth, one-time king of Babylonia!"

And then the *real* cheering began!

Seth watched happily as Het, not quite believing what he had heard, stumbled awkwardly onto the platform and stood blinking down at the great throng. Tharbis moved closer to him and threw an arm affectionately around his waist; the other hand was thrown heavenward to acknowledge the sustained cheers that rang out.

Balaam had not been popular with the army, but his spirited, rebellious daughter had been held in high regard for her robust, independent spirit and unwillingness to knuckle under to her father. The tale of how Moses and Het had slipped past the Nubian guards to open the gate and save the princess had traveled all over the camps of both winner and loser during the morning, and this inspired the cheers. It would be a day to remember.

There was even reason for Seth to be happy: He had found his son, Het, just as he was preparing to lose the surrogate son, Moses, who had become so dear to him. It should be a day of unclouded rejoicing, when the guilt and regret he had carried for two decades could at last be shed. He should be a happy man. But . . .

He shuddered and closed his eyes. His mind wandered, as it had done all morning. One by one he was exploring the chambers of memory, taking inventory of the great store of wisdom and learning he had amassed over his years of travel and study. . . .

It was as if he were walking along a desolate road through the desert hills. Suddenly, before him, half the landscape had vanished. First a mountain on the horizon crumbled and disappeared. Then the whole horizon itself shimmered and vanished, leaving no clear delineation between earth and sky.

He cried out, but there was no one to hear him. And now all the land to the left of the road vanished, leaving him standing on the brink of a yawning and bottomless abyss, a sickening chasm!

He recoiled to his right, but as he did, the land to the right of the road similarly disappeared! The road alone existed now! To right and left there was nothing!

Now the road itself began to crumble. He could see it dissolving before him. The line of the dissolution was coming closer and in a moment would be upon him, and he too would disappear. "No! No!" he screamed—

—and awoke on the hard ground, surrounded by a circle of anxious faces.

"Seth," Geb said, bending near him, "are you all right?"

He heard the same from the others. He knew the faces above him but somehow could not recall their names. The curly-haired one was his son, Het, but who was the beautiful young woman standing next to him, her arm around him? There were two tall, lean women, naked except for golden jewelry and weapon belts. Who were they? There were others: a general, gray-haired and tough looking; a striking, powerful, clean-cut young man with the bearing of a leader and the strong nose of a Canaanite. They acted as if he should know them.

He basked confusedly in the obvious concern they all held for him. What was he doing on the ground, and why did he feel so weak? If someone would offer a hand, he might be able to pull himself to his feet.

"Someone get a litter," ordered the general. "Are Tchabu

and Neku-re here? And bring the physician while you're at it. He may have hurt himself falling."

And then it was all tender solicitude as they made a little bed for him to lie in. Four strong warriors picked it up and carried him as if he were as light as a newborn baby. Where they were taking him he could not say; it was enough to know that they were apparently his friends and would do him no harm.

He closed his eyes and slipped into a restful sleep.

Weret came back from where the men had carried Seth. "He will be all right for now. Neku-re and Tchabu are not sure how completely he can be healed or how long it will take, but he will be in their hands."

Moses glanced at Het, then nodded solemnly. "Since you'll be taking him to the oasis, I was wondering—"

"Yes," Weret told him. "Baliniri's last message to me had to do with taking you into the desert with me to learn its ways—to live without food and water, to find sustenance where there appears to be none, and to judge location by the stars."

"I will do whatever you wish if I can be near Seth and help you look after him," Moses said. "I know I have a real father somewhere, a man named Amram, but a part of me will always think of Seth as my father."

"I will share him with you," Het said happily. "A man who has shared dangers with me, as you have, will always be my brother. How I wish I could accompany you into the desert."

"You've a busy life ahead," Moses consoled, now winking at Tharbis, "with a new love and a new title and a new destiny. I'll take care of him for you, and I'll make sure that he sends messages to you."

The two men embraced affectionately, and when Het stepped back, Tharbis moved up and hugged Moses close.

"Thank you for everything," she said. "For saving our country. For being a friend. For making Nubia whole again, when my misguided father had torn it in two."

"Don't be so hard on poor Balaam," Moses advised. "He was not a strong person, like you and Het are. In Apedemek's hands he was a fresh piece of clay, one that Apedemek could mold into anything he liked. I hope you and I will never know what it is like to be under Apedemek's spell, to be helpless as he does whatever he likes."

At this Tharbis and Het exchanged quick glances; the secret lay with the two of them only and would stay that way. "I'll try to think kindly of him," Tharbis promised. "And I'll remember your wise words for as long as I live."

"Fine," said Moses. "Carry my love with you wherever you go, forever—both of you. I will never forget either of you." He turned to the rest now. "Consider," he said in a powerful, ringing young voice that carried far, "what is necessary to heal the rift that came between us. Let us begin with a great feast, my friends! Let us sing and dance and eat our fill, and become friends again! And let there never again rise between Egypt and Nubia the contention that sets brother against brother!"

A great cry of thanksgiving roared out from a thousand throats and echoed up and down the valley so the hills sang with it!

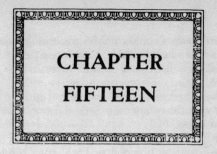

CHAPTER FIFTEEN

Down the Nile

I

"I can't say how grateful I am for your help," he said. "If I'd had to wait for the mail packet or to book passage by the ordinary means—"

"Think nothing of it," the fisherman replied. Naked and sun blackened, he stood in the stern manning the long steering oar and held the little vessel in the exact center of the downriver current. "You look like you probably couldn't have afforded the usual rate for passengers—not to insult you or anything. We've all had our ups and downs. I can tell when a fellow needs a helping hand. People have done the same for me in the past."

Apedemek's smile was ingratiating, and his eyes, mere slits from the bright sunlight, were unreadable. "I appreciate that. But I want to make sure that you know how grateful I am. Can I do anything to help?"

The fisherman looked over the side. "Maybe. It's getting

on toward lunch. I could catch us something, but I'd need an extra hand to mind the tiller. I don't want the boat swinging around on me. Could you do that?"

"I think so."

"Good. Let me get us out of the current." He pulled hard on the tiller, and the little boat moved toward the starboard shore.

Apedemek watched him, his expression betraying nothing. The fisherman dropped anchor, and as the boat came to the end of its tether, he stood and offered the tiller to Apedemek. "Just keep her pointed this way," the fisherman said. "If you can do that, I think I can find us some tasty morsels. Now where's that hand line of mine?"

Apedemek took the tiller and did as his shipmate had asked, sitting in the stern to do so. His eyes remained on the fisherman's skinny, naked back. The corners of his mouth briefly curled in a smile that lacked humor.

The first days downstream had been very difficult. He had found a coracle set adrift when the Egyptians had burned their boats, and he had tried to negotiate the rapids of the cataracts. The third cascade, however, had proved too much for the little boat, and he had foundered, taking a terrible beating on the rocks before he had finally made it to shore, half-drowned, his clothing in rags.

He had been saved by someone on the shore, taken home, fed, and dressed. The kindness of these upriver bumpkins was quite remarkable, he had decided.

So was their credulity. They apparently trusted everyone. His benefactor, who had lived alone, had owned a small boat. This Apedemek had stolen—along with his meager savings—after killing his host. The boat had made it through the rest of the rapids before finally being sunk by an underwater snag as Apedemek, inexperienced in the ways of the Nile, had foolishly steered too close to the shore.

There had been a two-day interlude during which he had walked—walked!—along the riverside track. That had ended when this fisherman had come into view.

And now his time, too, had come. The boat, he had said, was approaching Edfu, then El-Kab was just downstream. El-Kab would be a good place to go ashore and find out what the political situation was before plunging into Thebes. While Edfu was a backwater, El-Kab was a major population center and would be up-to-date on the status of the court.

He watched as the fisherman leaned over the side, his hand-held line dangling from one skinny hand. "Oh, by the way . . ." he said casually, his tone promising a continuation of his thought. But he said no more.

The fisherman's curiosity prompted him to turn his head. "Yes?" he asked, looking into Apedemek's eyes. Those eyes held him in a terrible grip. He could not move. He could not look away.

The faraway call for help sounded over the water. Kamose instantly sat up and looked across the Nile. He had been fishing by the river, thinking, planning, and scheming; now, galvanized by the high-pitched cry, he jumped to his feet and tried to get the faraway vessel into focus. Anchored, it flailed helplessly about, tugged by an eddy in the current.

The cry came again: "Help! Man overboard!"

The tall, skinny man in the boat waved both arms and continued to call out for help. It was a fisherman's boat, but fishermen always worked naked, and this man was dressed. What was the fellow doing?

"What's the matter?" Kamose called out in a powerful voice from the water's edge.

"My friend has fallen in! He hasn't come up! I can't swim!"

Without another word Kamose dived far out into the Nile, swimming with long powerful strokes. When he pulled up alongside the boat he asked, "Where did he go down? Where do I—?"

And then the eyes caught him, too, and held him fast.

Pedibast, head of the family in El-Kab that had been hiding Kamose, opened the door cautiously at his knock. "My lord! Come inside quickly!" But then he saw the tall stranger beside his king. "My lord! Who is this?"

Kamose ushered the stranger in. "This is my oldest friend in the world, Pedibast. I can vouch for him totally. We've known each other since we were children. He's going to help me with the great tasks I have ahead of me, restoring the kingdom. Treat him with great deference. There isn't a more important man in this great land of ours just now."

Pedibast and his wife exchanged puzzled glances. Their first glimpse of the stranger had not been reassuring.

Pedibast reminded himself that the king was not one to take kindly to the expression of doubt. Perhaps it was best to go along with him when he did something as odd as this, even if it seemed likely to lead to danger.

He smiled and looked the stranger in the eye. "Any friend of our friend's," he said, "is a friend of ours. You are welcome in our house."

And then the eyes had him. The eyes! The eyes!

Epilogue

The night was clear, so although the last ember had guttered and died, the tall, gaunt figure of the Teller of Tales remained clearly visible in the moonlight. He paused to look across at the rapt faces in absolute silence. Not even the wind rose to break the stillness.

"So came to an end the war with Nubia," he said. "For the first time a Child of the Lion formally ruled in one of the lands of the great Nile, and peace lay between the two lands. But the poison that had infected Nubia now invaded Egypt itself as the evil magus Apedemek brought his sorcery to Thebes.

"And as Moses and the rebel army lingered in the desert, praying for Seth's recovery, Apedemek consolidated his hold over the dissidents who challenged Amasis's regency, then reached out to the court itself. Prince Moses's impending return to Egypt was nearly suicidal as he moved into a world dominated by the deadliest enemies he had ever known.

"Yet the greatest peril lay not among his enemies but

484

among his kin, for among these was one who would betray him."

This brought from his listeners a great groan of apprehension. They knew the story, to be sure; but with every retelling their reaction remained strong.

"Thus the promised Deliverer of the sons of Jacob was driven from the land, and his wanderings began. But in exile he was to find the purpose his life had lacked. He came to know at last why he of all men had been singled out for the great destiny that lay before him.

"In time Seth returned from his own exile, weak and unsure but determined to test his strength against the deadly Apedemek.

"All hope was gone. The last of Apedemek's foes were exhausted. But new strength was forthcoming from unexpected sources, from the remote east and west. From the mighty line of the Children of the Lion, from the potent seed of Belsunu and Ahuni, a new leader, shrouded in mystery, would arise to bring the ancient wisdom of the Chalybians to bear on the crisis."

This, now, was something his listeners had not heard, and he could hear their expressions of anticipation. He silenced these with a wave of his elegant, long-fingered hand.

"Of all this shall you hear at the next moonrise," he promised. "Of the final confrontation between good and evil in Egypt, of the terrible plight of the Habiru, and of the return of their Deliverer, who would lead them from Egypt. You shall hear of the last days of Seth, greatest and wisest Child of the Lion, during that clan's sojourn along the Nile."

The murmur again rose, and once again he stilled it with a gesture. "Tomorrow," he whispered as the sleeping desert awakened in the darkness and as the soft wind began to sigh and carry his words away across the half-visible hills. "You shall hear these things tomorrow. . . ."

Coming in Spring 1989

THE CHILDREN OF THE LION
BOOK X

THE EXODUS

Look for another volume in the magnificent series that takes you back in time to a world aflame with passion and alive with magic . . .

In fulfillment of the ancient prophecies an Egyptian prince named Moses, known as the Deliverer, has risen to free the Haibru slaves from bitter bondage.

Moses will face the evil cult that holds Egypt in a deathgrip, and he will defy the tyrannical regime of Pharaoh, but the Children of the Lion will be his strength and his protection.

THE EXODUS is a seething saga of desire and hate, of faith and desperation, of a man of destiny and the woman he loves.

Look for **THE EXODUS** wherever Bantam Books are sold!

★ WAGONS WEST ★

A series of unforgettable books that trace the lives of a dauntless band of pioneering men, women, and children as they brave the hazards of an untamed land in their trek across America. This legendary caravan of people forge a new link in the wilderness. They are Americans from the North and the South, alongside immigrants, Blacks, and Indians, who wage fierce daily battles for survival on this uncompromising journey—each to their private destinies as they fulfill their greatest dreams.